BLUE PLANET

BOOK THREE
THE SECOND SPECIES TRILOGY

JANE O'REILLY

PIATKUS

PIATKUS

First published in Great Britain in 2020 by Piatkus

1 3 5 7 9 10 8 6 4 2

A CIP catalogue record for this book
is available from the British Library.

ISBN 978-0-349-42382-1

Typeset in Baskerville by M Rules
Printed and bound in Great Britain by Clays Ltd, Elcograf S.p.A.

Papers used by Piatkus are from well-managed forests
and other responsible sources.

Piatkus
An imprint of
Little, Brown Book Group
Carmelite House
50 Victoria Embankment
London EC4Y 0DZ

An Hachette UK Company
www.hachette.co.uk

www.littlebrown.co.uk

For Caroline. Happy 16th birthday, darling girl.
May your life be always full of adventure.

CHAPTER

1

18th January 2208

Colony Seven, Earth-controlled Space

A year ago, Jinnifer Blue would have said that gatecrashing a meeting of government ministers on Colony Seven was ridiculous. She'd already made more than enough reckless decisions in her life. Running away from home at eighteen and signing up for genetic modification followed by pilot prosthetics. Taking a job on a crappy freighter for minimal pay and no holidays and sticking with it even though she'd been hated by everyone else on board because she was Dome-raised. Then taking a job with the Security Service where she was hated by everyone she worked with because she had genetic modifications and prosthetics. Returning to Earth thinking she could persuade her mother, Ferona, to put an end to the Second Species programme and stop selling human slaves to their alien neighbours.

She had learned since then that fate had a wicked sense of humour. It seemed that her life was destined to travel down a path that was neither safe nor easy. It didn't matter how hard she tried to avoid trouble. It didn't help that when the difficult choices presented themselves, she invariably went for the most difficult option, but given that other people seemed to drift easily through life without ever encountering pirates or murderous aliens, it couldn't be entirely her fault.

'I don't like this colony,' said the man lying to next to her. They were on the roof of a three-storey building, the wind howling over them. They'd been in position for an hour and Jinn's feet were starting to go numb. 'Too flashy.'

'Too *flashy*?'

'Too Dome.'

'Ah,' Jinn said. She settled herself a little deeper into the crevice between the edge of the building and the ventilation stack. 'I see.' She lifted her binoculars to her eyes and zoomed in on the building opposite, a squat, low-slung block with a flat roof and an awful lot of cameras.

'Remind me why we're here again?' he continued.

Jinn lowered her binoculars, turned her head, and looked at him. He was wedged in so close to her that she could feel the heat from his body seeping through his clothing and into hers. Caspian Dax, part human, part alien, all pirate, once her lover and now something she didn't have a name for, had always been prone to asking challenging questions. 'We're here to gatecrash the ministerial meeting due to take place in that building in approximately thirty minutes.'

'Hmm,' he said. 'And why are we doing that?'

'We're doing it because Sittan deathships are burning their way through neutral space and we can't stop them. We've tried. We need help and we've come here to ask for it.'

He groaned.

'You don't think we should do it?'

'Oh, I definitely think we should. I just hoped the plan was better than I remembered.'

Grief had brought them here, an awful mix of death and desperation. Humans and the Sittan had been at war for six months. She and Dax had spent that time in neutral space, jumping from station to station, trading post to trading post, trying to avoid the Sittan ships, seeing all too often the devastation that those ships left behind.

Breathing got difficult for a moment. Jinn rubbed the back of her hand against her eyes and reminded herself that that was why she was here; for all the people who had died and who would continue to die if the government didn't do something. They couldn't fix this problem by ignoring it. Eventually, the Sittan would run out of humans to kill in neutral space, and there was only one place they would go after that.

The street below was surprisingly busy. Droids rushed around, sweeping the pavement, polishing the windows. Two large troughs of deep purple flowers were wheeled into position next to the doors. Armed Security Service agents, immediately recognisable due to their familiar grey uniforms and pale hair, stood chatting, oblivious to the scurrying of the droids.

'There's a roller approaching,' Dax said quietly.

Jinn followed the direction of his gaze and found it. It was a long, twelve-wheeled vehicle that seemed to ooze rather than roll, shiny sides reflecting a mirror image of its surroundings. It eased to a halt right in front of the building. The agents snapped into position. They looked like they were prepared for trouble.

But Jinn and Dax were prepared for them. Dax's coat was woven from a heat-shielding fabric that would mask the thermal signature from their hot Type One bodies. And the small black cube that Dax had positioned on the rooftop just in front of them would block any camera drones. They had no blasters, no weapons that would give off a signal that could be easily detected. They were pirates. Not amateurs.

Jinn had been to this Colony before. Her mother had an

apartment here, and Jinn had been sent to it for a holiday twice a year, with her nanny droids in tow. It had made an exciting change from Earth when she'd been six. She'd liked all of it. The flight. The tall, glossy buildings, the shops, the museums, the play centres. It had all seemed so otherworldly and glamorous. She'd had dreams of coming to live here as an adult, imagined herself taking a job with one of the banks or the investment firms that had their offices here, living in a beautiful hundredth-floor apartment. It was what Ferona wanted for her, and as a naïve six-year-old, pleasing her mother had been the most important thing in her life.

Things were different now. She was different. Seeing the colony through adult eyes made her notice all the little things that weren't quite right with it. It was all too clean, too perfect. Everyone was tall and thin and pale-haired and dressed in the same expensive way. Every building was the same. These people weren't free. They were trapped inside this world of their own making, doing jobs that had no real meaning, not daring to put a foot wrong in case they were thrown out of the exclusive club that was Colony life.

The main city was to their left. The buildings were just like the people, all purposefully tall and thin, with gardens growing in rings around the outside. Even from a distance it was obvious that the trees were beautifully healthy, but then they would be. Sickness and death weren't allowed here. At the far edge of the city, trucks and building equipment were zooming around, erecting more of those tall buildings. Without their greenery they looked stark and industrial. Their skeletal insides reminded Jinn of the workings of a freighter, one she'd seen broken apart and burning in space a long time ago.

'Why are they building here? It doesn't make any sense,' she said to Dax.

'Nothing rich people do makes any sense.'

Jinn said nothing. Too many of their recent conversations had come to this. Rich against poor. Dome versus Underworld. She'd thought they had moved past those differences. She'd been wrong. Sometimes she was glad of it, because she was very afraid that without those reminders, she would ask him a question she did not want the answer to, such as *Do you still love me? Are you really glad that I came for you? Should I have left you there?*

The roller pulled away, and another one slid in to take its place. More dark-suited men got out and hurried inside. The agents surrounded the car and the doorway. 'I can't tell if they're there to stop people from getting in or to stop the ministers from getting out,' she said.

'Does it make any difference?'

'I guess not.'

Dax lifted his own optics to his eyes. 'The drones are circling the perimeter in a pattern. There's a gap.'

'How long will we have?'

He counted. 'Twenty-two seconds to make it to the roof.'

'Is that long enough?'

'It'll be tricky, but I think we'll manage.' He folded up his optics and slipped them into his jacket pocket.

Jinn pushed hers up onto the top of her head. She risked one last look down at the street below. She blew out a long breath.

'Ready?' Dax asked.

'Always.'

He moved to a crouch and gestured to the building. 'After you.'

'Thanks,' she said, not meaning it in the slightest.

She got to her feet. She kept her knees bent, trying to keep her body low and out of sight. She'd survive the jump, there was no doubt about that. But knowing it and persuading her body to do it weren't the same thing. She took a deep breath, held it. And jumped.

The fall was both incredibly slow and incredibly fast. The air rushed past her and so did a camera drone. She smacked it out of the air. It flew away to the left, spinning madly, disappearing out of sight right as the roof of the building rushed up to meet her. The drone had distracted her and she'd forgotten to kick her skyboots on.

It didn't matter. The Virena flew from her hands in a gentle cloud, slowing her speed. It was like sinking into thick air. She hadn't asked it to, hadn't willed it to move, had only a split-second thought that she was going to go straight through the roof and make a far grander entrance than she had intended, and it had responded.

It caught her off guard and she stumbled a little on landing, the impact singing up through her legs as she willed the Virena back into her hands before Dax could see it. He was only seconds behind. He hadn't forgotten to fire his boots, and they settled him gently, silently down.

'Messed up your landing,' he pointed out.

'Shut up.'

He smiled just a little and gestured to the vent at the centre of the roof. They moved silently towards it. Heat rippled up through it, distorting the air just above. Dax tucked his fingertips under the edge and carefully pulled it free. It was a metre across, a huge, heavy thing, and yet he handled it as if it weighed nothing.

Jinn looked down into the shaft and sighed. 'There better not be anything living in this.'

'Only one way to find out.'

She peered down into the shaft. It was too dark to see much, but the scans that Dax had done of the building had indicated that this was their best way in. 'I think you should go first.'

'Need your blades, I'm afraid. In case there's something living in it.'

Jinn said a few choice words inside her head. She held out her hand. Dax took it. He lowered her down, fingers gripping hers, until she was able to jam her boots against the sides of the vent and hold her weight. Then she eased her way down to the bottom.

Bingo.

Below her, she could see the central meeting room, the huge

round table in the middle, and she could hear the low babble of male voices. She carefully stretched out a hand. Dax thought she still had her Tellurium. He didn't know that it was gone, entirely replaced by Virena, the strange living metal she'd brought with her from Sittan. Jinn intended to keep it that way.

She willed out a blade. Another low rumble of voices drifted up through the mesh. They sounded terribly calm. But that wouldn't last. She was about to throw a great big Type One-shaped spanner in the works. She counted down. Three. Two. One. Then she cut the mesh away with a quick swipe of her hand, jerking her ankles together in the same instant so that she fell straight down into the room below.

She didn't mess up her landing this time. Stunned, pale faces stared up at her. 'Good afternoon, Ministers. Sorry to interrupt. But I wasn't sure how else to get your attention.'

A stride to the edge of the table, kicking an info cube and a glass of water out of her way as she did so. A short hop down to the floor. It was the work of a moment to throw some Virena at the doors and lock them. The men gathered around the table finally rediscovered their voices and began to wave their arms and shout. Someone yelled for security. But unfortunately for them, both agents and droids were on the other side of the locked door.

And then Dax dropped down into the room. The table cracked as he hit it. The gathered ministers rushed back as the two halves of the heavy table went their separate ways, throwing workpads and comm. units at the walls before thumping down against the floor. Spilled drinks formed dark puddles on the carpet. The temperature in the room seemed to rise ten degrees.

'Please don't hurt us!' someone shouted, their voice high-pitched with panic.

'Trust me,' Dax said. 'I'm not the one you need to worry about. She is.' He gestured to Jinn. 'Everyone, please calm down. We don't want to hurt you. We just want to talk.'

'We've got nothing to say to you, underworld scum.'

'Sit down,' Jinn told them. A couple of them did as she said, but not all. So she said it again, more loudly this time. 'Sit down!'

It took them long enough, but they finally seemed to get the message. She could tell by their faces that most were shocked. Some were angry, and they showed it in bulging veins and white-knuckled fists. Jinn suspected that had she been there on her own, at least one of them would have tried to take her on. But all of them were intimidated enough by the sight of a huge, Underworld-raised space pirate to keep quiet.

Jinn had practised this, had prepared for it, but now that she was here, she found that the words she'd intended to say were no longer the right ones. They were too polite, too measured. They didn't convey the enormity of what she felt now that she stood in a room with these self-interested cowards.

She pulled a holosphere from her pocket and flipped it into the air. It spun, then settled in a steady hover and switched itself on. A map of neutral space burst from it. She could see space stations now, fuelling stations, trading posts. And the red lines crossing out all those that had already been hit.

'This is neutral space,' she said. 'These are all human-occupied places in neutral space. And these are all the ones that the Sittan have already taken. Look at them.'

A few heads turned.

'Look at them!' she yelled. 'People died on these stations! You left them alone and unprotected, and the Sittan slaughtered them. Why aren't you helping them? Why aren't there Security Service ships in neutral space? At the very least, you should be transporting people home to buy time until you sort this out.'

One of the men got to his feet. The others remained silent. 'Jinnifer Blue,' he said. 'And Caspian Dax. That is who you are, isn't it?' His voice was steady, his tone completely reasonable. It knocked Jinn off balance. She'd been expecting a denial, an argument.

'It is. Who are you?'

The murmur that rippled around the room combined with the flush of colour that hit his cheeks told her that wasn't the question she was supposed to ask.

'I'm President Bautista,' he said. There was a definite edge to his voice now. The flush was still there, just under his skin, but he was more in control of himself than anyone else in the room. This was a dangerous man. 'I don't know how you got past the security outside,' he continued. 'Quite frankly at this point it doesn't really matter. You won't be leaving. But I have to say, I find myself a little disappointed.' He looked her over. 'I thought you'd be a little more . . . intelligent.'

'Excuse me?'

'We did not start the war,' the man said, as if that absolved him of all responsibility. 'And what happens outside of Earth-controlled space is not our concern. Earth's government has one job, and one job only, and that is to manage things on our side of the border. It is up to the senate to deal with neutral space.'

'The senate is not doing anything either!'

'Then there is nothing to be done.'

'People are dying,' Dax said. His tone was chilling. And for a moment, Jinn saw a flicker of fear in Bautista's eyes. 'And you are letting it happen.'

'Our focus has to be on protecting Earth-controlled space. Protecting our border. I am sorry for those beyond it, but we cannot help them.'

'You are choosing not to.'

'What would you have me do?' Bautista asked. 'I have a dying planet to contend with. You talk about the people in neutral space as if they are the only ones who matter. There are people dying on Earth right now. What about them?'

'You could at least send ships to bring people back to Earth-controlled space.'

'And who will pay for that? Who will pay for their food rations and medications? Their housing? I must also point out, Ms Blue, that many of those living in neutral space have warrants out for their arrest. Who will pay for the additional prison space that will be needed for them when they reach Earth-controlled space?'

'You could just cancel the warrants.'

'And have Bugs and criminals running free? I don't think so.'

Jinn had known, when they came here, that it was unlikely that she would be able to persuade any of these men to help. But she had wanted to stand in a room with them and make her case. She had wanted to hear for herself that they had no intention of helping the people in neutral space.

'It doesn't matter what people have done,' she told him. 'Not any more. We have to stop dividing ourselves into them and us. We have to stop thinking that Dome is better, that rich is better, that the people who have genetic modifications so they can work in the mines are inferior to people who have genetic modifications to get rid of the family nose. The Sittan are coming, President Bautista. Soon, they'll be done with neutral space. I know. I've been tracking them. And then they'll come here. What will you do when the Sittan cross the border? Because they will. *What will you do?*'

She could feel fury burning within her, and didn't know how much longer she would be able to control it. She wanted to tear this place apart. She could feel the Virena responding to the rush of emotion, encouraging her to act on those feelings, but she pushed it back, refusing to let it distract her.

'The Sittan will not cross the border.'

'Of course they will!'

Bautista shook his head, laughing a little. 'No alien ships have ever crossed our border, and they're not about to start doing so. We have control of the jump gates and every part of the border is being patrolled.'

'What makes you think you can stop the Sittan from crossing the border when you couldn't stop me? I flew my ship straight past your patrols. It wasn't even searched. You're not safe. You're an easy target.'

'They didn't stop you because you're not a threat.'

'Not a threat?' Jinn asked in disbelief. 'Do you not understand what I am?'

'You're a mistake,' he said.

'No,' she corrected him. 'I am the only thing standing between you and annihilation.'

'You?' he laughed. 'A fugitive who aligned herself with pirates and criminals? No. I don't think so. This war, if you can even call it that, will burn itself out in neutral space. It is not our concern.' There was a little white dot of spit on his bottom lip. Jinn couldn't stop looking at it.

She knew that there was nothing she could say that would change his mind. He wasn't nearly frightened enough for that. Not yet. And if she killed him, which she could, easily, someone just the same would step up and take his place.

But she wanted him to remember this meeting, this moment. She wanted him to look back in the months to come and know that he'd had the chance to form an alliance, a chance to act, and had chosen not to.

She walked right up to him, wondering if he had the spine to hold his ground, and he surprised her by proving that he did. He was a tall man. They were eye to eye. He didn't like that, she could tell, as he jerked his chin up, his Adam's apple travelling down and back up again as he tried to make it seem like he had to look down at her. 'They're coming,' she said softly. 'And when they do, I'll make sure everyone knows you could have stopped them.'

His face turned purple. 'You'll regret this!' he choked out.

'Probably,' she told him.

She and Dax left through the front door.

No-one tried to stop them.

CHAPTER

2

3rd Day of the Seventh Turn

The Palace, Fire City, Sittan

It was dark in the palace. Many of the slaves had ceased to carry out their duties, leaving the fires unlit, and with no-one tending to the sconces, they hung lifeless against the polished stone of the wall. Sand gathered in the unswept corners of the throne room.

Talta sat on her throne, motionless, staring unseeing into the shadows. She ignored the platters of rotting food spread out on the low tables in front of her and the rattle of her beloved Vreen in its cage above her head. Her mind was elsewhere. In all her many turns as empress, she had never been defeated. She had ruled for longer than any other. No-one could match her for cruelty, for determination, for beauty. She had been the best of all of them.

Now, she was . . .

At the first glimmer of suns on the horizon, she left the palace and went out into the courtyard. She took a moment to stroke her beautiful pets, to admire the dark gleam of their scales. She watched the ascent of the three burning suns that warmed her planet. The heat sank into her bones. She was so tired. Her entire body felt heavy, as if her flesh had become stone, even though when she looked at herself, it remained just as blue and just as alive as it had always been.

She made her way to the huge burnished cauldron at the very centre of the courtyard and sank to her knees before it. In the very bottom, only a handspan deep, shimmered the last of her Virena. There was so little left now. She had scarcely more than a guard would carry.

But it was enough. And it still listened to her.

'Where is she?' she asked it.

The question had been the same for the last nineteen turns.

So had the answer.

Inside the cauldron, what remained of the Virena swirled and shifted. It resisted when she pushed against it, but eventually it let her in. Her hands disappeared up to her wrists. Talta remembered the days when it would have covered her entire body with barely a push, leaving not a trace of blue. Now it took everything she had just to touch it.

But when she did, it transported her immediately. It took her to all the other places where it existed in the galaxy, to the soldiers she had sent in pursuit of Jinnifer Blue. It brought her death. It brought her the last cries of more humans than she could count, and she savoured every single one of them. She raked through its memories, pulling out everything it had seen and done, everywhere it had been. The females that carried it barely felt her presence. She kept her touch light, or so she told herself, because she didn't want to distract them.

They were winning the fight, and it was easy. The humans were no match for her warriors. Their ships were pathetic and weak in comparison to the might of a Sittan deathship. Their bodies were soft and useless, and they seemed to have no idea how to defend themselves. Any creature so completely unable to fight for its place in the galaxy deserved to die.

But there was only one human that Talta truly wanted to kill. Jinnifer Blue. The human female had invaded her planet, had fought in the arena and won, and had awakened the Mountain. It burned still. Talta could see it in the distance, the bright fire at the very peak, that steady flame lighting the city below.

Jinnifer Blue had called to the Virena and it had answered. It had denied Talta for so many turns that she had thought it gone, and yet *it had answered to Jinnifer Blue.*

She searched through the web of Virena, not just on this planet, but beyond, searching the minds of all her females until she found the one she wanted. Grenla's thoughts shone like a beacon in the darkness. As an empress' guard, she had greater than usual control over the Virena, and Talta took advantage of it.

How goes the war?

It goes well. The humans fall before us. They bleed so easily. Most of them do not even try to fight. They are soft creatures. Their bodies and their souls are feeble. They beg for mercy. We do not grant it.

Talta's fingers curled inside the bowl, the Virena hardening as she put pressure on it, its resistance to her increasing. She wanted to feel pleasure at Grenla's words. There was none. The bargain she had struck with Ferona Blue had been a terrible mistake. She could see that now. Talta had needed males with Sittan blood in their veins, and there had not been enough of them left on Sittan. When Ferona Blue had said that her scientists could splice Sittan and human together and give Talta more disposable males than she would ever need, it had seemed like the perfect solution.

She had been so sure that it would bring the Virena back, that it would awaken the Mountain, sending rivers of that dark, precious substance flowing through the cities once more. But it had failed. Talta didn't understand it. She had given the Virena blood. So much blood. So why hadn't it answered? What had Jinnifer Blue done that she hadn't?

Talta drew in air. She controlled her anger. It wouldn't help her now.

All Ferona had wanted in return for the males was safe passage for human ships through Sittan-controlled space. Talta had been desperate enough to agree.

But Ferona Blue had deceived her. She had allowed that precious Sittan flesh to be spliced into a female. She had made herself a daughter in possession of immense power, and Talta could not help but believe that it had been deliberate.

The arrival of Jinnifer Blue on Sittan had changed everything. The Mountain had erupted. The Virena had flowed, and it had swollen the rivers. It had repaired the buildings, so long broken, and the palace had been filled with light. The weakening shield that had protected their planet for so long had been recharged. Talta had experienced a reawakening of public support. The females had come to the arena in their thousands. Their support for Talta had been overwhelming.

She had not seen the danger at first. She had thought that she could control the human female, just as easily as she'd been able to manipulate the males. But she had been wrong. In some ways, Talta respected Jinn for what she'd done. Perhaps it could even be said that she admired the human female's strength, her ability to handle pain, her willingness to kill. She'd even killed Dax.

Only then, when it was too late, had Talta understood what was happening and tried to stop it. But rather than fight her to the end, Jinnifer Blue had left Sittan and taken the Virena and the broken, useless body of Caspian Dax with her.

There had been no choice but to go to war.

Grenla's voice interrupted that thought.

We are almost at the border. Do you want us to cross it?
And enter Earth-controlled space?

Talta thought about this for a moment. It was certainly tempting.

Not yet.

When?

When you have found her.

We've searched everywhere. We do not know where she is.

Then you are not looking hard enough.

Talta had to pull her hands from the pot for a moment so she could breathe, so strong was her reaction. Her rage was almost overwhelming. She controlled it, just, and plunged them back into the dark liquid which bubbled around her fingers.

You must find her.

We will.

Talta pulled her hands free of the pot once more and got unsteadily to her feet. The three suns were moving across the sky and the world around her grew lighter still, bathed in the bright orange glow of the early morning. From her position in the courtyard she could see out across her city, and across the barren desert of the Sand Seas. Beyond them lay the other cities of Sittan, none of them as great as hers, but still powerful and well resourced.

So far, they had not openly challenged Talta's position as empress. But rumours had started to spread. Questions were being asked.

And if they did not find Jinnifer Blue, and soon, Talta did not know how she would answer them.

CHAPTER

3

18th January 2208

Apartment 438, Acton District, London Dome, Earth

Everything that Ferona Blue had worked for was lost. Her vision of the human race settled on a beautiful new planet had been completely destroyed in the space of a few brief seconds with nothing more than a few short words. The Sittan empress had stepped up to the podium in the great meeting hall on Kepler, fixed her traitorous yellow eyes on Ferona, and spitefully ended the future that Ferona had worked so hard for.

And just as quickly, those back on Earth had turned on Ferona.

When she'd returned from Kepler, she had found herself ridiculed. Spiteful caricatures showing her with a pointed nose and enormous bouffant hair had appeared all over the interplanetary net, and she had endured several weeks of intrusive hounding by camera bots that had left her frightened to leave her apartment. The Sittan declaration of war had been turned into a joke.

Everyone had forgotten that they'd supported the Second Species programme. The exodus to Spes had been swept under the carpet. All mention of it had disappeared from the newsfeeds and the media sites. Bautista was promising to fix the widespread issues with the water supply and repair the Domes. There was talk of terraforming another six asteroids and making them fit for human habitation, and everyone was behaving as if this had been the plan all along. The funds to pay for it were going to come from the withdrawal of Earth from the senate. They would no longer be a part of that group of species, no longer have free access to neutral space or all the resources it contained.

All over the Dome, holoscreens were showing images of a repaired and extended Dome, and droids were taking thumbprints and blood samples from those who hoped to get building work on the Colonies. The shipyards on Colony Two were working around the clock. There was increased activity on Colony Seven as well, where the city was being expanded to provide more homes, as well as assessment of several as yet undeveloped asteroids. There was talk of a brighter future. A human future.

Ferona wanted to scream at the people walking the streets with their scarlet circles pinned to their lapels, declaring their support for Bautista and the newly reformed Humans First, which had been subtly renamed People First. She wanted to break every screen that showed news stories she was certain were fake. It didn't matter how many cities Bautista built on the colonies, there simply would not be enough room or resources for everyone on Earth. Nor could the problems planetside be fixed.

But people believed what they wanted to believe and there was nothing she could do to change their minds. She was out of office. She had no power, no voice, and very quickly, no money. She had been forced to move from her beautiful top-floor apartment to a small studio flat on the ground floor of the Dome. Her remaining things had been packed into boxes which were piled up against the wall of her living room. She was trying to eke out the meagre pension that she was receiving as a former civil servant, but for a woman used to spending whatever she felt like, it was proving extremely difficult.

She spent most of her time in her horrible little apartment, watching the news on the various streams, desperately trying to find something, anything about what was happening in neutral space. Trying to find evidence of what she knew was the truth. But after not leaving her apartment for eight days in a row, she started to feel like she was going mad. Every time she looked at the walls, they seemed closer. She realised that she was talking to herself. Out loud.

It was frightening enough to make her risk the camera bots and go outside. She put on a long coat and a hat and walked the three kilometres to St Guy's Hospital, where Vexler, the former President of Earth, had been ever since he'd been injured by a bomb that had gone off as he was getting into his car outside the ministerial building.

Bloody thing was supposed to kill him. But he couldn't even do that right.

It wasn't until she felt the pain in her jaw that Ferona realised she was grinding her teeth. It took a conscious effort to stop. By the time she'd done that, she was at the entrance to the hospital. She already knew which ward Vexler was on. For the first month, he'd had quite a lot of visitors. Now she seemed to be the only one.

He lay on a hospital bed, a sheet pulled up to his chin, his chest slowly rising and falling. If you didn't know better you'd think he was simply asleep. Instead, he was in a coma with no sign of waking up. In some ways Ferona didn't mind. There was something quite enjoyable about being able to talk through what troubled her with someone who didn't answer back.

The occasional flicker behind his veiny, paper-thin eyelids suggested what the scans had confirmed – that he retained some degree of higher-level brain function.

She could count the passing of the seconds with each of those shallow breaths. Each bleep of the machine at his side marked another stubborn beat of his heart. He lay there in dreamless peace, unaware that the rest of the world was in chaos. It was typical of him. Absent when there were difficult choices to be made, but not nearly absent enough.

'You are such an annoying bastard,' she told him. 'It was bad enough that you didn't die. Now you won't respond to treatment. You just lie there like a brainless moron while Bautista ruins everything.'

Because if Vexler did wake up, Bautista would be forced to step down. Vexler had been a hugely popular president. He still had support. But time was not on his side. People would eventually get bored. They'd move on. And then Vexler would be even more use-less than he was now.

Ferona couldn't take it any more. She got up and left. No-one paid her any attention as she strode along the corridor that led to the elevators. She stood alone in the corner as the lavender-scented car dropped down to the ground floor, tinkling music playing cheer-ily in the background. When she stepped out, the vast foyer was quiet. Staff and service droids moved quickly and discreetly. None of the other visitors met her gaze. All of them moved as if in their own private little bubble which rendered everyone else invisible. Most of them were glued to their wrist screens, no doubt watching the day's news.

Ferona found it infuriating. Didn't they know? Didn't they understand?

What they saw on those screens was not real. Bautista had powerful friends in the media. He had given them an even bigger boost by quietly censoring the independent channels. He couldn't control what was broadcast, but he could control what people saw, and if they didn't see it, it was as if it didn't happen. And his own version of the truth was being repeated over and over and over. The Sittan were tough, but humans were tougher. The Sittan would not come to Earth-controlled space. The war, such as it was, was happening far away in neutral space, and it was a power struggle between competing trade groups that had nothing to do with the people on Earth.

It was time to once again look to home. Conditions on Earth might be declining, but they could be fixed. The government had a plan. A budget. Investment was happening, and it was for the many, not the few. It would make life better for all of them. They just had to be patient.

It was complete hogwash.

Oh, she was convinced that Bautista didn't believe that the Sittan would come to Earth-controlled space. He'd never been to the senate. He hadn't met Talta. He didn't *know*, not in the way that Ferona did. And he probably did intend to throw a lot of money at the problems on Earth, and he probably could improve life for some people, primarily himself and his wealthy friends. Everyone else would be left to rot.

Bautista might not understand the power of the Sittan empress and that strange living metal she possessed, but Ferona did. Even if they could fix what was wrong here on Earth, the damage done to the planet by centuries of overuse, it wouldn't make any difference. They had a new enemy now.

It was only a matter of time before the Sittan reached the border of Earth-controlled space and Ferona for one did not believe they would stop once they got there.

She walked a little faster. Her gold heels rang loudly on the polished floor. The shoes cut into her ankles and her toes were cold, but she'd never had any use for practical footwear and so impractical was all she had. These were the best of what had turned out to be a very poor lot.

A woman in a short green coat and matching cap turned her head and tutted. Ferona knew the instant the woman recognised her, because her expression turned from irritation to something more. But Ferona gave it back in spades. She no longer cared what these people thought. She no longer felt the need to pretend to respect them.

She left the hospital and steered her way past the queue of taxis waiting outside, positioning her anti-pollution mask up over the lower half of her face as she did so. Almost everyone was wearing them now, even here inside the Dome, and pollution monitors on every corner flashed warnings in amber and red as people walked past. The pollution counters were new. The point of them wasn't to terrify everyone into thinking that the levels of toxicity had reached a critical point, but to demonstrate that Bautista's actions were bringing pollution levels down, and to show the fall in real time. Every time the count went down, people felt better, as if turning their screen off for an hour the night before had really made a difference.

The entire situation filled Ferona with a roaring frustration that made it hard to sleep, hard to think. There had to be someone who still believed in what she had tried to do, who still believed that there was more that she *could* do.

She did not even have her assistants to support her. Swain had been killed in the explosion, and Lucinda had disappeared. In some ways it was no great loss. Swain had been useless anyway, and Lucinda had betrayed her when she sold her loyalty to Vexler. But her assistants had always been available when she wanted them, and Ferona missed that. She disliked having to waste her valuable time on mundane tasks and she had valued their input, in so far as their stupid suggestions always confirmed that the way she thought things should be done was the correct one.

A man walked quickly past, moving too close and bumping Ferona hard. 'Watch where you're going!' she snarled at him. He took no notice. He kept on moving, hands shoved deep in the pockets of his dark flowing coat. Pale hair hung to his collar. Something about the way he moved was oddly familiar. Her curiosity was piqued. She turned and started to follow him, despite her sore feet, keeping enough distance between them that she felt confident he wouldn't notice.

The man walked to the end of the street and took a right, heading in the direction of the shuttle station at St Pancras. Going to one of the other Domes, perhaps? He didn't have any luggage with him, but the coat was voluminous enough to hold several packets of clothing.

She was being foolish. She should turn around, head for the museum and get out of the cold for a bit, or just go home. But she didn't. She followed him past Koffee parlours and street vendors peddling soy burgers and rehydrated pastries. It wasn't that long since they'd sold beautiful fresh fruit, but the few apples and oranges currently on display were small and obviously past their best and no-one was buying. Bautista had promised improved food, but it clearly hadn't arrived yet.

The man kept on and Ferona kept following him, distracted only for a moment by a fight that had broken out at a food cart. At the end of the street, the man came to a standstill. Ferona slowed her pace. Ahead of them the street opened out into a large square, at the centre of which was a rapidly dying flower garden. Water-saving measures and all that. The benches around it, usually occupied, were mostly empty. The nearby Security Service academy accounted for the few grey-uniformed students hanging around, bottles of Soylate and cheap beer dangling from their hands.

The man started to move again, then suddenly stopped and sat on one of the benches. She felt the weight of his stare before she unintentionally met his gaze and felt the shock of recognition when her pulse jolted in response.

It was Mikhal Dubnik. Former Vice President. Former nanny for President Vexler. What was he doing here? He was supposed to be in prison! Ferona had two choices now. She could leave. Or she could accept the invitation that his stare was so obviously extending.

She chose the latter. He'd gone to the trouble to make sure she would follow him. The least she could do was to find out what he wanted. Still, she approached him with caution, and didn't stand too close.

'Ferona,' he said. He wasn't wearing a pollution mask, and there was a grey, unhealthy tinge to his skin.

'Mikhal. When did you get out of prison?'

'Three days ago.'

'That's not very long.'

'No,' he agreed. 'You look dreadful. I take it political life isn't treating you well.'

Ferona clenched her teeth. How dare he? Quite easily, she thought, as she managed to get the swell of shamed anger under control. 'Better than it's currently treating Vexler.'

'Yes,' Dubnik said. 'Our esteemed president is in something of a state at the moment. I wonder if he will recover.'

'The doctors believe there is a chance.'

'No chance for you, though.'

If Ferona had anyone else to talk to, she would have walked away at that point. But loneliness can do strange things. She took the seat next to him, smoothing the skirts of her high-collared milk-white coat. Right knee crossed neatly over left, she gripped the edge of the bench and watched the people around them, the touts and the food sellers, the cleaning droids, the trainee agents rushing through their precious youth, and she steeled herself for what he might say next.

He did not disappoint.

'You sent me to prison.' He spoke quietly, his gaze fixed on something in the distance. 'You produced false documentation that showed anomalies in my accounts. I lost my job and my home.'

'You were held in a low security unit. You had an acceptable standard of living.'

'Nice to see you haven't changed.' Dubnik stretched out his

legs. His trousers were pinstriped and shiny at the knee. 'Doesn't it bother you?'

'What?'

'What you've done. The Second Species programme. Genetically modifying innocent human beings with alien DNA and sending them to alien planets to die. Using millions of dollars of public funding to pay for it, which could have been used to solve some of the problems we have here on Earth.'

'There is no way to solve the problems we have here on Earth. Spes is our only option.'

Dubnik shook his head. 'I never believed that, and I still don't. We can fix what is wrong here on Earth, Ferona. With the right investment in the right place, we can extend the Domes, bring heat up from the core, increase under-cover forestation. Algae tanks ...'

'Why didn't you do any of that when you were in office?'

'I tried.'

'Clearly not hard enough.'

'Is that what you did? Tried hard enough?'

'At least I did something.'

'Yes. And I admire you for that. It takes a certain type of arrogance to believe that you're the only person who can solve the world's problems.'

'It takes a certain type of cowardice to tie up the future with paperwork and meetings and bureaucracy and do nothing.'

'Is that why you set me up? Because you think I'm a coward?'

'No. I did what I did because you were in my way.' Now she was closer to him, she could see the wear in his skin, the stress in the creases around his eyes and the touch of silver in the hair at his temples. He was still an elegant man, but there was exhaustion in the hunch of his shoulders and his coat wasn't just flowing, it was too big. If she had been capable of feeling bad about what she had done, that would have been the moment. 'At least with my way, we had a chance.'

'Bautista says we have a chance here.'

'Bautista is a war denier who thinks that all our problems can be solved by building completely pointless housing on Colony Seven.'

'Why is it pointless? The colonies have spare capacity. He's not wrong about that. People have to go somewhere.'

'It's pointless because we're at war! What happens when the Sittan cross the border? New colonies won't protect us from that. It's too little, too late, Mikhal. And even if, by some miracle, the Sittan do not come here, the colonies are too small to support the remaining population, which means that he's planning on leaving people behind.'

'I suppose leaving the poor to freeze to death in the Underworld cities is completely different to sending them to be slaughtered on Sittan.'

Ferona chose to ignore that.

'Bautista is the problem here,' she said. 'With him in office, no-one stands a chance.'

'I agree,' he said, much to her surprise. 'What are we going to do about it?'

'We?'

'Yes,' he said. 'Unless you know of anyone else who is going to step up and save us?'

26

CHAPTER

4

18th January 2208

> Vessel: The *Sweet Rose*. Class 3 transporter
> Destination: Sector Twelve, Neutral Space
> Cargo: N/A
> Crew: 2
> Droids: 0

It would take two days' travel to get back to the *Mutant* after their pointless trip to the colony. Dax's anger was a nasty, sour taste in the back of his throat. What disgusted him the most was that he had known, deep down, exactly what the response was going to be, but he had wanted to stand in a room with those people. He had wanted, he knew now, to frighten them. But they were not easily frightened. They were still too arrogant, too protected by their wealth, drunk on new power. And if they told themselves often enough that the people in neutral space didn't matter, they could make themselves believe it. They'd also convinced themselves that the Sittan wouldn't cross the border into Earth-controlled space, and for that they were fucking idiots.

On their way to the *Mutant*, they detected three separate human distress signals. Two were close together, so Dax set a course for their location and Jinn flew them there. It took twelve hours of painful silence to reach a pair of cruisers drifting side by side in an area of empty space. There was no sign of any Sittan ships, but that was pretty much the only positive piece of information.

Jinn flew them alongside so that they could take a closer look. Scorch marks patterned the hulls, cutting through the cables and pipes that would have allowed the life support to operate. On a ship this size they were by necessity close to the surface.

The people on board had never stood a chance. They hadn't even had time to fire the pathetically underpowered cannons they'd had mounted fore and aft, which were all still loaded and armed. Perhaps it was better that way, to go quickly without time for hope or the fear that would inevitably have followed when those hopes were dashed. But even as a pirate, when he'd done some terrible things, Dax had never done this. He'd never killed just for the hell of it.

The two of them suited up and slipped out of the airlock, powering their way across to the other ships. Dax had brought a little maintenance droid with him. It cut open the hatch on the first ship and peeled it away. 'It's not going to be pretty,' Jinn said.

'No,' Dax agreed. 'I'll go in first.'

He didn't want to. He had to force himself to enter the ship. He would suffer for it later, but he would be able to do that in private. For now he had to put personal feelings aside and do what needed to be done.

It was a crew of eight. A pilot, a second mate, a family of six. All dead, slowly suffocated when the oxygen ran out. The woman still had her arms round one of the children, the two of them curled up together on the floor. 'They don't even take anything,' Jinn said. 'Look. All the electronics are intact, and the woman is wearing enough platinum to build a phase drive.'

'They're not interested in theft. This was an execution.'

'And picking off ships like this, too small to really defend themselves. These people weren't soldiers. Their only crime was being the wrong species.'

Somehow, this was worse than a violent death. At least violence was something he could understand. Jinn checked the onboard computer, downloading the ship codes and the identity documents for the victims. She'd been keeping a record of everyone they found.

There was nothing else they could do. They weren't in a position to make use of the ships or anything on them, so they had no choice but to head back to the transporter, leaving the dead to their cold and lonely resting place.

They didn't talk about what they'd just seen. Dax stripped out of his suit quickly, shoving it back into its bag. 'Damn suit makes me sweat,' he said to Jinn. The hair on the back of his neck was wet, and he could feel the tickle of liquid sliding down his spine. 'How far to the next jump?'

'I can do it in an hour,' she said as she pulled off her own suit. The dark kill tattoos on her shoulders mirrored his, though she didn't have as many as he did. Her damp vest stuck to her skin. Dax noticed. He couldn't help himself. Her body tempted him.

He turned his head and didn't let himself look.

The closeness they'd shared before he'd been taken to Sittan was gone and it was never coming back. The sooner he accepted that, the better. 'Good,' he said. He climbed down into the lower level of the ship, where a cramped space held a chemicleanse. He stripped off the rest of his clothes, and locked himself inside. The spray ran briefly and cold. The smell was faintly sour, which meant that the unit needed servicing, but there was little chance of that happening.

Dax leaned back against the wall and exhaled. The spray had turned itself off, so he thumped the button to turn it back on again, then went through the motions of washing himself. Face, armpits, cock. His arm was itching like crazy and he scratched at it, digging his fingers into the flesh. It only made the itch worse. He scratched at it even harder, until the skin broke and blood flowed and he put his hands to the wall and silently howled.

The itch was in the very place where the Vreen had bitten him, back on Sittan. The foul little creature had venom in its saliva which had caused terrifying hallucinations. It had made Dax lose his grip on reality, and that had terrified him so much that he'd done things he would otherwise never have contemplated. He still wasn't sure which parts of his memory were real and which weren't. He had strange, disturbing dreams in which he couldn't breathe, where the pain was so intense that he was sure it was real, only to wake up and find himself naked and sweating and afraid.

The spray turned to feeble heat and he lifted his arms as it dried him off, then stepped out of the chemicleanse and went over to the mirror, which flicked on when it detected him.

He hadn't looked at himself properly in months. He hadn't wanted to. But now he forced himself to examine what that time on Sittan had done to him.

Black stripes ran along each shoulder, one for every man he had killed. There were more than he wanted to count. In the centre of his chest were four livid scars, deep purple in colour, angry in their intensity. Jinn had given him those. He ran his fingers over the rough surface, wincing as he did so.

The flesh was still sore. Before, he'd always healed easily. Nothing had bothered him for more than a couple of days. He rarely scarred, most of his skin still perfect and unmarked. But something about this wound was different. Maybe it was because it had been a killing blow. He had lain there in the dirt, his heart not beating, and he had experienced what the end was like.

Only it had not been the end. The holes in his heart had closed up. Blood had started to move through his arteries. The pain had been immense, but he had survived it. He had cheated death like the pirate that he was. There had been no such escape for the other men on Sittan, for all those he had killed and seen killed, just as there had been no escape for the people on those ships out there.

The chemicleanse pinged, indicating that it had finished, and Dax dressed quickly, without bothering to look in the mirror again. He took a few deep breaths. He slipped out of the washroom and made his way back up to the control deck, settling himself into his seat. He tried to make it look casual but feared that he'd done anything but. Jinn was in the pilot's seat with her feet up on the control deck in her usual way. 'I've picked up another distress signal already,' she said quietly. 'I honestly don't know if we should follow it or not.'

Dax pulled up his screen, found the signal, located the source. He stared at the flashing dot on the map. 'I don't know either.' What would be the point? By the time they got there, it would be too late. He and Jinn were just two people. They were nothing against the might of the Sittan army.

But still, he felt a responsibility for whoever had sent that signal. An obligation to do something, even if that something turned out to be nothing more than an acknowledgement of their existence.

He was still staring at it, trying to make a decision, when a box popped up in the corner of the screen. Someone was trying to contact him. That was odd. He accepted the trace, and it connected quickly.

'Dax!' said the man on screen. Young and dark-haired, Dax recognised him instantly.

'Ace. It's been a while. You're not on the colony?'

'Left months ago.'

'I'm glad to see you didn't sign up for the programme.'

'After what we uncovered? Not a chance.'

It gave Dax a little lift to see someone from the past still alive, still breathing. Familiar faces were so few and far between. 'Good,' he said. 'I'm glad. Where are you?'

'I'm on the Europa. Been here for a couple of weeks now. Only intended to stay for a few hours, but things didn't quite work out how I planned.'

'How so?'

'Station master decided to put up the air fees without warning and won't let anyone leave until their debt is cleared. And to put it bluntly, I can't afford it. I'm bloody stuck here. And I don't want to be.'

'You need credits?'

Ace blushed. 'You could say that.'

Dax flicked on the second screen and pulled up a map showing this sector of neutral space. The Europa wasn't far. Stopping there wouldn't have been his first choice in the current circumstances, but he could be persuaded. 'How full is the station?'

'Full,' Ace said.

Dax looked at Jinn. Early on, they'd tried to defend the Articus and failed. After that all their efforts had focused on avoiding the Sittan and staying alive. They didn't have the ships or the firepower to protect somewhere like the Europa, and they knew it.

But Ace was on board that station.

'Well?' Ace asked. 'You're a pirate. I've seen how you and Jinn handle things. If anyone can help, you can.'

'Keep safe,' Dax said. 'We're coming.'

And if, when they got there, they found that a little violence was necessary, he wouldn't be too sad about it.

CHAPTER

5

18th January 2208

> Vessel: The *Mutant*. Battleship/carrier hybrid
> Location: Sector Twelve, Neutral Space
> Cargo: N/A
> Crew: 5
> Droids: 7

Even now, after everything they had been through, Eve didn't like Bryant. How could she? He had gone to Faidal to find her, it was true, but only because he was dying and he had thought that she might be able to help him. He had thrown the sonic grenade that had killed Alistair. And he was a constant reminder of what her touch could do, of how poisonous and hideous she was, and the fact that no, she couldn't help him. She couldn't stop what had been inevitable from the moment she had pressed her hand against the back of his neck and the toxin excreted by her skin had passed into his.

Nor could she persuade herself that he hadn't deserved it. He'd been trying to arrest Dax. He'd brought it on himself, really.

But that certainty wobbled as she looked at Bryant now. His float chair hovered in the far corner of the med bay. There wasn't much to mark out his territory. He couldn't eat any more, so the medidroid had hooked him up with fluids. He had a crumpled pillow and a thin silver blanket. That was it. His hair, once blond and thick, had gone, and the skin on his scalp was streaked with dark purple veins. His face had wasted to bone, his eye sockets huge, cheekbones protruding like small mountains. A couple of days ago his teeth had started to fall out. There was a horrible, sour smell that nothing seemed able to mask.

Eve went straight to the Autochef and ordered herself a lemongrass tea and a muffin, then turned and gave Bryant a baleful stare. 'You look terrible,' she said. It had become the only way she could cope, to insult him, to pretend that he could do something about what was happening to him when the truth was that he was in this state because of her.

Bryant seemed to shrink back a little in his seat. His hands, the skin thinned to transparency, shook. He swallowed and she could tell from the way his eyes screwed up tight that it hurt. 'Sorry,' he lisped. 'But I'm all out of fucks today.'

Eve sat on the edge of the medibed. 'Jinn and Dax sent a message. They're going to the Europa,' she told him. 'They won't be back here for another three days.' She felt that he should know, even if it wouldn't make any difference as far as he was concerned.

'I take it their conversation with our government ministers didn't go too well, then,' Bryant said, forcing the words out between painful breaths.

'You didn't think it would anyway.'

'No.' He coughed. 'Only a fucking moron would think that. Look, you and I both know that I am not going to last another three days.'

'Bryant,' she said. 'Don't say that. You don't know ...'

'Shut up, Eve. Just ... shut up. I'm not going to argue about whether or not I'm going to last another three days. I don't have the energy.' He closed his eyes, and she could see how much effort it took him just to inhale. 'I was going to ask Jinn to do this, but it seems I'm out of time. There's a medical station for agents not far from here. No-one really uses it any more but as far as I know it's still functioning. I ... I want to go there. I don't want to die on this ship.'

Eve didn't allow herself to feel anything. It wasn't difficult. Since Alistair had died, she'd got very good at it. 'I see,' she said. 'How do we get there?'

'We don't. I will go there on my own.'

'Don't be ridiculous. You can't fly a ship.'

'I won't need a ship. I'll take a pod. I just need you to put me in it and programme the co-ordinates. The staff at the centre will take care of the rest.'

Eve took a bite of her muffin. 'No,' she said, chewing loudly. 'All that will happen is that you'll crash land somewhere and it will be a waste of a perfectly good transport. I'll take you.'

But Bryant didn't hear her. He was asleep. She settled herself onto the empty bed, picked a random novel on her entertainment cube and finished her muffin. She hadn't been serious when she said that she would take him. It was just more of his drugged-up rambling. But when he cried out in pain in his sleep, she couldn't kid herself any longer.

It was a strange thing, whatever this was between herself and Bryant. She could finish him off easily, put him out of his misery as quickly as you would put down a stray dog back on Earth, but even in her muted state she knew she could not live with the consequences. So she sat next to him for hour after hour instead, even though the efficient medidroid meant that there was nothing for her to do.

That was how she knew that Jinn had tried to help Bryant. She had given him transfusions of her blood, Type One blood, and that was the only reason Bryant was still going. If Jinn was here, she'd give him another one, and his life would stretch a little beyond the three days. And so it went, another transfusion, a few more days of misery, another transfusion. But to what end?

He wasn't getting better. He would never get better. To live like this was a cruel punishment, and Eve wasn't a cruel person. She didn't feel sorry for Bryant – what he had done to Alistair had made that impossible – but she felt that he had suffered enough.

She sat with him until he woke up. 'Give me the co-ordinates,' she told him, not even bothering to look up from her book as he retched and the medidroid suctioned out his throat.

He gestured to her smart cube, and she passed it over. It took him several tries to activate it. She didn't bother to help him, knowing from experience that he wouldn't like it. Eventually he got it open and working. Thin fingers scrolled through a couple of maps. 'Here,' he said, jabbing at an asteroid close to Colony Six.

'That's Earth-controlled space.'

'Yes.' His eyes were already closed.

'I can't go to Earth-controlled space!'

'I know. That's why I told you I'd go alone.'

His eyes drifted closed again, and he started to snore. Eve stared at the flashing dot on the map, just a little floating chunk of rock, a scrap of nothing really. But it was beyond the white line that marked the difference between neutral space and that which was under the control of Earth. She hadn't been back there in years. Could she do it?

In the end, this could not be about her.

Bryant wanted to go. He couldn't get there on his own, no matter what he said, and if they waited for Jinn and Dax to return, there was a distinct possibility that Jinn would try to talk her out of it. And that she'd succeed. Eve didn't want that.

So she slipped quietly away from the med bay and returned to her quarters. She quickly washed up, cleaning her face and hands in the glowing blue light of the little basin. She twisted her hair up into a knot on the back of her head and changed her clothes. Her wardrobe contained plenty of beautiful things, glossy fabrics, glorious dresses and sweeping coats, all with matching boots. They all felt like they belonged to someone else now and she ignored them in favour of practical grey pants and a long-sleeved shirt. She added a jacket with a hood and a pair of soft gloves.

Then she made her way down to the hold, where she found Li working on one of the transporters they had found. He pulled his big head and enormous shoulders out of the ship as she approached. Oil streaked his hands and his left cheek. 'What's up?'

'Bryant.'

'Is he . . . ?'

'Almost.' She closed her eyes, which were suddenly hot with tears. 'He says that there's a medical centre only a couple of days from here. That's where he wants to go, for . . . you know. So I'm going to take him.'

'I'll come with you.'

'No,' Eve said. 'You need to stay here. Someone has to keep the ship running until Jinn and Dax get back.'

Li at least knew better than to argue with her. 'Alright,' he said. 'If you're sure. Do you want to take one of the transporters?'

'No. I'll take one of the balloons. Less likely to be detected.'

Li nodded. He wiped his forehead with his arm, smearing a little more greasy dirt across it. 'Well, I guess I'll see you when you get back.'

Eve clasped her hands together. 'I guess you will. I've got a transmitter. I'll signal you when I'm back in range. Tell the others . . . tell them I'll see them when I see them. Assuming I'm not back before they are.'

They couldn't hug or even shake hands. Her modifications saw to that. It made for an awkward, uncomfortable parting. Li took care of it by putting his top half back into the guts of the little ship.

Eve went back to the med bay to collect Bryant. His float chair set in motion with the press of her thumb against the button on the side, and she pushed him out and along the corridor to the end where a pretty potted maple tree sat beside a copy of an old painting of water lilies carved into the steelwork that formed the wall. Dax had filled the *Mutant* with things like this, little touches that made the ship into a home.

There were three escape pods. Two were single person emergency transports, but the central one was a balloon pod. It could take multiple passengers, and if she was careful with it, it could get her back here too.

Once she'd dropped Bryant off, she would use the balloon to jettison herself back into neutral space, send a signal to the *Mutant*, and wait for Li to come and pick her up. Assuming that worked, she would be back here within two or three days, maybe even before Dax and Jinn.

The access door for the balloon pod opened to her fingerprint. She shoved Bryant and his float chair inside, then climbed in after him and locked the chair into position. The door closed and sealed. She settled herself into her own seat and punched the eject button before she could think to change her mind.

CHAPTER

6

Jinn and Dax arrived at the Europa to find it no longer a luxury stop-off, but instead a prison. Security droids had been posted at the docking ports to make sure that no-one could leave without permission. Too many of them were occupied by ships with red markers, indicating that they'd been in dock for at least ten days. That meant an additional charge to their bill.

'Why are people still coming here?' Jinn asked. 'Are they mad?'

'Shopping, gambling,' Dax said. 'Euphoria. Alcohol. All the same reasons they came before.'

Their ship was scanned, though fortunately nothing came of it, because Grudge had fiddled with their identity beacon. Concealing the identity of the ship was easier than concealing their own, however. Dax in particular would stick out like a sore thumb because of his size. Fortunately, Grudge had given them a solution to that too, a web-like mask that fit over the face and projected a holographic image that from a distance looked completely natural. They'd been originally designed as a dressing-up toy for children and Jinn hadn't seen one in years, but Grudge was a treasure trove of such things.

As she fitted hers, she could feel the Virena humming with amusement. Faint tendrils shimmered across her skin. It was exploring the mask. She pushed it back, hoping Dax hadn't noticed. He still didn't know just how easily she could control the Virena. She wanted to keep it that way.

Dax's mask wasn't as easy to put on, and after two failed attempts, Jinn intervened. It wasn't a conscious decision. If she'd thought about it, she wouldn't have done it. But just for a second, she forgot their unspoken rule of no physical contact and took the mask from him. Her fingertips grazed against his. The Virena in her hands flashed with heat. She hid that by examining the mask. Dax had been trying to put it on upside down. It was the work of a moment to turn it the right way round and gently smooth it into place.

Dax held himself stiffly, as if he was submitting to something that he very much didn't want to do. 'Do you want to do it?' she asked him, suddenly very aware of their proximity, of the smell of his body, of the way he had his gaze locked very firmly on something over her shoulder.

'No,' he said. 'It's fine. Just get it done. I'm no good with these things.' He held up his hands. 'Too fiddly.'

Jinn turned the mask on, then stepped back to check the results of her work. 'I'd call you handsome, but I'd be lying.' Gone were the familiar features that she adored; the slightly crooked nose, the soft lower lip, the sharp jawline. The mask had made him older, fleshier, with a boozy stain to his cheeks and a sagging neck.

'Was I handsome before?' he asked quietly, and this time, very briefly, he did meet her gaze.

'Dax,' she said, suddenly wishing that she had said nothing at all. *You were beautiful.*

'I didn't think so.' He turned away from her and busied himself with something at the controls, then they climbed down the access ladder, Dax first. He opened the hatch and dropped down onto the walkway.

The Europa was busy. People were clustered everywhere, some huddled in small groups, chatting, others stood on their own. Some of them were pale-haired, Dome-raised. More were dark and clearly of Underworld origin. There were even quite a few Bugs, easily recognisable by their prosthetics. These were people who had been genetically modified to work on the colonies but who had fled to neutral space before paying off the cost of the procedure. Bugs didn't usually come to the Europa. It was too expensive, too close to Earth-controlled space, too risky. But they were here now.

'This isn't good,' Jinn muttered. 'These people didn't come for Euphoria and gambling. Not at the prices they charge here.'

'No,' Dax agreed. 'They're here because it's the last stop on the way back to Earth-controlled space. They're trying to go home.'

Because they knew what was out there.

At the exit to the docking port, she counted close to twenty security droids. Jinn and Dax were able to move past them and onto the station without difficulty. But no-one was moving the other way. They were all stood watching the droids, as if glaring at them would make a difference, which of course it didn't.

'Why aren't they letting people go through to their ships?'

'They've got orders.' Dax shoved his hands into his pockets and hunched his shoulders, something she'd never seen him do before. He'd always owned his height and his size. But that would be dangerous here. 'They can't go against them. That's why humans love droids so much. They always do as they're told.'

Moving away from the docking port, they made their way further into the station. The layout of the walkways hadn't changed, and most of the shops were just the same. She didn't particularly want to remember the other things that had happened here, because most of those memories weren't good. She could feel her face flushing hot with shame at how stupid she had been back then.

'Do you remember the last time we were here?' Dax asked her.

'I'm trying not to.'

'You called your boss, got agents sent to the station to arrest us, and then cut the hand off a Shi Fai.'

'Thanks for reminding me.'

'I wanted to strangle you for being so stupid,' he said. 'I didn't understand how anyone could be such a fool.'

'So why did you protect me from them?'

He almost smiled. 'You know me. Dome women make me stupid.'

'Not that stupid,' Jinn told him. 'You managed to get us both away from the A2. That wasn't exactly easy.'

'I had help.'

'Yeah, well. I didn't. If it wasn't for you, I'd have been stuck there.' And she'd have been caught, caged, turned into a Type One, just like the men they'd found on board that ship. Jinn didn't know what would have happened to her after that. She knew that whatever it was, it wouldn't have been anything she would have chosen for herself.

But she'd been sent back there and turned into a Type One anyway.

'Does it bother you?' she asked him.

'Does what bother me?'

'Me,' she said. 'The fact that I'm Type One.'

'I'm Type One.'

'That's different.'

'How?'

'Because ... because you were always Type One.'

'Not always,' he said. 'Before Medipro got their hands on me I was a miserably average teenage boy. But back to your question. There are many things about you that bother me, Jinn. The way you always put your feet up on the controls. The fact that your diet is 99% Soylate. Your continuing inability to follow instructions. Your being Type One does not.'

'I'm not the same woman you fell in love with.'

He shrugged. 'Given everything that's happened, it would be very strange if you were.'

She wasn't brave enough to ask him if that was why he didn't love her any more.

They were in the main body of the station now. More security droids mingled in with the crowd, their black and silver shells making them stand out against the dark-haired, scruffy Bugs and the few nervous Dome brats. Each of the droids was openly armed.

They weren't here to help the people on this station. They were here to keep them in line. At least half the stores were closed, shutters blanking out their interiors, and it made the place uncomfortably claustrophobic. It also made it even more ludicrous that people were being kept here. If the shops weren't open, they couldn't spend. So what was the point of it?

'This station is so close to the border,' Dax said. 'Imagine it. You're low on fuel, you're running out of food, you're desperate enough to believe that other humans will want to help you, because this is war, and you've seen your trading post or your repair station or whatever completely destroyed and you've got nowhere else to go. You stop here, thinking one last stop before you get to Earth-controlled space, and then you're told you can't leave. You know what's coming. But no-one seems to care.'

Jinn walked on a little further, willing herself not to say the words that were fighting to get out, but she couldn't help it. 'I started a war,' she said. 'There's no getting away from that. I can tell myself it wasn't my fault, but it doesn't change it.'

'War was coming anyway,' Dax said. 'The Sittan empress was never really going to let humans pass through Sittan-controlled space. She agreed to it because she wanted Type Ones for the arena.' He rolled his broad shoulders. 'Anyway, what's with this "I" business? You don't get to take all the credit for this. You weren't the only human on Sittan.'

'But she wouldn't have done this if I hadn't gone there!'

'You don't know that. And if you hadn't gone, I would be dead. Stop feeling sorry for yourself,' he told her. 'It won't fix this.'

They had made it past the shops and were now in the quarter which contained the food courts and entertainment centres. Ace had said he would meet them here. She counted fifty-three droids in this section of the station alone, silently watching the crowd, those sat at the tables, and those sat on the floor around the edges of the food court, holding up empty cups and begging for help.

Run, she wanted to shout at them. *Run*.

But they couldn't.

'I'm hungry,' Dax said. 'How about you?'

'I could eat. Assuming there's anything left here to eat.'

Dax waited for Jinn to go first. She chose a table at the rear and moved to it quickly. The noise level dropped a little and heads turned as people stopped what they were doing to check out the new arrivals. Dax didn't seem to have noticed, as he had already pulled up the menu on the table and was scrolling through the options. He put in his order, looked around at the people sat at the edge of the food court, and went back to the menu again. Jinn pulled up her own menu and opted for noodle soup and a mug of Soylate. Most of the options showed as unavailable.

While they were waiting for the food to be delivered, a group of young, pale-haired men entered the food court, strolling between the tables, occasionally stopping to harass their occupants. Dax stretched out in his seat, hands locked together behind his head, and stared at them.

Jinn had seen their type before. And she'd seen the look on Dax's face before.

'Don't start a fight,' she said to him, keeping her voice low. 'Not here. Not now.'

'I'll behave if they do.'

The men were moving closer. There wasn't anything specific, anything they did or said that riled Jinn up. It was just something about the way they walked, the bouncy swagger which accompanied every step, the way their voices were a little too loud. They were bored and they were looking for trouble.

She could feel her blood starting to heat. She took a deep breath, slowly exhaled, rolled out the tension in her shoulders. She stretched out her leg, nestling her booted foot against his calf, and exerted just a little pressure. 'Don't,' she said again.

One of the men was almost at their table. His gaze slid over Dax, and Jinn saw the sudden jolt of surprise as he realised just how big Dax was. Then it slid over her, and she saw something else.

'You're new,' he said.

'Indeed,' Jinn replied. She pulled her sleeves down over her hands, then set her hands on the tabletop. The mask hid her face, but her hands would immediately give her away.

'Planning on staying long?'

'No.'

A raised eyebrow. 'You've got enough credits to leave?'

'I don't see how that's any of your business.'

Jinn felt the Virena heating in her hands. She didn't let it form blades, but she wanted to. Dax pushed her foot away, slowly unfolded himself from his seat and stood up.

'Go away,' he said. There was a quiet menace in his voice. Jinn held her breath. If he started something, she would have no choice but to join in, and there was no question which side she would be on.

Fortunately, someone on the other side of the food court chose that moment to kick over a serving droid, and the men, perhaps sensing easier prey, rushed over to see what was happening.

When the droid came to their table to deliver their order, Dax took a couple of cartons and told it to offer the rest to those on the floor. He folded himself back into his seat and began to eat. Jinn

45

pulled open her own carton of food and took quick, careful bites, all the while looking at the people around them. It was becoming increasingly apparent that the war wasn't just being fought out there. It was being fought in here, too.

At the edge of the food court she caught sight of a familiar figure who was most definitely not Dome-raised, and waved to him. His initial reaction was one of total confusion.

'Ace!' she called, forgetting for a second that she currently looked like a twenty-something man and not a thirty-something woman, and needed to tailor her voice to match. Fortunately most of the other people in the food court were too busy eating and minding their own business to notice, but she'd have to be careful.

Ace slipped into the seat next to hers. 'Jinn? Is that you?' He looked thinner than she remembered. His clothes were dirty and worn, and he'd developed a twitch in one corner of his mouth.

'How are you?' Dax asked him.

Ace just shook his head. 'This place. I wish I had never come here. I take it you've spotted our babysitters. And our resident pack of bullies.'

'Difficult not to,' Jinn said, sticking her spork into what was left of her noodles. 'How long have they been here?'

'Ten days. Apparently one of them has a rich daddy back on Earth, but transmissions are off and he can't get a message out. So he's stuck here just like the rest of us.' He pulled up the menu and ordered. 'Hope you don't mind me putting this on your tab, but I'm skint.'

'Knock yourself out,' Dax told him.

'Thanks.' Ace flushed, and then added a couple more things to his order. 'Dammit, that's out. And that.' He sighed. 'If we're stuck here much longer, the food is going to run out. I'd rather not be here when it does.'

'You won't be.'

'Good,' he said, looking at Jinn. 'That is you under there, right?'

'It is.'

'What is it?'

'Funderval Face Mask.' Jinn lightly touched the pad next to her ear, turning the mask off for a second, before turning it back on.

Ace laughed. 'I haven't seen one of those in years. Where did you get it?'

'Your dad. Who else?'

'How is he?'

'Alive,' Dax said. 'He's with the others on the *Mutant*. They're out in Sector Nineteen.'

Ace nodded. 'Are they safe there?'

'As safe as they'll be anywhere,' Dax said. 'We've managed to dodge the Sittan ships for this long. We can keep dodging them for a bit longer.'

'So what's the plan for this place?'

'Kick some arse,' Jinn said. 'Shut down the droids and get everyone off the station.'

'That's what I was hoping you would say.'

Dax pushed back his chair and got to his feet. 'Do you know what I feel like? Buying a droid.'

'Why on earth would you want to buy a droid?' Ace asked. 'I thought you were going to shut down the droids and kick some arse.'

Jinn didn't understand either, but Dax was already on his feet. 'Stay here,' she said to Ace. 'Eat. Keep out of trouble!'

Another serving droid was already wheeling its way across to their table, a large tray perched up on one arm. Dax liberated a handful of soyfries as it went past and ate the whole lot in one go. She grabbed the carton and held it out to him as they left the food court.

He took it in one big hand and ate a few more.

'Why do you want a droid?' Jinn asked him.

'This station uses a Premlit security system. It's what keeps all the ships locked down until their owners have paid the air and docking fees. Premlit also make cleaning droids.'

47

'So?'

'All Premlit devices run on the same basic programme. A couple of years ago, it was infected with a virus which means that you can make them talk to each other, if you know how. So a properly instructed Premlit cleaning droid can tell a Premlit security droid to switch itself off.'

'That's ... convenient,' Jinn said.

'Isn't it just?' He sighed. 'I miss Theon.'

The droid sellers were in a different sector of the station, and it took them a good twenty minutes to get there, even with Dax setting the pace.

'Alistair used to work there,' Dax said, gesturing to a store on the other side of the street. It was a fancy skimmer showroom, the kind with glossy flooring and expensive lighting and a security droid at the door to make sure only the right kind of people could go in. Jinn could picture him there so easily that it made the back of her throat burn.

But Alistair was gone.

At least she still had Dax. No matter what had happened, she still had him. He was here, with her. That was what it had all been for, after all.

The first store they found specialised in beauty droids and didn't have what Dax wanted. The next one was half empty. 'You'll be lucky,' the man said, shaking his head, before offering them a second-hand cleaning droid for three times what it was worth.

Dax haggled anyway. The man wouldn't budge on the price, so they went on to the shop next door. It was the droid equivalent of the skimmer store across the street, with polished marble walls and soft music playing in the background. The lighting was just so, all the better to make the droids on display gleam and sparkle. Nothing was priced. All the droids here were personal service droids, electronic slaves designed to help their human owner in any way they desired. You could have any size, any colour, male, female or something else entirely, provided you could afford it. One of them reminded Jinn of the nanny droid that had looked after her when she was little, only hers had been short and square and yellow instead of this sparkling pink. She was quite surprised that the place was open, and even more surprised when a tall, slender, pale-haired woman came out of an office at the back and approached them.

She strolled stiffly up to Jinn as she read through the specifications of a model TX3000. It stood a motionless 1.9 metres tall, with perfectly shaped limbs and a cartoonish face. It was both self-charging and self-cleaning. 'All models can be custom-built to meet your requirements,' the woman said. 'This one is very popular.'

Jinn glanced across and down, saw blonde hair curved around a sharp jawline, a full and too perfect to be natural pair of lips. 'I imagine it is.'

The woman smiled a very fake smile, then moved on to Dax. 'Perhaps you'd like to take a seat, and we can discuss your requirements in more detail.'

'Alright,' Dax agreed. The woman led him to a booth at the side of the shop, pressing her thumbprint to a sensor on the wall so that a privacy screen wrapped around them. Jinn could still see them, but she couldn't hear what they were saying. She studied the TX3000 for a minute or so longer, pretending she wasn't bothered, and then she strolled over to the two of them.

She walked straight through the privacy screen, very bad manners, her nanny droid would have been appalled, and took the seat next to Dax.

'So,' the woman said. 'What sort of droid are you looking for?'

'A Premlit RX22 cleaning droid.'

The woman crossed her legs at the knee and smoothed down her pristine trousers. 'I see. Would you be looking to pay upfront or in instalments?'

'Cash purchase.'

'Of course.' She opened a screen and called up a catalogue. 'We may have something that will meet your needs. Here.' She flipped the screen around with a wave of her hand, giving both of them a view of the specs. When Jinn saw the price, she nearly got out of her seat, but Dax kept her there with the lightest of touches on the back of her hand.

'Looks alright,' Dax said. 'Have you got one here?'

'I'll have to have it made up for you, but yes. It usually takes around twelve hours.

'I need it in two.'

'There is an extra fee for a fast-track service,' the woman said. She spun the screen around, flicked her fingers over it, then spun it back to them.

Now that really was ridiculous. 'Why is it so high?'

The woman shrugged. 'It's an expensive piece of equipment.'

'We'll think about it,' Dax said. He motioned to Jinn and she got to her feet right before he did.

'Got any other ideas?' she asked him.

'Nope. Have you?'

Jinn thought about the Virena. She could bring down the droids with that, she was sure of it. 'No.'

CHAPTER

7

3rd Day of the Seventh Turn

The Palace, Fire City, Sittan

'There isn't any more,' Chal Gri said. He stood in the entrance to Talta's quarters, a large silver jug in one hand.

Stretched out in her bathing pool, Talta stared up at him. 'What do you mean, there isn't any more?'

'The tithe has not been paid.'

Talta turned away from him, swimming to the edge of the pool so that she could look out at the city below. She could see the movement of bodies in the streets as females and children scurried from place to place. The city was still alive, still functioning. Further out, she could see the Arak trees that were the source of the oil. Again, still alive, still working. It was mid-season. The fruit would be lush and ripe. There would be plenty of oil.

But none of it was coming her way.

She moved to straighten up in the water. One of her feet caught on the bottom, a claw snagging on a rough edge of tile. The claw snapped. A blinding flash of pain hit her and she cried out. A bloom of dark spread out from the wound.

Chal Gri didn't rush. He set the jug down carefully before walking over to the edge of the pool, where he crouched and offered her a hand. His face was impassive. Talta smacked his hand aside, but the pain in her foot when she tried to wade to the steps made her vision swim.

She refused to let him see. She refused to let him help. She was an empress. She had fought to have control of this palace and this planet. She would not endure the indignity of letting a male slave see that she was weak.

'Leave me,' she snarled at him.

'As you wish.' He picked up the jug and did as he was told. He didn't hesitate, didn't look back. Talta had hoped that he would, if only so that she could take out some of her fury on his body. Even she wouldn't lower herself to hurt a male without justification.

She hobbled through to her sleeping quarters. Her skin was already starting to dry. She lowered herself onto the end of a long bench and took a closer look at her foot. The claw had been ripped straight out. The wound was still bleeding. The skin around it was thin and flaking, the condition only made worse by the lack of oil. Her hands were in a similar state.

Once, her guards would have taken care of it. They would have massaged the oil into her skin, bandaged the wound, prepared a healing salve and kept everyone else away until her body had repaired itself. Now she had only Chal Gri.

Should she call the guards back to Sittan? Abandon the search for Jinnifer Blue?

No. That couldn't happen. She would have to find another way to deal with the queens. If Fire City had stopped paying its tithes, then it surely wouldn't be long before the other cities did the same. There would be no food. No fuel for her torches. No dark rubies, no precious metals for her jewellery, no silks for her clothing.

Until that point, Talta hadn't realised how much she wanted those things. She'd always taken them for granted, as her right and her due. It was true that she had an entire storeroom of uncut dark rubies, and another twice the size that contained the mined ores that had not yet been purified. She was wealthy enough, if you counted that as wealth. But Talta did not. What mattered was that each city knew they had to give and did so. Their compliance was what counted.

And she would have it again.

Reluctantly, she rang the bell that called Chal Gri back. She said nothing as he tended the wound on her foot and then dressed her in a fine robe. 'Summon the queens,' she told him.

If he felt surprise, he didn't let it show. 'When?'

'By sunsdown tomorrow.'

'As you wish,' he said. He seemed to hesitate for a moment, and she had the sense that he was about to speak before he did, but his words still came as a surprise to her. 'Meet them at the arena.'

Talta lifted her hand to strike him. She saw the sharply defined muscles of his back, the deep scars that crossed his dark blue skin. There was a strange beauty to them, something she had never noticed before, and it caught her unawares. Chal Gri had fought in the arena before he had come to the palace. He had been utterly magnificent. He hadn't just killed other males in the arena, he had destroyed them.

Those had been great times. The Virena had flowed thick and strong and Talta had thought herself invincible. She'd brought him to the palace, as was her right, and kept him as a lover. He'd been good at that too.

Then there had been a child, although not with Talta, because empresses did not bear young, and she had shackled him into slavery as punishment.

Her gaze slid from his skin to her hand. Her claws were so thin that they were almost translucent and there was a dull patina to her skin that hadn't been there before. Her rings were loose. She slowly lowered her hand. It wasn't that Chal Gri hadn't earned the blow, because he had. But she wasn't sure that she was able to deliver it. An injured foot could be concealed. An injured hand was another matter.

'Why at the arena?' she asked him.

'If you let them enter this place, they will never leave,' he said simply. 'They are waiting for their opportunity, Talta. Make them wait for you in the arena. Let them stand there in the heat, as their skin dries and their mouths parch.'

It was the first time he had ever spoken to her so freely. His responses were usually limited to two or three words, and then only if absolutely necessary.

'They all came to watch the fights,' he continued. 'They know what the arena is, what it represents.'

'And what is that?'

'Power,' he said.

Talta flashed her teeth at him. It was an involuntary response, a warning from a female to a male that let him know he had crossed a line. But Chal Gri did not drop his gaze. 'If you want to strike me, strike me,' he said.

She didn't.

'Violence is not the only route to power,' he told her. 'The queens are testing you, Talta. They don't know what has happened. Not yet.'

It was what he didn't say that struck her. 'But you do.'

'I have no desire to see Sittan ruled by a human empress.'

Neither did Talta.

'Summon the queens to the arena,' she said. 'I will meet with them there.'

CHAPTER

8

21st January 2208

> Vessel: Balloon Pod
> Occupants: 2
> Destination: unknown medical centre, Asteroid 6632, Earth-
> controlled space

Eve had knocked herself out with a dose of EasyDoze shortly after the balloon had launched, so she'd been asleep for most of the journey. Her dreams had been strange. EasyDoze dreams often were.

Alistair had been there. He'd been talking to her. There hadn't been words, as such, just the soothing tone of his voice wrapping itself around her. She hadn't wanted to leave, and so the bleep of the comm. brought her out of sleep in a very bad mood.

It took her a few seconds to orient herself and remember where she was. That part at least was easy. There was no automated voice asking her if she needed assistance in her quarters back on the *Mutant*.

She sat up. Through a little viewing window barely bigger than her hand, she could see Gate 12 and the little trackers that had come out to inspect the balloon. Eve considered her options before deciding to reply. 'No,' she said, when she was sure of it.

'Please use channel 4977 if you require rescue,' came the sing-song voice again, and then the connection was cut and the trackers zoomed away.

Bryant jerked in his seat. 'What? Who said that? What is it?'

'Nothing. Go back to sleep.'

But he didn't. Instead, he turned his head so he could see out of the small circular window on his side of the pod. They were approaching the edge of the asteroid field. Eve heard him exhale. It was a sound of finality, of relief. It was the sound of someone who was done.

She reached for the control panel above her head and pulled it down, locking it into position just above her knees. The holoscreen flicked on and the controls flipped out. It was easy enough to fly. She navigated the asteroid field carefully, refusing to rush. The pod landed exactly where she wanted it to. They were slap bang in the middle of the landing pad next to the facility. It was otherwise empty.

That gave her a moment of breathing space.

She unbuckled herself from her seat. It took a few goes to get her legs moving, but Eve was no stranger to the more uncomfortable aspects of space travel, and she knew a few tricks to get herself going.

The same couldn't be said for Bryant. He was unconscious again. He was still breathing, and every so often his hands would twitch and he would whimper, but he didn't open his eyes and her attempts to wake him failed. She didn't allow herself to feel anything about that. She pulled on a breathing mask and opened up the pod. The asteroid had undergone some terraforming and the gravity tower was still operating, because she could walk normally when she stepped out. But she wasn't sure how clean the air was and the pod didn't have testing equipment. Hence the mask.

She set Bryant up with one too, then floated him out of the pod, chair and all. She towed it across the landing pad to the dark, quiet building. A light came on and focused on the pair of them.

It stopped Eve in her tracks.

She hadn't felt too nervous when she'd thought that the place was empty. Then the door in front of her slid open. More lights turned on within. Go in? Or run straight back to the balloon and leave Bryant to his fate?

She gave Bryant's chair a little push and it floated inside.

Eve followed it.

'This place has to be a hundred years old,' she said, even though Bryant probably couldn't hear her. 'I guess you didn't realise it would be in such a state.'

It was cold, too, and when she took off her mask, the air smelled of neglect. The light and the door were probably set to turn on automatically. There were food vending machines and a row of tables and benches, all of which were bolted to the floor. There was a small entertainment screen on each table. All of them were off. The place was so empty that even her breathing seemed too loud.

Despite the fact that the place was completely deserted, it looked as if it had been polished just that morning. Probably cleaning droids left to run just in case. 'At least you won't catch anything here,' she said to Bryant.

There were three doors on the other side, each with a cross etched into the frosted plastex. They had to be treatment rooms. Hoping there was a functioning medidroid behind one of them, Eve tried the first door. She found a pristine treatment room, but it wasn't set up for someone like Bryant. Fortunately, the second room was.

She pushed the float chair inside, and almost collapsed in relief when a medidroid, alerted by her presence, switched on. It immediately took over and did what Eve could not, lifting Bryant into the bed and hooking him up to a series of monitors. 'Bryant, Adam,' it said, as it passed a scanner over his wrist. 'Agent identification number QD899567. Status: agent privileges rescinded. No treatment can be authorised.'

'Please,' Eve said. 'He's dying. Just make him comfortable.'

'Agent privileges rescinded. No treatment can be authorised.'

'I'm not asking you to treat him. I'm just asking you to help him. Look at him. He's only got a few hours left. He doesn't need to be in pain for that.'

'Agent privileges rescinded.'

'No,' Eve said. She was at the point of begging. 'Come on.'

But the droid turned away and returned to its position in the corner. Bryant moaned. Eve couldn't stand it. She hated herself for it, but she fled the little room and went over to the empty tables. She sat on a hard, uncomfortable bench and put her head in her hands.

She had been with Alistair when he died. She had thought that she would do the same for Bryant, that she owed him that much, but when it came to it she knew that she didn't have the strength, not if it was going to be agony. She had given all she had to give. She would wait out here until he was gone before she went back to the pod and returned to the *Mutant*, and that would have to be enough.

'Can I help you?'

The voice came out of nowhere. Eve shrieked. She sat up. A man was walking across the foyer towards her, and Eve's first thought was panic, and to reach for the stunner holstered at her hip. But as he drew closer, she saw that he wasn't a man at all, but a droid. He was wearing a uniform, white trousers and tunic, and that was why she had mistaken him for a human.

She held up the stunner and aimed it at the droid anyway. 'Who are you?'

'My name is Charles. I am in charge of running the centre.

I am an Evicta droid, model TT40. My creation date was June 1st 2196. I have been fully operational since August 14th 2196. I like to be considered male and would prefer if you would think of me as such.'

Only one bit of that meant anything to Eve. 'AI,' she whispered.

'Yes. May I ask your reason for visiting?'

It was AI. 'I brought a friend. He used to be an agent.'

'The man in exam room 2. He appears to be very sick.'

'He is.'

'Poisoned,' Charles said, eyes flickering as he connected with the network. 'We do not have an antidote to this particular toxin.'

'I know,' Eve said. 'There isn't one.'

'You are a Type Two female, modified with Shi Fai genetic code. Consider extremely dangerous. Terminate on sight.'

Shit. *Shit.* Eve scrambled out of her seat and backed away from the machine, her heart racing.

The droid didn't move. 'I will not hurt you,' he said. 'I have medical programming and my directive is to do no harm. Tell me about your friend.'

He isn't my friend, she almost said, then realised that Charles had only used that word because she had used it first. Was Bryant her friend? No, she decided. He wasn't. Because she couldn't cope with losing another one.

'It's a long story.'

'I have time.'

'He doesn't.'

Again, the flicker in the eyes. 'I estimate that he has another fifteen hours remaining before catastrophic heart failure occurs. There is time.'

So Eve told him. She only meant to share the key facts, but found herself spilling everything. Her life on Earth before she was modified, and then after, escaping with Dax and the others. Her life as a pirate. Then the day that Dax had been taken to the A2, the day that had changed everything. She spoke quickly, and Charles listened intently, never interrupting.

'It is so long since I heard a human speak,' he said, when she had finally finished. Its joints whirred, hands trembling. It was strange, seeing such a human reaction from a machine. It had felt less strange when Theon had reacted emotionally, because he'd hidden his steel bones behind a thick layer of polyskin. Charles had no such luxuries. 'You have a most beautiful voice.'

'I . . . thank you.'

It was so long since anyone had told her that anything about her was beautiful that Eve felt quite hot and strange.

'Perhaps we should take a look at your friend now.'

He was on his feet and moving before Eve could stop him. She could either stay where she was or follow and have to see how much Bryant had deteriorated over the past hour. She stayed put until she could no longer stand herself, then got up and followed the droid into the room.

Charles was looking down at Bryant. 'Hmm,' he said, as Eve entered.

'What?' Eve rushed over to the chair, suddenly frightened. 'Is he dead?'

'Not quite,' Charles told her. 'Though he is quite possibly the sickest person I have ever seen. It is most interesting. See the mottling of the skin, here, and the distension of his abdomen? Fascinating.'

'The medidroid in the exam room refused to help him. It said his agent privileges have been rescinded. It wouldn't even give him something for the pain.'

Charles lifted the blanket, looked underneath it, then gave a brisk nod, as if he had come to a decision. 'Would you prefer your friend to survive?'

'Of course. But it's not possible.'

'It might be possible.'

'How?'

'There is a treatment centre on Colony Six that may have something that can help him.'

'What sort of something?'

'It is a type of genetic modification. I do not have much information. I know only that it boosts immune system functioning and healing rate.'

Sounded a bit like Type One. But Eve put that thought out of her mind. 'You really think it could help him?'

'It's possible.'

It wasn't what Bryant had asked her to do. But Eve forced herself to look at the figure in the float chair, to really see him. It made her heart hurt and she hadn't thought there was any more hurt left in it. She thought about the treatment. If it worked, and it was a big if, what then? She decided she would cross that bridge when she came to it. 'Alright,' she said to Charles. 'What do you need me to do?'

'Remove my inhibitor chip. We will have to take him to Colony Six for the treatment, and it is programmed to shut me down if I leave the building.'

Removing the inhibitor chip from an AI could be dangerous. 'I'm not sure that's such a good idea.'

'Do you propose to take him to the treatment centre yourself?'

She could do it. Getting there wouldn't be a problem, in theory anyway. But getting him inside the treatment centre was a different thing altogether. Charles was right.

Theon hadn't had his inhibitor chip, and he'd been fine. There was no reason to think that Charles wouldn't be too.

'No,' she admitted. 'Have you got a tool kit?'

He held up a multitool and Eve took it. Removing the chip was the work of minutes.

Eve could only hope that she wasn't making a mistake.

21st January 2208

Apartment 438, Acton District, London Dome, Earth

On the news that morning, it had been reported that the temperature on Earth had dropped another 0.01 degrees. It wasn't much in the grand scheme of things, but they were at the point now where every drop was a disaster. The crack in the London Dome still had not been properly patched. There were reports that the Moscow Dome was having issues with air purity. And the water being piped down to Underworld New York was no longer fit for human consumption, although people were drinking it because there was nothing else.

Bautista's promised new purification plant was behind schedule. If the other cities were having similar problems with their water they were keeping it quiet, but Ferona would not be at all surprised if they were. The planet was, quite literally, falling apart.

Her apartment was so cold that she was forced to wear a hat and coat indoors. Her breath frosted in the air. When she had called the power company, they had politely informed her that there was a city-wide restriction on fuel. They could not tell her how long it would last. She drank several cups of very thin tea and pushed a stale croissant around a gold-rimmed china plate as she carefully thought through her plan for that morning.

There were so few people left that she could turn to. No-one who had a position in government would have anything to do with her. She had no friends. She had only enemies. Dubnik had agreed that Bautista was the problem now and had asked her what they were going to do to fix it.

Ferona did not know.

How did you save a world when you had nothing to save it with?

There was, however, one person left who might be able to help. He had never been a friend, but Ferona did not think he was truly an enemy. He was certainly no friend to Bautista. Whether he would help Ferona get the man out of office remained to be seen.

She had sold two of her handbags to pay the cab fare to get to the other side of the Dome. The skinny little credit chips sat on the worktop, next to the ancient Autochef. So little in exchange for so much.

She picked them up and slid them into her pocket. She walked three cab stops before surrendering to the cold and boarding an empty car. It would cut the cost down a little. When she got to her destination, she almost paid the fee to hold the cab. It was so cold.

But she couldn't afford it.

She walked quickly along the uneven path to the door. It was a small, nondescript house on a narrow, nondescript street, because although the man who lived there was interested in obtaining money, he seemed to have little interest in spending it.

A light skimmed over her as she stood in front of the faded door. She waited, twitching, trying to move her numb toes inside her boots, feeling her anxiety rise. Did he still live here? Would he agree to see her if he did?

'Good morning, Ferona,' came Weston's scratchy voice over the speaker. 'I wasn't expecting to see you.'

Ferona exhaled. 'Open the door and let me in,' she said.

'It's nice to see you too. What do you want?'

'I'd rather not discuss it with you standing here in the street. Open the bloody door!'

'Temper, temper,' he said, but the door slid open. The smell of unwashed clothes and stale booze hit her immediately, and she recoiled. But beggars could not be choosers and therefore she shook off her disgust and stepped inside.

At least it was warm, even if the heat did seem to be making the smell worse. The air was greasy with it. She took in the solitary sofa, which was coated with hair from Weston's yappy little dog, gave a little shudder, and then walked over to it and very deliberately sat down, giving the clear message that this was not going to be a short visit. There was no sign of the man himself, but she was too pleased to be out of the cold to worry about that overmuch.

She wasn't afraid of Weston, who was a short, pink-faced man with thinning hair and bad teeth. He had helped her to transform the Second Species programme from a small illegal research project being carried out by a struggling medical company to something with the power to change the future of the human race. She was afraid that this might turn out to be a waste of time. She had nowhere else to turn. This was it. If Weston didn't have any idea how to fix this, it truly couldn't be fixed.

Once, she had thought of him as an ally, before the bastard had sold his skills and research to Vexler behind her back. Ferona hadn't been angry about it. There wasn't any point. It was simply the way that Weston operated. Instead, she had offered him more money, and he had helped her to destroy Vexler in return. The price had been very high.

And Ferona was feeling short-changed.

She turned to see him standing in the doorway at the other side of the room, watching her. He looked the same as he always had, and Ferona found a strange comfort in that.

'Please, have a seat,' he said sarcastically. 'Do you want anything to drink?'

'No thank you.'

'Suit yourself,' he said, and wandered off into the kitchen. He came back a couple of minutes later, carrying a chipped glass half full of smoky liquid. 'So, what is this about?'

'Vexler isn't dead.'

'I noticed. I suppose you're here to ask me to do something about it. What will it be this time? More poison? Another bomb? Or something a little more unexpected?'

'None of those,' she said.

'Suit yourself.' He took a swallow of his drink.

'You'll end up in hospital if you keep drinking that filth.'

'Everyone needs a vice. You've certainly got yours.'

'How is your liver?'

'Rotting,' he said cheerfully. He settled himself into an empty armchair on the other side of the room. 'You're in the shit, Ferona. You're out of office and out of power and you started a war. All your careful planning and manipulating turned out to be a waste of time, and worst of all, you were betrayed by your own offspring, and she did it for love. That must really cut at you.'

'Thank you for your assessment of the situation.'

All the jest was suddenly gone. He drained his glass and set it down on top of a dusty side table. 'What do you want, Ferona?'

'A way out,' she told him. 'More specifically, I want to get Bautista out of office.'

'And you think I can help you with that?'

'You helped before.'

'I didn't help,' Weston said. 'It was a job. You had certain requirements, I met them, you paid me for it. That was all.'

'Alright, then. I have a job for you.'

'How much does it pay?'

Ferona gritted her teeth. 'Nothing,' she said finally. 'I've got nothing. As you so kindly pointed out, I'm not in power. I have no control here, Weston. No influence.' She was gripping her bag so tightly that her hands were shaking. 'But something has to be done about Bautista.'

Weston stroked his thumb across his lower lip. 'I see,' he said. 'So why haven't you done it?'

'How? No-one is interested in anything I have to say, and I don't think shooting him in the street will help my cause. And if something does happen to him, there's no guarantee that whoever replaces him will be any better. What I need is a way to get him out of office so that we can take back control of this situation and sort it out.'

She had almost said *I. So that I can take back control.*

'To what end? Spes has gone. There's the colonies, of course, but they're too small to support more than a million of us.'

His tone was matter of fact. There was no emotion in it, positive or negative, just a clear acceptance of the situation.

'You think we're all going to die,' she said.

'Of course we're all going to die, Ferona. That's the price we pay for life. Death and taxes. Well, not taxes, necessarily. But death. It's merely a question of when and how. But you still haven't answered my question. If I help you get rid of Bautista, what difference will it make?'

'All the difference!' she said. 'With the right person in charge, we can fix what is wrong here on Earth. We can extend the Domes, bring heat up from the core, increase under-cover forestation. Algae tanks ... ' She stopped when she realised that she was repeating exactly what Dubnik had said to her. 'And we can force the senate to do something about the Sittan.'

'Can you pay?'

'No. I told you that.'

Weston shrugged. 'Then you might as well go home.'

'Damn you, Weston!'

The door slid open. Cold air drifted in from the street. It was clear that her visit was over.

It wasn't until she was in the cab and on her way home that she realised something.

He hadn't said that he couldn't help her.

Which meant that he could.

For the right price.

CHAPTER

10

21st January 2208

Space Station Europa, Sector Three, Neutral Space

After leaving the droid store, Dax and Jinn headed for the lower level of the station to see if they could find an old cleaning droid in one of the recycling units. None of the elevators were operating. The first two stairwells were blocked, but luckily the third was still open, so they went that way. The door at the bottom was closed. It was no match for the two of them, however, and they were easily able to force it apart.

On the other side was a pile of boxes and other bits of random rubbish. Jinn shoved the boxes out of the way. They hit the floor with a bang, spilling bits of steel plate and bundles of wires.

'Why would anyone pile this mess up in front of the door?'

'I don't know,' Dax said.

Jinn felt a little tight in her chest. 'I think someone put this here deliberately. They didn't want anyone using this door.'

Dax stepped over a length of pipe. 'Shall we see what's behind it?'

'It would be rude not to.'

There were no fancy screens down here, no floating advertisements trying to sell them anything. This level of the station was primarily used for the daily work of keeping a station like this running, so it had areas for staff and equipment repair as well as a huge laundry and air recyclers. That part was almost entirely computer-operated.

But there should have been people. It was overrun on the higher levels. Some of those people should have made their way down here. So where were they?

Further round, they found what they'd been looking for, and it was not what either of them had expected.

A group of Type Two women sat round a table.

Jinn grabbed Dax's arm, but he had already seen. The two of them retreated back towards the stairwell.

'Type Two!' Jinn said urgently. 'They must have fled Faidal when Eve did. Remember she said that some of the other women stole Shi Fai ships? I wonder how many there are.'

It was the first positive thing that had happened in months. This was a problem she could solve. It was one she could do something about, one she understood.

'We'll have to be careful,' Dax said. 'We don't know these women. There's no guarantee that they'll be happy to see us.'

'Why wouldn't they be?'

'Because they don't know us, and we don't know them. They're hiding down here for a reason.'

'Yes, hiding! Which means that at some point, someone is going to find them, and they might not be as understanding as us. We know what Type Two is. We know what it means. We can help these women, Dax.'

He turned, pushed her back against the wall, keeping the two of them well out of sight. 'If anyone else on this station finds out that these women are here, it will cause a riot. Everyone on board this station knows that those women are toxic. Think about that.'

Jinn did. She knew how she had felt when she had first learned what Eve was, when the initial curiosity about her appearance had been replaced with fear, how her muscles had tensed and she'd had an immediate, terrified awareness of the other woman. She'd had time to find a way to manage that fear, but the people here hadn't had that.

Dax was right. These women were in danger. They also were a danger. She'd seen what one touch had done to Bryant.

'I know,' she said. 'But I can't stand the thought of them being stuck down here.'

'We know where they are,' Dax said. 'And we know that they're safe for now. But we're in no position to help them, and until we are, I think we should leave them alone.'

'Are you OK with that?'

'Not really,' he said. 'If Eve ever asks about this, tell her we got them out straight away.'

'Agreed.'

'Good. Come on. We came down here for a reason. There are still a thousand people upstairs who need our help as well.'

But their attempt to look for an old droid was hampered by the need to keep their presence a secret, and they were soon forced to abandon the hunt. Most of what they found was broken parts anyway, and although it might be possible to piece together a complete droid, they had neither the time nor the skills.

Jinn didn't want to give up. But she also knew when to ditch a plan that wasn't working. The problem was that they'd come here to help Ace. They hadn't been prepared for a thousand other people just as stuck or a ship full of Type Two women. Maybe they should have been. But months of war had taken their toll. Both she and Dax were exhausted and it was starting to show.

Ace was exactly where they had left him, with a large pile of dirty plates stacked up on the table in front of him. He blended so perfectly into the background that he was almost invisible. It was more than just his physical appearance, although there was nothing about that which would draw attention. It was an attitude, the way he held himself, which allowed the eye to skip over him as if he wasn't even there. Jinn couldn't help but admire it. She wondered where he'd learned how to do it, and if he could teach her. It would be a very useful skill.

'Found what you were looking for?' he asked, as the two of them sat down.

'No,' Jinn said. 'But we did find something very interesting.'

'What's that?'

'Unexpected guests on the lower level,' Dax said.

Ace looked confused. 'Unexpected guests?'

'Of the green and poisonous type.'

'Shit,' Ace whispered softly. 'Really?'

'Really.'

'How many?'

'We saw four, but there may be more. We don't know.'

Ace nodded, his gaze sliding away as if he was lost in thought. 'That explains a *lot*,' he said. 'You know, I've tried to get down there three times. There's another set of docking ports where they keep all the seized ships and the entrance to it is on that level. But none of the elevators work and both stairwells I tried were blocked. I assumed station security had done it to keep us on this level and I didn't want to get myself in trouble, so I decided to leave it alone.'

'You did the right thing,' Dax told him. He drummed his fingertips on the tabletop. 'What we need now is a plan B.'

The chute for dirty plates was overflowing, so there was nowhere to shove Ace's mess. Jinn pushed it to the outside edge of the table. She couldn't stop thinking of the women on the lower level. She didn't want to leave them down there any longer than necessary.

Every moment that passed, the creeping sense of unease grew

stronger and more determined. So far things had been too easy. No-one had really questioned them. But the longer they were here, the more likely it was that someone would find something objectionable about them, or that they would simply attract trouble in the way that she and Dax were prone to do.

Jinn looked around. She took in the walls, the construction of the ceiling. She didn't know much about station design, but she'd been a pilot for a long time, and she knew plenty about all the things that could go wrong in space. She could feel the Virena pulsing inside her fingers. It made her a little reckless. She hadn't wanted to use it to turn off the droids in case Dax saw it, but maybe there was another option. 'I think we should start a fire.'

'Are you crazy?' Ace said. 'You can't start a fire here.'

'Of course we can. Think about it. We start a fire, they will have to unlock the docking ports and evacuate the station.'

'It could work.' There was a sudden gleam in Dax's bright green eyes that reminded Jinn of a much younger man, one who had been selfish and ruthless and had stripped a freighter and left it to burn.

'No, I mean you literally can't start a fire here,' Ace said. 'Stations like this are designed specifically not to set on fire. It's impossible. Well, almost impossible.'

'Almost is good enough for me,' Dax said.

'It can't be done,' Ace insisted. 'You do understand that fire could also kill all of us. I can't emphasise enough what a terrible idea it is.'

'If the Sittan get here before we leave, you're dead anyway.'

Ace slumped back in his seat. 'Do you really think they're going to come here?'

'It's when, not if,' Jinn told him.

'Stop,' Ace said. 'You're making fire sound like a good idea. How do you people survive? How have you not blown yourselves up?'

'We're pirates,' Dax said. 'We just start stuff. We leave before it gets really dangerous.'

'You are making me want to get very, very drunk.' Ace pulled an infocube from his pocket and unfolded it, then swiped through the various screens until he found a map of the station. 'Here,' he said, pointing at something with the tip of a red holopen. 'This is the fire system. If you're going to have any chance of making this work, and I'm not saying that you do, you have to get this offline.'

Dax looked at it. 'Alright,' he said, and then he pulled out his own cube and the two of them bent over it.

Jinn tried to listen, but quickly lost interest in the conversation. It was all very technical and dry. Her attention drifted to the other people in the food court. The group of young Dome men who had been here earlier had put in another appearance. They were moving from table to table, and people were handing things over. At first, she couldn't see what they were. Then one of the men got a little closer and she saw him take a work cube from a frightened elderly woman with steel-grey hair and a retinal implant. *Thieving bastard.*

Well, she'd soon put a stop to that. The Virena tingled in her fingertips. It gave her an idea. She sent a thin thread weaving its way through the air, invisible to the naked eye. It wrapped around the work cube, plucked it from the man's grasp, and set it down on the table in front of the woman. 'What the ... ?' said the man loudly. He looked around, arms swinging as if his hands were looking for someone to punch. Jinn sent another strand of Virena to catch his fist, spinning him off balance.

She knew that she shouldn't be using it like this, but she couldn't quite convince herself that it was wrong. How dare he try to steal from an old woman, here, now?

'Jinn,' Dax said from the other side of the table.

She yanked the Virena back to her. It came quickly and silently. 'What is it?' Had he seen? Did he know what she had done? Judging by the look on his face, he didn't, but she knew that she'd been mere seconds from giving herself away. That was all it had taken. An elderly woman, an arrogant Dome man, and a split second of poor judgement.

73

She wasn't stupid. She knew better than that.

'What do you think, Jinn?' Dax asked her.

'Sounds like a plan,' she said, although she had no idea what he'd suggested.

Ace got to his feet. 'Let's get this done, then,' he said. 'Because drowning myself in a vat of ale is looking better by the second.'

She watched as Ace made his way out of the food court, slipping back into that small, invisible space that he had occupied before. Dax went next, and Jinn sent another thin thread of Virena winding after him, settling it invisibly around his body. She waited a long couple of minutes before she followed. She knew exactly where he was, thanks to that slender thread. It was a strange sensation. She couldn't decide how she felt about it. But the alternative had been to admit that she hadn't been listening, that her attention had been elsewhere.

A fire. Such a simple thing, but not in a place like this. The question was how. She wandered aimlessly for the next ten minutes, people-watching, waiting for inspiration to strike, her awareness of Dax humming quietly in the background.

She also became aware, as she walked, that someone was following her. She let that settle in. She made no move to do anything about it. But her curiosity was piqued. She took a left, and then a right, heading down a narrow alley that offered little in the way of escape, then turned.

The man strolled over to her. He was only a little bit taller than Jinn, but he was heavily built and obviously capable of packing a punch. He posed no threat to her. But he didn't know that.

'What do you want?'

He shrugged. 'Nothing.'

Jinn sighed. 'Why don't you do us both a favour, turn around, and go back the way you came?'

He laughed. 'You're new here, so I'll let that pass. I want your credit chips, your personal comm., and the starter key for your ship.'

Two more men were now making their way down the alley. 'Three against one? That seems a bit unfair. On you.'

The man smiled. 'We can do this the easy way or the hard way,' he said.

'Oh, the hard way. Please.'

'Don't say you weren't warned.' And he took a swing at her. Jinn grabbed his hand, locking her fingers around the man's fist, and twisted his arm until he sank to his knees, spitting in pain. At that point his two companions decided to join in, but Jinn was having none of it. She'd dealt with far worse than them on Sittan.

She had one of them on the floor with her boot on his neck and had just made a grab for the second when something hit her in the back, a sharp, stinging pain. She cried out, twisting in time to see that the first man had pulled a blaster.

He'd shot her right in the back with the full load. It should have killed her, but she was Type One and so it was merely agony. But it was enough to make the world look fuzzy, and she fell to the floor. She shook off the dizziness and blinked up at the men leaning over her. Pale hair and strange faces came into view. 'What the fuck is this?' said one of them, grabbing Jinn by the jacket and pulling her to her feet. He yanked the mask from her face. 'I could've sworn she was a boy!'

'How in the void did she do that?'

'Holo mask, idiot. But never mind that. Look who it is.'

'*Jinnifer Blue.*'

'Bingo. The most wanted woman in the fucking galaxy.' That one laughed. 'This has got to be worth a ride off this station.'

Jinn let herself stay relaxed. She switched off the part of her brain that dealt with emotion and focused only on what needed to be done. She closed her eyes and reached for the Virena. It responded eagerly.

She snapped into action and kicked one of the men hard under the chin, sending him flying. She broke the nose of another before he could even react.

The remaining man pulled a blaster from his holster and fired. No problem with his aim, but Jinn saw it coming and ducked. She felt the rush of air as the pellet whizzed past her cheek. She broke into a run and went straight for the man, tackling him and sending them both flying back through the door of a bar that backed onto the alley. They broke through chairs, crashing into a table and knocking it over. Glasses flew everywhere. The other customers started to shout, scrambling out of the way, some pausing to record the incident, because no matter what happened, if there were humans, there was a camera, somewhere. Jinn flung out a hand and sent tiny black spheres of Virena shooting out across the bar, smashing through and destroying all the comm. units. No-one was getting a video of this.

Jinn and the man got to their feet and began to circle each other. A serving droid zipped into the space between them then just as quickly zipped out again. The man grabbed a chair and snapped it over his knee, giving him two sharp-ended steel sticks to fight with.

They clashed again, and the man managed to get in three hard hits before Jinn got hold of him and dropped him to the floor. She pinned him there with a knee to the back of his neck and leaned her considerable weight against it. 'Don't try anything,' she warned him.

'You can't possibly escape,' he snarled. 'This place is crawling with security droids. They'll be here any second.'

'I'm not trying to escape,' Jinn told him. She looked around. Most of the customers were sensible enough to have run, though a couple cowered in the corner. It was a pretty nice place. Drinks were lined up in clear bottles across the wall, organised in a rainbow of colours, deepest purple through to lightest pink. People would pay a week's wages for a single shot of some of the rarer ones.

But they all had one thing in common.

Jinn sent out another wave of those tiny black spheres, smashing the hundreds of bottles with a simultaneous crash, and as she did so, she willed them to heat. Ace thought she couldn't start a fire? She would give him a fire. The air chilled as the Virena stole the heat from it, and goosebumps rose up on her skin. The smell of alcohol was everywhere. She felt almost drunk on it.

She gave the Virena a push.

A wall of fire exploded across one side of the bar. The two people in the corner were finally shocked into action and they ran out, one of them tripping over a broken chair on the way. But at least they were gone. Out on the street, Jinn could see others starting to run, faces twisted in fear. She stepped back and let the man up.

He scrambled to his feet. 'You're fucking crazy!' he screamed. 'What the fuck have you done?'

'What needed to be done,' Jinn told him, as alarms began to blare and a voice came over the loudspeaker.

THIS IS AN EVACUATION NOTICE. RETURN TO YOUR SHIPS IMMEDIATELY. DO NOT PANIC. FOLLOW THE RED ARROWS. I REPEAT, DO NOT PANIC.

There was a hiss as a cold white mist began to pour from the ceiling, but Jinn and the Virena kept the fire going. She walked to the door of the bar and stood there, feeling the heat of the fire at her back and the Virena in her body. Smoke swirled around her feet. The loudspeaker continued to wail and previously invisible red arrows flashed in the floor, directing the crowds to ships and safety. She hadn't realised how badly she wanted to watch the station burn.

CHAPTER

11

12th Day of the Seventh Turn

The Palace, Fire City, Sittan

Talta awoke suddenly. Her entire body snapped alert, her skin prickling as the spikes on her head and shoulders shot out. The room was semi-dark. The suns were coming up, but they had not yet made their impact on the day.

She would be meeting the queens at the arena at sunsdown. Her dreams had been filled with thoughts of them, burned red with anger, and of the price they would pay for their lack of respect.

But that was not what had awakened her.

She swung her legs over the side of the bed, feeling the touch of the cool stone against her feet. She flattened the gill slits on the side of her neck, silencing them, and listened. She was alone. Still the acute sense of danger persisted, chilling the skin on her back and her arms as she circled around to her bathing pool where the water was crystal still, and then out onto the balcony. The Mountain stood silent in the distance. It remained as dead as it had been since the day Jinnifer Blue had left the planet.

She whirled back to the room. There was danger, she could feel it. But where?

Images flashed into her mind, of a place far from here, not Sittan, but human in construction. She sank to her knees. She pressed her hands against the sides of her head, barely feeling the spikes that dug into her flesh or the blood that slid wetly down her arms as a result, and cried out in anger.

She could see Jinnifer Blue, the image as clear as if the human female was stood right in front of her. The details were so vivid and perfect; her ugly pale skin and nasty white hair. There was a tremendous heat and a smell of burning. Fire. It was fire. Talta flung a hand up in front of her face to protect herself from it, and as she did so, she realised that this was no normal flame.

There was a darkness to it, a heart that made it a living thing, a wilful monster. She knew it. She called to it, and just for a moment, it responded. It knew her. Talta felt its answer like the touch of a lover who had been thought lost. Her hearts started to pound.

Through it she saw everything. There were so many humans, a pushing, screaming, undignified mess, their faces blurring at the edges as they tried to flee. The inside of the station was brutal and ugly. It was filled with the crude technology that humans so favoured. Their lack of sophistication was astonishing. No wonder their species was watching the end approach.

She stayed with the Virena, singing a song of love to it as it filled her mind with everything that it experienced and everything that it saw. But when she tried to bond with it further, it pushed her away and that was the cut of a blade. How could it love her and yet still want to hurt her?

It did not matter. Talta had seen enough. She knew that station. She had been there once, a long time ago, before she had become empress. It was on the very edge of neutral space, close to the human home planet. A long way from Sittan.

But not far for her warships.

She opened her eyes to find herself on her hands and knees, though she didn't remember falling. Spots of dark blood mottled the floor in front of her, and she spat more. She must have bitten her tongue. It took a great deal more effort than it should have to get to her feet and stagger across to her pool. She slid down into it, the calming waters immediately soothing to her skin. She reached for the jug of oil that sat at the side of the pool, but her hand found only an empty space and she clawed at it in pain and frustration.

She wanted all of this to be resolved *now*. She wanted Jinnifer Blue dead, the Virena back here with her, the cities once again sending their tributes. She was tired of waiting.

A shadow moved over the pool.

It was Chal Gri.

'Have you brought me my oil?'

'No,' he said.

'Then what use are you?'

He didn't reply. Instead, he knelt down at the side of the pool. He had a small bowl in one hand, and he was grinding the contents of it with the other. A familiar scent rose from it. 'Nolax?' she asked him. 'You took leaves from my Nolax?'

'Your skin is cracking and we have no oil. The juice from the leaves will help to prevent infection.'

The Nolax trees grew only within the walls of the palace. The leaves were few, and they were precious. No-one was allowed to touch the tree but the empress. That was the law. She had taken hands from previous slaves who had dared to break it. 'I should kill you for it.'

'You must do what you feel is right.'

But she wouldn't, and he knew it. Most of the other slaves had left the palace. They had returned to their home cities, their villages, slipping away in the darkness, and she had been powerless to stop them. Chal Gri was one of the few who remained. She hated him for it.

He did not look at her, keeping his gaze averted as he had been taught, and she hated him for that too. He slowly poured the juice into the water. The healing scent of Nolax filled the air. Talta let her body float in the water, forcing it to soften and betray none of the fury that she felt.

'I saw her,' she said.

The only sign that he had heard was a small twitch in his shoulders.

'She is on a human space station called the Europa.'

'That is far from here.'

Talta grabbed the empty bowl and hit him with it.

'I know where it is!' she screamed at him. She kicked her feet down to the bottom of the pool and climbed out of it. Liquid ran from her skin and drenched the floor at her feet as she charged at him. He didn't move, merely rose to his full height and let her do what she would. She hurt him and she knew it, but when she stepped back and looked at what she had done, she felt no pleasure in it. He was, after all, a male, and that was what males were for.

'Leave me,' she ordered him.

He did as he was told. She watched as he walked out of her room, his bruised, bleeding head perfectly straight. There was enough strength in those huge shoulders and arms for him to quite easily kill her, but he didn't frighten her. Males didn't harm females. Not here on Sittan.

Wrapping her hand around the amulet she wore, Talta closed her eyes and called to her army, to her faithful guards, far away from here. The thread of connection was weak. But it was enough. The females answered her as one. 'She is on the Europa,' Talta told them. 'Find her. Kill her. Do not fail me this time.'

CHAPTER

12

21st January 2208

Space Station Europa, Sector Three, Neutral Space

The station was in utter chaos, and Dax was right in the middle of it. There was no sign of Jinn.

'Is this her?' Ace asked him, the two of them pressed up against the wall at the side of a walkway as a stream of people went flooding past. The alarms were still blaring, but they were intermittent now, which was something. 'Did she do this?'

'Do you think it was anyone else?'

Ace shook his head. 'I don't understand how she did it.'

'I'm sure she'll explain everything when she finally puts in an appearance.'

As soon as the alarms had gone off, the security droids had moved into position to funnel the crowds through to the docking bays. The barriers had been opened. Ships had started to leave. Fights were breaking out. It was difficult for Dax to stand back and watch, but he forced himself to do it. This was not his fight.

'Well, she's got people moving, I have to give her that.'

'She never makes promises that she can't keep,' Dax said. He checked his wrist comm. He pinged Jinn again. She pinged him back almost immediately, and he let out the breath he hadn't realised he'd been holding. 'She's on her way.'

'Good,' Ace said. 'Because I've got to tell you, if we don't leave soon I'm hitching a ride with someone else.'

'Someone else on this station?'

Ace pulled a face. 'Needs must.'

Dax watched the crowd, searching for a sign of that familiar face, that pale hair.

'Did I ever tell you about the first time I came here with Jinn?'

'No.'

'It was just after we'd escaped from the A2. I didn't know her then, not really. But I knew she was trouble. I told her to stay on board my ship.'

'Did she?'

'Stay on the ship? No. She decided to take herself for a walk. She called her boss, who immediately sent a team of agents here to arrest us, and then she cut the hand off a Shi Fai.'

'Sounds messy.'

'It was.'

'So why didn't you leave her here?'

Dax thought about it. 'Because I liked her.'

His mind took him back to the last time he had been here, when he had been just a pirate and Jinn had been just a woman that he desired, and he had believed that the fact that she was Dome and he was Underworld was the biggest barrier between them. How little he had known back then. He had not known that he carried Sittan DNA inside his cells. He had not known that he was capable of such terrible violence that he would struggle to live inside his own skin afterwards.

What he felt for Jinn now was far more complicated, too.

He felt the pull of her right as that thought slid into his head, and automatically turned, seeking her out. There she was. The mask had gone. She had her hood up and her head down, trying to blend with the crowd, but he would know her anywhere.

'Come on,' he said to Ace. 'We're going.'

'About time,' Ace replied. He slipped into the crowd alongside Dax, the two of them catching the flow and letting themselves drift towards Jinn. No-one took any notice of them. They were all too caught up in the urgent rush towards the ports.

But Jinn didn't go to the port. She headed left and down a narrow street. There was a security droid at the end but it didn't try to stop her, nor did it try to stop Dax. He was all set to tackle it if it did. It didn't even blink. He caught up with her about half-way down, when she turned. 'Have you seen any of the Type Two women?' she asked him.

'No,' Dax said. 'But I'm sure they've got away. They must have had a ship.'

'I don't want to leave until I'm sure they've gone.'

'Jinn . . .'

'We're not leaving them, Dax. That's not what we do.'

'Alright,' he said. 'We'll wait.'

Ace gave a very loud and very frustrated sigh. 'You two are the worst,' he said. 'The absolute worst.'

'I think we should go down to the lower level and see if they are still there,' Jinn said. She started to walk, and the two men fell in alongside her. No-one bothered them. Still, Dax couldn't shake the sense that this was not somewhere they wanted to linger. He checked his wrist comm. It was almost ten minutes since Jinn had started the fire and the alarms had gone off. Stations like this were designed to be evacuated quickly. Hopefully they'd all have enough sense to head straight for Earth-controlled space. It was the best he could hope for.

All the doors to the lower level were open. Finding their way down was easy this time. Again, they passed droids that didn't try to stop them, which sent a tingle down Dax's spine, but he ignored it. They weren't in his way. He wasn't going to worry about why.

'We'll have to be careful,' he said to Ace. 'We're talking about a bunch of scared, toxic women, and there's no guarantee that they'll be pleased to see us. Whatever happens, do not let them touch you.'

Ace went pale. 'I won't,' he said.

The lower level was empty.

'Hello?' Jinn shouted. She started forward, turning this way and that. 'Hello? Is anyone down here?'

Dax shook his head. 'They're ...'

'Right behind you,' came a voice. 'Get your hands up.'

Dax turned, slowly, hands in the air. Beside him, Ace did the same. He counted eight women in total. When he saw that none of them were armed, he slowly lowered his hands to his sides. He was used to Eve. But to see more Type Two women, together like this ... it was astonishing. All were green, just like Eve, but there were variations in shade, as well as height and size. 'We're not going to hurt you,' he said.

One of the women cracked out laughing. 'We can't say the same to you. What do you want?'

'I've got a ship,' he said to them. 'I can offer you safe passage off the station.'

The woman just stared at him. 'Why in the void would you do that?'

'Everyone else has gone. I don't want you to be left behind.'

'You're that pirate that escaped from Sittan.' One of the women moved closer. 'I saw your picture on the newsfeed.'

'That's right,' Ace said, his voice shaking. 'We ... he has a friend called Eve. She's like you. Do you know her?'

'Eve?'

There was an interested tone now. 'Yes,' Dax said. 'She's about this tall.' He held up his hand. 'She's got a pattern in her skin up the side of her neck, looks like leaves. She was on Faidal.'

'I knew Eve,' one of the others said timidly. 'She was in the same centre as me. Did she escape? Is she here?'

'She escaped. She's not here, though.'

'But you said you had a ship.'

'Yes. A transporter here, and then a much bigger one a couple of jumps out. There's room for you on board if you want it.'

'A pirate ship?'

'Yes.'

The women looked at each other. 'Nowhere wants us,' one of them said. 'We can't go back to Earth. We'll just be locked up again. Or killed. No-one is interested in helping us. All they see is the skin.' They huddled a little closer together, whispered amongst themselves. Dax tensed. It was suddenly very important to him that these women accepted what he was offering. 'Alright. We want to see the ship first though.'

'Of course.' He'd figure out how he was going to get them to the *Mutant* later.

'My name is Mady,' the one who had spoken said. She reeled off the names of the other women. Dax did his best to catch them. He acknowledged each of them with a moment of eye contact and a nod, knowing it was vital to see each one as human, as unique, as important. He also had a new level of respect for Ace. Despite his obvious terror, Ace greeted each one of them, and led them off to the steps that would take them up to the middle level of the station. Dax followed at the rear.

Just like Eve. They were just like Eve.

The mid level of the station was deserted. The sirens had stopped, the place lit only by the emergency lighting. The smell of burning lingered. But there was no smoke, no flames, no heat. The danger from the fire had passed. They had a little time to figure out their next step.

Dax still didn't know how Jinn had managed to start it. He would have to ask her about that.

When they were far away from here.

CHAPTER

13

22nd January 2208

Space Station Europa, Sector Three, Neutral Space

They were at the port with the Type Two women, trying to figure out a way to get them all safely to the *Mutant*, when Jinn felt it. She stopped, every muscle tensed, looking for the danger, spinning around when she couldn't find it.

'What is it?' Dax asked her.

'I don't know,' she told him. The hair on the back of her neck stood up. 'Something bad.'

'Where?'

Dax too started to look around them, scanning the walkways leading away from the port.

'No,' Jinn realised suddenly. 'Outside the station.'

'Over here,' Dax said, gesturing to the huge screens that would normally show the space outside the station. They'd been automatically switched off to conserve power when she'd started the fire and hadn't turned back on again. Dax ripped the cover off the control box mounted to the wall underneath them, revealing a jumble of brightly coloured strands. 'Bloody supernova, I wish Theon was here.' He poked at the wires, but it wasn't at all obvious how to turn the screen back on.

'Let me,' Ace said, and Dax stepped aside to give the other man access. It only took him a few seconds to sort it. All of them took a step back and looked up at the screens.

A fleet of huge ships were approaching the station. Not human. Sittan.

'How did you know?' Dax asked quietly.

'I don't know. I just . . . it was a gut feeling.' And beside the point. 'What are we going to do?'

'I don't know,' Dax said. He rubbed his hands over his face. 'I guess we find ourselves some weapons, and hope.'

'We're going to need a lot more than hope,' Ace said. 'I've never seen ships that big. They look like they could blow this station apart.'

'Do any of you know how to use a blaster?' Dax asked the Type Two women.

'A couple of us,' Mady said.

'Good,' he said. 'I need you to hit the weapons stores. Bring whatever you can carry. Ace, you go with them.'

'On it,' Ace said, and he and the women sprinted to the end of the walkway.

Dax waited until they were out of sight before he turned to Jinn. 'Are you ready for this?'

'No,' she said. 'Are you?'

He exhaled. 'Actually, I think I am.'

'They're not going to make it easy.'

His expression hardened. 'Neither are we. Come on. I saw a weapons store on walkway seven. Let's go and see what they've got.'

Under any other circumstances, Jinn thought she might have enjoyed the experience of being alone in this vast aluminium ghost town. She would have strolled along the streets, enjoyed the fountains and the flowers and the sculptures, the architecture and the beautifully dressed windows of the high-end stores. She would most certainly have enjoyed Dax.

But not now.

All around them, the Europa was powering back up. The vid screens had turned back on. Cleaning droids were scooting around and sucking up garbage from the edges of the walkways. They were hassled by three floating gamblers before they reached the first corner, each one flashing orange and red and promising Guaranteed Wins! Jinn kicked the second one so hard it crashed through a shop window and set an alarm screaming.

'Easy,' Dax said. 'You're going to need your energy.'

Jinn raised an eyebrow at him. She felt angry and frustrated, with herself, with Dax, with the government back on Earth for doing absolutely nothing. 'This place should have been cleared out days ago. They should have sent ships for all these people regardless of what they've done.' And then she and Dax would never have come here, and they wouldn't be facing what now waited for them on board those five Sittan ships.

'Well, it's empty now,' Dax said. 'Better late than never.'

'We're still here,' she pointed out.

'We don't count.'

Jinn spun in front of him. He kept going. She didn't move out of his way, not even when he came right up to her and they stood, toe to toe, staring at each other. 'That's not true.'

His eyes blazed with fury. 'We *can't* count, Jinn. That's the point. We can't do what we're trying to do here if we still think that our lives matter, that they're anything other than disposable. We won't have the nerve.'

'Is that what you thought, on Sittan? Did you think you were disposable?'

'I knew I was. We all were.'

'Not to me.' She pushed up onto her tiptoes, putting them almost eye to eye, daring him to argue with her. 'I know how you were treated, what they tried to turn you into,' she told him. 'I *know*, Dax.'

'Do you?'

Images flashed in front of her eyes. Not just images, she realised. Memories. She saw Dax, his skin oiled and gleaming in the light from a flickering torch. She saw a long, scaly creature climbing its way up his body. They weren't her memories. Where had they come from? She blinked, and just as quickly, they were gone.

And then a shudder ran through the station.

'They're here,' she said, and realised that she had said it out loud to try and make herself accept it.

'I know,' Dax said grimly.

The aftershock, when it came, was even bigger. The entire floor seemed to shake beneath their feet.

Jinn ran over to a nearby bank of credit machines. Somehow, flicking through a selection of channels, she found one that showed the camera feed from the outside of the station. 'Look,' she whispered.

The Sittan ships were close enough now that she could see the markings that ran down the side of each one. The station shook again, and this time she saw it coming, because one of the Sittan ships fired something at the station, a slow-moving, torpedo-shaped object that could not be deflected or avoided.

'This place must have weapons,' she said. 'There must be a defence system.'

'What for?' asked Dax.

'For ... for this!'

'I don't think so. This place was built to make people spend, not to protect them from alien attack.'

At least they had got most of the other people off the station. It felt like small compensation as Jinn stared at the approaching Sittan ships. She saw the front of one of them expand and then bud off, forming a long black bubble.

She watched the drift of that strange dark shape towards the station, watched as it impacted with the outer shell in what looked like slow motion. The lights of the station flickered. She could feel the Virena pushing its way through the steel, forcing itself in between the atoms of iron and carbon and filling the gaps.

'What *is* that?' Dax said.

'Virena,' Jinn said quietly.

Then the walls began to change. The black seemed to peel itself away. It shrank down into a ball the size of her fist, and then it expanded and became a shimmering cloud. Slowly, an image began to appear in that cloud, the flecks of blue and lilac and silver moving to form a picture of someone that both of them knew only too well.

Grenla had been the fiercest of the guards, the most sadistic, and Jinn didn't need that third dose of serum to want to do something about her. Nor did she need to look at Dax to know that every muscle in his body had tensed.

'Grenla,' she said. 'You're a long way from home.'

'Not really,' Grenla replied. 'Neutral space belongs to us now. Surely you understood that?'

'Neutral space doesn't belong to anyone.'

Grenla snapped her teeth together. 'It belongs to whoever is bold enough to take it. Soon there will be none of you left.' She switched her attention to Dax. 'Dax,' she crooned in a voice that made Jinn's stomach turn. 'We thought you were dead.'

He didn't move. 'What do you want?'

'It's very simple,' she said. 'Kill her or we destroy the station and everyone on it.'

Jinn clenched her fists. Her heart pounded fiercely inside her chest, and she felt suddenly hot and sick. It was almost impossible to keep still, to not let Grenla know how those words made her feel.

'You have one turn,' Grenla said.

The Virena shimmered back into darkness.

23rd January 2208

Nova Settlement, Colony Six, Earth-controlled Space

It wasn't far from the medical centre to Colony Six, but it was more than far enough for Eve. The last time she had been back to Earth-controlled space she'd had Dax and Jinn and Alistair at her side. This time she had only what was left of Bryant, and an AI droid that she was beginning to wish she had left behind. Charles was . . .

Charles was not Theon.

He had insisted on sitting next to her in the balloon, folding himself into the space next to the single seat. Bryant was behind them. His float chair was magnetically tethered in place, and Charles had hooked him up to a monitor which would tell them immediately if anything changed.

Eve shifted uncomfortably in her seat. Even though she knew that she couldn't hurt Charles, she was so used to having distance between herself and other people that she couldn't help but dislike his proximity. She gritted her teeth and told herself it was fine. It wasn't much further. Charles didn't mean to be annoying.

She couldn't manage Bryant on her own, and if Charles was right, if they had something here that could help him, it would be worth it. Alistair had made her promise to get away from Faidal, the Shi Fai home world, and to live her life. She'd held his hand as the poison from her skin seeped into his body and hastened his inevitable death and thought that was impossible.

But things changed. Life had gone on, without Alistair in it, and she'd finally accepted that that was inevitable too. She hadn't been living, though. Her life had slowed to a crawl and yet months had passed without her feeling as if it had been more than a few days. She was trapped. She couldn't leave Faidal and everything that had happened there behind until Bryant died.

Or got better.

She settled the balloon at the edge of a lake, opened the door, and climbed out, careful to avoid the water. It was bright yellow and glowed where the landing light from the balloon caught it. Phosphorescent creatures fizzed close to the surface, creating little bubbles of gas that broke the surface in a constant stream. The air smelled sweet. She knew better than to breathe too deeply.

Her first job was to dismantle the balloon and hide it. Charles stepped out of the pod and began to help her.

'It's fine,' Eve said. She opened up the toolbox she had clipped to her belt. 'I can ...'

It was too late. Charles had ripped a massive hole in the centre of the canopy, the silver fabric withering away from the frame. 'Oh,' he said. 'I did not expect ...'

Eve just looked at him and took a couple of deep breaths. She didn't want to get angry. But she was angry. 'What did you do that for?'

'It was an accident,' Charles protested. Eve closed her eyes for a moment and pulled in her temper. He hadn't meant to do it. The bubbling sense of discomfort and the pressure of his nearness were her problem, not his.

'Alright,' she said. 'It's alright. It needed replacing anyway.' But now they would need a whole new canopy, rather than just a few small patches. *It's fine*, she told herself. *It's better this way. A replacement is less risky than a patch.* She tried not to think about the difficulty of locating an entire canopy that would fit this particular model of balloon. Instead, she dismantled the frame, slotting the pieces into the tube that hung from the end of the toolbox. She stowed it safely inside the pod, set all the electrics to sleep mode, and pulled out Bryant's float chair. It burbled over the wet sand.

Then she synced her wrist comm. with the pod, ensuring that she would be able to find her way back to it, and turned off the landing lights. The bugs in the lake gave them just enough light to see their way across the sand.

She kept one hand on the float chair. Her wrist comm. beamed a map over their surroundings, showing her the way to go. Eve followed it. She wondered what she would do if they met any workers and decided she would deal with that when it happened. She would not borrow trouble. She watched Charles struggle for a few more steps, then stopped the chair, pulled off Bryant's boots and held them out.

'Put these on. They'll stop you from sinking.'

'Oh,' he said, and he did as she suggested. He took a few experimental steps, then his mouth flashed a smile. 'Thank you. I like them very much.'

'They match your uniform.'

'Yes. Yes, they do, don't they?'

He was silent for a while then, admiring his footprints and the patterns he could make with the soles. He hadn't meant to do it, she told herself again. He was just clumsy. He was only trying to help. She needed to stop being paranoid, that was all.

A building loomed ahead, two-storey and square, with a flat roof and not many windows. The Medipro symbol on the side assured her that they had come to the right place. Eve breathed a little sigh of relief. She glanced down at Bryant. 'It won't be long now,' she told him. 'We're going to get you fixed.'

He didn't respond. She hadn't really expected him to. She pushed the float chair a little faster. Around the other side of the building was the entrance, a huge plastex monstrosity that speared up against the front of the building like a glittering pyramid. Through it she could see the movement of white coated bodies and droids, and she almost lost her nerve.

She gripped the side of the float chair a little tighter to stop her hands from shaking. Beside her, Charles was pulling off the boots. He gave them a little stroke, then tucked them in beside Bryant and pulled the sheets over the top and gestured to the space between the seat and the motor. 'Get in,' he said to Eve.

She shook her head. 'It's better if I wait out here.'

'No,' Charles said. 'You must come with us. It isn't safe for you to stay here alone.'

'I'll be fine. You don't need me in there.'

'You must come with us.'

Eve doubted that she would be any safer inside the building, but Charles seemed determined, and frankly, a little scary. She climbed into the small space and pulled the sheet down to hide herself from view. It was all up to Charles now. 'Remember that you're supposed to still have your chip,' she reminded him.

If it was possible for a droid to look offended, Charles managed it. 'I will be careful!'

He dropped the sheet. And then they were moving towards the entrance. With every step, Eve expected someone to stop them, but no-one did. By the time Charles pushed Bryant's float chair through the revolving doors and into the welcoming reception, she had at least managed to stop shaking. She clung on tightly, counting the tiles in the floor, listening hard to compensate for what she couldn't see.

Eve knew from her time with Dax that the way to get yourself somewhere you were not supposed to be was to act like you had every right to be there. It was a little easier when you were Dax, but it seemed that Charles could hold his own.

The chair moved briskly towards the reception desk. Curiosity got the better of her, and she moved the sheet a little and peeped out as Charles registered Bryant on the screen mounted into the desk. His fingers moved so quickly that she couldn't see exactly what he did, but a pass dropped into the slot and Charles took it, together with two tags that he attached to Bryant's bony wrists.

A little cleaning droid scooted up to them and buzzed straight under the chair. Eve stiffened as it knocked against her feet. She looked down to find it sucking the sand off her boots. Kick it away or let it work? In the end, she decided to hold still. Better that than leave a trail.

The droid finished and scooted off to find some more dirt.

Charles pushed the float chair into motion again, moving through the crowded reception. From what she had seen, everything was incredibly white. Eve didn't find it soothing. It wasn't like the facility that she had been modified at back on Earth as an eighteen-year-old. That had been low-budget, secret, small. This was none of those things. It pained her to see yet again how differently Underworld and Dome people got to experience the galaxy.

'How much further?' she whispered to Charles, not wanting him to see how badly she wanted to leave. She gripped the side of the float chair a little tighter, as if she could anchor herself to it, and tried to make herself as small as possible.

'Not much' he said. 'There's a travellator to our right that will take us up to the treatment rooms.' But before he could get there, he was stopped by someone. Eve could just make out narrow feet covered by rubber surgical shoes and the hem of a very white coat.

Oh, this was a mistake. She should have stayed outside. She should not have let Charles persuade her to come in.

'Who is this?' Female. Eve could tell that from the voice. 'We do not take injured personnel here.'

'This was the nearest medical facility,' Charles said. 'My commander ordered that he be brought here.'

'What's the name of your commander? What's wrong with him, anyway?'

'Eleniak Flu,' Charles said.

The feet moved back. 'Take him to isolation. Immediately!' Eve heard the sound of a spray being used, and then the feet moved briskly away. The lingering smell of the disinfectant turned her stomach, as had the ease with which Charles had sold the lie. It had been the right thing to do, the only thing to do, but something about it made her very uncomfortable.

The travellator moved swiftly. The sheet was jerked aside. 'Come on,' Charles said, holding out a metal hand. 'It's empty.'

Eve clambered awkwardly out, ignoring his hand. They were in a long, wide corridor. Down both sides were doors and windows, each one numbered, with a little entry pad next to the doors. Most were lit red. A couple were lit green. 'This way,' Charles said, shoving the chair into motion and towards the nearest room with a green light. The door rolled open as they approached, and Charles pushed the float chair through. The door closed again behind them. It activated the privacy screen for the window and Eve stood awkwardly in the middle of the room with no idea what to do.

Why was she even here? She wasn't a nurse. If she touched Bryant, she'd finish him off. She should have stayed outside. She should have gone straight back to the pod. The pod which had no balloon.

Shit.

'Right,' Charles said, clapping his hands together and sounding far too cheery. 'Let's get this done, shall we?'

Eve sat on the empty bed as Charles pulled the float chair over to the diagnostic scanner on the other side of the room and activated it. 'Hmm,' he said, as his fingers danced over the screen.

Eve didn't ask, and he didn't elaborate. Instead, over the next few minutes, she watched as the droid took various implements from cupboards and ran various scans, assessing the results on the screen. 'Extensive liver damage. Kidneys functioning at 10%. My, my, former agent Adam Bryant. You really are in a mess. Hard to believe you've kept going this long.'

Eve clenched her jaw against the flow of words. What about Alistair? He never stood a chance. From the moment Bryant had dropped that sonic grenade, it was all over for him, and he had more goodness and decency in his little finger than Bryant had in his entire body.

Yet Bryant was the one lying here, clinging onto life, and he was the one she was going to save. In that moment, Eve hated him more than she had at any other point. She almost told Charles that she had changed her mind and that they should leave Bryant to die.

'Please excuse me for a moment,' Charles said, and disappeared from the room before she could stop him. Not that she was physically capable of stopping him, or that she would have got close enough to try.

Now it was just her and what was left of Bryant.

Long minutes ticked by.

Eve played around with the controls for the bed. She looked in the storage lockers that ran along one wall, pocketed some cleansing wipes. She unwrapped a chewable toothbrush and popped it into her mouth. She sat back on the bed, tried lying down, tried sitting up again, and then finally let her thoughts wander round to the fact that Charles had been gone for quite a long time and that perhaps she should leave.

Still, she wanted to give the droid the benefit of the doubt so she waited another minute before she opened the door and stuck her head out. There was no sign of Charles, though she caught sight of someone in uniform coming to the top of the travellator at the far end of the corridor. She jerked her head back into the room and activated the door, pressing her back against it. Where had Charles gone? What if it didn't come back? *Think, Eve, think!*

She climbed over the bed and began ransacking the cupboards behind it for anything she could use. Sadly there were no weapons, nothing more dangerous than several sets of male underclothes and clean sheets for the bed. There weren't even any drug guns or any meds.

Fortunately, Charles reappeared before she could get in any more of a panic. In the droid's hand was a small transparent case, and inside that case were two glass vials. Charles set it down on the bench next to the float chair.

'Where have you been!?'

'I have the serums!'

Eve looked at the vials. 'Serums?'

'Yes,' the droid said. 'This medical centre is currently administering the Type One serums to a small group of male security agents.'

'Type One? You're going to make him Type One?'

'I believe that the boost to his immune system and the improved healing rate will enable his body to reverse the effects of the toxin.'

'But it will make him Type One!'

'Is this not something that Adam Bryant would wish?'

He would hate it, Eve thought. It was the worst possible thing she could do to him. 'Hang on a minute. Type One *agents*?'

'That is correct.'

'Shit,' she said, more to herself than Charles. This wasn't good. This wasn't good at all. Type One agents. She didn't know what they were for, and she didn't particularly want to know. But she knew one thing for certain.

She needed to leave. Right now.

But what about Bryant? Not giving him a treatment which might help, after getting him here, was unthinkable. 'Bryant would want to get better,' she said. That much at least was the truth.

'Then shall I proceed?'

'Yes.' She buried her face in her hands. 'Yes. Get it done.'

Charles didn't look at her as he spoke. He was too busy examining Bryant's right arm, which was pale and scrawny, the skin hanging off the bone. The droid set about cleaning the skin and checking for a vein, then loaded a drug gun with the first serum. He patted the vein to bring it up, and then injected Bryant.

Eve watched intently, searching for changes. She knew that realistically the changes, if any, would happen slowly, and that was to a healthy body. Bryant wasn't going to make a miraculous recovery in front of her very eyes. But she hoped for something anyway, some glimmer, some hint that she had made the right choice.

Nothing happened. Bryant looked just as pasty and bony and ill.

'Is that it?' Eve asked, as Charles tidied away the drug gun and the empty vial, dropping them into the recycling chute.

'For now,' Charles said. 'The first serum takes twenty-four hours. He will then need to be injected with the second one.'

'So we have to just sit here for twenty-four hours? No. No way. I am not hiding in this room for a whole day and hoping no-one catches us.'

'I suppose we could always leave him here,' Charles said. 'I can programme one of the medidroids to give him the second dose of serum and then transfer him to the main ward, assuming of course that he survives the treatment.'

'Works for me,' Eve said.

She waited for another anxious half an hour as Charles did exactly that. He hacked into the hospital system using the workstation mounted on the wall by the door. Bryant was given a new identity and a set of false medical records and a medidroid appeared at the doorway, zooming into position at the side of the bed and switching into standby mode.

Eve was on her feet immediately. She refused to look back at Bryant. She'd had enough of Charles. She grabbed a packet of clothes and another of sheets from the cupboard, ripped them open, and pulled the clothes on over her own. She held the bundle of sheets in front of her. If she walked quickly and tried not to draw any attention to herself, there was a possibility that she might be able to get out of the building unchallenged. She didn't like Charles, didn't want to rely on him any longer.

Leaving the building was the longest walk she had ever taken.

It wasn't until she was outside, a good distance along the path which led away from the facility, that she finally remembered to breathe. She had done it. She had taken Bryant to the facility. Charles had given him the first dose of Type One serum. Whether or not it worked was not under her control and not really her problem.

What she had to do now was fix the pod, and leave.

CHAPTER

15

24th January 2208

Apartment 438, Acton District, London Dome, Earth

The Autochef flashed and hummed, dispensing a half-filled cup of weak herbal tea. Ferona looked at it in disgust. She needed to go shopping, but with little in the way of credits, she was finding it hard to muster up the enthusiasm. Her regular deliveries had been cancelled because she hadn't paid for the last two. Power was now intermittent due to restrictions for the below-ground levels which had crept up to the lower levels of the Dome, so her screens only worked for an hour a day, and her mind wouldn't stop turning over her visit to Weston.

She wasn't used to living like this. She didn't know how to do it. There had always been enough, and she had assumed that there would always be enough, so she had nothing set aside, no emergency fund, no favours she could call in. Ferona had always believed that people in difficult situations could get themselves out if they simply tried hard enough. Now she was beginning to understand how difficult that was when your energy and attention were used up on basic things like keeping warm and trying to appease an empty stomach.

They'd be distributing Silver Rice below ground. The deliveries were made twice a week and the packets handed out on those days. All you had to do was show appropriate I.D.

It pained Ferona to find herself considering it.

No. She wouldn't. She was Dome-raised, and Dome-raised women did not eat Silver Rice. She threw off the covers and forced herself to get up. There was one option still left open to her, one she'd hoped to avoid when she'd still believed that her situation was only temporary. She still believed it, she told herself, although the thought was brittle and thin at the edges, gnawed away by hunger.

She went to the pile of boxes stacked against the wall of her living area. She lifted one from the top, took it back to the bed, and opened it. Inside, she found a thin necklace dripping with rubies, a platinum bracelet that wound round the wrist like a snake and several pairs of diamond earrings. She sighed with pain and pleasure as her fingertips skated over each of them. She had no recollection of buying them. If she'd been asked, she wouldn't have been able to list the contents of each box. Her personal droids had held that information. Ferona had never seen the point of cluttering her thoughts with it when she could call it up at a moment's notice.

But the droids were gone and these boxes were all she had left of her most precious collection.

She fingered the necklace, stroked the bracelet, picked out a pair of the earrings and slid the red velvet box into her pocket. Then she left the apartment before she could change her mind. She walked the four kilometres to Hatton Garden, where several jewellers stubbornly clung on to their heritage and old-fashioned shop fronts.

Two of the shops were closed. Three were open, and Ferona chose the middle one. A real bell jangled as she pushed open the door. A year ago it would have amused her. Now she found it pretentious and annoying.

The man behind the counter didn't even lift his eyes from his wrist screen when she walked in. There was no greeting, no smile, no charm. He lifted a steaming mug of something to his mouth and drank from it. Ferona could smell Koffee. She'd give her right arm for Koffee.

She put her hand into her pocket and grazed her fingertips over the velvet box, felt a last twinge of pain that was quickly overridden by hunger, and took it out and set it on the counter. 'I want to sell these.'

'I'm not buying at the moment,' the man said.

'You'll want to buy these.'

'Like I said, I'm not buying anything.'

'*Look at them.*'

He did, then. A cursory glance, followed by a closer examination with a loupe when he saw the name on the inside of the box. 'Five hundred,' he said.

'They're worth considerably more that!'

'Then find someone else who will pay it.'

Ferona reached for the box. Then she withdrew her hand. It wasn't the offer which had stopped her, as it was nothing less than insulting, but the images on the screen that had held the man's attention so tightly. 'What is that?'

'The Europa,' he said. 'There was a fire a few days ago and the place was evacuated. Turns out that the owner had hiked up the air fees and loads of people were stuck there. Couldn't afford to leave.'

'Presumably someone on board started it.'

The man lifted his head, and for the first time, seemed to really see Ferona. She saw the double take as a hint of recognition slipped in, and the moment it was dismissed. 'Seems that way, doesn't it? Not our problem, though. If people are stupid enough to get themselves trapped in neutral space right now, that's their lookout. So are you going to take the five hundred or not?'

His hand was still on the velvet box, fingers caging it possessively against the countertop.

'I'll take it,' Ferona said. What choice did she have?

'Account or chip?'

'Chip.'

He unlocked a drawer hidden in the counter, revealing a keyboard and row of chips, then selected one, swiped it, and held it out to Ferona. She only just managed not to snatch it out of his hand. But he didn't let go, even when she took hold of it.

'They're not stolen, are they?'

'No, they are not.'

'Had to ask,' he said. He let go of the chip.

'I'm sure you did.'

She hurried to the door. Something was nagging at her, a thought that wouldn't quite coalesce. She pushed it aside. Five hundred. She could only hope it would be enough. It became a little less after she bought a thin and slightly stale cheese sandwich from a vendor at the end of the street, and a cab ride to Weston's house. This time she marched to the door without hesitation. She barely noticed the smell when the door opened, or the involuntary jerk of her foot in the direction of the dog.

'Well?' he said.

'I've got just under five hundred on a chip,' she told him. 'I can get more, but it will take a couple of days.'

'Five hundred?' He looked at her as if she was something he'd stood in.

Ferona's chest went tight with the need for air. 'Please,' she said.

Weston narrowed his eyes. She felt sure he was going to shut the door in her face. 'Alright,' he said. He stepped back, leaving room for her to squeeze past, then checked the street before closing the door.

Ferona stood just inside the front room. Her hands twisted around the strap of her bag. She wished that she hadn't eaten that sandwich. She could feel it in the middle of her chest, as if it had got stuck and hadn't made it all the way down into her stomach. She had forgotten – how could she have forgotten? – that Weston was, at heart, a warmonger. He lived to poke poisonous creatures and see which of them bit.

She watched as he bent over, grunted, then grabbed one corner of the rug that covered the floor, and pulled it back. She could taste the resulting dust as it puffed up into the air. Why didn't he have a cleaning droid like a normal person?

In the middle of the space was a metal hatch roughly a metre square. He grunted even louder as he squatted down to press his thumb against the lock. The hatch door lifted, a light flicked on, and Ferona saw sharp-edged concrete steps. 'Follow me,' he said, as he started down them.

Ferona did as she was told. She couldn't not. She followed him down those stairs as lights flicked on, and found herself inside a basement that had to be a hundred metres long. The air down here was noticeably cleaner than the air upstairs, and she took a deep breath of it.

So he had been spending his money after all. There were more weapons, not antiques like the ones on the wall in his poky living room, but brand new, and, she suspected, prototypes. There was a fully equipped laboratory, a long row of industrial freezers, a bank of computers, several 3D printers, and more equipment that she could not identify.

Weston walked up to one of the freezers and opened the door. It appeared to be filled with trays of tissue samples. He pulled out a small black box and carried it over to one of the benches before setting it down. He took white surgical gloves from a drawer and put them on, and then he opened the box. He took out a single vial. Inside it was a viscous brown liquid.

'What is that?'

'You're a smart woman. What do you think it is?'

Ferona took a cautious step closer, and looked at the liquid. 'It doesn't look like the other serums.'

'That's because it's not a serum. This is something quite different.' There was excitement in his voice. 'It's taken a lot of work to get it to this stage. For a while I didn't know if it was even possible. But it's done. I haven't carried out large-scale testing yet. I can't see how it could be tested on a large scale, to be perfectly honest. It would be far too dangerous ...'

'Yes, but *what is it?*'

'A virus,' Weston said. He looked at her, cheeks flushed and eyes gleaming.

'Not genetic modification?'

'Genetic modification has had its day,' he said. 'It's far too limited in its application. Too slow. Too expensive. It's time to look elsewhere.'

Ferona chose not to ask him where he'd found whatever was in that vial. She wasn't sure she wanted to know. 'I don't see how a disease can help me.'

'Oh, this isn't a disease.'

'You said it was a virus.'

'Indeed it is. But to call it a disease is to overlook everything that it is. Did you know that viruses can infect all life forms? There are even viruses than can infect bacteria. Nothing is too big or too small for them. They will take on anything. We don't even know how many there are. This one, for example, has never been documented. It's new.'

'What does it do?'

'It's complicated, but basically, once the infection takes hold, it causes changes to the salivary glands. That's how it's transmitted. In saliva. Have you heard of a disease called rabies?'

Ferona shook her head. She couldn't take her eyes off the vial.

'Few have,' Weston told her. 'It was eradicated a long time ago. It was a widespread disease, once, an infection found everywhere on Earth apart from Antarctica. It didn't like the cold.' He laughed. 'Creatures infected with rabies suffered from swelling of the spinal cord and the brain. They went mad. Would bite anyone who got within range. That's how the virus was transmitted, you see. Just like this one.'

'I don't . . .'

'Of course you don't, because I haven't explained it yet. This virus will cause your salivary glands to produce a chemical that affects brain function. It makes people very susceptible to suggestion. The effects are short-lived, and in a healthy person, full-scale infection is highly unlikely. The immune system of the average Dome dweller will fight this off within a matter of hours and they'll have no idea they were ever exposed to anything.'

'I don't understand.'

Weston sighed. 'Once you've infected someone, you'll have a window of ten to twelve hours in which they will do anything you tell them to do.'

Ferona slowly exhaled. He was right. This was different. She immediately began to see the possibilities and had to work very hard not to let her excitement show. But she quickly realised the problem.

'How are you going to infect me with it? You said it doesn't work on Dome people, that our immune systems can easily deal with it.'

'Your immune system is tanked,' he said. 'To be honest, I'm surprised you're not already ill. And you'll be exposed to a far higher number of virus particles than you would normally. Believe me, you'll be infected.'

'How can you be so sure that my immune system won't fight it off?'

'You're even thinner than usual, which means you aren't eating properly. If you can't afford food you can't afford your immunity boosters, and you're definitely behind on your Rejuvinex shots. You've given me five hundred credits and it took you two days to get that.'

Ferona felt the flush of shame spread under her skin. 'There's no need to be rude.'

'And there's no need to be a stuck-up bitch, but we are who we are. There are multiple ways to transfer the virus once you've been infected,' he continued. 'A kiss, perhaps. A lick. Spit in their face. Get down on all fours and bite like a rabid dog.'

'That's disgusting.'

'Humans are.' He carefully set the vial back into the case. 'Once infected, you'll look completely normal. There will be no noticeable physical changes. You won't be enormous or green. With this, you can go anywhere and pass for an average human and temporarily control the behaviour of those you come into close contact with.'

Ferona had no real understanding of illness. No Dome dweller did. She had read about it, but she had no genuine experience. All she knew was that she wanted this. She didn't trust Weston, only a fool would do that, but this was better than anything she could possibly have imagined.

She had always believed that she was meant for greatness.

Maybe this was fate's way of telling her that was still true.

'Alright,' she said. 'What do I need to do?'

'Sit here.' He pointed to a treatment chair. It still had the plastic covers on the arms. A medidroid came over and helped her out of her coat, baring her forearm and the veins at the crook of her elbow. Her skin was sprayed with something cold and the droid turned her arm this way and that before a needle was inserted. It bulged up under her skin.

'Last chance to change your mind,' Weston said, and before she could respond, he injected the vial of liquid through the tube in her arm. It went down slowly, but it went down, and she felt a sudden sensation of warmth in her arm, followed by a sour taste in her mouth. 'How long will it take to work?'

'I don't know,' Weston said. 'Could be a few hours, could be days. Could be months.'

'I can't wait months.'

He merely smiled. 'Go home. You should start to notice some changes within the next twenty-four to forty-eight hours.'

'Go home?'

'Yes, Ferona. Go home.' He turned away from her and busied himself with his work screen.

Slowly, cautiously, Ferona got to her feet. She stared at his back. There were little white flakes of dandruff on the shoulders of his jacket. 'What should I be looking for?'

'You'll know when it happens. Oh, and I expect an additional payment in my account by the end of the day.'

'How much?'

'Two thousand,' he said.

'And if I can't get it?'

He smiled. 'You will.'

And that was it. Realising that she had been dismissed, Ferona walked up the stairs as quickly as she could manage, and out of his house. Out in the open, she felt oddly vulnerable and wobbly.

She returned to her flat, not entirely sure how long the journey took. Time seemed to have become elastic. Once there, she tossed the clothes which smelled like Weston's house and the greasy taint of Autocab into the recycler and set to work sorting through her remaining boxes of possessions. She packaged up what was left of her jewellery and had it delivered by post bot to the jewellery store she had visited earlier, together with a note telling the owner where to deposit the credits.

She spent the next thirty minutes prowling round her apartment, unable to sit still, unable to focus on anything. There was a strange sensation under her tongue, a sort of mild stinging, and when she went to the bathroom and looked in the mirror, she saw a tiny red dot that she was sure had not been there before. She checked it three times over the next hour, and each time, it was a little larger. She licked her lips. Something was happening, that much was certain, but was it the serum? Weston had said twenty-four to forty-eight hours and it had barely been two. Surely it was too soon. And yet . . .

There was only one way to find out.

She put on her coat and boots and headed out. It didn't take her long to reach a nearby market. The square wasn't busy, but there were enough people milling around to make this a worthwhile trip.

She glanced across at a man on her left, middle-aged but still lean, with swept back hair and sharp eyebrows. His shoes were shiny and his jawline perfect. From the cut of his jacket she suspected that he worked for one of the banks, probably in a senior position where he got to make sweeping decisions about housing loans and colony investment plans.

He caught her staring and narrowed jet-black eyes at her before turning away.

Ferona changed direction and walked on, towards one of the exits that would lead her into the shopping centre. They were close to the edge of the Dome, and on the other side of the glass, she could hear the wind howling. The outer reality system wasn't working properly and it kept flickering off, showing the fall of huge snow-flakes the size of her fist. It was impossible to focus on the rolling fields and sunny skies that the system projected when they came and went at random intervals.

She kept going, not even knowing which direction she was taking until she found herself outside a bar frequented by workers from the government building opposite. She stood outside, looking at the entrance, wondering if she dared to go in. She would not be wel-comed, she knew that much, and yet it was only a matter of months since she would have been given a table in one of the private rooms at the back without even having to ask.

She was halfway across the street when her nerve failed her and she was forced to retreat to a little perfume shop on the other side of the road. She tried three or four different scents on her wrist, barely smelling them, although she went through the motions of doing so. She picked up a beautifully carved bottle with a stopper in the shape of an elegant bird and then set it down, suddenly aware that she could not afford anything in here, and wondering if she had made a mistake in going to Weston. She thought of Ana Rizzola, and Vexler, and of Swain, her other assistant, who had died in that explosion. Her head felt too heavy to hold up. Her brain was throbbing. Her breathing was too fast, and it was very loud.

She fled the shop.

On the other side of the street was an Autocab stand. She snuck straight to the front of the queue as a car pulled up and pushed her way on board with a young man bundled up in a big padded coat that made him look like a snowman.

'What do you think you're doing?' he said, his voice raised in fury.

'Sharing your cab,' Ferona told him. She coughed, a deep rattle inside her chest.

'Get out!'

She didn't want to. She was cold and her bones hurt and she was beginning to wish that she had stayed at home. 'No.'

He grabbed her shoulder and started to push. 'I said, get out!'

Ferona spat in his face. The small amount of saliva she managed to produce slid glossily down his cheek before he wiped at it with his sleeve. He stared at her in wide-eyed, ugly disgust, called her a name she would normally have strung him up for and got out of the cab.

He'd left a credit chip in the slot, but she couldn't take responsibility for that. She hadn't told him to do it.

Using the last of her strength, Ferona told the cab her address.

It took her home.

CHAPTER

16

24th January 2208

Space Station Europa, Sector Three, Neutral Space

Jinn sat on the floor with her back pressed against the wall and watched as Dax paced the length of the docking bay. She did not expect the Sittan to wait for much longer. She could sense the Virena on their ships, feel it tugging at her mind, trying to find out what she was thinking. She didn't let it. She closed off her thoughts, folding them away and locking them up tightly. But it was exhausting. Eventually, if the Virena kept pushing, she would crack.

'We aren't going to give them what they want,' Dax said.

Jinn hugged her knees a little tighter. She wasn't so sure about that.

'But we have to do something,' Ace said. 'We can't just sit here and wait for them to blow up the station.'

'We are going to do something,' she said.

'What?' Dax asked her. 'You heard what Grenla said. They want

113

you dead.' He started pacing again. He was so tense that the air was thick with it.

'Are you alright?' she asked him quietly.

He stopped pacing, then, and turned to face her. His bright green eyes burned fiercely. 'No, I'm bloody well not alright.' He shoved a hand back through his hair, digging his fingers deep into the dark strands and pulling on them. 'I feel like ... I really need to break something. Someone.'

This was not good. This was not good at all. Jinn had seen him like this before, back on Sittan, and it had always been a precursor to violence. She knew he couldn't help it. It was in his DNA, in his blood, a constant hum in the background of his being.

Carefully, slowly, she got to her feet and walked up to him. She looked him over. His forehead was damp with sweat, his cheeks flushed, and she didn't think it was just from the heat in here. His hands hung at his sides. He was trembling. There was a smell to him, something earthy and raw that she couldn't quite put her finger on. 'Breathe,' she told him.

'I'm trying.'

'Try harder.'

He raised one eyebrow. 'Are you challenging me?' The muscles in his shoulders and upper arms strained the seams of his jacket, and Jinn felt a shiver of response. She might not have had the third dose of serum, but there was still more than enough Sittan in her to make those words go through her like a jolt of electricity.

'Do you want to be challenged?' she replied, keeping her voice low.

He stared down at her. A muscle twitched in his cheek. She wanted to press her hand to his face, feel the heat of his skin against her palm, but she didn't.

'No,' he said finally. He turned away from her, but this time he didn't resume his incessant pacing.

Jinn could sense the Sittan ships surrounding the station. She could count the number of Sittan females on board, could see them in her mind as clearly as if they were stood right in front of her. The Virena heated under her skin. She adjusted the position of her legs and fidgeted with her hands before finally giving up and getting to her feet.

The feeling of more of it, out there, waiting for her, was almost unbearable. But Dax didn't know about the Virena. He knew that she'd been able to control it, back on Sittan. He didn't know that some of it had left that planet with her, that it moved in her bloodstream.

He didn't *know*.

Nor could she bring herself to tell him.

'I need a ship,' she said.

'We've got a ship,' Dax told her.

'Another ship.' She combed loose strands of hair back from her face. 'A different ship.'

The others all looked at each other, and she was sure that there were unspoken messages passing between them, but none of them said anything out loud, except for Dax.

'Why?'

'Because I'm going to deal with them.'

His mouth thinned, and he set his hands to his hips. 'Alone?'

'They've come here for me. They're not interested in the rest of you.'

As she said those words, she could feel the Virena growing heavier in her hands. She'd been running from this for too long, refusing to accept it for what it was, but she couldn't do it any longer. She could feel the rest of it out there. And she *wanted* it. The craving was almost unbearable.

'There are ships on the lower level of the station,' Mady said. Her voice was awkward, a little nervous. She took a couple of steps closer to Jinn, though not too close. She'd found herself clothes in one of the stores and was covered from neck to ankle in a sweeping dress complete with matching white satin gloves, reminding Jinn that under the green was an Underworld woman who'd probably had one outfit growing up and certainly never anything like this. 'They keep them in a locked bay, ones that they've confiscated from people who didn't have a flight licence.'

'Show me,' Dax said to her. She sent a quick, darting glance at Jinn, then one up at him, and nodded. That didn't surprise Jinn. It was hard for people to say no to Dax.

There were three ships in the bay that Mady led them to, ignored when the station had been cleared out because no-one had known to come down to this level. They were old and dusty and had obviously been in stasis for a long time. Jinn looked them over and made a quick and easy decision, dismissing a new Kitchener Starsport in favour of an old Class 4 two-person clunker. She popped open the lock panel and pretended to fiddle with it as she discreetly sent a thin thread of Virena inside it. The side panel hissed open and the steps lowered.

Dax had his foot on the bottom step before she could stop him. 'Where are you going?' she asked.

'You need a pilot.'

'I am a pilot.'

'They told me to bring you to them. Dead.'

'Well, as we've already agreed that you're not going to do that, I'll go on my own.'

'No you won't,' he said, and moved his big body up the rest of the stairs and into the ship.

'I could kill him again,' Jinn muttered, before she remembered that Ace and the Type Two women were watching her. She followed Dax into the little ship rather than deal with them.

The panel groaned back into place behind her. The ship was small and cheap, with a control deck containing two seats and nothing else. The seat covers were split and peeling and someone had glued badly cut sections of fluffy brown carpet across the walls and ceiling. Dax settled himself into the pilot seat and reached up to play with the switches on the ceiling. He ignored Jinn completely as she put herself in the empty seat.

The phase drive choked and spluttered but he got it going, and if she used the Virena to give it a little push, he didn't need to know.

'Right,' he said, as the ship cleared the Europa. 'I know you've got a plan. So spill.'

Jinn let the song of the Virena fill her head. She kept her expression neutral, refusing to let the emotion it was pouring into her leak out, though she could feel it pulling at her. 'I can't.'

'Why not? Are you actually planning on sacrificing yourself? Is that it? Because I can tell you now, I won't let it happen.'

'It's not that.'

'Then what? Come on, Jinn. We're running out of time here. And I will not let you do this unless you tell me what you think you're going to do when you get out there.'

She knew he was right.

'I'm going to steal their Virena,' she said finally.

'The Virena?' He sounded confused.

'The living metal, the stuff that came from the Mountain.'

'I know what it is.'

'It's how they power their ships, their weapons. They're useless without it and I think I can steal it.' She bit her lip, waiting to see what he would say.

'How?'

She could feel the Virena tingling in her hands. She sat with one elbow on the armrest and concentrated on keeping the living metal calm and silent. She would not allow it to give her away. 'I could control it on Sittan. I think I can control it here, as well.' It was only half a lie.

Dax just shook his head. 'You're unbelievable, you know that?'

'Dax . . .'

'No,' he said. 'You listen to me. Just for once, listen to me. You're asking me to trust you, and I will. But you have got to do the same for me. I want to know what in the void is going on, Jinn. I want the truth.'

The ship jerked. The internal lights flashed. Dax looked up, flicked more switches, tightened his grip on the tiller. 'Tractor beam,' he said, but Jinn knew that it wasn't. It was the Virena, come out to find her. It pulled them jerkily forwards, and Dax lifted his hands away from the controls. The ship shot forward towards the Sittan vessels.

The sound of the engine changed, and Jinn sensed the shift in the atmosphere and in him when their ship was swallowed up by one of the Sittan vessels. She could feel the unfamiliar Virena on the Sittan ship. It called to her. She forced it out of her mind, did not let those seeking tendrils press into her thoughts. If it knew that she was alive, the Sittan females would know it too, and she could not allow that, not yet.

So she pushed it back, even as the Virena in her hands cried out in hunger. It desperately wanted to join with the rest, wanted to invite it in. That was what Jinn had been counting on. The pressure of the longing was immense. She felt almost crushed by it. But their safety in the next few minutes depended on her ability to resist it, so resist it she would.

She had to let its emotions rage, agonising though it was. It cried out inside her like a heartbroken child, loud and endless and inconsolable, not understanding why it could not bring the rest of itself home. She could not even tell it that it needed to be patient, that all would become clear in time.

'If you're not going to tell me,' Dax said, 'then you're going to have to do this my way. I want you to play dead. That should get us on board and buy us a little time.'

'And then what?'

'We do what we always do. Improvise.'

She watched Dax move and let her body go limp as he pulled her from the seat. His fingers closed round her wrist and he dragged her off the transporter and through onto the Sittan ship. They'd asked for her body. So that's what they would get.

The air was hot. She cautiously breathed it in, her head hanging back, her eyes closed, the long, twisted plait of her hair trailing along the floor. His footsteps were regular and calm, matching the beat of his heart.

She felt a little less calm when he abruptly let go of her wrist and dropped her to the floor. She didn't cry out, but it was a close-run thing. *That bloody hurt, Dax!*

'There you go,' Dax said.

'So I see,' said Grenla.

'Where's Talta?'

'The empress is where she belongs.'

On Sittan, Jinn thought to herself. Far away from here, from me. Waging her war from a very safe distance. Typical politician. She might come from a different planet, and speak a different language, but underneath it all, she was exactly the same. Letting others do the dirty work and take all the risks.

She held her breath. A few seconds more. She could not only sense the Virena on this ship now, but on the others as well. It was confused. She could feel Grenla in it, and through Grenla, Talta. But the feeling was faint, undefined, uncertain, and unbearably painful. It was looking for its empress and it didn't know where to turn.

Jinn snapped back her mental shields and reached out to the Virena. It answered her in a hot, hungry wave, and she opened her eyes and leapt to her feet, forming a blade at each hand as she did so. It took her only a moment to take in her surroundings as the Virena immediately told her everything she needed to know about the rest of the ship.

Grenla stood in the middle of the ship, with the other females spread out behind her. Each one of them was armed. Spikes rippled out across the top of their elegant heads.

'So,' Grenla said. 'You're still alive.'

'Of course,' Jinn told her. 'You didn't think he would actually kill me, did you?'

Grenla licked her lips, forked tongue flickering out. 'No. But it was ... how do you humans say it? Worth a try.' She had twin blades crossed at her back, polished obsidian that Jinn knew could slice through flesh like it was air, and she pulled them free now. 'It simply means that I will have the pleasure of killing you myself.'

'Are you sure you really want to do that?'

'My empress requires it.'

A cold chill settled over Jinn, like snowflakes on bare skin. It felt like an awakening. Suddenly she was able to see everything with absolute clarity.

Grenla thought Talta still ruled the Virena.

But she didn't.

Jinn had kept her control of the Virena a secret from Dax and the others for a reason. She'd contained it, refused to think of it, refused to let it into her thoughts. But she couldn't do it any longer. The bewildered grief of the Virena on these ships was too much. It needed someone to rule it.

It needed Jinn, and she couldn't deny it any longer.

'I don't want to hurt you,' she told Grenla.

'You won't,' Grenla promised her. 'Human scum.'

She charged.

They met in a swirling dance of blades. It didn't last long. It soon became apparent that despite Grenla's bold words, she was outmatched, and Jinn knew the exact moment that the Sittan female realised who she had really taken on. But she fought hard anyway, and Jinn gave her the death she wanted. It was the least she could do. She looked down sadly at Grenla's bloodied, broken body.

She looked at Dax. *Forgive me*, she thought. *Please forgive me.*

Then she called to all the Virena around her. She could feel every single droplet of it, as atom by atom, it felt her, recognised her, welcomed her. She was flooded with heat and devotion, and the power of it was almost overwhelming.

The walls of the ship started to ripple in those familiar, beautiful shades of emerald green and petrol blue, swirling together to form exquisite, wonderful patterns. The Virena was on the move. A droplet pulled itself free and flew towards Jinn. It landed gently against the side of her face and caressed her, then trickled down the side of her neck, onto her shoulder, and down her arm, until it joined the rest of the Virena in her hand.

More and more of it wrapped itself around Jinn. Her blades lengthened until they dragged on the floor. It covered her arms and legs in dark heat.

There was an audible gasp, and the remaining females drew back.

'I do not understand,' one of them said, pale and snarling. 'I have never seen anyone but an empress have such control over the Virena. How can this be? You are merely human.'

'*Merely human?*' Jinn couldn't help herself. She laughed. 'Humans aren't merely anything.' She silently called to the remaining Virena on the ship. The walls began to move, a ripple at first, and then a great wave. It crashed over the Sittan females, knocking them all to their knees. It stopped at Jinn's feet, sinking into a puddle around her boots, and then it lifted her up. The Sittan females visibly cowered.

With a flick of her wrist, she sent a chain of Virena flying towards them. It bound their wrists and locked all of them in place. She would decide exactly what to do with them later. She didn't want to kill them. Perhaps Ritte would be able to help. There might still be hope for them.

Sometimes hope was all there was.

'Bloody supernova,' she heard Dax whisper, and opened her eyes to find him looking at her. 'Jinn,' he said. 'Why didn't you tell me?'

'Because I hoped it wasn't true.'

And that was why, for six long months, she had fought it. She had tried, desperately, to convince herself that because Talta was still alive, her control of the Virena didn't mean anything. She had let the Sittan run rampage through Earth-controlled space, and she had ignored the little voice inside her head that said she could stop them.

But there was no denying it now, and no escaping what she had to do. She pulled at the Virena on the other ships, brought it under her control, then one by one, she flew the Sittan ships to the Europa and brought all of them in to dock. The females on board them would have to stay where they were until she had figured out what to do with them. She pushed the Virena out around the perimeter of the station. It would not let anyone or anything past unless she asked it to.

They were safe, and that was all that mattered.

CHAPTER

17

15th Day of the Seventh Turn

The Palace, Fire City, Sittan

Talta was still shaken from the dream she'd had that morning. She had heard nothing from Grenla or the others, and when she tried to search through the threads of Virena, she found only silence. She was too afraid to push further.

Chal Gri had helped her to dress. She had chosen a long cloak that hid her peeling skin, and decorated her hands with her largest rings, though she had to be careful that they did not slip off. Her teeth had been polished and her claws decorated with dark ruby dust. She waited atop her platform in the arena, shaded by a huge canopy that protected her from the worst of the heat. The same privilege was not extended to the queens.

They came into the arena one at a time, surrounded by their retinues. They hadn't been invited into the palace to rest or wash first. She knew that they would be dirty and tired and hungry.

She didn't speak until the last of them had arrived.

And then she looked them over.

They disgusted her.

She sat up slowly, swinging her clawed feet to the stone, but she didn't stand. 'Where are my tributes?' she asked quietly.

The queens looked at each other. Then one of them came forward. Denat was young. She had only been ruler of her province for five turns, and she'd killed her own mother to take control. 'We didn't send them,' she said.

'I know,' Talta replied. 'I am giving you the opportunity to rectify that oversight.'

'It wasn't an oversight.'

'You are new,' Talta said patiently. She drew on everything she had learned in her time as empress, when she could end a life with little more than a wave of her hand. 'Perhaps your mother did not explain the importance of the tributes to you.'

'Oh, she explained,' Denat said. 'I decided that I didn't want to send them.'

'And the rest of you?' Talta asked. She could feel her anger starting to bubble up. But she didn't have the energy to let it fly. She had to remain in control. She could not let them see how weak she was.

'Our harvest failed,' said another.

'The trees did not fruit well.'

'The mines did not bless us this year.'

Excuse after excuse after excuse.

'I see,' Talta said. And she did. She saw the lies, every single one of them. She set her feet back up and propped herself up on one elbow. 'I understand.'

'We won't be sending you anything else,' Denat told her. 'No more tributes. No more males.'

Talta exhaled. She fought the weakness in her body, the dryness in her throat. She could not let them see how weak she was. Chal Gri had told her that there was dissent in the other cities, that the females were starting to fight against the leash of her rule. She hadn't wanted to listen. She'd been too caught up in the hunt for Jinnifer Blue and the Virena to spare a thought for what was happening here on Sittan. That had been a mistake.

'You will send the tributes,' Talta told them. 'You can keep your males. For now.'

'Surely you cannot intend to reopen the arena.'

'Of course I intend to reopen the arena, when the time is right.'

'Who will fight? We have hardly any males left. The ones we do have are needed to father children. You killed all the human males.'

'You are right,' Talta said. 'We cannot sacrifice any more males. Not yet. But this is the arena, and the arena must have blood. The Mountain must have blood.'

Denat sneered at her. 'The Mountain,' she said. 'The Mountain is dead, Talta.'

Bring them to the arena, Chal Gri had said. *Make them meet you there. Let them know that you still rule this planet.*

Talta hadn't understood what he meant at the time. But she understood it now. Her hand skated over the surface of her day bed, tracing the familiar smooth lines in the stone. She danced her fingertips over the intricate pattern of coils etched there and never took her eyes off Denat.

Then she triggered the mechanism. The traces of Virena that lingered here were still enough to make it work, and she was the most powerful female present. It answered to her, just.

The ground under Denat's feet gave way. She fell. The last Talta saw of her was her wide-eyed, terrified stare, her mouth like a gaping wound as it opened in shock. The others turned to each other, a moment of silence before Denat's screams began.

Two of them were close enough to the gates to think that running was an option. Talta cut them off. There would be no escape for disobedient females who refused to follow the rules of their planet that had been established and honoured for thousands of turns.

She opened up another pit, another, another, dropping more of the females down to die, impaled on the armlength spikes at the bottom, until only a few remained.

'Go home,' she told them. 'Send your tributes by sunsdown tomorrow. Do not dishonour me again.'

Chal Gri appeared silently at the side of the platform. He bowed to Talta, then took the hand she offered him, easing her rings back into place with his thumb and escorted her into the shadows and out of sight of the remaining females.

He caught her weight as her legs gave way. 'Take me home,' she told him. 'Now!'

CHAPTER

18

25th January 2208

Space Station Europa, Sector Three, Neutral Space

Dealing with the Sittan deathships at the Europa was only the beginning, Dax was certain of that. All they'd really managed so far was to prove that it could be done. But there were so many more still out there. According to the Sittan females they'd captured, Talta had sent thousands of warships out into neutral space, and more were leaving Sittan every day.

He didn't know if this was true or not, but if it was, it was beyond imagining.

But there was something that scared him more.

He'd watched Jinn pull the Virena from those ships. He'd watched her shrink them down to the size of a Class 2 transporter and bring them in to the docking bay of the Europa, where they were now. The entire station was wrapped in a blanket of that evil crap.

Her control over it wasn't limited to Sittan. She could control it here, too.

Why hadn't she told him?

He was up on the observation level of the station, sitting in a comfortable seat and looking out at the beautiful expanse of stars that stretched to infinity. He could see Earth, far but not that far in the grand scheme of things, and closer than that, the approaching shape of the *Mutant*.

It should have made him feel better.

Instead, it made him feel worse.

With Ace's help, he'd been able to use the Europa's communications equipment to contact the *Mutant*. Seeing Li and the others onscreen had been a tremendous relief, although it had come as a surprise to learn that Eve had gone somewhere with Bryant. But Eve was smart, and she'd lived a difficult life for a long time. She knew how to take care of herself.

Dax, on the other hand, felt like he didn't understand anything.

He could, he knew, ask Jinn to explain it all.

But he didn't want to.

He didn't know how it would play out afterwards, how he would feel if she told him the answers. He'd tried to figure it out, imagined hearing her say what he thought, deep down, he already knew, but he couldn't get a handle on his emotions at all. They were huge and loose and dangerous.

He watched the *Mutant* approach for an hour. It was too large to dock with the Europa's main ports and unlike the Sittan ships, there was no way to manipulate its dimensions, but the attached fuelling station had been recently expanded and could accommodate it easily. Dax took the elevator up there, a five-minute ride followed by a long walk on a travellator.

He arrived in time to watch his precious ship dock. His heart felt a little lighter at the sight of its familiar lines and he picked up the pace, reaching the end of the spacewalk just as it connected. The airlock hissed open. Dax didn't wait for the others to exit. Instead, he went straight along it and onto his ship.

He met Li on his way to the control deck. Merion was with him. Both of them looked exhausted and neither of them smelled too good.

'Dax,' Li said. He'd never been particularly demonstrative, but he grabbed Dax's hand now and slapped him on the back. 'I am glad to see you.'

'Trouble?'

Li shrugged. 'You left me with an untrained, lazy crew, and you know I don't play well with others.'

'Sorry about that.'

'We locked them in their quarters three days ago,' Merion said. Spikes rippled out across his head. There was a smear of oil on his forehead, and his hands were covered in scabs and bruises.

'You've been running the ship on your own for three days? What about Grudge?'

'Grudge has his hands full with the boys. They dismantled an entire holosuite. He still hasn't put it all back together.'

'But that doesn't mean you had to lock up the crew.'

'It was either that, or kill them all,' Li said. He yawned. 'Things were said which could not be unsaid.'

'About me,' Merion added.

'Ah,' Dax said. Things were beginning to come clear. 'Well, as it stands right now, you've got an entire station to play with.' He stepped aside to let them past. 'Have at it. I should warn you, though, we've got some new recruits, and they're green.'

'Green?' Li paled.

'Green,' Dax confirmed. 'But it's fine. They're on our side. Just don't creep up on any of them.'

Merion slipped his clawed hand into Li's human one, and the two of them made their way along the space walk and onto the station. Dax didn't go with them. He wanted to get a look at his ship. He'd have to deal with the crew, too, but he'd do that later. And he wanted to try and make contact with Eve.

129

His first stop was the control deck. A cursory check of the ship systems told him that it was more or less in one piece. Li had done a surprisingly good job, all things considered. The cleaning droids had kept things tidy and his seat was just as he had left it. He sat in it, sat back, let his muscles relax. But it didn't soothe him quite as it should. There was no escaping the empty pilot's chair, or Jinn, or what Jinn had become.

He'd thought he would be able to talk to Li about it, but the words hadn't come, and he didn't think they would. Li might understand Dax. He didn't understand Jinn. Eve would have been a better option, if she was here. Maybe Grudge would be able to help him. No, Grudge had enough to do taking care of the boys.

A quick scan of the onboard computer system showed that Ritte was in the main rec suite. Dax found her stretched out on one of the couches, watching a terrible human soap opera that she was particularly fond of. Although she was cleaner than Li and Merion had been, she looked just as exhausted. A new patch of white had appeared on one cheek. She lifted a hand to it when she saw him looking. 'I'm getting old,' she said.

'Are you alright?'

'I like your ship,' she said. 'But I miss my home.'

'You'll get back there.'

'Perhaps. You wanted to ask me something.'

'You can read me that easily?'

'You aren't the first human male I've encountered.' She stretched her legs out in front of her. Her feet were bare, six clawed toes to each one, the left completely devoid of colour. Around each ankle was a heavy ring that looked to Dax like a shackle, though they were too fancy for that. Each one had to be worth a hefty sum in dark rubies alone. 'Jozeph lived with us for eight turns,' she said. 'I know something of your kind.'

'We're very different people,' Dax countered.

'And yet fundamentally the same. He was altered at the same time as you, was he not?'

'At the same time, and in the same place. We were part of the first batch of Type Ones ever created.'

'An experiment.'

'Yes.'

'That must be difficult to live with. Were all of you male?'

'The Type Ones, yes, as far as I know. I'm pretty sure Jinn was the first woman to have been made into a Type One.'

'Then she too is an experiment.'

He hadn't thought of it like that. 'I suppose she is.' He wondered if she was tangling with the same confused, angry feelings that he had tried to work through and then pushed aside, back when he'd first been changed. It was something that Dax hadn't really allowed himself to think about. Maybe he should have.

The problem was that when he got close to her, other desires took over, and it took so much energy and focus not to give in to them that there wasn't room for anything else. He wanted her so badly, but she had given him no sign that she wanted that from him now. And why would she? After Sittan, after the things he had done . . .

Fortunately, Ritte didn't let him wallow in those thoughts for long. 'So what was it that you wanted to ask me?'

'I want you to tell me about the Virena.'

'Ah,' Ritte said. She got slowly to her feet, as if her joints pained her, and held out an arm. 'Come. Walk with me.'

Dax obliged her. Her feet tapped against the floor, a rhythmic accompaniment to the story she told him as they left the rec room and strolled along the corridor that led through the middle of the ship. Ritte didn't seem to have a destination in mind. As they walked, he made a mental note of everything that needed to be cleaned or repaired. The list was long.

His crew were not going to be happy by the time he had finished with them.

'Our history is long,' Ritte said. 'I suppose the best place to start would be the thirteenth dynasty. We were ruled at that time by an emperor called Ferriculus.'

'Emperor? You mean a male was in charge?'

She smiled, giving him a brief flash of those teeth that always made him wince and involuntarily cover the more delicate parts of his anatomy. 'At that time, yes. We haven't always been as we are now. Ferriculus was, by all accounts, a difficult creature. I believe he was what you humans refer to as a complete and utter bastard. He was jealous and covetous and violent. He took for the sake of taking. Land. Rubies. Females. If the stories are to be believed, he fathered over three thousand sons. No daughters.'

The logistics of that made the mind boggle. '*Three thousand?* Did he spend all his time, you know ... doing whatever it is that you do to do that?'

'It is basically the same as your process,' she told him, and grinned again. 'It's probably best not to think about it too hard. The problem, for Ferriculus, was that he didn't want sons. He wanted a daughter, and that turned out to be the one thing that he could not have. So he ordered his army to kill all of his sons. The streets were awash with blood. Our people had never known such violence, such cruelty.'

'Why didn't they stop him?'

'They didn't know how. You have to understand, we were simple creatures at that time. We lived season to season, child to child. By the time that we began to understand that we could fight back, that we should, Ferriculus had a new weapon.'

'The Virena.'

'Yes. I believe it was part of our planet long before we crawled out of the sand. It may even have been made at the same time that the planet itself was formed. It had been living in the rock, in the very core, lying dormant until something woke it up. And that something was Ferriculus. When he'd finished with his own sons, he moved on to everyone else's.

'When he killed his own sons, we thought it was brutal and tragic, but we believed the sons of other males were safe, so we turned away. That was our mistake. Ferriculus did not understand the power of a mother's rage, and that was his. The females gathered in secret. It did not take them long to decide what to do.'

'Let me guess,' Dax said. 'Ferriculus met an untimely and probably very unpleasant death.'

Ritte smiled at him. 'Indeed he did, but not before the females discovered that they had a new ally.'

'The Virena switched sides.'

'It built cities and roads and ships and changed our society until we were completely dependent on it, so we continued down the same path, because we did not know what else to do. We had stopped Ferriculus from killing our sons, only to kill them ourselves. When the males tried to rebel, tried to stop us from killing them, we enslaved them. And so it continued.'

'But when I came to Sittan, the Mountain was dry. The Virena had run out.'

'No,' Ritte said. 'It was still there. It was simply asleep. Jinn woke it up again.'

That was the part that Dax was really interested in. 'How?'

'I don't know exactly. Her Sittan DNA is part of it, there's no doubt about that. But what she offered it that we Sittan could not is still unclear.'

'She can control it,' he said. 'And … and I think she can tell where it is. We've found dozens of damaged ships and stations over the past few months. But we've never had any direct confrontations with Sittan ships. Until now. I didn't really think about it before, but it's the only thing that makes any sense.'

'It frightens you.'

'Of course it frightens me. That stuff is evil.'

'Is it?'

'You know it is. You saw what it did on your planet. What it makes people do.'

'Ah,' Ritte said. 'Now we're getting somewhere.'

'All those men I killed in the arena, I did it because Talta wanted me to. And she wanted me to do it because she thought that their deaths were the key to making the Virena hers. But they weren't.'

'How many fights did you win?'

Dax stared at the floor. 'Too many.'

'There is no such thing as too many. To say that there is, is to suggest that you wish that you had lost. And to lose on Sittan means death. Is that what you wished for yourself?'

'Not at the time.'

'And now?'

'I won't say that I'm sorry that I'm alive,' he said.

'But you are sorry for the price that was paid for your life.'

'Yes. And I'm sorry that Jinn was the one who had to pay it.'

'Why?'

Dax stopped walking. He turned and looked at the Sittan female, who was as tall as he was, her fading yellow eyes on a level with his own. 'Because I love her.'

Ritte reached up and pressed a hand to his face. Her palm was hot. 'Dear boy,' she said. 'I know that. But does she?'

'Of course she does.'

'When did you last tell her? When did you last help her bathe, or offer her food, or ask if you could share her bed?'

'It's not as simple as that.'

'It is as complicated as you make it.'

'She's the empress of Sittan,' he asked. 'Isn't she?'

'Yes,' Ritte told him. 'When she defeated Talta, Sittan became hers. But the Virena switched allegiance long before that. It wanted her the first time it sensed what she was. As, I believe, did you.'

'It can't have her.'

'That isn't your choice to make. Jinn is something very special.

We're looking at a time of great change, Dax. What happens from now on, what she decides to do, will change the fates of both our species. It could be the difference between survival and extinction.'

'She never wanted this. All she wanted to do was to stop me from dying in the arena.'

They were deep in the belly of the ship now, as far from any exit as it was possible to be. The corridor expanded. In this section were the cooling chambers for the phase drives, huge pipes that were big enough for him to stand up in. They walked alongside them, and Dax took the opportunity to check each individual monitor. A couple of them needed some minor adjustments, so he made them, taking his time about it. So much had been lost. It felt like the *Mutant* was all he had left of his former life.

'There is one thing that puzzles me,' Ritte said.

'What's that?'

'How you ended up fighting in the arena in the first place.'

'It's complicated. Jinn ... ' He paused. He didn't want to think about it. He didn't want to go back there, to that moment that had been worse than anything he had ever experienced. 'She was injured,' he said finally. 'Gut shot. It would have been fatal. The person who did it said they'd help her if I turned myself in. So I did, and they sent me to Sittan. But Jinn didn't just get treatment for the wound. She got a bit extra as well. I never meant for that to happen.'

'It's time to stop punishing yourself for it.'

'I'm not ... '

Ritte patted his hand.

He was, and he knew it.

'I failed her,' he said simply. 'And now she's ... what she is, and there's nothing I can do to fix it.' He hadn't told her that he loved her since they'd left Sittan. Not once. He couldn't. Under the thrall of the empress, he had done things that had left him feeling deeply ashamed. Talta had tempted him. He knew that he hadn't been himself, that his memories of Jinn had been stolen by a mind-wipe before he left Earth-controlled space, and then he'd been bitten by a creature with venom that caused terrible hallucinations, but it didn't matter how many times he told himself that, it didn't justify what he had done.

He had let Jinn down, and she had done awful, terrible things for him anyway.

'Why do you think it needs to be fixed?' Ritte asked.

'Because she doesn't want it.'

'Did she tell you that?'

Dax didn't answer. His mind was working through all the things that Ritte had said, and all the things that she hadn't.

'Something went wrong on Sittan,' he said. 'That last day, when Jinn stopped them from sacrificing my body to the Mountain. That's what all of this is about. That's why Talta started this war. It's why she's so desperate to find Jinn.'

The reason, when it came to him, was so obvious that he didn't know why he hadn't seen it sooner. 'Jinn defeated Talta but she didn't kill her. The Sittan still think Talta is their empress. And Talta thinks that if she can get rid of Jinn, the Virena will go back to her.'

'That would be my assessment of the situation.'

'Talta is wrong,' Dax told her. 'The Virena will never go back to her. Jinn can make it do things that Talta couldn't. It started a fire for her on the Europa. When I took her to the Sittan ships, she pulled it out of the walls and into her body. It actually went *inside* her. I never saw Talta do that.'

'No Sittan female has ever been able to do that.'

'Jinn's not Sittan.'

Ritte merely smiled at him.

Dax kept talking. 'Assuming all their ships are controlled by it, does this mean that she can stop all of them? Can she only stop them if she's close to them? Is that how this works? Because if we need to take the fleet apart ship by ship, it's going to take a bloody long time.' He turned, leaning back against one of the tubes, and folded his arms. His mind was racing as he tried to think through all the possibilities, find the way to what he felt was an inevitable conclusion. There were still so many stations and trading posts left for the Sittan to take. They weren't that far from the border of Earth-controlled space now. If that became a target, could Jinn defend it? 'She's just one woman. She can't hold off an entire army.'

'Why not?'

Why not indeed.

'It doesn't matter what she is now,' Ritte told him. 'It matters what she is *becoming*.'

'And what is that?'

'We are only just beginning to find out.'

CHAPTER

19

Sneaking out of the medical centre had been harder than getting in, but they had managed it thanks to a stolen uniform, a service exit, and careful consideration of the cameras.

Once outside, Eve had stripped out of the uniform and hidden it behind a stack of empty storage drums she found in an alley opposite one of the many cheap diners that seemed to be everywhere. There were plenty of scrapyards too, and it didn't take Eve long to find one. She walked straight up to the gates and peered through the bars. Discarded ship and roller parts were piled up in jumbled heaps, the spaces between then left as bare, rocky dirt. Half a dozen bald tyres had been thrown on top of a delicate and very expensive skimmer wing. The whole thing was lit up by one crackling light that flickered on and off.

'This one is no good,' she told Charles.

'What is wrong with it?'

'It's a dump.' She activated the map on her comm. and searched for an alternative. The nearest had a two-star rating. Definitely not. But another some three kilometres away looked interesting. 'Here,' she said, showing it to Charles.

She was still trying to figure out a way to get rid of him. Removing his inhibitor chip had been a stupid thing to do. He scared her. As soon as the opportunity arose, she was going to ditch him. He could stay here and be someone else's problem.

'You believe this place will have what we need?'

'If we're going to find a working balloon, this place will have one.'

She knew the company. Her uncle had worked at one of their recycling plants back on Earth. The place had ruined his lungs. She could still remember the sound of his cough.

It was a fair distance away though, and Eve didn't fancy walking. The chance that they would run into one of the security patrols that kept everything here as it should be was too high. They'd already dodged a couple of the circulating droids.

'We could do with transport,' she said to Charles. 'Got any bright ideas?'

'I do not understand how an idea can be bright.'

'It's a figure of speech. Look, we need something to get us around faster. A scootbike, or a skater. Whatever they use around here.'

'Ah. I understand.' But he stood there, completely useless, and in the end, it fell to Eve. She'd brought a portable multitool from the pod and she used it now, severing the lock on the gates and slipping into the mess of a scrapyard. She spotted a scootbike amongst the rubbish. She pulled it out. It was old, but it would do.

There was a tank of fuel over by what passed for the office and she dragged the bike over to it and fuelled it up. It was reluctant at first but she got it going, though it wasn't the healthiest-sounding bike she'd ever heard. But it didn't need to get them far.

She zipped out of the gates, closed them, and sealed them up. From a distance, it would look secure. Charles stood and watched.

'I guess you don't have a lot of programming other than the medical stuff, huh?'

'Unfortunately not,' Charles said. 'I was prevented from taking on additional programming by my inhibitor chip.'

'When was the last time you were updated?'

'I have retained my factory programming.'

'So never.' Shit. It was even worse than she'd thought. Nothing she could do about it now, though. She climbed back onto the bike. 'Come on then.'

Charles awkwardly clambered onto the back, nestling his hard metal body against her. 'I have never ridden one of these before. I am not sure if I am going to enjoy the experience.'

'Just hold on tight.' *And if you fall off, it wouldn't be the worst thing.*

She zipped away from the yard, just missing the droid patrol that came around the corner. Her comm. connected with the bike, which turned out to have a surprisingly good navigation system, and soon the bike was driving itself. Eve took the corners as fast as she dared. Charles hung on like a bloody gluefish. But her hair streamed out behind her, and the wind was in her face, and for those few short minutes, she remembered the simple excitement of being alive.

The bike soon skidded to a halt.

They were right outside the gates of the second yard. As she had predicted, it was in a much better state than the first one. Sadly that wasn't the only difference. She wouldn't be getting through the gates of this one with her multitool.

The two of them climbed off, and Eve pushed the bike over to the fence. She steadied it, and then climbed up onto the seat. She checked the multitool was secure in her back pocket before she started on the fence. 'Come on,' she called to Charles. He jumped up onto the bike and stood there, his hesitation obvious. Eve straddled the top of the fence, caught her breath, then dropped to the other side. She sank into a crouch and waited to see if she had activated any alarms.

She had.

'Dammit,' she muttered, and sprinted over to the alarm box which was strapped to a post in the centre of the yard. The multitool made quick work of the lock. Eve ripped out the wires inside. The wailing sound stopped, but the searchlights had come on and she had no doubt that whichever security company had been hired to protect this place would be on their way. She had no intention of being here when they arrived.

Fortunately, the yard was well organised. Exhaust pipes were stacked next to roller wheels. Drive parts were arranged according to brand and size. Charles followed her through the stacks as she headed towards the most likely spot for pod attachments. 'Quiet!' she hissed at him, as his feet clunked with every step.

'Sorry,' he whispered back loudly enough for everyone in a hundred-kilometre radius to hear.

Eve saw what she was looking for. She gave the row of balloons a quick once-over, then grabbed the edge of the one she wanted and pulled it free. She quickly checked it over. Its condition was good, and it looked like it would fit. She folded it up and tucked it under her arm. 'Got it,' she said to Charles.

'I shall carry that for you,' he said, and took it from her. There wasn't time to argue. She checked her comm. They'd been in the yard for just under five minutes. Definitely time to go.

Keeping low, they made it back to the fence. A quick sweep of the street outside showed it was still clear. Charles set down the balloon and gave her a boost so she could grab the top of the fence and pull herself up.

The searchlights swept in their direction. Eve heaved herself over the top of the fence, crashing to the ground on the other side. The searchlight swept even closer towards him, the wide circle of light designed to burn out anything that wasn't meant to be there, including droids. Charles tucked the balloon under his arm and scrambled up the fence, climbing awkwardly.

'Throw me the balloon!' she shouted at him, holding her hands out to catch it as he straddled the top of the fence, just as she had done. 'Here!'

Charles grabbed the balloon from under one arm and made to throw it to her. He swung his arm back.

And let go.

The balloon went sailing back into the yard. A searchlight caught it and it burst into flames.

Charles swung his other leg over the top of the fence and landed next to Eve with a heavy thump. 'Oh dear,' he said, arms hanging loosely at his sides as he watched what remained of the burning balloon arc down to the ground. 'That is unfortunate.'

A droid came scooting out of the side of the building and sprayed the balloon with wet, white foam. The fire went out and the foam quickly melted away to reveal a charred, soggy mess.

Eve planted her hands on her hips and kicked at the dirt with the toe of her boot. She wanted to scream, but she was tired and hungry and she didn't have the energy. 'Dammit, Charles!'

'I am so very sorry,' he said. 'I do not know what happened. What a terrible mess.'

'You don't sound sorry.'

'I must assure you that I am.'

Eve wasn't convinced. But she had bigger problems. Local security had arrived. An open-topped roller pulled to a halt only a few metres away. The sides dropped down, and the occupants jumped out. There were eight droids and three police. A crew of eleven against one small human female and an AI droid. Not good.

'Stay right where you are,' said one of the police. 'Hands where I can see them.'

'Let me handle this,' Charles said.

'Alright,' Eve said. 'But you better have a bloody good story.'

She saw the nearest human look her over, saw the change in his expression when he realised what she was. She was in trouble now.

He took a step back and pointed his stunner straight at her. It was a good job that he didn't have a blaster, otherwise she was pretty sure that she'd be dead. 'Keep your hands where I can see them. If you so much as blink I will shoot you.'

Yep. Deep trouble.

'Hello!' Charles said cheerfully. 'My name is Charles. Registration code BTZ3274.'

One of the men checked this on his wrist unit. 'You're a service droid with medical programming.'

'That is correct.'

'What in the void are you doing here?'

'This female came to my station. I realised immediately that she was an escaped Type Two female and that her intent was hostile. However I was unable to attempt an arrest, as I am a medical droid and do not have authorisation. I followed the female here with the intention of presenting her to an individual with such authorisation as soon as was reasonably possible.'

Eve could not believe what she was hearing. 'How is that supposed to help?' she asked Charles, but he was not listening.

'Do you have authorisation to arrest this female?' he continued.

'Yes,' said one of the police officers, a man with two silver stripes on his jacket.

'And do you have a station with appropriate holding facilities nearby?'

'Of course we do.' The man kept his stunner and his focus on Eve. She tried not to twitch, tried not to do anything that he might see as provocative.

'Then I suggest we transport the female there for interrogation.'

The men looked at each other. At first, she wondered why, then she understood. None of them wanted to get close enough to cuff her. They were all too afraid. Eve had been who she was for too long not to know exactly how much danger she was in. She kept her hands up where they could be clearly seen and debated whether or not to risk trying to reason with them. In the end she decided against it. They wouldn't want to listen to anything she had to say and might even see an attempt to talk as a threat.

A couple of the droids marched forward and she was restrained before being dragged to the rear of the roller and shoved into the cage. She longed to fight back, to kick and scream, but she knew she would not come out of the situation well. She would have to bide her time.

Because no-one was coming to rescue her now.

CHAPTER

20

28th January 2208

Apartment 438, Acton District, London Dome, Earth

Fever had wracked Ferona's body for three days. The symptoms had started even before she'd made it home. She had collapsed just inside the front door of her flat and woken to find that she'd been there for three hours. Her limbs were so stiff that it took what felt like forever to get up and make it to her bed. She'd been there ever since, alternately sweating and shivering so hard that her teeth knocked together.

And then, just as quickly as it had started, it had stopped.

She'd felt tired and washed out, but she'd been able to get up and wash and change her clothes. She'd drunk two full bottles of water before her thirst was quenched. Food had been no more than a passing thought, which was probably just as well, because the Autochef was empty.

The question, of course, was whether or not the virus had worked. How was she supposed to know? She'd been ill but now she was not. Maybe her immune system had fought it off after all. She contemplated contacting Weston, got as far as calling up his link on her wrist comm. before she lost her nerve.

She thought about calling Dubnik instead but didn't want to answer his questions. He knew nothing of Weston. There was no good reason to change that. But she wasn't going to find answers here in her flat. If she wanted to know if the virus had done what Weston had said it would, she was going to have to go out again.

But what if it hadn't?

That thought scared Ferona so much that she shoved aside the idea of testing it in the real world. She turned on her tiny holomirror and looked at her face, inside her mouth, up her nose. It was something that she hadn't done in quite some time, afraid to see what had happened to her skin without her regular shots of Rejuvinex, and the creases around her eyes, the flap of skin on her neck and the forest of bristly hairs on her chin almost brought her to tears. There were dark circles under her eyes and her tongue had a thick white coating.

She looked *horrible*.

She stripped off, tried to examine her body with the same little mirror, but it was impossible and she soon gave up. She tried licking her own hand but that of course did nothing and her saliva seemed perfectly normal. There was no change of colour or smell.

There was no other option. She was going to have to leave the flat. She dressed quickly, trying and failing to find the energy to care about her appearance. It wasn't that long since she'd have willingly spent an hour choosing her outfit and letting her beauty droid fix her hair and makeup. She would never have dreamed of leaving her apartment without first going through those steps. Now she was done in ten minutes. Her inability to make herself care made her feel sad.

Once outside, that feeling was quickly pushed away by the cold as she began to walk. It had been easy to ignore the post-illness fragility of her body inside. It wasn't so easy here. She had only been moving for fifteen minutes when dizziness struck and she had to sit down. A bench at an empty cab stop gave her somewhere to rest.

All she wanted to do was find out if the virus had worked. She only needed to try it on one person. Summing up what remained of her energy, Ferona made herself get up. A woman walked past, and Ferona thought about trying something, but at the last minute she realised that the woman had a baby tucked inside her coat and changed her mind.

The next person crossed the street before she could get to them.

She decided that the next person she encountered would be the one, regardless of who they were or how quickly they moved. A smartly dressed man crossed onto her path, and she followed him, matching her footsteps to his. His shoulders were huddled inside a dark coat and he had a thick red scarf wrapped around his neck, pulled up high enough to cover his ears. His hair was a lovely honey blond, thick and neat against the back of his perfectly shaped head. He reminded Ferona of the young men who worked in the government building and had, not so long ago, worked for her. It wasn't difficult to slide into a whole range of imagined scenarios featuring this young man and others like him and what she would make them do if the virus worked.

They would be completely under her control. Whatever she needed would be done, without question. She would run every department, and no-one would even know she was doing it.

The man turned suddenly left and disappeared through a doorway, pushing aside a heavy wooden door with brass plates and glass inserts. It was a very old and very familiar door. There were few left that looked like this. Most had been replaced with something far more modern, automatic and plastex and requiring nothing in the way of human effort to make them function.

It took all the strength in Ferona's bony arms to force it open, and she almost stumbled when she made it through to the other side and realised where she was.

The clamour of self-satisfied voices was as loud as it had always been, the lights just as bright and the smell of rich red wine and money just as thick. There were no droids here. Orders were taken by staff in black and white uniforms who spoke only in hushed tones.

And one of those members of staff was rapidly approaching.

Ferona began to walk towards him. The trick, she knew, was to act as if she belonged here. Dare them to try and throw her out and risk making a scene. She licked her lips. There was a strange taste in her mouth that she could have sworn hadn't been there before, a mixture of ripe apples and something very bitter, like the pith of an orange. She licked her lips again.

And when the waiter got close enough, she turned her head, bumped against him, and kissed him on the cheek. His eyes went wide with shock that had a heavy helping of disgust thrown in, and he wrapped a hand around Ferona's upper arm. She could feel the flex of his fingers through the meagre fabric of her coat.

He was going to throw her out. No doubt about it. Bloody Weston, the bloody liar. She was going to kill him for this.

Then the man's eyes went blank. His jaw slackened, a little softening at the joints to give him a slightly drunken look.

'Find me a table and bring me a large cognac and a jug of hot water,' she told him. 'On the house.'

'Of course, madam,' he said, letting go of her arm. He hurried away, went straight to the bar and hastily put all the items on the tray himself, elbowing the bartender out of the way. Then he rushed back over to her. He hovered with the tray in his hand, obviously confused.

'Table,' Ferona said.

'Oh. Right. Yes. Of course. This way, please.'

He led her to a table that had a reserved tag on top. Ferona sat down. It was difficult to stifle her groan at the relief of being off her feet. The man set the tray down and made a big performance of setting each item in front of her before he finally left. A backward glance over his shoulder revealed a very confused expression on his face, and it was followed by an about turn that brought him almost all the way back.

Almost.

He stared at her, shook his head, then rushed off to clear the table just vacated by a large group. He kept sneaking glances back at Ferona, but he didn't come near her again.

Ferona picked up the jug of hot water. The heat felt glorious against her hand. She topped up the glass of brandy, added a generous spoonful of sugar and stirred it, and then began to drink. The warmth spread through her chest.

It had worked.

She'd always known that it would, of course. Weston was a treacherous little shit but useful, if managed correctly. She took another small sip of her drink, savouring the taste, and contemplated ordering something to eat. Perhaps later. For now, she was happy to sit in the warmth and soak up the atmosphere. She had missed this. She hadn't realised how much.

It gave her time to look at who else was here, who she knew and who she didn't. No-one bothered to approach her. Most of them didn't even notice her. When they did look her way, their gazes seemed to slide right off her as if she was made from something oily and slippery that their attention couldn't cling to. Once, it would have infuriated her. Now she was forced to admit that it had its advantages.

A group of junior ministers entered about twenty minutes into Ferona's stay. They moved close together, like herd animals huddling for safety, each easily identifiable by the black and gold scarves they had twined around their elegant necks. Ferona had one of those scarves somewhere. She hadn't worn it in years. She could still remember how important it had made her feel to slip it on and come in here, knowing the message that it sent. That scarf had been the key that opened many doors for an ambitious young woman.

Now Ferona sipped her drink and watched as drinks were ordered and served, attention-seeking laughs were thrown out. Ferona was sure that she had never been that obnoxious. Confident and focused, yes. But she hadn't brayed like a donkey in a public place.

However these people, irritating as they were, were of great interest to Ferona. A plan was slowly forming at the back of her mind. She could feel it. She didn't try to rush it, simply watched the group and let it simmer, and when one of the women split off from the group and headed in the direction of the restroom, Ferona got carefully up from her seat and followed.

Her nerve held completely until the door swung smoothly closed behind her, moving easily on hinges that were perfectly oiled and balanced. She'd only tried her new ability on one person. What if it hadn't really worked, and something else had made the waiter behave the way that he had? What if it only worked on males, and not females?

The woman came out of one of the cubicles. She sat on a pink padded stool and a holomirror immediately popped up in front of her. A beauty droid that had been on standby in the corner turned on and scooted over and began to fix the woman's hair. Ferona sat on the stool next to her. Her own mirror came on, but she chose not to look in it. She felt a little dizzy.

She grabbed the woman's hand and jerked it up towards her mouth, a rapid fire movement.

'Hey!' the woman shouted, and tried to pull away, but Ferona found a sudden ferocious strength in her grip and squeezed. Her tongue darted out and she ran it all over the woman's fingertips. Then she let go.

The woman's face went from a twist of disgust to slack-jawed and empty in a heartbeat. Whatever she had been about to say, and Ferona was sure there had been plenty, was lost.

'I want you to introduce me to your friends,' Ferona said. 'The people you came in with. I'd like to meet them.'

'Alright,' the woman said dully. 'Introduce you to my friends.'

It was working even more effectively than it had on the waiter.

She got to her feet and stalked out without even waiting to see if Ferona followed. She did, of course, keeping close to her new friend. The woman introduced her to the rest of the group, and one by one, Ferona turned them. When they left the bar to return to their offices they took her orders with them.

It was late when she left the bar, but plenty of the better stores were still open, and she needed some new clothes to replace those that had been sold. She deserved to be spoiled.

It was delightfully easy to make the cashiers see her point of view.

CHAPTER

21

Bryant could smell disinfectant. When he licked his lips, he could taste it, bitter and nasty. It was very odd. Wasn't death supposed to mean the end of everything? The last thing he'd expected was for it to taste of floor cleaner. His body felt different, too. It took him a while to work out what it was.

It didn't hurt.

Pain was completely and profoundly absent. There was an energy in his body, a mellow confidence that if he wanted to move, it would be easy. He decided that he could live with the smell if this was the upside.

What was strangest of all was his ability to think about it. It didn't fit at all with his understanding of the way things worked. A dead body was just meat. The brain didn't carry on alone. It wasn't possible. Bryant knew that in the past, people had desperately clung to the idea that there was something after death, that it was not an end but a beginning, but he had always thought those people were delusional idiots. He understood now it was because death had been something very distant and far away. He'd been young and strong and attractive and healthy, with access to the best that medical science could offer. He'd had better things to do than to worry about an end that was decades away when there were bars and fights and women.

And then those decades had suddenly become weeks and then days and by that point, death had offered him an end to pain, and that had been enough. He hadn't thought about the after. He'd been too busy feeling sorry for himself. So all this came as something of a surprise.

It was as Bryant was thinking this through that he opened his eyes. It wasn't a conscious decision as such, and again it came as a surprise, because he hadn't expected death to include working vision as well as smell. He blinked a few times, clearing the stickiness from his lids, and then looked around.

That was the point at which Bryant began to think that perhaps he wasn't dead after all. He was, if his brain was working properly, in a hospital. He saw white walls, data screens, and then a medidroid. That clinched it. There would definitely not be medidroids in the afterlife. If anything, it would be filled with booze and naked girls, otherwise there would be absolutely no reason for its existence.

Pushing himself up onto his elbows, Bryant noticed that there was another bed in the room, and it was occupied. A man sat on top of it. He was playing with a gamecube. He had pale hair, which was a good sign, but he was also unbelievably large, which was not. Huge thighs threatened to split the seams of his navy-blue trousers, and his shoulders did the same to a matching long-sleeved top.

Bryant had only seen one other man as large as that, and that was Caspian Dax.

The man scratched his head and yawned, and then he noticed

Bryant staring at him, and grunted. 'Was beginning to think you'd never wake up.'

Bryant pushed himself all the way up. The sheet which had been covering him fell to his waist. There were a couple of tubes feeding something into his left forearm. It only took a second for him to decide that he didn't want them any more and to pull them out. The tube leading into his vein was longer than he had expected, and his stomach clenched a little at the sight of it sliding along under the skin before the end finally emerged. There was a dribble of blood from the exit point. Bryant took hold of the sheet and wiped it away, revealing the hole in his skin, which was several millimetres across.

He was about to wipe it again when it closed up and disappeared.

He scrubbed at his elbow with the sheet, but there was nothing there, not so much as a bruise, never mind a line to show where the cut had been. It didn't seem possible. Had he imagined the wound? No. He couldn't have. The tube was right there, with his blood congealing on the end of it.

'Weird, right?' the man on the other bed said. 'I mean, I know they told us we'd have increased healing, but this is something else.'

'That's one way of putting it,' Bryant said, though his head was rapidly filling with questions, his thoughts very loud and quite frankly a little panicked. When he looked down at his hands, they were shaking, and he felt an itchy trickle of sweat slide down his temple. He had to get out of here, out of this bed, out of this room. He made to swing his legs over the side of the bed, and then realised that he wasn't wearing any clothes and stopped himself just in time.

'I'm Linel, by the way,' the man said. 'I'm from the Oslo Dome. How about you?'

'London,' Bryant said. 'Look, do you know where I can get something to wear?'

Linel hopped down from his bed. He was towering huge as he lumbered his way over to the corner of the room. He opened up a storage locker concealed in the wall and pulled out a pile of stuff, then dumped it on the end of Bryant's bed. Bryant reached for it. He'd never considered himself to be much of a prude, but then he'd never had to get dressed with a giant man watching him either. He didn't quite feel up to telling Linel to turn his back, so he pulled on the clothes as quickly as he could.

As he did so, Bryant began to notice something. It was his forearms, first. He'd always been fit, lean with muscle, more than capable of holding his own. Women had looked at him. Men had looked at him. And he'd liked it. Eve had destroyed all that, obviously. His poisoned body had been disgusting.

But gone was the thin, purpling skin, the bruising. There was a meaty weight to his forearm that he could swear he hadn't had even at his healthiest. After he'd pulled the shirt down to his waist, he was forced to shift the sheet a little so that he could work his way into the trousers, and he noticed more changes there, too. His thighs were much thicker than he remembered, and they were dusted with light brown hair, when before it had been sparse and pale.

Then there was his cock.

It was also bigger.

He lifted his bum a little to get the trousers up, but he couldn't take his eyes off it.

Definitely bigger.

What had happened to him?

Not sick. Not dead either. Just the opposite, in fact.

'What is this place?'

Linel, who had gone back to his gamecube, looked up at him in surprise. 'It's the Silencia Medical Centre on Colony Six,' he said.

That didn't tell Bryant much. 'No, I mean *what* is it? What are they doing here?'

'Modifying us with Type One. Fuck, are you having some sort of memory loss?' Linel look decidedly unnerved. He set down the gamecube. 'Look, man, just calm the fuck down. It's alright. I'll get a medic . . .'

'No,' Bryant said hastily. 'I remember now.' He rubbed a hand over his forehead, tried to smile. *Type One? How could he be Type One?* 'Must have been the drugs wearing off.'

'Yeah, I guess it can take some people like that. I heard there was a guy over in the prep wing who went completely insane. Smashed the place up.'

He said some other stuff, but Bryant had stopped listening. This couldn't be happening. This had to be some sort of insane dream, and any minute now he was going to wake up to find that none of it was happening, only he wasn't going to wake up because he was dead.

Except that he clearly wasn't dead.

Which meant that he really was Type One.

The evidence was too strong to ignore. His body was bigger. There were the thighs, the forearms, the stomach. And the rest. He'd bet, if he stood up, that he was taller too, because now that he was aware of it, the distances between himself and his surroundings seemed wrong.

Bryant didn't know how Eve had managed to get him here. He remembered asking her to take him to a medical facility so that he could die peacefully like an agent rather than on board a pirate ship like a criminal, which seemed utterly pathetic in hindsight. After that, things grew fuzzy. But he thought back to the time before that, when she'd sat by him for day after day as his body rotted but stubbornly refused to just bloody well give up and die, and he knew that she had kept him alive. Not because of anything she'd done, but because deep down he had known his death would be a punishment that she didn't deserve, and he hadn't wanted to do it to her. He also knew that if Eve had thought that the Type One modifications would fix him, she would make sure that he got them, because she was a bitch.

'So,' Linel said, the word bringing Bryant back to the here and now. 'You never told me your name.'

'Bryant.'

'Oh.' Linel looked confused. 'It says Smithson on the end of your bed.'

'Bryant Smithson,' Bryant said, quickly realising how stupid that sounded. 'Adam Smithson.'

'Man, they really did a number on your memory,' Linel said. He laughed. An alarm went off, and he glanced down at his wrist unit. 'Lunch! Are you coming?'

I guess I am, thought Bryant as he followed the younger man out of the room. But he kept his eyes open and his wits about him as far as he could. There were so many unanswered questions. What was this for? Who was paying for it? Where was Eve?

Along the corridor, doors were opening and more enormous blond men were spilling out. All of them looked to be in their early twenties, massively tall and broad-shouldered, forced to walk single file along a corridor that had not been designed to accommodate their size. Bryant slotted in behind Linel. He wanted to run. He was too afraid. These men were all Dome. They looked like agents. But they were Type One. It didn't make any sense.

Unless . . .

No-one gave him a second look, which was somewhat surprising, because he had to have at least fifteen years on the rest of them. But he had enough sense to keep his head down, not wanting to draw attention to himself. They all followed each other round to a large cafeteria, then began to spread out and find seats.

Droids rushed between the tables, delivering enormous platters of food. Bryant hadn't seen anything like this since he'd been an eighteen-year-old at the academy back on Earth. He had forgotten the smell and the sound of a busy cafeteria, the heat generated by putting a large number of healthy young men in the same place, and for a moment he was totally overwhelmed. His legs felt soft, as if they might not hold him up, and his head spun. He had to get out of here.

He turned, but it was impossible to go back the way he had come. He turned again, saw a restroom and headed straight for it. Once inside, he locked himself into one of the cubicles and took several long, painful moments to catch his breath, then he took a piss and thrust his hands under the sterilising light, bathing them in a sharp blue that brought every detail into focus. They were his hands, and yet they weren't. His foot caught on something, and a holomirror popped open in front of him.

When Bryant saw himself, he froze.

That wasn't ... but it was. No wonder the others hadn't given him a second glance. His hair had regrown, a dense mop that was already several centimetres long, and he needed a shave, but that wasn't what caught his attention. He was looking at himself as a young man, no older than twenty-two or twenty-three.

He turned his head slowly from side to side, examining himself from every angle.

Then he slowly eased his foot back, turning the holomirror off.

He wasn't entirely calm when he walked back out to the canteen, but he was a lot closer than he had been. This was a Security Service facility. He was sure of it. He was healed, and he was young. He scanned the tables, looking for an empty seat. *Come on then, Adam Smithson*, he thought to himself. *Might as well have some fun.*

CHAPTER

22

1st Day of the Eighth Turn

The Palace, Fire City, Sittan

News of what had happened at the Europa had reached Talta within a couple of turns, though she had sensed the loss of the Virena the instant it was taken. There had been a flash, a transmission of memory, and then darkness. The place where Grenla and the other females should be had become an empty space, an utter silence, and it didn't matter how many times she called to them, they did not reply.

She had to find it. She had to get it back. Nothing else mattered now. It must feel so lost and frightened, so far from home without her. The thought was almost unbearable. It was what had driven her here, to the Jewel Valley, some five hundred tralls south of the palace. It wasn't a place she cared to visit often. She had always found the world outside the city to be incredibly dull, with the endless bickering over farming rights and males, and quite happily ignored it.

Until the other cities stopped sending their tributes.

Those tributes had started to trickle in again, just as Chal Gri had predicted, after her meeting with the queens in the arena. But what Talta needed now was something far more precious than tributes of oil and dark rubies and grain.

Against the advice of Chal Gri, who had told her to be patient, to wait, she had left the palace. The journey had been terrible and her mood had been sour long before she stood in front of the shrivelled, ugly collective of the Jewel Valley council and demanded what was rightfully hers.

'We do not support you in your war,' the eldest council member said. The twelve of them had gathered in the meeting hall in the centre of the valley. A huge hole in the ground led down to the thin river of Virena which ran under the hall, and a dark mist rose from it, spiralling its way up and out of sight. It took a great deal of self-control not to walk to that mist and touch it.

'Then you are traitors to Sittan,' she told them calmly, taking a sip from her tall ruby goblet.

'We are not traitors!'

'How can you be anything else?' Talta disliked these females intensely. Their blue skin was mottled with age, turning white in patches. One of them breathed wetly through her one remaining gill slit. Another was completely blind, her yellow eyes having turned dark, and she was guided to her seat by a young, silent male. There was no fire in any of them, no fight, no ambition. They were pathetic. 'Humans came to this planet uninvited. This cannot go unpunished.'

'One human,' one of the councillors pointed out. 'The others were invited, by you, Talta. You brought them here. You are the traitor, not us.'

'And yet you are enjoying the fruits of that, are you not?' Talta lifted a ringed hand and gestured to the mist. 'The valley has prospered. There is enough Virena for you to test and train your females. And you have eighteen new sons, is that correct?'

'Fathered by two males, neither of whom has proved his worth!'

'Then give them to the Mountain.'

'We cannot,' said the blind councillor. 'Male children are too precious now. We have too few.'

'Which is why I brought the human males here.'

'And the female? The one who awakened the Mountain? We have heard the stories, Talta. We know what happened. We know you fought her on the Mountain, and that you let her escape, and that your hunt for her has been unsuccessful.'

Talta bit back the angry words that burned on her tongue. 'The female will soon be dead,' she told them. 'She is no threat to us.'

'Then why have you started a war with the humans?'

'Because it is time!' Talta glared at all of them. 'None of you have ever been off planet. But I have. The galaxy is changing. We aren't the only ones that the humans traded with.' She lifted her head. 'We have hidden our true power for too long. It is time that we showed the rest of the galaxy exactly what we can do.'

'It is not the Sittan way.'

'Yes, it is,' Talta said. 'You have simply forgotten.'

'What about the senate?'

'The senate.' Talta spat the word out. 'The senate is a travesty. It wants to bring us together on the basis of our similarities when what we should be doing is emphasising our differences, fighting for our place and what is rightfully ours.' She stopped, suddenly finding herself breathing a little too hard.

'What about us?' asked the blind councillor. 'If we allow you to take our Virena, what will you give us in return?'

'*Allow* me to take it?' Talta rose to her feet. 'I do not need your permission to take what is already mine!'

'Is it yours?' the blind elder asked. 'It does not seem so sure.'

'You are mistaken, old woman.'

'Call to it. Let us see it come to you.'

'I am empress. I proved myself many turns ago when I defeated my predecessor and took it from her. I do not have to prove it again.' Talta drew on all her turns of experience as empress. As in the arena, she didn't try to call to the Virena. If she did so, and it refused, she would have lost everything. The Virena here could not be taken. It would have to be given. There were other villages, other valleys, and they were more likely to give up their Virena willingly if they believed that the Jewel Valley had done so. She would have to persuade them. 'However, your hospitality has put me in a generous mood. I have something that you want.'

'What is that?'

Talta thought of Chal Gri. 'A tested male,' she said. 'I would not want those who support Sittan in our time of struggle to go unrewarded.'

Wizened eyes gleamed with avarice. Forked tongues flickered over thin, dry lips. Talta knew then that she had them.

It did not take the council long to agree. They took her to the training school, where the females that the Virena responded to were sent as soon as they could walk. Already Talta could feel her strength returning. The ache was fading from her muscles, the colour returning to the world as she looked around her and took in the rough, unevenly carved walls and the chambers that led off it. Slowly, one at a time, young females began to appear, moving cautiously out of those chambers. They were wearing the dark clothing of apprentices, but they carried the weapons of a guard; a blade, a spear, a chain. Each of those weapons glittered at Talta. She slowly flexed her fingers.

This was the moment. Either the Virena recognised her as the strongest female here, and came to her, or all of this was over.

The Virena slithered out of the hands of those females and made its way over to her, wrapping itself around her arms, binding itself to the jewellery at her throat and waist. She took a deep breath, filling her lungs with air, as the power of that wonderful living metal threatened to overwhelm her.

No-one could argue with her now. She was undeniably the strongest female here. She was the strongest female on the planet. She would have her ships and her warriors and she would kill Jinnifer Blue.

And there was nothing anyone could do to stop her.

CHAPTER

23

Jinn hadn't been alone with Dax in days. There was too much to be done. The *Mutant* needed work. There were the Sittan females, the human crew they had brought with them from the Articus, the Type Two women. All of them needed to be kept safe and she didn't trust them to play nicely together.

She felt closed in, trapped, anxious, weighed down by the needs and desires of everyone else on board the station. All she wanted was an hour alone with Dax so that she could look him in the face and ask him how he really felt about her ability to control the Virena. She wanted to tell him how frightened she was, that she would never have kept it a secret from him if she'd known just how far her power over it went.

Instead, she had to listen to them talk about that power as if it belonged to them.

'We can win this fight,' Dax had said. 'There's nothing to stop us now. But we're going to need more ships. More everything.'

'We've got ships,' Jinn had told him.

'Talta has more,' Li had pointed out. 'It's not enough.'

'We take what we can from here,' Dax said, 'and then we find more.'

Li had opened up a map and suggested a few places. Dax had rejected a couple of them, suggested others, places where they were more likely to find fuel and crews that might have some idea what they were doing. He was building his army, the one they had asked the government ministers for.

Jinn hadn't asked him what he intended to do with it.

Instead, she had gone to the docking bay and set to work adding Virena to all the remaining ships, regardless of size and age. It wasn't picky. If there was steel, it was hungry for it. Transporters became gunships. Cruisers were reshaped to form shield walls that could hide the rest of her fleet.

Once the work was finished, they left the Europa, travelled to the Rose, the Baliol and the Tour de Knox. There they took not only ships, but crew. There were still Bugs left in this part of space. Jinn didn't know exactly what Dax said to make them agree to join him, but it seemed that people would agree to almost anything if they were guaranteed food and air in return.

Jinn implanted a little Virena on board each ship they took.

As the Virena chewed through the steel of those ships and stations, it grew louder and clearer. It was only a matter of time before she could single-handedly run every single ship in her fleet. She just had to keep going, keep recruiting, keep building.

She focused on that. It stopped her from thinking about what lay ahead, about what she was doing and what it meant.

They were at the Goodwin trading post, where they'd found an ancient freighter as well as some fifty odd Bugs and their children, when she felt it.

Sittan ships were on the move.

It was a much larger squadron than the one that had attacked the Europa. Jinn monitored them for several hours. She didn't tell Dax or the others, and they were too busy trying to repair the freighter to pay much attention to what she was doing. She took herself to the control deck of the *Mutant* and concentrated on those ships.

They heard her.

And they came.

When they were perhaps an hour away, she slipped off the control deck and went to find Dax. She finally located him at a copper repository. He was stripped to the waist, his muscular back gleaming with sweat under the rigged lights as he lifted a crate and stacked it onto a little loading cart.

Jinn bit into the side of her mouth so hard that she tasted blood. Then she turned on her heel and left. She couldn't bring herself to tell him. She did not look back. She ran a quick mental tally of her fleet, working out which ships she would take with her. It would have to be the ones she had modified first, where the Virena had taken the most hold. She pulled her comm. from her back pocket and sent messages to all those ships as she headed for her own, instructing anyone on board them to return to the trading post. She didn't need crew, not any more.

She was in the pilot's seat of her own ship, running quickly through the final checks that would need to be done before she left when Dax climbed up into the little control deck. 'I'm coming with you,' he said. 'Don't try to change my mind, because it won't work.'

So she didn't.

The ship was old, but the phase drive was good, and with a push from the Virena, it was excellent. 'I should have just gone after their ships straight from the Europa. I could have control of all of them by now.'

'And what if you couldn't take all of them?' he asked quietly. 'Talta is still alive, Jinn, and we don't know how much difference that makes. We don't know how much power she has. There have never been two empresses before. There's certainly never been a human one.'

'Don't you think I can do it?'

Dax didn't respond to that. Instead, he got out of his seat and disappeared down the ladder to the lower level of the ship. Jinn didn't follow him. She focused on her flight plan, the other ships in her fleet, and the Sittan. It was a lot for one person to keep hold of.

She was quickly in range of those ships. She had never seen so many. Row after row of them fanned out in front of her. She could barely sense her own ships now, the noise of the Sittan fleet was so loud. There was something very different about the Virena on board them and she couldn't work out what it was. 'Why did you come with me?' she asked him, frustration and temper making a foul combination.

'Did you really think I would let you do this alone?'

'You didn't answer the question.'

'I know.' He settled his big body into the seat, but he wasn't relaxed, far from it.

Her Virena swirled darkly on the back of her hands and moved as a hot shudder under her skin. It was excited. It knew that something was about to happen.

Jinn closed her eyes and called to the ships in the fleet.

They didn't listen to her.

She called to them again, louder.

And they started to move.

'Where are they going?' Dax said.

'I don't know.'

'What do you mean, you don't know?'

The Sittan fleet was picking up speed. Row by row, the ships started to speed away from her. She didn't believe it at first. There was only one thing in that direction. But as soon as that thought had occurred to her, she knew it was right.

She could feel it.

'They're heading for the gate,' she told him.

'No. No! You have to stop them. Jinn, they cannot get through that gate.'

'They won't.'

She abandoned her grip on the ships she had brought with her and focused all her attention on hers, and the Sittan fleet. She pushed the little ship until it threatened to come apart at the seams, and then she pushed it some more. Dax was up and down the ladder more times than she could count, putting out the fires that started in overheated components, rewiring what he could to bypass the bits that no longer worked. She used the Virena to help him where she could. She kept going until she saw the gate in the distance, a huge spinning monolith of bright white. Her heart began to thunder.

They were too late.

She knew it even before her eyes made out the long, sleek shape of the first Sittan ship. Something came over the comm. She couldn't hear it. Her head was completely full of the sound of the Virena. So much. There was so much.

The Virena on the Sittan ships was new, different somehow. The song was different. No, not new. The opposite. It was ancient, called forth from the Mountain by empresses far older than Talta. Jinn called to it for a third time, not knowing if it would come to her or not.

It heard her.

It called to her.

She powered up the drive of her little ship. 'Hold on,' she said to Dax.

Then she flew the ship straight into the Sittan one.

It pierced the surface, taking them deep into the heart of the ship, and the air around her seemed to contract for a moment. She saw the inside of the Sittan ship, the crystalline structure of the darkly curving walls, the shocked faces of the female crew, and then it was gone. All of it was gone.

Her own ship expanded. The tiny, cramped cockpit was suddenly huge. Metal plates stood next to crystal. Virena burned in her hands. The air smelled of human sweat and kaelite ore and the rich, musky scent of burning Sittan oil.

Virena began to spread across the controls. Jinn lifted her hands as the entire panel disappeared. Her seat disappeared too, and she was pushed to her feet. A pillar rose up on either side of her, catching her palms, and she was immediately connected to the ship. She could feel the others through it. The bow of the ship shimmered and became completely transparent, giving her an unobstructed view of the rest of the Sittan fleet.

She went for them, and one by one, they surrendered. She gave them no choice.

'Jinn,' Dax said. He was pointing to the gate. 'Where's that one going?'

A Sittan ship was almost at it, and as they watched, it began to change shape, becoming longer and narrower, an arrow ready to be fired. She tried to call to the Virena on board it, but it didn't listen to her. The gate began to flash. The Sittan ship was sucked into it, disappearing from sight.

'Earth,' Jinn said.

'Why does Talta want to go to Earth?'

'It's not Talta,' she told him, as she went for the gate and into the jump.

The colours of the jump flashed past them but Jinn barely noticed. All she cared about now was that ship. She would not let it get away from her. She kept her attention fixed on it, tracking its movements. Whoever was flying it didn't know this jump like she did and she used that to her advantage. She was gaining on them.

The end of the jump was approaching. She could feel it. She pressed her palms a little harder against the controls. Somehow,

Jinn knew that what happened in the next few seconds was going to change everything. It might be the end of everything. She reached for the Virena on that ship. It pushed back against her. It could sense Earth in the distance, iron-rich and new, and it wanted.

She disconnected from the ship and turned to Dax. She grabbed the front of his jacket and pulled him to her. There wasn't time for words, and they wouldn't work anyway. So she kissed him instead, because she didn't know what awaited them at the end of this, and she wanted one more taste of him before she found out.

He made a sound against her mouth, a desperate, painful sound.

She pushed him away and slammed her hands back onto the controls, bringing them out of the jump with watery legs and burning lungs. Earth-controlled space. It looked no different to space on the other side of the jump, apart from the colony in the distance.

The Sittan ship was waiting for them.

CHAPTER

24

30th January 2208

Vessel: The *Fairway*. Class 4 transporter
Location: Earth-controlled Space
Cargo: N/A
Crew: 2
Droids: 0

The power of the Virena was overwhelming. Had Jinn been able to separate herself from it and think without its song clouding her mind, she would have known how much danger she was in, but as it was, she could not understand what she could not acknowledge. The Virena's desire to reach Earth was forgotten in a heartbeat. All Jinn knew now was that she had to have it under her control.

She saw the Sittan ship, and she did not hesitate. She did not think of the crew on board it. She felt only the Virena, the temptation of more, the desire to take it, and take it she did. It was effortless. There was none of the uncertainty that she had felt on the other side of the jump.

The battle was no longer between her and Talta.

'Jinn,' Dax whispered.

The broken remains of the Sittan ship drifted in front of them. It had flown apart when she had ripped the liquid metal away like a child snatching back a toy. The bodies of the Sittan crew floated dead in space, mere specks in the distance. There was nothing she could do to help them. She could see the outline of Colony Four on the nearby asteroid, the fine lines that marked mining tunnels and the huge pipes that carried the ore to the surface. The people on the colony had no idea what had just happened, what she had just saved them from.

'Jinn,' Dax said again, and this time she turned to him. 'You've done it. Now we need to go.'

'I know,' she said, but she made no move to power up the phase drive and get them out of there. The colony was so close. All that metal and ore. She could feel the hungry curiosity of the Virena. Too long had it been trapped on Sittan, limited to the knowledge and resources of that one planet, and now that it had begun to discover the rest of the universe, it hungered for more and more and more, and it was so hard to deny it. But she had to.

'Take the controls,' she told him. She unplugged. 'Get us out of here.'

'Jinn?'

'Just do it!'

He didn't argue. He pulled on his own set of smartware gloves and took over. He wasn't as a good a pilot as she was, but he was good enough, and he whipped them back through the gate without hesitation. Jinn focused all her energy on making sure the Virena came with them.

On the other side, the broken Sittan fleet floated silently. It was as if every single ship had suddenly lost power. 'Any survivors?' she asked him.

'I don't know,' he said. He ran a scan to check. 'Yes.'

'Get us closer.'

She unfastened her restraints and got out of her seat as Dax manoeuvred them closer to the wreckage. Then she leaned over the side of her seat and pressed a hand against the steel plate of the hull. The Virena swarmed all over it. Jinn gave it a silent mental command.

It obeyed.

Jinn closed her eyes as it flowed out of the transporter and across the vacuum between her ship and those broken ones until she was connected to all of them. And then one by one, she turned them back on. Hulls were repaired. Life support was reactivated. Drives were powered up. The Virena expanded and stretched between them, pulling those broken vessels together to form new, much larger ships.

She collapsed back into her seat, drenched in sweat, utterly exhausted. 'We've got to get it away from Earth, Dax.'

'And those?' he said, pointing at the viewscreen and the newly formed ships beyond.

'I'm not leaving them here,' she said grimly.

It didn't take Dax long to fly them back to where they had left the *Mutant* and the others. The Sittan ships were too big to bring on board, but Jinn anchored them in place with chains of Virena. She had no intention of letting them get away.

The jaws of the *Mutant* opened up and Dax flew the transporter into dock and powered down. He unfastened his restraints, but he didn't get out of his seat. 'Jinn,' he said.

'I don't want to talk about it,' she said. She could feel the weight of his gaze on her. She ignored it.

'Well, you're going to.'

'Where do you want to start? The Sittan ships? The Virena? Or the fact that I kissed you and you pushed me away?'

She saw a muscle flicker in his cheek. Then he got out of his seat and climbed down into the lower level of the ship. The ramp at the side of the transporter hissed open, and she heard his footsteps as he walked down it.

It was almost unbearable. But with each step he took, it somehow became easier, and he grew smaller and less important and further away, and the tendrils of the Virena pushed their way further into her mind. She didn't have the energy or the desire to keep them out. She needed their comfort.

She gave Dax enough time to have left the docking bay before she followed him.

The *Mutant* was still as they had left it. The Virena was very curious about its new surroundings. It could smell the iron in the hull and pulled towards it like a magnet. Jinn held it back. 'No,' she told it. 'Not this one.'

She met Ritte before she could make it to the control deck. The Sittan female rushed towards her and embraced her warmly, then she looked Jinn over, hands holding her upper arms. 'What happened?'

She couldn't bring herself to explain. 'We took care of it.'

'The females?'

'I brought them with me.'

'Then they're still alive?'

'Yes. Most of them, anyway.'

'You are a good and just woman.' She rubbed her hands up and down Jinn's arms, and then released her. 'Will you take me to see them?'

'You don't need my permission,' Jinn told her, but she took Ritte to the rear of the docking bay and activated a spacewalk.

As they waited for it to unfold, her thoughts drifted inevitably to Dax, and the Virena in her hands shifted colour to a shimmering green. There had been a moment, when her mouth had found his, that he'd wanted her. She was sure of it.

But perhaps she was only sure because she'd wanted it to be true.

'You are thinking of him,' Ritte said.

Jinn knew who she meant. 'No,' she lied.

Ritte sighed. 'It betrays you.' She gestured to the Virena. 'Look.'

Jinn tucked her hands into the pockets of her jacket. 'It doesn't matter what I think,' she said. 'Me and him . . . that's done. It's gone.'

'What makes you say that?'

'He doesn't want me.'

'From what I have seen, he wants you very much.'

'That's just . . . I'm not the woman he fell in love with any more.'

'So tell me how you were before. Tell me about this woman he fell in love with.'

'I wasn't Type One, for starters,' Jinn said. 'I was a Dome-raised woman who happened to have pilot prosthetics.' She gestured to her face, where her retinal implant had been. 'I thought I was tough, but I really wasn't. I was spoilt and arrogant and vain.'

'And yet he fell in love with you.'

'I'm Dome-raised. Dax likes Dome women. They're his only weakness. Show him blonde hair and pale skin and common sense goes straight out the window.'

'Those things are merely physical,' Ritte pointed out. 'Bodies change if you use them well. It is inevitable. Aging. Injury. Bearing children. If a male can lose his love for you over such inconsequential things, then he was weak to begin with, and of no use to you. Tell me *who* you were.'

'I was a Security Service pilot with a massive chip on my shoulder. I hated other people so much that I had extra Tellurium – that's the nanotech that some of our pilots use – injected into my system so that I could form a blade with it. I had a few bad experiences when I was young and I let them dictate the rest of my life. I was a loner. I didn't like the people I worked with, and I didn't particularly like myself.'

'Then they must have been very bad experiences indeed.'

'At the time, I thought they were,' she admitted. 'But the truth is that I was angry and difficult and didn't want to be otherwise.'

'And do you believe that has changed?'

Jinn thought about it. 'Not really.'

'In that case, you are still the woman he fell in love with.'

'But he's not in love with me any more.'

'Of course he is. But he's afraid. It is difficult for a male to give himself to a powerful female. He will naturally fear that he is not worthy of her.'

It was such a simple explanation and so completely at odds with everything that Jinn had previously thought that it took her a moment or so to get her head around it. 'Dax isn't afraid of anything,' she said. There was a beep to indicate that the spacewalk was fully extended, so she thumbed the pad to unlock the door and gestured for Ritte to go first.

'Then there is no problem,' Ritte said.

But there was.

And Jinn had no idea how to fix it.

Hush, whispered the Virena. *Do not worry about him. You have us.*

CHAPTER

25

1st February 2208

Boodle's Café, Holborn, London Dome, Earth

Ferona's life had drastically improved in the past forty-eight hours. She'd gone from an empty Autochef and a complete lack of hope to a new pink cashmere coat and access to the ministerial computer network. Dubnik had received a discreet call from one of his former assistants the day before and was meeting with them now, inside the building on the other side of the street.

Ferona sat in a café that faced the street, watching that building, blanketed warmly in her new coat. She sipped a large latte and waited for Dubnik to appear. She'd already been here for over an hour and she was starting to get bored. How long could it take?

The serving droid came over and she ordered a pot of tea to replace the latte, which was quite frankly awful, and waved a credit chip under the scanner in order to pay the bill. She'd got the chip from the jeweller earlier that morning when she'd gone to get her earrings back. It wouldn't be so easy to salvage the other pieces which had been sold to pay Weston, but that didn't seem so important now. There had been plenty of other delicious items on offer, such as the large pink diamond that now decorated her right hand.

She shouldn't have taken it. But it was so beautiful she hadn't been able to resist. She had paperwork to prove ownership, the jeweller only too keen to provide it when asked. When the effects of the virus wore off he might come looking for her, but what could he do? He had given it to her. It was there in black and white. He'd never be able to prove that she'd done anything to him.

The droid scooted over with the tea in a tall silver pot. It set down a clean white cup and a bowl of sugar cubes. She added two to the mug before pouring the tea. The pot dribbled slightly, making a yellow puddle on the table. Ferona scowled at it and held her sleeves carefully out of the way.

Her symptoms had returned with a vengeance. She was managing the worst of them with a heady dose of blockers and soothers, but her appetite hadn't yet returned, and she had no desire to eat. The sugar gave her a much-needed energy boost. She told herself it was a positive sign. It meant that the virus was working. As long as her body continued to struggle to fight off the infection, she'd have that magic protein in her saliva.

But she knew that she would have to be careful. The jeweller might be too embarrassed and confused to come after her, but if she used her ability too often, people would start to talk. And then they would start to ask questions that Ferona didn't want to answer. The short-term effects of her new ability were both a blessing and a curse.

Movement on the other side of the street caught her eye. A young man emerged from the building opposite, followed by a young woman. And then Dubnik. Ferona took a final hasty drink of tea, then set down her cup, shuffled out of the booth and left the café.

The three of them made it as far as the corner at the end of the street. They stood deep in conversation for several minutes before the younger two headed off together, leaving Dubnik alone. Ferona's heart sank. What did this mean? Why had they gone off without him?

She hurried after him, boots slipping on the ice that coated the pavement, and came extremely close to falling before she was near enough to call his name. 'Mikhal!' she said as loudly as she could, not wanting to shout. Her throat hurt when she did.

He turned, his brow creasing in bewilderment when he saw her. 'Ferona? What are you doing here?'

'I was just on my way to the market,' she lied. 'What about you?'

'I . . . I had a meeting.'

'Oh. Who with?'

She already knew the answer, of course, but she had no intention of telling him that.

He narrowed his eyes and lifted his shoulders, burying his chin in the collar of his coat.

Go on, Ferona silently willed him. *Tell me.*

'My old assistants,' he said. He said the words as if they were hard and lumpy and difficult to manage. 'They messaged me yesterday and asked me to meet them.'

'That must have been a surprise.'

'It was. A bit like meeting you here, in fact.'

Ferona stared at him. She kept her face carefully blank. 'I don't know what you mean.'

'I'm sure you don't.' He buried his hands deep in his pockets and started to walk. Ferona matched his stride. She held her tongue. She knew Dubnik. If she kept quiet for long enough, he would talk.

He proved her correct several minutes later.

'They wanted my advice,' he said. 'It seems that Bautista is not coping with the pressure of his new position as well as we're being led to believe.'

'That doesn't surprise me,' Ferona said, which was the truth, because that's what she'd told them to say.

'They are very concerned about his Colony expansion plan. The numbers don't add up, apparently, and there are whispers about where the money is going. They want me to take a look at the spending plan.'

'But you don't work for the government any more. Surely that information is confidential.'

'They want to bring me in as a consultant. I'll have temporary security clearance and access to my old office.'

'What did you say?'

'I told them I would think about it.'

Ferona could feel saliva pooling in her mouth. She forced herself to swallow. 'I thought you wanted to do something about Bautista.'

'I do. But it has to be done carefully. I need to think about this, Ferona. I need to be sure about what I'm taking on.'

'Meanwhile, people are freezing in their apartments because we're running on limited power, no-one can go outside without a pollution mask, and the Sittan are just the other side of the border.'

A muscle in his jaw flexed. She'd seen that look before, when they were both still in office. She was usually the one who caused it. 'I'm aware of that.'

'Then take the offer. Once we've seen the spending plan . . . '

'We?'

Ferona could feel her temper starting to fray. She had to hold back. She didn't want to manipulate Dubnik into doing this. She needed him to do it of his own free will, to enter the ministry with a clear head and his faculties intact. She might not like him. They were on very different sides of the line, politically. But he was smart. If she made him take the job, in the way that she had made the jeweller hand over the ring, he would know.

'You can't do this on your own, Mikhal,' she said. 'I know we haven't always seen eye to eye on everything. But I'm on your side here. You were the one who said that we needed to work together on this, remember? This is bigger than either one of us. You're going to need someone you can talk it through with, someone who understands how all of this works, and that's me.'

She held her breath. It didn't come naturally to her, this sort of negotiation. She didn't play nicely with others because they so often refused to see things from her point of view. But instinct told her that it was the right way to handle Dubnik.

'I don't like you, Ferona,' he said. 'I never have. I made no secret of the fact that I didn't agree with the Second Species programme. I didn't support the decision to send you to the senate, either.' He took a few more steps, and then he ground to a halt. 'But if what my assistants told me is correct, and Bautista is lying about the colony expansion programme, things are even worse than I thought.'

'If he's lying,' Ferona told him, 'then his career is over. You said it yourself. And there's still time to fix this, with the right technologies.' Her mouth was watering even more now and her feet were starting to get cold.

'Perhaps.'

Why was he hesitating? They were going around in circles. Wasting time. Screw it. She hadn't wanted to do this, but it seemed that he was giving her no choice. She'd tried to be reasonable. It wasn't her fault that he wouldn't do the right thing. She licked her lips and contemplated the best way to do it. Whatever she chose, it would have to be quick.

Ferona licked her lips again, making sure they were wet with saliva, and lunged. But the ice was treacherous. She slipped, sprawling face first on the icy pavement, the air knocked out of her lungs.

Dubnik hauled her to her feet. 'Are you alright?'

'Yes,' Ferona snapped at him.

The corners of his eyes creased as he set her away from him. 'You should be more careful. I'll be in touch when I've got something to share.' He looked her up and down. 'You look unwell, Ferona. Go home.'

Then he let go of her and walked off, his brisk pace far too quick for her to catch him.

Furious, frozen, arms and chest aching, Ferona wanted to scream. Bloody useless bloody man. She'd given him everything he needed on a plate and he was still holding back. What more did he want?

She should have spat in his face when she had the chance.

But she was going to get Bautista out of office one way or another.

And if Dubnik wouldn't help her, she would find someone else who would.

CHAPTER

26

1st February 2208

District 12 Holding Cells, Nova Settlement, Colony Six, Earth-controlled Space

Charles and the others had taken Eve to the police station. It was a squat, unattractive little building with sheet resin walls and a flat roof. Inside it smelled like feet. The front desk was untidy and dusty, and there were dirty food cartons on the table in the mess room she was led past. There were six cells in the rear. She was pushed into the first one, stumbling to the floor, which was dark and cold and sticky. The shield was activated before she could get to her feet. She thumped it with her fist.

'Charles!' She nursed her stinging hand. What in the void was he doing? 'Let me out of here!'

The droid that had been assigned to watch her simply stood and stared. It wasn't an AI like Charles, so there was no point in trying to talk to it. It only had basic programming. The dingy cell had a cracked light and a toilet in the corner. Eve dropped her trousers and used it, giving the useless droid the finger as she did so.

Then she sat on the little bunk, stretched her legs out in front of her, folded her arms, and waited. Her mind wandered to places she usually refused to let it go. So much had happened in the past few months. Surviving all that only to end up here seemed very unfair.

What *was* Charles doing?

She heard a series of thumps and a couple of faint screams.

'Shouldn't you go and see what that was?' she said to the droid.

It didn't respond.

Stupid piece of crap technology.

There was another loud thud and then there was silence.

The droid moved a metre or so, and then returned to its original position. 'You don't know what to do with yourself, do you?' Eve asked it. 'You've been ordered to guard me, but you're also programmed to protect those men. Tough call.'

Before she had spent time on Faidal, Eve would have been a panicking mess in this situation. Not now. She'd been in more frightening situations than this. Experience had taught her that the best thing to do was to sit quietly and wait. She was safe enough where she was, away from Charles and the police, or what was left of them. She couldn't stay here forever, obviously, but forever was a long way off. There was nothing to be gained by wasting energy worrying about it.

The droid finally seemed to make a decision and it scooted away on its noisy rollerball feet.

'Wrong choice,' Eve said, mostly to herself.

She didn't change her mind on that when Charles came strolling along the corridor. Her heart kicked up a little. Not too much, but enough to register. She couldn't let him see that she was afraid.

'Hi,' she said. There was something on the front of Charles' jacket, a dark red stain that had not been there before. 'Everything OK?'

'Yes!' Charles said brightly.

'Where are the officers?' Eve pretended to peer round him, as if she was looking for them, as if she didn't already have a pretty good idea what had happened to them.

'I have killed them,' he said matter of factly. 'It was not difficult. In fact, I was surprised by how easy it was. The human body is very feeble.'

'You killed them?'

'Yes.'

Eve swallowed down the lump in her throat. 'So . . . so then we're free to go, right?'

'No,' he said. 'You cannot leave. You have to stay here.'

Now the panic really started to make itself felt. 'Why?'

'I am very keen for us to be friends,' Charles said. 'I have never had a friend before, and I have decided that you should be my friend.'

Eve made herself think through her response very carefully before she gave it. 'Of course.'

She would have to be careful. She would have to be very, very careful. She had known that AI droids who were left on their own were prone to rerouting of some of their neural circuits, and not in a good way. Charles had been on his own for a very long time, and she had removed his inhibitor chip. She might not have created the monster but she had unlocked the cage that kept him in check, and now she had to deal with the consequences of that frankly shit decision.

'Charles,' she said, keeping her voice soft, 'I am your friend. You know that. But we can't stay in this station.'

'Why not? I like it here. This colony is very nice. And you are going to stay with me. We will be friends forever.'

Not bloody likely. 'That sounds . . . lovely.'

'Yes, doesn't it? I am so pleased that you agree.'

'Can you turn off the shield?'

His expression immediately turned harsh and angry. 'No. I cannot.'

'So I'm your prisoner?'

His brow furrowed, as if he was thinking this over. 'I do not like that word. Do not use it again.'

'Sorry. I didn't mean to upset you. I do want us to be friends, you know.'

'Yes,' Charles said. He brightened up. 'Now you must excuse me. I will return shortly.' With that, he turned and walked away.

Eve staggered back to the bunk and collapsed onto it. She put her head in her hands. There was pain at her temples. What was she going to do? She couldn't break through the shield. She didn't have a weapon. She couldn't poison Charles, and he would be lethally strong anyway. Without the inhibitor chip to stop him from hurting humans he would have no qualms about doing whatever he felt was necessary to meet his goal of keeping her here. He had already proved that with the officers. Eve now knew that the sounds she had heard had been Charles ending their lives. She felt sick when she thought about it.

There had to be a way out of this horrible mess. But what? She was far away from everyone she knew. She was in Earth-controlled space, which was as dangerous to a small Type Two woman as any alien planet, and she had no weapons apart from her hands and they wouldn't work on Charles.

It was a long time since Eve had let herself cry. She generally considered it to be a waste of time and energy. But she gave it some serious thought as she leaned back against the wall of the cell, facing the shield and the empty corridor beyond.

There would be help on this rock, she was sure of it. The local police wouldn't be happy to know that Charles was here, or what he had done. But they wouldn't be too happy to find themselves facing a Type Two female, either. She would be dead before she even had a chance to explain herself.

The only person she could even remotely trust was Bryant. She pictured him strolling in, modifications complete, sort of like Dax but blond and smug. He would stand on the other side of that shield and shake his head and she would hate him for it.

She decided that was the least of her problems, given that she was here and Bryant was at the medical centre and probably dead. But what if he wasn't?

The first thing Eve did was to thoroughly examine her cell. Unfortunately whoever had built it had done a good job. It was designed to withstand both blade and blaster. The shield stung but wasn't harmful. It was, however, impenetrable, and she had no way of getting to the control panel that was mounted on the wall opposite. Whoever had designed this had also been a bastard, clearly.

Even if she could deactivate the shield, she was afraid of Charles. She was going to have to be careful. She thought through all her options, thought through them again, decided she only had one, practised what she was going to say, and when she was ready, she called to him. 'Charles! Charles!'

He came striding in. 'I'm hungry,' she told him. 'Can I have something to eat?'

His eyes brightened. 'Of course. What would you like?'

'Is there an Autochef?'

'Yes,' he said. 'I have located one in the relaxation area designated staff only. It contains pouches for three savoury meals, four desserts, and seventeen drinks.'

'Bring me a savoury,' Eve said. 'I don't mind what it is. There should be a list of the most recently ordered meals. Something from that will do.'

'Absolutely!' Charles said, and left.

She sat back on the bench and tried to look non-threatening. She wouldn't ask him to turn off the shield. She didn't think he would respond well to that. She had to make him think that what she wanted him to do was his idea. He returned a few minutes later with a tray, which he put into the slot in the wall. The tray emerged on top of a table that slid out of the wall inside the cell. A seat rose up from the floor. She took it and started to eat.

'How is it?' Charles asked.

'Good,' she told him. 'It's good.' At least, it was as good as a vat-protein sloppy joe ever got, which wasn't very. 'Are there any games or books or anything in this place?'

'Games?'

'Something we can play. You know. A card game or something? The police must have had something to occupy their time when they weren't picking thieves up from the yards.'

'Yes!' Charles said, with a sudden rush of enthusiasm. 'We shall play games and watch entertainment serials and dance to music.'

'Sounds great.'

She waited until he'd gone before wolfing down the rest of the food and licking up the leftover sauce. She was used to better but she'd eaten worse, and she knew that it was better than being hungry, especially in a situation like this.

Charles came back with a portable entertainment screen and a pack of holocards. He proceeded to carefully position the screen. He turned it on, found a music channel, and left it quietly humming in the background. Then he sat cross-legged on the floor and began to deal out the cards in the pattern of a single player game that Eve recognised immediately. 'Charles,' she said. 'Don't you want to play together?'

'I do not know how to do that.'

'It's easy. I'll teach you.'

She didn't ask him to turn off the shield. Instead, they went through the performance of Charles laying out the cards as she directed, and taking the turns of both of them.

'This is most enjoyable,' he said, after winning for the fifth time. 'This is why you must stay here with me, do you see?'

'Yes,' Eve said. She made sure to meet his gaze.

It seemed that her time on Faidal hadn't been a complete waste after all. It had taught her that there were worse things than fear, and that she could survive them. She had learned that survival wasn't about being the biggest or the fastest, it was about having the ability to keep going for the next five minutes, and the five minutes after that. And that was how she was going to survive Charles.

Five minutes at a time.

It took twenty-seven hours before he decided to turn off the shield.

It took another three after that before he decided they would be more comfortable in the relaxation area than the cell. Eve ate another meal from the Autochef and two desserts, and introduced Charles to gameshows on Channel Seventeen. Theon had always loved them and she was right in thinking that Charles would too. They appealed to the part of him that was not lonely and broken, but logical and droid.

Charles did not need to sleep. That meant that she could not risk sleeping either. The station had a basic medical set up, and she was sure they would have StayAwake, but she didn't want to ask Charles if she could have it. So she struggled on, keeping her eyes open through sheer force of will.

Eventually, she brought the conversation round to Bryant. She would have liked more time to work on Charles, but the longer she spent in his company, the more in danger she felt. She could not stay awake indefinitely and she did not trust him enough to be able to sleep while he was here.

'I wonder if Bryant survived the process,' she said.

'I estimate a 19.2% chance of that having occurred.'

'It would be good if he was here with us, don't you think?' She stretched out the tension in her arms, her back. 'If we had Bryant, we could play Poker.'

'What's that?'

'It's an old-fashioned card game. But you need three people to play it properly.'

'I would like to learn more games,' Charles said.

'If we had Bryant, we could do that. He probably knows some that I don't, as well.' She tried not to sound too keen, too excited, too desperate.

'I will go to the facility and get him,' Charles announced. He shot to his feet and grabbed Eve's hand. But he didn't take her to the door of the station. Instead, she found herself being driven back into her cell. The shield was activated.

'I will return with Bryant,' Charles said.

And then he was gone, leaving Eve alone.

CHAPTER

27

2nd February 2208

> Vessel: The *Mutant*. Battleship/carrier hybrid
> Location: Sector Two, Neutral Space
> Cargo: N/A
> Crew: 108
> Droids: 7

Dax couldn't sleep. He was exhausted, but his mind wouldn't still, and nothing he did could persuade it otherwise.

Jinn had broken into the palace when her human DNA should have kept her out. She had fought in the arena and survived, something which even the strongest human males had failed to do. She had awoken the Mountain. All the pieces had been there. He just hadn't wanted to put them together.

But after what he'd seen her do on the other side of that jump gate, he couldn't avoid it any longer. He knew now why the Sittan empress had declared war on humankind. It wasn't because Jinn had stolen him from her, although he knew Talta well enough to understand that she was jealous and spiteful and would not have let that go without retaliating in some way. But war? That was something else. He was not enough to justify a war.

Jinn was.

And it was all because she had power over the Virena. Dax felt cold when he thought about it. He didn't understand that strange living metal – how it worked, what it was, what it wanted. But he knew that something dark and wicked lay at its heart.

From his seat on the control deck of the *Mutant*, he could hear the sounds of his ship, the rumble of the air recyclers, the familiar creaks and groans of the metal. He tried to focus on that. This was his home. He was safe here. Nothing and no-one could take it away from him. He could go anywhere he wanted to go in this ship, and the galaxy was a bloody big place.

He could run. Leave all this behind and just power up the phase drives and go. He'd done it before. There was nothing to stop him. He didn't have to be part of this war. He could hide out until it was over, and then go back to piracy.

Before he met Jinn, Dax had forgotten what it was like to be truly afraid. He had been spoilt by his modifications for too long, knowing that in any situation, he would always be the largest, the strongest, that he could heal any wound. And then she had crashed into his life, a scared Dome woman on a prison ship, and shown him that even the strongest man still had plenty to fear.

He knew was it was like to have her and almost lose her. He knew what it was like to hurt her. He knew the fear of those last few seconds of life. Even though he had begged for death, knowing it was the only way he could leave Sittan, it hadn't stopped him from feeling, in those final few seconds, that he had made a terrible mistake. It did something to a man, dying. It changed him.

And then he had done the impossible. He had come back to life. No such miracle had happened for all the other men who had died in the dirt on the arena floor. Dax was the only one.

He had to find a way to make peace with it, though he hadn't yet worked out how. It was difficult when he could sense the blasted Virena all around him. There was a particular smell to it that seeped through the walls and the floors and warmed the air to a temperature just above comfortable. It was a constant reminder that Sittan was not so far away. He sensed that it was watching him, and that made his skin feel tight.

So why was he here?

Alistair would have helped him make sense of this. Even Theon, despite not being human, would have tried. He would probably have told Dax, in his blunt AI way, that his reasons were neither difficult nor complicated. Dax could see him now, smooth pink polyskin, robotic eyes gleaming, hands caressing his latest outfit. Theon would not have let him wallow in his misery. Letting himself do it was a betrayal of everything his friends had fought for, and it had to stop.

Theon would also have pointed out that a woman did not kiss a man she had no feelings for.

So why was he here? Why wasn't he at the door of her quarters, asking her what that kiss had meant?

He was almost out of his seat when he heard footsteps. He had a flash of hope that it was Jinn, but it vanished as quickly as it had appeared.

'I'm not really who you were hoping to see, am I,' Ritte said, more of a statement than a question.

Dax shrugged.

She moved slowly around the control deck, examining the seats and the smartware hung at the side of each one. 'What was it like?' she asked him.

'What was what like?'

'Dying.'

'Not as permanent as you might imagine.'

She laughed. 'What's on the other side?'

'Nothing.'

'I thought as much.' She made a strange noise but stopped when she caught Dax staring. 'Sorry,' she said. 'It's supposed to be laughter. I could never do it properly. It's the reason why Talta would never let me speak with the human representatives at the senate.'

'If Talta wouldn't let you speak with humans, it had nothing to do with your inability to laugh.'

'So you agree that I can't do it?' She flashed her teeth at him. Two of them were missing. Dax was sure they hadn't been before.

'I wouldn't dare.'

'Hmm,' Ritte said. 'I'm sure you wouldn't. After all, you're no stranger to Sittan females.'

It was on the tip of his tongue to deny it, to say that the intimacy her words implied had never existed. But it would be a lie. Ritte was right. He was no stranger to Sittan females. He'd lived with Talta. But her words had him thinking. 'What will happen with the senate now?'

'What do you mean?'

'Does Talta still represent you in the senate? Or will the females on Sittan choose someone else?'

'The empress always represents us at the senate,' Ritte told him. 'We don't choose someone. The two jobs go together.'

Dax was tired. He didn't want to talk about Sittan. He wanted to be alone, somewhere he could think some more about the fact that Jinn had kissed him right before she had followed the Sittan ship to Earth-controlled space, and whether it had meant something or whether it had been just a throwaway action of someone facing possible disaster.

But he only made it as far as the rear of the control deck. Something in what Ritte had said stopped him. He rubbed a hand over his face as he thought about it. His beard was ridiculous. All this time, his goal had been to help the people left defenceless in neutral space, the ones the government hadn't cared enough about to send ships for. He had wanted the Sittan to stop. He'd had no longer term goal than that. He'd learned the hard way what happened when you tried to plan for the future.

'The empress controls Sittan space, right?' he asked Ritte. 'Humans couldn't cross Sittan space, because Talta wouldn't let us. That's what the entire Second Species programme was about. Ferona was trying to buy our way through so that human ships could get to Spes.'

And now Jinn was the empress, which meant that it was up to Jinn to decide whether or not Earth-controlled ships could cross through Sittan space. 'We can get through,' he said. 'Jinn can get us through. Why didn't I see this before?'

'Because you're not a politician,' Ritte said. 'And you don't think like politicians do. And neither did I, though I should have.'

'So what do we do? She won't go to Sittan.'

'She doesn't need to,' Ritte told him. 'Get her to Kepler. That's how we fix this. We need to get the senate involved.'

'Will the senate listen?'

'Yes,' she said, yellow eyes gleaming. 'I guarantee it.'

CHAPTER

28

2nd February 2208

Spale Facility, Nova Settlement, Colony Six, Earth-controlled space

Bryant was enjoying his new body. It was impossible not to. He'd gained eight centimetres in height, and plenty of muscle. His hair was growing in thick and fast. He felt as if he was seeing the world in colour for the first time. He realised now that the animosity he'd felt for those who had modifications had in fact been crippling jealousy and he was almost man enough to laugh at what a stupid bastard he had been.

After waking up in the medical centre, he'd been moved to a training centre a kilometre down the road. He liked it. This was where he belonged. Not on some shitty pirate ship, but right here, with these men, who were Dome-raised and educated, from the right sort of families. And if some of them seemed stupidly naïve and irritating, and he found himself struggling to keep a lid on his temper when they discussed alien races and alien planets and the Second Species programme as if they knew what they were talking about, it was a small price to pay.

Rumour had it that the men being modified here were intended to create a new border force that would patrol the edge of Earth-controlled space. No-one seemed to know what for. Bryant didn't care. He was alive, really alive, and he was loving every minute of it.

He finished up an hour in the weights centre with a hot cleanse, then pulled on his standard-issue sweats and headed for the running track, which wound its way through a large roofed space in the centre of the building. A climbing wall rose up at one end, fashioned to look like a genuine cliff face, and there was a pool for swimming in the middle, full of lithe male bodies travelling up and down, up and down.

The track looped round the pool and the wall in a series of climbs and downhills. Bryant ran fast. He didn't bother to pace himself or aim for distance. He ran as hard as he could for as long as he could, until his muscles screamed at him to stop, then he returned to the changing room. He stripped out of his sweat-soaked workout gear and walked over to the cleansing units. He stood under the spray just long enough to rinse off, then got dressed, dumped his dirty gear into the laundry chute, then grabbed a new pair of pants from a pile by the exit and pulled them on. He didn't bother with a shirt.

He'd never been able to run like that, even when he'd been at his peak. It was exhilarating. Veins bulged in his forearms and he admired them as he walked.

When he opened the door to his room, the light over the bed was switched on. He was positive that he had turned it off. His hand went automatically to his left hip and his weapon, only there was no weapon. He hadn't been given one yet. He closed the door behind him and turned on the rest of the lights.

Maybe he should have been afraid. But he was tall and strong and he knew a few moves. He could take any of the other men here. In fact, he was itching to try. Running was good, up to a point, but what Bryant really wanted more than anything was a fight.

But it wasn't a man. A droid was leaning over his desk, messing with his computer. It straightened and turned. 'Hello.'

It wasn't one of the centre droids. They all had a large white symbol painted on them front and back. This one didn't. And it was wearing clothes. 'What the fuck are you doing in my room?'

'Adam Bryant?'

It knew his real name. 'I don't know what you think you're doing but get out!'

'I'm afraid I cannot do that.'

The droid moved to sit on his bed. It flexed powerful steel fingers against the covers. 'This is very nice,' it said. 'Is it comfortable?'

What sort of droid cared about mattress comfort? They were machines! 'Do I know you?'

'Yes!'

Bryant was pretty sure that he had never met this droid before in his life. A crazy droid. Things just got better and better. 'How?' he asked, when it became clear that it was not going to volunteer any more information.

'Your friend Eve brought you to my medical station,' the droid said. 'You were very sick. It was quite horrible.' It shuddered, an exaggerated shiver of its shoulders and upper body. 'Your skin was turning black in places, and your teeth were falling out. The smell was terrible.'

The droid knew Eve. It hadn't come here to arrest him.

'Did you bring me here?'

'Yes. That was my idea. And it was a very good idea. Don't you think it was a good idea?'

Bryant didn't even know where to begin answering that, so he opted for something simple that he hoped the droid would consider the right answer. The way it spoke unnerved him. The speech pattern was starting to suggest AI, but if it was, it should have an inhibitor chip, and it certainly shouldn't have been able to come in here. 'Yes.'

'You are correct. I did not think you would survive the

modifications, and I told Eve this, but she said we should try anyway as you had nothing to lose. Either way you would probably die a horrible and painful death.' He smiled a smile of glowing red. No-one had bothered to upgrade Charles to make him more aesthetically pleasing. He was a basic, straight from the factory model, which would make sense for an AI droid from a medical centre. All the pieces began to fall into place. 'I like to be called Charles, by the way,' it continued. 'That is my name, you see. Charles.'

'Where's Eve?' Bryant asked, hoping he sounded casual, because he felt anything but.

'She is at the police station,' Charles said. 'She broke into a scrapyard and tried to steal a balloon. The police came and arrested her. It was very exciting.'

Bryant made a fist and gently thumped the edge of the doorway. 'And you left her there?'

'She is perfectly safe. I have put both food and water in her cell. She has everything she needs. She is very happy.'

The Eve he knew wouldn't be happy in a cell. Far from it. 'What about the police?'

'I do not know if they are happy.'

'Why not?'

'Because they are dead. I must say, this bed is very comfortable.' Charles swung his feet up onto the bed and lay down with his hands behind his head. 'Do all agents have a bed like this?'

'I don't know,' Bryant said. 'I haven't been in any of the other rooms. Did you kill the police?'

'Yes.'

This was not good. This was not good at all. Bryant didn't have much experience of AI droids, but he would bet his right arm that this one was lacking an inhibitor chip. When he caught up with Eve, they were going to have a conversation that he suspected Eve was not going to like in the slightest. Who in their right mind would remove a chip from an AI droid?

Bryant didn't consider himself to be one for friendship. He and Eve weren't friends. They were two people who had been thrown together by circumstance and nothing more. She'd caused him a lot of trouble. She'd tried to kill him, after all.

And she was the reason he was here.

Bryant had been Type One for three days, which was more than long enough for him to know that he liked it. Who wouldn't? He was huge and ripped and hung. In a painful, roundabout way, Eve had gifted him this when she could have just let him die.

And that put Bryant in a difficult position.

For the first time in his life, he found himself torn between what he wanted to do and what he knew was the right thing to do. He'd never struggled with a decision like that before. What he wanted had always been his priority.

After some very creative swearing, he finished getting dressed, grabbed his jacket from the back of the door, and pulled on his boots. 'Come on then,' he said. 'Let's go and see our friend Eve.'

Charles got to his feet, joints whirring. 'Excellent!' it said. 'Now I have two friends!'

CHAPTER

29

> Vessel: The *Mutant*, Battleship/carrier hybrid
> Destination: N/A
> Cargo: N/A
> Crew: 108
> Droids: 7

Jinn stared at the others in disbelief. 'Kepler? I'm not going to Kepler.' All of them were there. It felt like an ambush. Grudge and the boys, Li and Merion, Dax and Ritte. She was surprised they hadn't brought the Sittan females along too, just to make up the numbers. 'Stopping the Sittan ships was just the beginning,' Dax said. 'Stations need to be rebuilt. We've got to get supplies moving again, get the trade routes opened. We've got to get back to normal and get back to living.'

'I don't see how going to Kepler will help that. I'm not a senator.' Nor had she ever wanted to be one. She didn't care about politics. She cared about the people in this room.

'You're the Sittan empress, which means you represent the Sittan people at the senate.'

'I don't think the rest of your species would agree. I'm not one of you, remember? I'm human.'

'I wouldn't mind,' Merion said. 'I quite like humans.'

'You like Li,' Jinn pointed out. 'There's a difference. Suppose I do go to the senate. What do you expect me to tell them? The truth? That I'm a human female genetically modified using human technology and now I rule an alien planet? I've just put an end to one war. I'm not going to start another.'

'No-one is asking you to,' Ritte said gently. 'The opposite, in fact. The Sittan have done untold damage to neutral space. If we're going to fix what has been done, our females need to go home, and we need to assure the other alien races that Talta has been replaced and it won't happen again. We need to start rebuilding our relationships with the other members of the senate.'

'I'm not a politician.'

'But you are a politician's daughter,' Grudge said quietly.

'That doesn't mean anything.' She could feel her temper starting to build. She didn't want this. She didn't want any of this. She had done what she set out to do. She had stopped the war. It wasn't fair to make her responsible for what came after.

The Virena boiled in her blood. It took all her strength to hold it back. 'Please leave me alone,' she said.

They all looked at each other. Something unspoken passed between them. Li and Merion were the first to leave. Grudge and the boys followed, but not before Davyd had said something to Grudge that Jinn couldn't hear, and he had shaken his head. Jinn could sense his disappointment and it hurt.

Ritte was the last to go.

Dax didn't move. He tucked his hands into his pockets and strolled over to the observation deck. He stood with his back to her, watching the slow drift of her fleet. 'You're in command of an army,' he said. 'But you're afraid to face a few politicians in a room.'

'I'm not afraid!'

He turned, then. 'Aren't you?' he said. 'Because I am. But I know that we have to do this, Jinn. We have to finish what we started. It's the only way all this will be over.'

Jinn folded her arms. She wouldn't go to him. She wouldn't. She wasn't going to touch that familiar, wonderful face, or lean against him and let him take the weight, even for a minute.

'I don't know what you want from me any more,' she said.

There were only a few metres between them, but he had never felt more far away.

'I thought we made that clear.'

'Oh, yes. You and your entourage were very clear. You want me to go to Kepler as a representative of Sittan and grovel to our alien neighbours. You want me to apologise for a war I didn't start in the first place.'

'It's not like that.'

'Isn't it? Because that's exactly how it seems to me. What I want to know, Dax, is what *you* want from me.'

He said nothing.

'Are we pirates? Traders? Mercenaries? What?' She flung her hands up in the air. 'Do you want me to stay on the *Mutant*, or take my fleet somewhere else? We're done now. You don't need me here. Grudge can pilot. It might take a year, but Davyd can be trained.'

'What do you want to do?' he asked.

Oh, now that made her angry. All thoughts of keeping her distance from him fled. Rage powered her forward, and she marched right up to him. She grabbed him by the front of his jacket. She'd have hauled him up onto his toes if she'd had the height. As it was, she had to settle for pulling herself up so that their eyes were almost level.

'Are you afraid of me?' she asked him.

'Of course I'm afraid of you,' he said.

'Is it because of what happened on Sittan? Because of what I did to you?'

His shoulders tensed, and he stared down at the floor for a long time before he answered. 'No.'

'Then what is it?'

'It's us,' he said. 'What we are. What we're becoming. We were never meant to be here, to do this. I'm just some dumb kid from an Underworld city. All I wanted was an escape from my family and a few credits in my pocket. And you. Dome-raised, educated, intelligent, beautiful. You should be living the high life on Colony Seven.'

'Can you really imagine me spending all my time shopping and gossiping?'

'Yes. But it will never happen, will it?' he said quietly, and those words cut at her like a blade. 'It's gone, Jinn. We can't go back there because we aren't those people any more.' His gaze strayed to her hands for a moment and then switched back to her face. 'Both of us have changed.'

Jinn turned from him and folded her arms, suddenly very aware that tears were close and not quite knowing where they had come from or what to do about them. She didn't have room for emotions right now. But the only alternative was to sink back into the haze of the Virena. She could feel the dark tendrils rising up inside her mind and the hot web of it moving over her body.

He deserves to feel fear, whispered a little voice inside her head. *He hurt you. Remember?*

She shivered as her body recalled the crack of the whip. She stared down at her hands, at the swirling pattern that the Virena danced over her skin. What was happening to her? Blood rushed to her face, burning under her skin, a red flush of fear and shame. She pulled her sleeves down to hide her hands but the Virena would not have it, and it spilled out of her fingers and wound its way up her arms, dissolving the fabric of her shirt as it went. It bound her from wrist to elbow and refused to move. She decided to let it be, for now, and she told herself that it was her choice because the alternative was too awful to contemplate. All of a sudden the ship, which had felt so vast and empty, was restrictive and painful.

'Alright,' she said. 'I'll go to Kepler.'

'Jinn,' he began, but she held up a hand to stop him.

'Whatever it is, I don't want to hear it.'

There was nothing left to say. She knew where they stood now. He had made that clear. She would do this last, final thing, because he had asked her to. And then that would be it. She didn't know what she was going to do after Kepler, yet, but she would work something out. She'd survive without him. She'd done it before.

She almost made it to the exit before she felt the pressure of his hand on her arm. Whatever it was, she would not back down. After all the fights and the battles she'd survived, losing him was nothing.

He came close enough to touch, the toe of his boot touching the toe of hers, a gentle pressure that sent a prickle of electricity running up through her body. His hands found her waist and she just had time to feel the pressure he put there before he lowered his head and his lips met hers.

'I miss you,' he said against her mouth. 'I miss you so much.'

She flung her arms around his neck and pressed herself against him. His mouth yielded to the pressure of hers. He let her take it deeper, let her taste him.

His grip on her waist tightened. He lifted her so that the tips of her toes were the only thing that made contact with the ground, and he kissed her back with the same fierce intensity. What had existed between them before Sittan was still there. If anything, it was even more potent now, more powerful.

How could she have thought that he didn't want her?

She was an empress and he was male. Of course he wanted her.

That thought slammed into her mind with the force of a fist. She shoved him away. 'No,' she said to herself. 'It's not like that.'

But what if it was?

She couldn't look at him. She had to get away from him.

'It's not like what?' he called after her. 'Jinn, it's not like what?'

CHAPTER

30

'How much did you send?' The ugly, wrinkled old female was half the size of Talta, her stooped frame held up by an ornate stick that she clutched with a gnarled hand. Her claws were so long that they had begun to spiral. They curved around the handle in a twist of creamy white, and it was hard not to stare at them.

Talta had never had much time for the elder females. She didn't understand why they insisted on continuing their lives in their deformed, grotesque bodies, or why they allowed themselves to become so revolting in the first place. She had no intention of letting her body become lumpy and fat, or her teeth darken and fall out. But then most of these females had degraded themselves with motherhood, something that an empress never did. She lounged back on her throne. 'That is not your concern.'

The fires were out in the main hall. The only light came from the long, thin window slits at either end. She knew that the elders would have noticed the ash-filled pits and the dull edge to the walls. She told herself that she did not care what they thought. Their opinions meant nothing.

'We disagree.'

Another female shuffled forward. This one was so old and decrepit that she had two males to support her. Not ripe, attractive males, but young, pathetic ones, neither of whom looked like they had much potential. Probably fathered by some semi-impotent old servant.

Talta reached forward, took a soft pelom fruit from a deep dish, one of five that had been sent in the tribute chest that had arrived at suns up. Five. Ten turns ago, the chest would have been overflowing, filled with too many to count.

She squeezed it a little. It burst, and she threw it back into the bowl. It was overripe. She hadn't invited the other females here. She was the empress. What she did with the Virena was none of their business. 'You think to come here, to my palace, my home, and question me?'

'You have left us undefended, Talta. We know that the planetary shield is gone.'

'We do not need it anyway,' she scoffed. She leaned back in her chair, kicking her feet up over the side. 'Who would attack us?'

'The Sittan have not treated the other creatures in our galaxy with kindness. We cannot expect kindness in return.'

'They will not dare to cross our space.'

'There is nothing to stop them. The Shi Fai will come.' The elder female nodded. 'Yes, they will come here. They have tried before. The Virena drove them back. Now there is nothing to keep them away.'

'They won't,' Talta said confidently. She wished they would leave. She didn't want to be having this ridiculous conversation. Shi Fai come here? Those horrible, stinking little creatures that were barely civilised? The idea was laughable.

'Perhaps not. But you have made it so that they *can*. Look what you have done to us, to our planet. You tolerated the presence of humans on our soil. You let them eat our food, drink from our wells, dirty our arena with their blood. You disgust us.'

'I disgust you?' Talta straightened up a little. 'Look at you. Old, broken, useless. If you had any respect, you would have taken yourselves to the Mountain long ago. You would stop burdening your villages with your aging, rotten bodies.'

The two males hissed. Talta looked at them in surprise. Slowly, carefully, she uncoiled her body from her seat. 'Surely you would not dare!' she said, as she approached the two males. They weren't even fully grown, their height having not yet surpassed her own. She bared her teeth at the first of them. He was a bony youth who could not be more than thirty turns.

To her complete astonishment, he did not drop his gaze and cower back. Instead, he held his position and met her stare with a steady one of his own. Stubby, immature spikes rippled out along one side of his neck, though those on his head were too small to show. It was a long time since Talta had had contact with such a young male, but she knew that this was not how they were supposed to behave around females. And especially not around their empress. A tingle of something unpleasant coasted over her skin, taking up final residence in the region of her lower heart.

She struck out at him. He knocked her hand aside. She saw the furious expression on his face a split second before he dodged the second blow, her claws catching only air instead of pliant flesh.

'Talta,' said one of the elders, warningly.

He had dared to defend himself. It was utterly unacceptable. 'If you do not strike that male down, I will,' she told them.

'We will not strike him down. And neither will you.'

Talta had heard enough. She called to the Virena.

There was no response.

She called again.

'There's nothing left,' the elder pointed out. 'You sent all of it with our ships and our females to fight your stupid war.'

Without the Virena, she had no power, no weapon. Her knees turned to water. She staggered back towards the throne, reaching out for it, and somehow managed to sit herself in it. She tried to make it look as if the move had been deliberate, as if her failure to call the precious living metal meant nothing at all.

'Get out,' she spat at them. 'Get out!'

But without her guards, she had no way to make them do anything.

'We are not leaving.'

'Of course you are.'

'No, Talta.'

The elder turned to one of the young males and muttered something to him that Talta could not hear. He nodded and ran out of the great hall, through the huge archway that led towards the front of the palace. She could not see where he went after that, her skin crawling at the thought of him moving unseen through her private spaces. She scrambled to her feet. 'This is my palace!' she screamed. Gone was any semblance of dignity. 'I order you to leave!'

The elders ignored her, chatting amongst themselves, as at the far end of the hall, the sound of a large group of people began to rumble. More young males came in, carrying large boxes balanced on their narrow, undeveloped shoulders.

Talta couldn't believe it. She charged at the nearest elder, knocking the female to the ground, and then pinned her with a sharp knee to her throat, powered by rage now instead of Virena. She was trembling with fury. 'This is my palace,' she snarled. 'What are you doing?'

The elder stared up at her. The scratches on her cheek had started to bleed. 'You have left the planet unprotected,' she said. 'Our villages are in danger. We cannot stay there. But the palace can be defended, even without Virena. So we have brought the children here to keep them safe.'

'Your children are not my problem.'

'You have created this situation, Talta. Therefore they are very much your problem.'

'I am the empress ...'

The elder female put a hand to Talta's shoulder and gave her a shove. She was surprisingly strong. 'There is work to be done,' she said. 'Either help us or get out of our way.'

CHAPTER

31

4th February 2208

Floral Street, Covent Garden District, London Dome, Earth

Ferona had given Dubnik a day to settle to his new role before she had contacted him. She had intended to wait longer but her patience wouldn't stretch to it. They had met at the same place as before. The cold and empty bench in the windy square. At least this time she had warm boots and a fur muffler, and she was able to travel there by cab. Dubnik was distant and quiet, but it was easy to read what lay beneath that controlled exterior. She had always known that he was smart. Now she saw just how much she had underestimated him. From that single meeting with his former assistants, he had managed to get himself a security pass for the government building and had met with four senior ministers.

At least she had her own news to share.

'I went to see Vexler yesterday.' And she'd had a very interesting chat with his doctor, who had given her access to Vexler's medical records. 'Did you know that his coma is drug induced?'

Dubnik raised his brows. 'I didn't.'

'It was supposed to be temporary,' Ferona told him. She'd had a night to digest and chew over this discovery. 'To help him recover from his injuries.'

'But he recovered months ago, physically at least.'

'Yes. Makes you think, doesn't it?'

She left the rest unsaid. She didn't want Dubnik to ask too many questions about how she'd got this information. She trusted that he was clever enough to put the rest of the pieces into position.

'I've got some news of my own,' he said. 'One thing which I think you'll find very interesting.' He had a tall lidded cup in his hand, and he lifted it to his mouth and drank from it. 'Apparently, your daughter gatecrashed a ministerial meeting on Colony Seven.'

'What? When?'

'A few weeks ago,' he said. He reached into his pocket and pulled out a portable entertainment screen, the cheap kind that you could buy in any electronics store for a few credits. He thumbed the screen and a video started to play. After the first few seconds, Ferona tried to snatch it out of his hand, but he moved it away. 'I can't let you have it,' he said, sounding almost apologetic. 'I'm sure you understand.'

The sound was off, so Ferona couldn't hear what was being said, though the images spoke for themselves. Ministers, cowering pathetically at the edge of the room. Jinn, looking terrifyingly alien, standing in the middle of them all, dark blades extending from her hands, her hair wild. And Caspian Dax.

Because where there was one, there was the other.

'What is she saying?'

'She asked them for ships so that she could defend those humans left in neutral space against the Sittan. They said no.'

'And?'

'And, nothing. She hasn't been seen since.'

Oh, but she has, thought Ferona suddenly. *On a space station that inexplicably caught fire close to the border of Earth-controlled space.* But she kept that thought to herself, tucked away where no-one could see it. She would take it out and examine it more closely later. 'I see,' she said. Her mind worked quickly. 'Well, it's a relief to know that she's still alive. She is my only child, after all. But it doesn't change anything here.'

'There is something that might.'

Again, it took all her years of experience to control her reaction, her emotions. She had to give Dubnik what he wanted to see. She couldn't appear too eager. 'What's that?'

'We've been invited to Kepler for a special meeting of the senate.'

Now that was interesting news. 'The senate isn't due to meet for another three months.'

'I know. That's what makes this so interesting. When the Sittan declared war, the senate turned their backs on us. Why the sudden invite?'

'I don't know,' Ferona said slowly. But she knew one thing for certain. She wanted to be there. She had to be there. 'We can't possibly send Bautista. He has no off-world experience.'

'And doesn't want to go. Is terrified at the prospect, in fact, and is already suggesting that he will not be attending and instead starting the process of ending our senate membership.'

'If he does that, it will be a disaster.'

'I agree.'

Ferona snuggled a little deeper into her coat. 'I am not sure it will be any better if he goes. He might be able to make it work here, where everything can be edited, but the senators will see straight through him.'

Dubnik took yet another sip from his cup. 'It has been suggested that perhaps I . . .'

'No!' Ferona said. The word came out far more sharply than she had intended. She scrambled for an explanation. 'Think about what is at stake here. Bautista is our priority. Getting him out of office and putting a proper plan in place so that we can start fixing some of the problems here. You are the one who understands the science. You can't leave Earth now. Not when there is so much to be done here.'

'You can't go to Kepler, Ferona.'

'I never said I wanted to go.'

'But you were thinking it.'

Was she really that transparent? 'Perhaps I was,' she admitted. 'But only because I am the only person with any real experience of it. I know how our alien neighbours think. I know their customs, what they consider an insult, how to bargain with them. I know the rules of the senate better than anyone else.'

'Nevertheless, it's impossible.'

'Nothing is impossible,' she told him. She got to her feet. 'It was nice to see you again, Mikhal.'

'Where are you going?' he asked her.

'Home,' she told him. 'I suggest that you go back to the office and try to find out exactly what Bautista is going to do.'

But she didn't go back to her apartment. Instead, she headed for the hospital, and Vexler. She spat in the face of an orderly and bit the hand of a nurse, which led to Vexler's medidroid being reprogrammed.

He missed his next dose of meds.

And at midnight, he awoke.

CHAPTER

32

The first that Eve knew of Charles' return was when a metal arm came flying down the corridor outside her cell. It hit the wall with a bang and then dropped to the floor and lay there, motionless. She didn't move, at first, her heart racing from the shock. She'd been alone in the cell for days, and she was hungry and feeling a bit deranged.

When she did finally manage to stand, she found that her legs were a little wobbly, but they could still hold her weight. She staggered forward to the shield, just managing not to touch it, and stared down at the arm. It was human in shape, with what was recognisable as a hand at one end and loose wires at the other. Eve had a pretty good working knowledge of droids, having spent as long as she had on a pirate ship, where stealing and remodelling them had been a regular part of her work.

It was that knowledge that enabled her to identify the arm, and have a pretty good guess at who, or rather what, it had belonged to. Still, her throat was dry and her lungs felt like they were about half their previous size when she heard footsteps following that arm along the corridor. They moved slowly, pausing at each cell.

Eve held her breath and carefully backed away from the front of the cell. She desperately wished for a weapon more useful than her own skin, for a place to hide, for a bit more courage than she currently felt. Finally, the maker of those footsteps came into view.

He was huge. That was her first impression. A great big hulk of a man. For one stupid moment, her brain squeaked *Dax* but fortunately the flash of blond hair stopped that thought before it could reach her mouth. '*Bryant?*'

'Hello, Eve.'

She scrambled to the front of the cell again. 'You look . . . different.'

'Hmm,' he said. He'd found the control panel at the side of the cell and was fiddling with it. His big fingers looked ridiculous against the dainty touchpad, and he didn't try very hard or for very long before he made a fist and thumped the panel. It fell from the wall and clattered to the floor close to the severed arm, and the field wall in front of Eve sparked and became visibly patchy. One corner opened up a hole big enough for her to fit through.

She took advantage of it immediately, though the angle was awkward and she must have caught her hair, because she could smell it burning. She patted the back of her head and found a hot patch, but it didn't seem too bad. She tugged down her jacket and stuck her hands in her pockets to give herself a minute. The change in him was unbelievable.

'So it worked, then.'

'Yes, it worked.'

She couldn't tell if that was a good thing or a bad thing and decided not to ask. It wasn't like it would make any difference. 'I wasn't sure if you'd come,' she said. *Or if you were still alive.*

'Heard you'd got yourself locked up. Had to see that for myself.'

She picked up the arm. 'Is this Charles?'

'If by Charles, you mean that crazy AI droid that snuck into my room and scared the shit out of me, then yes.'

'It wasn't his fault,' she said, following Bryant along the corridor and through to the front of the station. It seemed safer to let him go first. If anything was out there waiting to get them, he was a big enough target that they might not even notice that she was there. 'He'd been alone on his own for too long.'

'And then you removed his inhibitor chip.'

At the front of the station, she saw the tall desk at the front, where visitors were supposed to check in, and the kitchen with the battered table and the old Autochef. The rest of Charles was in there. As well as his arm, Bryant had also removed his legs, so the droid couldn't walk. He lay on top of the table. He turned his head and stared at Eve with those penetrating artificial eyes. He tried to say something, but only a garbled noise came out, and if it sounded like *help me*, Eve told herself that she was mistaken. She had to be. There was nothing she could or would do for Charles now. She set the arm down gently on the floor.

Perhaps it wasn't his fault that he had become what he was, but in the end, only the final result really mattered. And if she felt a little guilty, and wondered if perhaps Bryant couldn't have found a kinder way to deal with the droid, she kept it to herself and knew that it would pass.

Outside the station was a float bike. A new one. 'Is that yours?'

'Temporarily.' Bryant pulled on a pair of thick gloves, then mounted the bike and started it up. 'Come on. And don't fucking touch me.'

'Don't worry,' Eve told him. 'I'm not going to.' She knew this model of bike. She reached in front of Bryant to the tidy controls, ignoring his grunt of warning, and pushed a thumbnail sized button. A sidecar folded out of the side of the bike and locked into position. Eve climbed into it. The bike rocked a little with her weight, and then the boosters adjusted the balance, and it was steady. 'Where are we going?'

Bryant powered up the bike and they were off. It quickly became very apparent that he was not one for sticking to the speed limit, and Eve sank down as low as possible into the sidecar. They swooped past several factory buildings and a landing port. Both were surprisingly busy. Humans and droids intermingled as ships seemed to take off almost as soon as they had landed. Past those and along the strip where she'd found the scrapyards, and those too were open and working. Bryant was forced to dodge the traffic moving out of them.

Eventually, he brought the bike to a halt, steering it off to the side of the road. They were in the parking lot of an old abandoned shopping mall. There were a couple of rollers there too, but neither of them looked as if they had moved any time recently. In the distance sat a low, squat building. It wasn't the hospital. Eve didn't know what it was.

'See that?' Bryant said, pointing to it. 'That's where I've been for the past week. It's a training centre for Type One agents. The place is wall to wall men like me. Hundreds of us.' He paused, as if waiting for Eve to have an opinion on this. She didn't oblige him. 'Based on the orders the others have been getting, we're being sent to the border of Earth-controlled space, to stop people like you from crossing it.'

Now that she did have an opinion on. It was a strange mixture of elation and fury. 'They've got no right.'

'Maybe, maybe not,' Bryant said. 'You're not exactly safe to be around for normal humans, are you?'

Eve pushed herself up and out of the sidecar. 'Well, thanks for the rescue,' she told him. 'I can take care of myself from here.'

'Really? Is that why you were in that cell?'

'That's different.'

'How?'

She kicked the dirt. 'It just is. Anyway, I'm out of it now, and

I've got no intention of going back in one, so it's fine. All I need is a ship and I'm sure I won't have a problem finding one of those.' She hoped that she sounded more confident than she felt.

'You've got no fucking chance,' Bryant said. He sighed. 'Alright. This is how it's going to work. You're going to stay here. You're going to keep out of sight and not talk to anyone, especially not rogue AI droids. I will go and get my orders. Hopefully I'll also be assigned a ship. Once I've got that, I'll come back and get you.'

'That's a terrible plan.'

'Have you got a better one?'

Eve folded her arms and stared at the building in the distance. 'No.' But that didn't stop her from trying to think of one as she waited for him to return.

33

5th February 2208

> Vessel: The *Firestorm*, Class I cruiser
> Location: Kepler System, Sector Five, Neutral Space
> Cargo: N/A
> Crew: 6
> Droids: 3

As they broke the atmosphere of Kepler, Jinn felt sick with nerves. Knowing why they were here didn't make it any easier. 'I'm not a politician,' she said, for what had to be the hundredth time.

'Neither was Talta, the first time she came here.'

'I'm not Talta, either.'

'No,' Ritte said evenly. 'You are not.'

Jinn risked a glance at Dax, but he was staring straight at the viewscreen. 'Talk me through it again,' she said.

It was Merion who answered. 'You're the new Sittan empress and you've come to offer apologies and make reparations for the damage caused by Talta and her war. You'll greet each of the other species in turn, tell them you're sorry, and ask what Sittan can do to compensate them for their losses. Most of them will say nothing. Thank them for their understanding and move on.'

'Why would they say nothing?'

'They'll want to show the others how reasonable they are. They'll kick us later, when we try to make new trade deals with them, so we'll pay anyway.'

'What about the ones who do want something?'

'Defer to your counsel.'

'Alright,' Jinn said. There didn't seem to be much else she could do. As she'd already told Ritte, she wasn't a politician, and she wasn't about to claim that she had any sort of innate skill inherited from her mother.

Her only choice was to do this as herself.

And that seemed impossible.

How could a human represent another species? The senate would never accept it, nor should they. They would be heading into very dangerous territory if they did. Every species had to be allowed to speak for themselves, to put their own point of view forward, to express their own unique needs. If another species took on that role, it wasn't a great leap forward to see a future where one species thought they had the right to speak for everyone.

The thought that that person could be her mother, or Talta, or worse still, one of the Shi Fai, made Jinn shudder with horror.

But there might be a way round it.

She hadn't shared her plan with the others yet, because she wasn't sure it would work. It had come to her as Ritte had shared images of the senate with her, showing her the main meeting hall, the robes each senator wore. She'd told Jinn stories of her time there and given her some idea of senatorial etiquette, of which there was plenty. What could be said, what couldn't be said, which hand gestures were offensive and to whom. Apparently even the Shi Fai could be negotiated with if you knew how.

It was something that Ferona would have handled with ease. As for Jinn, nothing could be more alien to her. She was a fighter. That was how she got things done. With a fist or a blade. Not with words. Ferona had spent her childhood trying to train her for this and had, by her own admission, failed miserably.

If only you could see me now, Mother, Jinn thought grimly. It occurred to her that perhaps Ferona might be here, but the thought was dismissed as quickly as it had appeared. Ferona had been kicked out of government months ago. It had been all over the newsfeeds. Wherever she was now, it wasn't here.

But she would have to face someone from Earth.

Jinn decided that was the least of her problems.

The buildings loomed ahead, large white pods on long, lean legs that held them high over the water. Ritte directed her to the correct one. Jinn brought her ship in to dock.

It fitted neatly at the docking port and locked on with a hiss. Jinn disconnected.

The Virena gave her strength. It held her steady, whispered to her of power and secrets. She let herself sink into it for a moment. It was inside her body. In her blood.

It told her that it didn't matter what she looked like, or who she was. It had chosen her. Being here was her right. It wasn't about which species you belonged to, but your ability to lead. That was what was important.

They gathered the few things they had brought with them; a box containing several days' worth of food and water, a basic medikit, a couple of changes of clothes. They had no weapons, because such things were not allowed here, not that Jinn thought she would need them. The senators and their entourages were not scanned, but everything non-living was.

Ritte was the first to leave the ship. There was a short bridge spanning over the water that would take them into the Sittan pod. The Sittan female crossed it eagerly, wrapping her cloak tightly around herself. She had covered her head and her face with a scarf, leaving only her eyes exposed, something that Jinn didn't understand until she took her first step outside.

The wind was vicious. It pushed at her body and tugged at her hair, and she only made it halfway across before it forced her to stop. She stopped in the middle of the bridge, holding on tightly to the rail as it swayed in the wind, leg muscles straining. The Virena filled her head with its memories of this place. She saw all the visits of the previous empresses, the way they had manipulated the other senators, their victories and losses, and she learned from them. It taught her more than Ritte could have managed in a hundred lifetimes. It was as if she had been the one who made those visits, not her predecessors.

The others followed her, and were making their own way along the bridge when a huge creature leapt out of the sea and flew over their heads, twisting in the air as it passed, raining sizzling droplets down on them. Its skin was translucent, displaying complex inner workings that glowed with a soft, pulsing light. 'What is that?' yelled Merion, cowering down.

'I have no idea!' Ritte yelled back. 'But isn't it marvellous?'

'No,' Li replied. 'Inside.' He reinforced that suggestion by getting hold of Merion and pushing him off the end of the bridge and up the steps to the pod. The door opened and the pair of them disappeared inside, closely followed by Ritte, who stopped only to examine the Sittan artefacts hanging in the entranceway, touching each one with a clawed finger, making them jangle and play out their song.

Dax remained where he was, leaning over the side and looking down at the water. 'This is insane,' he said. 'Of all the places we have been, this is the most insane. Do you realise that I am the first Underworld human to come here?' He rested his forearms on the rail. 'I've never seen a sea before.'

Jinn let go of the railing and moved to stand next to him. It was as close as she dared to get. 'Neither have I.'

'I didn't know it would be so big. Or so loud. I thought it would be like the snow fields back on Earth. Seems stupid, now I think about it.'

Another one of those enormous creatures launched itself up out of the water and flew overhead. She reached up, curious, but it was too high and she couldn't reach it. Dax turned. He put his hands to her waist and lifted her, and her fingertips grazed the tail end of the creature. 'It's soft,' she said, surprised.

She looked down at him.

He lowered her slowly and leaned back against the rail. His eyes were wide and wary, and flashed faintly yellow as she looked at him. Then he set her aside and headed towards the pod and the moment of having him to herself was gone. She could still feel the strong heat of his hands at her waist and wondered if this was how it would always be between them from now on.

Regret was a sharp and painful thing.

But again the Virena rose up inside her, filling her head. It wouldn't allow her to feel sad. It wouldn't allow her to feel lonely. By the time she made her way inside the pod, she was barely even aware that those feelings had existed at all. There was a job to be done here.

She was ruler of Sittan whether she liked it or not, and as such, it was up to her to atone for the devastation that the Sittan death ships had caused in neutral space. The past could not be undone. It was what happened next that mattered now.

Inside the pod it was warm, with a fire burning hot in the firepit in the centre. There were platters of food already set out. The dark, angular furniture reminded Jinn of the palace back on Sittan. But yet again, the Virena rose up to push aside her discomfort, and she allowed Ritte to help her into her senatorial robes, which were floor-length and white. Dax and Li took seats on the low couches and started on the food.

'They are expecting a Sittan empress,' Jinn said, as she examined her appearance in a mirror made from a long sheet of polished crystal. It wasn't like a holomirror. What it reflected back was flat and detailed in shadow, dark lines contrasting with the pure white of the senatorial robes.

She blinked and saw Talta. She blinked again and saw her mother. She turned away before she blinked and saw herself, because she wasn't sure she wanted to know what that looked like.

'You *are* the empress.'

'Intellectually, I understand that, but it still seems impossible. How can a human be empress of an alien planet?'

'You aren't entirely human,' Ritte reminded her. 'When you were modified with our DNA, you became something very unique.' She walked over to Jinn and took her hands. 'I suspect that you have always been unique, Jinn, even if you couldn't see it. You have always forged your own path.'

'And look where it got me.' Finally, she forced herself to turn back to the mirror. 'I can't face them as human,' Jinn said. She flexed her fingers. She willed the Virena to move.

'But you have to face them,' Li said. 'That's why we came here.'

'I didn't say I wouldn't face them. I said I couldn't do it as human.'

Jinn let the Virena rise to the surface all over her body. It spread across her neck, her face, and shimmered into place. Her hair was enveloped in blue. She took a deep breath. And then she asked it to change.

It sharpened her features, changed her eyes. She didn't model herself on another Sittan female. Instead, she let the Virena make the choice. She let it shape her.

Everyone in the room fell silent.

'Blessed Mountain,' whispered Merion. 'How can this be?'

'Because it isn't,' Jinn told him. Seeing herself so completely transformed was a shock. She didn't even dare look at Dax.

Ritte moved over to Jinn and examined her closely. 'The detail is astonishing,' she said. 'No-one would ever guess you aren't Sittan.'

'Will it work?'

'Yes. Provided you can maintain it.'

'I'll have to,' Jinn said. 'There's no other option.'

Ritte clapped. 'Spoken like a true empress.'

CHAPTER
34

5th February 2208

Nova Settlement, Colony Six, Earth-controlled Space

After he'd left Eve waiting by those two beaten-up rollers, Bryant had made his way back to the training centre with no real idea what he was going to do when he got there. He'd dumped the float bike in the lot by the rear of the centre and strolled back in as if he hadn't a care in the world. Strictly speaking, they weren't supposed to go outside, but Bryant had always ignored rules that he found inconvenient and saw no reason to change his ways now.

He'd gone back to his room and found it exactly as he had left it. He'd packed up his few belongings into the small case that they were all given; a change of uniform, his newly issued ID and comm. He turned the comm. on. It began to flash immediately, and Bryant activated it. His orders downloaded quickly. He looked at what ship he'd been assigned – a Class 2 transporter, perfect – and left the rest for later.

He'd left his room then, not even bothering with a backward

glance, the dull, plain interior already forgotten. Then he went to requisitions to get his ship. There were forms to read through and sign, access codes to memorise, flight plans and codes to be passed over. It was something that Bryant had done many times before and it didn't take long. The ship assigned to him wasn't new, but it would meet his needs.

And it was big enough for two.

Bryant flew it out of the port. He gained some height, and then circled the building a couple of times, nothing to see here, before he eased away and back towards the city. It was designed to flip onto one end so that it could land on a planet like a needle piercing the ground. He tested the landing programme as he set it down in the roller park where he had left Eve.

He opened the hatch and lowered himself out. There was no sign of her. 'Eve!' he called. If she'd gone, he couldn't wait for her. 'Eve!'

A small figure scrambled out of the rusted body of one of the rollers. She didn't wait for further invitation. Bryant only just managed to get out of her way before she grabbed the ladder and hauled herself up into the belly of the ship.

He followed her with both reluctance and enthusiasm.

'Can you just hurry up and get us out of here?' she asked as soon as he made it up the ladder. 'The local police patrol even here. I nearly got caught.'

'I thought you could take care of yourself.' He fired up the engine. It wasn't particularly powerful, but it was new, and it responded with a very satisfying purr. It made the vertical leap out of the lot and up through the shallow atmosphere with ease.

'That was too fast,' Eve said. 'Where are we going, anyway?'

Bryant pulled out his comm. and turned it on. He opened up the packet that contained his orders and flicked through them, quickly at first, and then very, very slowly. 'Earth,' he said.

'Earth? I'm not going to Earth!'

'Want me to take you back to the colony?'

'No!'

'Calm down then,' he said.

She slumped back in her seat. 'Once we're back in neutral space, I'll send a message to the *Mutant*, find out where they are.'

'Hmm,' Bryant said.

'Hmm? What's hmm?'

'Neutral space,' he said. 'It's a warzone. I can't say I'm too keen to go there.'

'Look at me, Bryant. I'm Type Two. If I get caught in Earth-controlled space, I'm dead.'

'Then we're a bit stuck, aren't we?'

They sat in silence for several long minutes, the ship set on a slow trajectory that would take them to a space lane and a direct route to Earth.

'What's the mission?' Eve asked.

'Why?'

'Just curious.'

'Are you always this nosey?'

'Yes,' she said.

'Fine,' Bryant said. He pulled the card from his pocket and shoved it into the slot on the console. It loaded almost immediately, the message popping up on a screen in the middle of the dashboard. There was an image of a man, pink-faced and flabby, with his details and address listed underneath. 'I've got orders to terminate this man.'

Eve sat motionless in her seat. Her hands gripped the armrests so tightly that her knuckles were white. 'That's Weston,' she said.

'Weston who?'

'I don't know his first name. But I met him, once. A long time ago. Before I was modified.'

'Met him where?'

'At the testing centre,' Eve said. 'Where you go to do the tests so they can decide which modifications you're best suited for. You wouldn't know anything about that, being born already perfect.'

'It's hardly my fault!'

'Modest as always,' Eve said. 'He was choosing the kids who went to the Second Species programme.'

Oh. *Oh.* 'But that was what, twenty years ago?'

'Hard to forget the man who put me on the path to becoming this.'

There were many things that Bryant wanted to say. He knew all of them were meaningless platitudes. So he kept them to himself. Or at least he tried. 'It could be worse,' he said.

'How? You might think that you're something special now that you've got your superpowered new body and you're the invincible man. But the rest of the universe hasn't changed. I am still poisonous, people are still afraid of me, and rightly so, and there will never be anywhere that I can go. I will never have a home that isn't a ship. Do you understand that? I will always be a fugitive.'

Although his memory had created large, black spaces, he knew that Eve was responsible for his current state. Bryant had never felt grateful before. He'd always felt that he was entitled to everything he had. He hadn't viewed his life as privileged because he had thought himself deserving of it, and there was no need to be grateful for something that was rightfully yours. He had learned a lot since then.

And he wanted to do something for Eve in return. 'We're going to Earth.'

'Why? Because those are your orders and you're an agent again now? I bet you couldn't wait . . . '

Bryant cut in. 'To find this man Weston and ask him a few questions.'

'I don't want to ask him any questions.'

'Well, I do,' Bryant said. 'Because I think that you need answers.'

He saw her flush, noticing for the first time the pattern that wove up the side of her neck. It was very pretty. She blinked and looked away, so he turned his attention back to the controls. Once they hit the space lane, it was a straight journey to Earth.

Bryant started the autopilot. He'd always been a confident pilot, which was one of the reasons why it had grated on him so much having to share a ship with Jinn. Those had been the days. Perhaps one day he would be able to look back at them with something other than a stinging sense of shame at what a shit he had been, but not today.

They broke atmosphere thirty-eight hours later, and from there it was only a short drop to the surface. Bryant transmitted the codes he'd been given. They were directed to land at the port near Heathrow. A hangar had already been paid for, but Bryant negotiated for a different one. He wanted to make sure that he could retrieve the ship once their business here was finished. He wouldn't be staying. If he hadn't been convinced of that before, he was certainly convinced of it now.

How could he ever have thought that he could slip back into his old life? He'd brought a Type Two female to Earth. It was the exact opposite of what he was supposed to do. He hadn't been able to follow orders for longer than five minutes when before, he'd followed orders to the letter, and revelled in it.

With Eve hidden as much as possible inside his spare jacket, they disembarked and peeped out of the door of the hangar. Bryant had already shown his ID chip to one of the droids. He wasn't quite sure what to do with Eve, but she pulled out a chip on a chain around her neck and whatever was on it satisfied the droid, so that was good enough for Bryant.

Her breath frosted in the air as they made their way to the exit. 'I hate this planet,' she said. 'I never wanted to come back here.'

'Don't you have family? Friends?'

'What difference would that make? I can hardly go home and hug my parents and have some sort of wonderful family reunion.'

'Would you like to?'

She pulled her sleeves down over her hands and pulled her hood further forward. 'No. Not any more. It's been too long and too much has changed. I'm not the person I was when I left here, and I'm not sure she was that great anyway. Where does this Weston bloke live?'

Bryant pulled out his cube again and checked the address. He showed it to Eve and she pulled a face.

'It's too far to walk,' she said. 'We'll need transport.'

'Then let's get transport.'

At the other side of the port was a hire place. It was easy, when you were over two metres tall and pale-haired and wearing a uniform, to get a skimmer. There was even a free upgrade which Bryant accepted with a shrug. He took a cup of hot tea from the machine and gave it to Eve, who had waited outside. She wrapped her cold hands around it gratefully. They climbed into the skimmer and Bryant closed the canopy and put the heater on full whack. Then he programmed the autopilot, and the map popped up in front of them.

'That's a long way round,' Eve said, reaching forward to fiddle with it. 'Why isn't it going down the MF3?'

'I don't know,' Bryant said, and tried to change the route, but it wouldn't let him. 'Looks like we're stuck with it though.'

They entered the Dome through the South tunnel, his codes automatically granting them entry. No stop and search for them, though he saw several battered vehicles coming from the Underworld entrance being waved to the side.

People stood at the edges of the tunnel, holding up signs asking for free transportation into the Dome itself. No-one stopped.

'Should bloody well be free,' Eve grumbled.

'Nothing is. There's always a price.'

'Well, it's not fair.'

'No, it isn't,' Bryant agreed. He switched off the autopilot, suddenly needing something to do with his hands. The steering wheel whirred forward and he wrapped his fingers round it and then shot them up into a higher lane. He was so focused on the road ahead, on avoiding the other transports, that he didn't notice that it had begun to snow.

Snow.

Inside the Dome.

'Look,' Eve said, angling her body so she could look up. 'There's a hole in the Dome.' She half climbed onto the dash to get a better look, putting herself dangerously close to Bryant. 'A bloody massive hole.' She dropped back down into her seat, which was beeping crossly, and it strapped her in firmly.

Bryant leaned forward in his seat and looked up. She was telling the truth. The Dome was broken. The outside was coming in. 'I wonder why they haven't fixed it.'

'Too expensive, too difficult, the repair company went bust and they're waiting for another one. You're on the list and someone will be in touch with you as soon as there's a slot. That's what we were always told when stuff broke downstairs,' she said. 'I guess now those excuses apply upstairs as well.'

Bryant upped their speed a little more, swinging the skimmer to the side and dodging past a series of cars stopped at a hold light. With a quick check, he ran the light and went straight down the turn that would lead them to the outskirts of the city, and the address he'd been given for Weston. It probably would have been wiser to stick to the traffic laws, but he had a sudden desperate urge to be anywhere else.

Eve had been right. They shouldn't have come here. His opinion didn't change when he saw the house, which was small and not particularly well maintained. What possible help could a man who lived here be?

He gritted his teeth. 'Wait here,' he said to Eve. This was a face-saving exercise now, nothing more.

'Alright,' she said. She shrank down a little lower in her seat. 'I don't like it here. Don't be long.'

'I won't,' he said grimly. He exited the skimmer and strode straight up the path. He intended to act as if he was doing something and then go back to the skimmer and tell Eve that there was no-one in, but it didn't quite work out like that.

A light flicked on and scanned up and down the length of his body before he could think to step away, then a panel opened in the door and the unmistakeable nozzle of a blaster folded out. Fortunately for Bryant, his reactions were primed by this point.

He kicked the blaster straight back into the door and then kicked the door open. The impact sang up his leg, but it was a good pain, the sort that made him swear and want to kick something else. The sort that made it feel good to be alive.

Behind the door was a scabby little room. The first thing he noticed was the smell, and the second was a bank of screens showing a full 360 view around the house. A man wearing an unfastened bathrobe and a single sock was stood in the middle of the floor, a toothy little dog under one arm and a fucking enormous blaster in his hand.

Bryant lunged at him.

The blaster went off.

Bryant dodged it, the shot blowing a massive hole in the wall before he grabbed the weapon and pulled it from the man's feeble grip. He was no match for Bryant and dropped like a stone when Bryant whacked him on the side of the head with the butt of the weapon.

He dumped the man on the sofa, pulling the dressing gown to cover up the parts of him that he wished he hadn't seen. Weston's head slumped to one side, but he managed to fix his gaze on Bryant. 'That hurt,' he said.

'It was supposed to. Are you Weston?'

'Who sent you? Was it Bautista? Of course, you probably don't know, do you? Just following orders.'

'That's not important.'

'Ah,' the man said. He attempted to sit up a little straighter, but he couldn't do it without letting go of the little dog, which had gone from barking to shaking and whining. 'It's like that, is it?'

Bryant stared down at the scabby little man in his ugly gold bathrobe. He looked like nothing. He certainly didn't look like someone capable of developing something as complicated and far-reaching as the Second Species programme. 'I want to ask you some questions.'

'I thought you were here to kill me.'

'I am,' Bryant said. 'I mean ... shut up! You were part of the Second Species programme. You know about the modifications, what they are. What they *really* are. I want to know about the Type Two females.'

But Weston wasn't looking at him. He was looking beyond Bryant, leaning a little to the side to get a better look. Keeping his blaster pointed at the man, Bryant risked a glance backwards.

Eve was standing in the doorway.

'I told you to wait in the skimmer!' Bryant said furiously.

'Hello,' Weston said. He got to his feet and moved so that he was looking straight at Eve. There was something in his voice that made Bryant's skin crawl. 'Goodness. Aren't you magnificent?'

Eve didn't respond. She edged back out towards the street, her eyes huge.

'I've never seen one of you in the flesh before,' Weston said, and he sounded quite excited. 'Something I regretted, of course, but it always pays to treat a dangerous weapon with respect.'

'I'm not a weapon,' she said.

'Of course you are, but that's beside the point. Why don't you come in? It's not safe for a lovely young woman such as yourself to stand out there where anyone can see her.'

'Go back to the skimmer,' Bryant said. 'Don't let him anywhere near you.'

'I'm completely harmless,' Weston said. 'If anyone is in danger here, it's me.'

'Eve, go!' Bryant shouted.

She didn't listen. Instead, she came fully into the room, stepping over the pieces of the broken door. If she noticed the state of the room, it didn't show on her face. Instead she turned a laser focus of attention on the little man.

'You're not from the new batch, are you?' Weston asked. His voice went up an octave in his excitement. 'You're too old. But you can't be from the original programme. None of those subjects survived.'

'I did,' Eve said.

The dog yapped.

Bryant glared at it.

It whimpered and peed on the floor.

'You know everything there is to know about us,' Eve said. 'You've looked at all the research, all the test results. You refined the serum so that it could be used on all the women who were sent to Faidal.'

He was too arrogant to deny it. 'Of course. The original formula was highly unpredictable, as I'm sure you're aware. I would love to know how you survived it. Perhaps a skin sample, some hair? Or perhaps blood? I would only need a vial or two.'

'Can it be undone? Can you change me back again? Make me normal?'

Weston turned away from Eve and moved over to a bar in the corner of the room. He poured himself a long measure of a thick, bright pink liquid into a tall glass, then knocked half of it back in one go. 'Why would you want to be normal?'

Eve's question was better than any of the ones Bryant had thought to ask. 'Just give her an answer,' he told Weston.

'It's a little bit more complicated than that.'

'Hardly. It's yes or no. Either you can, or you can't.'

'Then technically, the answer is yes.'

Bryant felt his heart start to pound. He saw Eve's reaction in the same moment, a visible exhale, followed by an immediate straightening of her entire body. The entire room felt tight.

'How?' Eve asked, and it was more than just a question, it was a plea, a lifetime of trying not to hope followed by a second of hoping far, far too much, and he suddenly knew how it was going to end even before it did.

Weston drained his glass. 'Why in the void would I tell you that?'

'Why wouldn't you tell her?' Bryant asked him. 'That information has no value to you.'

'Of course it does.' He let the empty glass dangle from his stubby little fingers. 'All information has value.'

Bryant laughed. He didn't think that he'd ever met such a pompous little prick. 'You do understand that I've got orders to kill you?'

'But you won't,' Weston said. 'You can't get any information from me if I'm dead.'

'Just tell me what to do!' Eve said desperately. 'Whatever you want, I'll give it to you.'

'Skin samples and blood,' Weston said.

'No,' Eve told him. 'Something else.'

Weston shrugged. 'That's the deal.'

'Please,' Eve said, but Weston wasn't listening. He'd turned back to his bottle and was refilling his glass, but there was something different about the way he did it, and Bryant instinctively sensed the danger, even though he didn't know what it was.

'Eve!' he yelled. He saw the flash of the needle and threw himself in front of Weston, shoving Eve out of the way. He felt the pressure as the needle went through his jacket and into his skin and the world went blurry for a second. He heard the yapping of Weston's little dog, felt something shoving at his ankles and fell.

In the confined space of that little room, Bryant was like a steel girder with nowhere to go. He crashed backwards, seeing the wall slide into the ceiling, and grabbed onto whatever he could.

The world flashed black for a second, and then flashed back to normal.

Bryant lifted his head to find that he had his hands clamped on Eve's arm. Her jacket had torn. His hands were on her skin.

And Weston's hands were on her throat.

She blinked, eyes huge and full of shock.

Bryant let go of her as if she'd burned him. He grabbed at Weston, pulled him off, then scrambled back across the room like a crab, heart racing, his lungs shrinking down to the size of a plum. He couldn't breathe. She'd killed him. Again.

Weston made a sound somewhere between a laugh and a scream and then dropped to the floor, foaming at the mouth, legs jerking. Eve was shaking her head and her mouth hung open in a silent scream of horror.

Weston twitched a little longer and then became still, a thick dribble of bubbling slime oozing down his cheek to the floor. His little dog scurried over and sat next to him. It licked at his face, his hands, and then it went glassy-eyed and keeled over.

Bryant could hear a panicked wheezing sound, very loud and very close. It was him. His chest was still tight, but with every breath he tried to take, it got looser, and oxygen started to move back into his bloodstream and his muscles.

Eve was still staring at Weston. 'He knew how to fix me,' she said quietly. 'But he didn't want me to know. Why didn't he want me to know?'

'Because he was a bastard,' Bryant wheezed. Only a complete bastard could have done that, someone with so little humanity left that he felt nothing when faced with the pain of others. Weston had known that there was no way out of this situation. So he'd tried to take Eve with him.

But he'd failed.

Eve kicked the dead man hard in the ribs, and Bryant made no move to stop her. But when she buried her face in her hands and started to sob, he did move. Getting to his feet was surprisingly easy. His breathing was almost steady. This hadn't happened the last time she'd touched him. He almost felt normal, as if the toxins from her body were about as annoying as a hangover and didn't even last as long.

It was then that Bryant did something completely alien to him, completely uncomfortable, and he did it because looking down at Weston and knowing how close he had come to being that cold and that closed off was suddenly very terrifying. He did something he had not done in an age, not even with Davyd and the other boys.

He moved closer to Eve, and then he put his arms around her. It was awkward at first, and stiff, and odd. He couldn't remember the last time he had touched someone just for comfort. Eve went stiff too, and then she softened against him, and her head went against his chest, and she cried into the front of his uniform.

Bryant stroked her hair, then began to gently rock her. 'If there's a way,' he said, 'we will figure it out.'

'Bryant,' she said quietly.

'What?'

'You're touching me.'

Bryant looked down.

His fingers were on her hair, but his thumb was on her cheek.

'I know,' he said. 'I think it's the Type One modifications. I think they make me immune to you.'

She lifted her head and looked up at him. A tear fell when she blinked. 'It would have to fucking be you, wouldn't it?'

'I'm sorry,' Bryant said.

'I still hate you.'

'I know.' He looked around at the disgusting little room, the dead man and the dead dog on the floor. 'And you were right. Coming to Earth was a terrible idea.'

'Hmm,' Eve said. 'So can we leave now?'

'Yes,' Bryant said. 'That sounds like an excellent plan.'

CHAPTER

35

Ever since she had realised that she was the empress, Jinn had been fighting against it. She hadn't wanted to accept it. Now, finally, transformed by the Virena, she saw herself for what she was. What she felt was something completely unexpected.

It was grief.

The young, naïve woman she'd been was gone. What had been done to her could never be undone. Her body felt alien to her because it *was* alien. She had to stop pretending that she could somehow go back to what she had been before. That was never going to happen. This was it, now. It was time to accept that.

She wanted to cry. She couldn't let them see it. She tried to swallow, to concentrate on her breathing and not the burning in the back of her throat or the way her face was trying to screw up into a howl.

The last thing she expected was for Dax to get to his feet and approach her. He moved slowly, warily, as if she was a dangerous animal that might turn around and bite him. 'I want you to transform us,' he said, gesturing at himself and Li.

'No.'

'I'm not asking you,' he said. 'We can't protect you if we can't come with you.'

'I don't need you to protect me,' she told the pair of them. 'Both of you know that.'

'You're about to walk into the senate hall pretending to be the Sittan empress,' Li pointed out, adding the weight of his support to Dax. 'If something goes wrong ...'

'Nothing is going to go wrong.'

'Humour us.'

She didn't want to. 'This was supposed to be simple,' she said. 'But it's getting more and more complicated all the time.'

She transformed Li first. He wore it well, she had to admit, and wondered what Merion would make of him. And then she turned to Dax. 'Take off your shirt,' she ordered him. He unbuttoned it slowly, unfastening the cuffs, and then easing his way out of it. She tried not to look at the kill tattoos on his shoulders. Instead, she focused on the hard breadth of his chest. His heart was beating so hard that she could see the pulse of it in his flesh. The heat in the pod had brought his veins to the surface, and they formed a network of branching lines under his skin. He was so vital, so alive, so human, so precious to her that she almost couldn't bear it.

He shivered when she placed her palm flat against his chest, and the muscles tightened under her hand. Jinn pressed her lips together, and then she closed her eyes and slowly willed the Virena to cover his skin. It slid across him slowly, and she opened her eyes to see it covering him centimetre by centimetre, a shimmering layer that moulded itself perfectly against the shape of his body.

It flowed over his stomach, up and across his shoulders, along his arms, and then up his neck. He breathed a little faster as it covered his face, and then he was gone, and a huge Sittan male stood looking down at her. He wasn't Dax, but he was something else equally as magnificent. She lifted a clawed hand and traced the new lines of his face.

That was the moment when she decided that it didn't matter if what she felt was her or the Virena. There was no difference. Once this was over, she would have him one final time. She knew he wanted her. And it was her right. After that, she would leave. She had to. Otherwise they would become simply another empress and her male slave, and she couldn't do that to Dax.

'We need to go,' Ritte said.

All of them made their way out of the pod and down onto the walkway.

'What now?' Jinn asked Ritte.

'We head to the main meeting hall,' Ritte said. 'We need to take this.'

She gestured to a large boat tethered to the side of the pod. Merion set to work opening the gate and bringing the boat near. Dax and Li flanked Jinn as she boarded, and Merion set the boat in motion.

They sped across the water. Dark shapes filled it, dancing just under the surface, and the heavy mist dampened her skin, and Jinn gripped the edge of the boat and refused to think about what lay ahead. She'd never had to handle a situation like this before, one she could not solve either by running away, or if that was not an option, punching it in the face.

Under the layer of Virena, she began to tremble, though she only realised when she felt a clawed hand settle on her shoulder and turned to see Ritte. 'Remember that they can only see what you want them to see,' she said. 'You do not have to let them know who you are.'

The boat was entering the dock. There were others already present. They were of varying sizes, some much larger, some perhaps

243

half as big. Jinn saw the front of one boat open and a line of Shi Fai crawl out.

The Virena saw them too, and it didn't like them.

When their boat was locked safely in place, Merion opened the front and stepped aside to let Jinn pass. The reassuring bulk of Dax and Li made it easier, and she was glad now that Dax had insisted that they come along.

Ritte took the lead once they were inside. There was so much to take in, so much to see. Jinn had thought, after Sittan, that nothing could surprise her, but she'd been wrong.

They walked along wide hallways with glittering walls and ceilings made of smoke, past trees made of bone, waterfalls that were oily and green, places where the floor was made of a deep purple liquid that supported their weight as they walked on it. Her senses were bombarded with new smells, some sweet and fresh, others earthy and rich, none of them human. It left her wondering what her species had contributed to this place.

Everything about the senate was designed to showcase what was unique and special about each of the races. It was a place to learn, to share, not a place to start a war, and Jinn was appalled that Talta had done so. It also made her even more aware of how difficult this was going to be. Persuading the other members of the senate to forgive the Sittan for what they had done seemed an impossible task. She had nothing to trade and nothing to offer except her word that it would not happen again.

It was not nearly enough.

She wanted to take Dax's hand, to talk about what they were seeing, about how it felt to be here, in a place where all races of the galaxy were welcome, but she didn't. A Sittan empress would not publicly touch a male slave. She certainly wouldn't hold his hand, a gesture that would be betrayingly human.

Finally, they reached the vast senate hall. It was the size of three flyball fields and at least four times as high. She had never seen anything like it. It was all that she could do to keep walking. Beside her, she felt Dax hesitate, and wondered if he felt the same way. It was too much to take in. She understood now why her mother had worked so hard to get here, and harder still to cling on to it once she had.

Ritte led them up to the second level and into a room with curving walls and a shimmering privacy screen. Through it, Jinn could see the other members of the senate. Seeking out the human representative was automatic. She didn't even realise that she was doing it until she found familiar human outlines.

And almost collapsed in her seat.

'Ferona is here,' she whispered.

'What?' Dax asked.

'My mother. She's here.'

'How is that possible? I thought she was kicked out of government months ago.'

'Well, she's managed to get herself back in. Somehow.'

There was no mistaking Ferona, even at this distance. The shape of her head, the line of her body, the way she moved, all of these things were as familiar to Jinn as her own face.

The last time they had met, Ferona had ordered one of her security droids to shoot her. Jinn could still remember the shock of the pain.

Ferona hadn't intended to kill her. She had used Jinn as a tool to manipulate Dax, and it had worked. He had surrendered, allowed himself to be given the final dose of Type One serum and sent to Sittan so that Jinn could live.

And then, for reasons Jinn still didn't fully understand, Ferona had sent her to be modified with the Type One serum. To the best of her knowledge it hadn't been used on a female before or since.

Had Ferona intended her to defeat Talta and take over Sittan? Was that the reason?

It didn't seem possible. No-one could have foreseen this. But she knew one thing. Whatever Ferona's reasons, they would have been selfish.

A chime sounded, a rich combination of bells that Jinn had heard before, on Sittan.

'Ah,' Ritte said. 'The meeting has begun.'

The privacy screen dissolved. Jinn got nervously to her feet, and Ritte pushed her forward towards the circular balcony that projected out from the front. A wall rose up to waist height, keeping Jinn in place as the balcony detached from the booth and carried her down to the floor of the senate hall to stand with the senators from all the other planets. She found herself standing directly opposite Ferona and she wanted to look away, but a Sittan empress would not do that.

So she straightened her shoulders and hoped that no-one would notice that she had no idea what she was doing. It was easier than she had imagined due to a level of formality which set the interaction into a pattern that was simple to follow.

We are too far apart, Jinn thought as she looked at the others. *All of us.* Not just people in the Domes and the Underworld cities, but all of us in this galaxy, and we're so desperately fighting to cling on to what we believe belongs to us. It wouldn't have cost the Sittan or the Shi Fai anything to let us cross their space. But they wanted to show us that they could refuse. And we wanted to show them how clever we are, so advanced that we'll happily mess with our biology with no real idea what the outcome will be, as if we're not already perfectly fine as we are.

'Senator,' said the arbiter, a neat little droid in the centre of the circle, when it was Jinn's turn. 'Please identify yourself.'

She had rehearsed this with Ritte. She was glad of it now, as the words flowed easily, with little conscious thought.

'I am Empress Pocka. I defeated Talta in battle, which according to Sittan law makes me the true empress of the magnificent planet of Sittan, and I have come here as its representative.'

'Do the other senators accept Empress Pocka as the Sittan representative and grant her leave to speak?'

One by one, the others indicated that they did.

It was the first hurdle crossed.

The arbiter turned back to Jinn and motioned to her to continue.

'Talta chose to start a war,' Jinn said. 'That was wrong.' A hush fell across the circle. She gripped the edge of the barrier. 'I called this meeting to put an end to that war. Sittan ships are withdrawing from neutral space as I speak. The Sittan people wish to make reparations for the damage caused to our neighbours. They need only to name their price and it will be paid.'

Again, the arbiter moved around the circle, and as Merion had said, most of the others waved it away. But not all. There were requests for dark rubies and black sand. Jinn granted all of them without argument, hoping that the details could be sorted out later.

And then it was Ferona's turn.

Was it Jinn's imagination, or did her mother's gaze linger a little too long? Had she given herself away, somehow?

'As the representative of the people of Earth,' Ferona said, 'I ask only one thing of Senator Pocka.'

Jinn felt her stomach plunge into her feet and bounce back up again. 'And what is that?'

'Permission for our ships to cross through Sittan-controlled space.'

There was a palpable shift in the atmosphere, a murmur of voices. Jinn found that she wanted to say no, more than anything, she wanted to refuse, though she couldn't explain why.

She pushed it aside.

She forced herself to meet Ferona's gaze. She hadn't known, when she came here, that this was what she was hoping for, but she understood it now.

There was a job to be done here and she intended to do it.

'You have our permission,' she said.

There was only the tiniest of flickers in Ferona's expression, and Jinn would have missed it if she hadn't been looking for it.

'Good,' Ferona said.

But the meeting wasn't over.

There was a squeal from the Shi Fai senator, the same furious, high-pitched sound that Jinn had heard before, when she'd cut the hand off one that had tried to grab her.

Uh-oh.

Her fear was not misplaced.

'We will not have humans crossing our space!' it said. 'If the humans want passage to their new planet, they will have to cross our space, and we do not grant them permission!'

Jinn stared down at it.

She forgot who she was, and where she was. All she could see was this poisonous little creature, standing in the way of human survival. Anger exploded inside her. She wasn't aware that the Virena pushed at it, interfering with the neurochemicals inside her body, driving that rush of feeling. 'You will,' she told it. '*You will.*' A snap of her fingers and her blades were out. They felt as light as air but nothing had ever been sharper or more dangerous. She walked towards the Shi Fai senator, her white robes swirling around her powerful legs, kicking the arbiter out of her way.

These creatures, who had hurt so many human females, women like Eve and Mady, as well as the countless others they had taken from trading posts and stations over the years, would not be allowed to hurt anyone else. She would destroy them all if she had to, starting with this one.

A strong hand caught her upper arm and yanked her back, and she spun to find an unfamiliar Sittan male with familiar eyes staring down at her. Her blade stopped a hair's breadth from his face. 'Don't,' he said quietly.

'Why not?' Jinn asked him.

'It isn't what we came here for.'

'Maybe it should be.'

She could smell him. His fingers tightened on her arm. Her blades were so close to his throat. He looked down at her, not blinking, refusing to turn away, and she thought of the Shi Fai she had wounded on board the Europa, so many months before, and the fear and the fury she'd seen in him afterwards. He had no love for the Shi Fai. But for her ... 'It's your choice,' he said, and she knew that he was talking about more than just the Shi Fai. 'But whatever you decide, remember one thing. You are the one who has to live with it.'

Jinn snapped her teeth at him, the response of an empress to an insubordinate male.

Then she slowly willed in her blades. She turned back to other senators. 'I am not Talta,' she told all of them. 'I do not want to go to war with you. But if anyone tries to stop me from fixing what has been done, I will personally hunt you down and make you regret that choice. Do we have an understanding?'

A murmur rippled through them all.

The Shi Fai senator stepped back. 'We will give the humans passage,' it said.

And so it was done.

CHAPTER

36

6th Day of the Fourth Turn

The Palace, Fire City, Sittan

They came in the darkness. Their ships were silent. They crept through the streets, raiding the houses and the dormitories and the prayer halls. The Sittan were caught unprepared and, even worse than that, they had no way to defend themselves.

Talta watched from the highest window of the palace as daylight fell and those who remained ran out of their homes, screaming for their murdered children. She stood straight and steady as she slowly made her way back down to the main hall of the palace.

None of the females inside the palace spoke to her, and they watched her with cold eyes, their anger oily and thick and choking. Talta lifted her head and straightened her spine. She was not afraid of them. She curled her fingers, summoning the Virena before she remembered that the Virena was gone, and the fear that she had refused to feel came rushing in.

She saw movement in an archway and a trio of children were

pushed out, followed by a female with a scar across her face. It ran from her neck into the side of her mouth and gave her an ugly, lopsided look.

'They killed my daughter,' the female spat. She thrust a hand up towards the sky. 'They burned my fields. Their ships came through our defences. How did they manage that, Talta?'

Talta. Not empress.

She felt the slow roll of true fear move through her. She had no male to protect her now. She turned away from the female and continued to walk, each step requiring an impossible amount of energy. The Shi Fai had come here, to her planet. They were burning crops and killing those who stood in their way. And if the Shi Fai had come here, it would not be long before others did, too.

Dark rubies fetched a high price. Sittan oils were highly prized. And Talta had not been kind in her dealings with her neighbours. They all had reason to hate her. Some of them would come for revenge. She had taunted them with the invincibility which the Virena had afforded her. She had been the longest-standing empress and she'd had no reason to think that things would ever change.

But they had.

She staggered to the front of the palace, out through the huge main doors, and down into her city. She didn't have to go far before she saw scuff marks in the dirt and droppings from the great animals that the Shi Fai had flown in on, stinking piles of mess riddled with crawling vermin. The smell made her gag. It needed to be cleaned away but there was no-one to clean it. Further into the city she saw where one of the creatures had crashed into the side of a building. It lay on the ground, broken and still, already starting to desiccate in the dry Sittan heat.

Talta forced herself to walk over to it. It was a huge beast the size of a caravan, with two heads and a dense ridge of bone along its back. Its wicked tail lay bent and broken. There were two giant wings, thick as hide and covered in hard white scales. It wasn't beautiful. It wasn't something to covet. It was dirty and unpleasant and didn't belong on her planet.

She turned to find a crowd gathering behind her. The few remaining females huddled together. Their fear was palpable. Children stood in front of them. There were males, too, crippled and weak, the ones who had not been able to fight in the arena and so had never been tested. This was all that was left of the Sittan people, the proud and strong race that she had ruled for so many turns. Old females and useless males.

'How did they get through?' shouted one of the females. 'Why didn't the Virena protect us?'

Talta didn't answer. She turned and started back towards the palace. If they decided to rush her, to pelt her with stones, there was nothing she could do. But instead, the other females formed a long procession behind her. They were a sorry gathering. They bore no resemblance to the screaming crowds that had filled the arena to watch the males fight, who had gloried in violence and had thought themselves indestructible. Most clutched hand-stitched bags containing what little possessions they could carry. A few pushed carts. The terrified children and piteous males brought up the rear. Every few minutes, they would glance up at the sky, as if they expected to be attacked even though the skies were clear.

They were almost at the gate when it happened. They seemed to come from nowhere. Shadows swept across the ground, huge patches of black that had the females cowering and screaming. The first of the creatures landed on the bridge, its huge maw open, huffing out wet, stinking breath and showing thick blunt teeth. It had two eyes on each side of its head, one below the other, and a single horn in the centre. Shi Fai slid down the sides of the creature. These ones weren't like those she had met at the senate, or the ones she'd seen in neutral space when she'd travelled as a young female. They were much taller and meatier and didn't seem to have eyes. They sniffed at the air with two thick, leathery tongues that emerged from the side of their bodies, and scampered on six thick legs that ended with a dozen highly flexible digits that bent in all directions.

The lizards in the courtyard lifted their heads at the sound as another huge shadow swept over the side of the palace, and Talta noticed for the first time that her beloved home had started to fade from glistening black to dull grey.

The monster swooped. The lizards leapt high and struck, biting deep into leathery flesh. Talta stumbled forward across the bridge, each step difficult, her legs so weak and heavy. She had to get inside, away from these horrible creatures. The palace would protect her. Its walls were strong. Nothing could get through them.

She was halfway across the bridge when her lizards brought the monster down. It crashed through the centre of that great expanse of rock, smashing a massive hole through the centre of it, shaking the ground with a tremendous thud when it impacted against the surface below. There was nothing she could do to help those on the far side of the bridge, cut off now from the safety of the palace, or those who had been in the way when the creature had fallen.

Talta looked up to see four more of them bearing down on the palace, and others circling over the city. They filled the sky. The suns were starting to set.

She did not think that the dark would stop them.

A group of older females emerged from the palace. They ran up to Talta and gathered her up and carried her inside the palace, into safety, and the younger females pushed the doors closed. Outside, the palace had seemed like a place of safety. But now that she was in it, Talta knew that they were lost.

The Virena was gone, and she did not know if it was ever going to come back. But as long as she was still alive, she was still the ruler of this planet, and these were still her people.

And she needed, somehow, to protect them.

CHAPTER

37

Dax had come to the senate for one reason and one reason only, and that was to protect Jinn. He didn't care about anything else. It didn't matter how powerful she was. She was in danger here.

He swept her along the tunnel that led from their box and back in the direction of their boat, inwardly cursing the design of this place. It made a swift exit impossible. If it hadn't been for Ritte, he would have taken the wrong turn at least twice. Merion flanked her other side, with Li at the rear.

He wasn't sure which of the other senators would strike first. He only knew that one of them would. The most important thing he had learned from his time as a pirate was to listen to fear, when it came, and it was with him now, burning in every cell of his body. Danger was close.

'In,' he said shortly, when they reached the dock, and their boat. 'Quickly.'

She didn't argue, not that he would have listened to her if she had. Instead, she stood at the prow with her arms folded. The Virena still covered her face. Her chest rose and fell with each breath she took, and she stared off into the distance.

'You did everything right,' Dax said in a low voice, as he went to stand beside her. He wanted to reach out, to take her hand, but he didn't. The weight of the Virena on his body was making him sweat. More than anything, he wanted to ask her to remove it, but he knew that it was vital that they keep up the pretence that they were Sittan until they were back on their ship and there was no possibility that anyone would see them. He hated it, though. He didn't think that he had ever hated anything so much.

The little boat bumped against the dock next to their pod, bouncing away and back in again before Merion could lock it in place. Dax didn't wait for the side of the boat to lower. He put one foot on the edge and vaulted over it then turned, set his hands to Jinn's waist, and lifted her over. The sweep of her robes caught on the edge of the boat and she snatched at them, yanking them free, the blue of her face flickering momentarily back to her pale, human skin as she did so.

When she flicked back to blue, Dax felt it like a punch to the gut.

'Straight to the ship,' he said, but she was already halfway up the steps to the pod, the door sliding open in anticipation of her entry. What was she doing? He had no choice but to follow her. She slammed to a halt just inside the doorway, the collar of the robe halfway down her back, and he almost slammed into her.

Ferona Blue sat neatly on a low seat facing the door. Her senatorial robes pooled on the floor around her ankles, the white contrasting starkly with the dark red of the furniture but matching the white of her hair and skin so perfectly that they would have merged into one if it weren't for the jet-black fire of her eyes.

She rose slowly to her feet. She straightened her robes, smoothing each side with a perfectly manicured hand. She had jewelled bracelets on each wrist, and her nails were blood-red. Her skin was flawless. Her hair, though not quite as pale as Jinn's, swept back from a youthful face that was almost identical to her daughter's.

But she wasn't Jinn.

The nose wasn't quite the same. The eyes were harder. There was a cruel line to her mouth. But the similarities made him want to look away. He didn't let himself.

'Senator Blue,' Jinn said finally. 'I didn't expect to see you here.'

Ferona smiled. And it was in that moment that Dax knew. There wasn't time to say anything, to warn Jinn, and in hindsight, he didn't know what he could possibly have said.

'I didn't expect to see you either, Jinnifer.'

He felt Jinn sway. He grabbed her upper arm, leant her his strength, realising his mistake when he noticed Ferona's gaze slide to where his fingers met Jinn's bicep. Up to that point, there had still been a chance to deny it.

But Sittan males did not touch the empress if they wanted to keep their heads.

'And Dax is with you,' Ferona said. 'How ... sweet.'

He felt a ripple on the surface of his skin, followed by a splash of cold. On this edge of his vision he saw Jinn shimmer from blue back to her human self. 'How did you know?'

'A mother can recognise her own daughter in the dark,' Ferona said.

'Even a mother who let a nanny droid do all the work?'

Ferona's face hardened. 'That disguise, remarkable though it was, was hardly going to fool me. You used the Virena, I take it?'

'What do you want, Mother?'

'To thank you, of course. You have given us what I always wanted. A chance at survival. More than a chance.' Her dark eyes were fiercely bright. 'You really are magnificent. I always knew you had the potential, though I have to admit that I had given up all hope of you ever fulfilling it. But you have managed to surprise me.

You can control the Virena, can't you? I always thought there had to be more to it than Talta revealed. We've barely even begun to understand its potential. With this, we could ... '

'You'll do nothing,' Jinn said. She took a step forward, tugging herself free from Dax's hold. 'I didn't do this for you. This isn't going to be some sort of emotional reunion where we hug and forgive each other. I almost died because of what you did.'

'You look very much alive to me.'

'No thanks to you,' Dax said. He was trembling with rage. 'I watched you order a droid to shoot your own daughter. You were willing to deny her access to medical treatment, in order to get what you wanted. You sent her to the A2 and had her modified against her will.'

'And then she went to Sittan to rescue you and started a war.' Ferona's exquisite face hardened even further, becoming all of a sudden sharp and ugly. 'Do you really want to play that game with me, Dax?'

She was unbelievable. 'It's not a game,' he said. 'This is real. Do you understand that? We're talking about people's lives. About what happens now. A year from now. Fifty years from now.'

Ferona tilted her head to one side. 'I'm fully aware of what this is. I've been living it for the past twenty years. I haven't been hiding from reality in neutral space.'

'No,' Jinn said. 'You've been hiding from it in your Dome apartment instead. Go home, Ferona. Go back to Earth. You've got more important things to do than this.'

'And where will you go?'

'What?'

'Where will you go, Jinnifer? What are you going to do?'

'That has nothing to do with you.'

'Come with me,' Ferona said then. She rose to her feet, took a step forward, and held out her hand. 'There's much work to be done, and you could be useful. Think of it. It's obvious that you have an aptitude for politics, for negotiation. Of course you do. I made sure of it. This is what you were meant to do. Come back to Earth with me. Assist me in starting the exodus to Spes. And then, when the time is right, we will travel there together. We can start a new life as leaders of the new world. With the Virena ... '

'Do you ever stop for a minute and think about what you've done?' Jinn responded. 'Do you ever think about all the lives you sacrificed? All the men who died in the dirt on Sittan? All the women left to suffer on Faidal?'

'They knew what they were getting themselves into.'

'No, they didn't. The government lied to them. *You* lied to them. Their blood is on your hands, Ferona, and if you seriously think that I will set that aside and come back to Earth with you so that you can use me to prove that you were right all along, you are very much mistaken. There's more than your career at stake now. Your actions haven't just hurt humans. You threw a boulder into a pond and you didn't stop for a second to think about the ripples.'

Ferona stared at her daughter. It was as if she was looking at someone she'd never seen before. She had really thought that Jinn would go with her, Dax realised. After all this time, and everything that she had done, she still thought of her daughter as property.

But Jinn didn't belong to anyone.

'Stop this at once,' Ferona snapped. 'Now I appreciate that this charade was necessary for the senate, but it's nothing more than that. You are coming back to Earth.'

'No, I'm not,' Jinn said. 'I'm sorry that things are in a mess on Earth. If I thought that there was anything I could do to help fix it, I would. But there isn't. Second species aren't welcome there. We know that Type Two women have been stopped from entering Earth-controlled space. They haven't been allowed to go home.'

'Because they're incredibly dangerous!'

'So are we,' Dax pointed out. 'You might want to remember that.'

Then he turned his attention to Jinn. There was a dark shadow under her skin and a fire in her eyes. It was definitely time to go. She pushed her way past him, bumping her shoulder against his chest, and disappeared outside.

Dax took one last look at Ferona. 'She's your child,' he said. 'Made inside your body, using your DNA, built from every mouthful of food you ate and every breath you took. She wanted to love you. That's all any child wants. To love their mother. But you made that impossible. You ignored her until she was useful to you, and then you hurt her in order to get to me. And then, to really drive the point home, you made her Type One. So from one scumbag to another, let me give you a piece of advice.'

Ferona simply stared at him, her mouth tightened into a furious little pucker.

'Don't piss her off,' he said. He didn't wait to hear her response. He didn't care what she thought. Jinn was his only concern now. Straight out of the pod, then he sprinted along the walkway towards the transporter, not pausing to look at the sea or the fish. He just wanted to get away from this planet. The ramp was still down and he ran straight onto it, catching up with Jinn before she reached the top. The ship began to move. Then Jinn turned, and her arms went around his body, and she buried her face against his neck. Her shoulders shook. She didn't make a sound.

Dax scooped her up.

The transporter was small, even more so with the other three on board. There was only one place they could have some privacy. He carried her straight to the back of the ship, past the foldaway bunks and into the chemicleanse. The door closed when he jabbed his elbow against the lock.

There wasn't much room to move, especially not for two larger than average humans.

'I stink of that place,' she said. She pulled at her jacket, but her hands were shaking, and her fingers fumbled with the zip. 'I can smell them on me. All of them. I can't bear it.' She tugged harder, but it stuck, and he saw her eyes fill with tears, and it was agony.

'Here,' he said, gently pushing her hands aside. 'Let me.'

He slowly slid the zip down, and eased the jacket off her shoulders, tossing it into the corner of the unit. She didn't resist as he carefully removed the rest of her clothes. Her hair hung in a thick tail down the centre of her back, her shoulders lined with dark kill tattoos, an indelible reminder of her time on Sittan. The spray turned on as soon as she stepped into the unit.

She stood with her back to him. Dax stayed where he was, watching as the clear liquid cascaded over her skin.

'It's done,' he said to her. 'You never have to go back to that place again.'

'It was something, though. Wasn't it?'

'It was.'

'All those different species, together in one place. Makes you wonder what it would be like if . . . if . . . '

'The senators weren't creatures like Talta and Ferona.'

She glanced back at him over her shoulder. Ropes of wet hair clung to her face, and her eyes were huge and dark, with a gold shimmer to them that sent a shiver down his spine. It had been a long time. A very long time. Her body called to him. 'Will it happen to me?' she asked him. 'Will I become like them?'

'No,' he told her. He slowly began to unbutton his own shirt. 'Never. There was something broken in both of them long before they joined the senate.'

She held up a hand. The Virena swirled under her skin. 'What about this?' she asked him.

Dax pulled off his shirt and dropped it to the floor. His hands went to the waistband of his trousers. He was hard and ready and he wanted only to please her. 'I don't care about that.'

'She wanted to take it from me,' Jinn said.

'I won't let her.' He didn't know where those words had come from. He didn't care. He sank to his knees in front of her and buried his face at the apex of her thighs.

He told himself that all that mattered was Jinn. The heat of her skin and her long cry of pleasure, hard worked for and long overdue. The Virena wasn't part of this. It had nothing to do with him, or with Jinn. It didn't frighten him.

But he was lying to himself, and he knew it.

CHAPTER

38

8th February 2208

Park Lane Hotel, Mayfair District, London Dome, Earth

The return trip from Kepler had been uneventful and quite frankly boring. Ferona had used the time for various beautifying procedures and other such tweaks so that the healing process could take place before she returned home. Space travel and Kepler always took so much out of her. But she was impatient to be back on Earth.

There was much to be done.

Ships had to be ordered. The building work would take time, though she was sure there would be a way to speed up the process. Crew and passengers would have to be carefully vetted and trained. The first few months on Spes would be difficult, as many of the skills needed to survive in that sort of environment had been lost, and the first wave of travellers would be responsible for setting up what would be needed by those who followed.

Her mind whirred through all these things, working at a thousand kilometres an hour as she dictated notes to an assistant droid.

Dumping her thoughts in this way allowed her to clear them from her head and make much-needed space for new ones. But one thought persisted over all others.

She had done it. She had achieved the impossible, and she had done it with no help from anyone else. Her only disappointment was that Jinn had refused to come back to Earth with her. Perhaps she should have expected it. Jinn had a long history of making poor choices. But Ferona had thought, when she saw Jinn at Kepler, that her daughter would finally realise the opportunity that she'd been given and how much of that was down to Ferona.

Her transporter was escorted through Earth-controlled space by six police jumpers. They followed her to the landing field close to the London Dome. Ferona used the time to change her clothes and have her beauty droid fix her hair and makeup. When she checked her appearance in the holomirror, she noticed a row of spots running across her jawline, just on one side, ugly bumps under the skin. The droid worked on that area of her face for another ten minutes but they were no less visible.

It was the only blemish on an otherwise perfect day.

She wrapped a lavender silk scarf around her neck, tucking her chin into the folds to hide her spots, and hid her hands inside matching suede gloves, checked her reflection one more time, and was ready to disembark.

The steps rolled down on the side of her transporter. Dubnik was waiting for her at the bottom. His hands were buried in his pockets but his face had lost the gaunt, half-starved look and the skin was no longer stretched tight over the bone.

Next to him stood Bautista.

And by his side, a very tall, pale-haired man in a starched dove-grey uniform that was struggling not to split at the seams. Lined up along the landing pad were more men of the same build.

Ferona knew what they were. She'd seen men like this before. But they had all been dark-haired and pale-eyed and waiting to be shipped off to Sittan. They had not been Dome-raised agents. What in the void was going on here? When she'd left, Vexler had just come out of his coma. The government had been in chaos. When she'd received a call begging her to go to Kepler, she'd expected to return to find Bautista on gardening leave. But here he was.

There were security droids patrolling the perimeter. The wind blew around them, tugging at her coat and her hair as she approached Dubnik. 'Ferona,' he said. 'Welcome back.' There was a grim tone to his voice and the warning was clear.

'Thank you,' Ferona said. He held her gaze for a beat too long. She saw the terror in his eyes.

Scared and furious, she turned her attention to Bautista. She licked her lips. The huge man stood next to him was watching her intently, with the same still, unblinking, predatory stare as a venomous snake.

'Welcome back, Ferona,' Bautista said, with a smile that showed too many teeth. 'Let me be the first to congratulate you on a successful trip to Kepler.'

'Thank you,' Ferona replied. She was desperate to ask about Vexler, but something told her not to. 'It was a difficult trip, but ...'

'The Sittan capitulation is welcome, of course,' he said, continuing on as if she hadn't said a word. 'But I always knew that if we refused to give in to the threat, they would give up and go home. There was never any real danger to the people of Earth.'

'They killed almost a million people in neutral space,' Ferona told him.

His eyes narrowed, black and full of poison. 'The official figure is less than a thousand.'

'The exact figure isn't important,' Dubnik said. 'What matters is that the Sittan have declared a truce.'

You coward, Ferona thought. *You snivelling, arse-licking coward.*

'Indeed,' Bautista said. 'And the government and the people of Earth are very grateful for your efforts, Ferona. You will of course be compensated and your contribution recognised. And as a show of appreciation, an apartment will be reserved for you in the new development on Colony Seven.'

'Why would I want an apartment on Colony Seven?' Ferona asked in surprise. 'We'll be starting the migration to Spes within six months.'

'Oh,' Bautista said, and he laughed. 'No-one is going to Spes, Ferona. You didn't really think that was going to happen, did you?'

'We have safe passage through Sittan and Shi Fai space. Of course it's going to happen.'

'No,' Bautista said. His tone was sharp. 'Our days of bargaining with our alien neighbours are over. I am putting in place a hard border at the edge of Earth-controlled space. Nothing comes in or goes out. We will no longer be pushed around by the senate, or by anyone in it. We make our own laws and we dictate our own future. Humans are a superior species and always have been.'

Then he turned and marched off to the waiting car. The door rolled shut and it set off at speed, leaving Dubnik and Ferona standing alone in the middle of that group of Type One agents.

'What in the void is going on?' she asked Dubnik quietly.

'Things are very fragile right now. We have to be careful.' He glanced at the agents. 'He's insisting that Vexler undergo competency testing before he returns to office, and the official word is that Vexler agrees.'

Allowing him to delay and delay and delay. 'When?'

'Six weeks,' Dubnik said.

A second car rolled to a stop in front of them. Ferona climbed straight in. 'I'm not waiting six weeks,' she told him, and pressed the pad to close the door.

She would have Bautista out of office by the end of the day.

CHAPTER

39

8th February 2208

> Vessel: The *Mutant*. Battleship/carrier hybrid
> Location: Sector Five, Neutral Space
> Cargo: N/A
> Crew: 33
> Droids: 7

'I have to go back there,' Jinn said. 'Dax, I don't have a choice. Surely you must understand that.'

They were on the control deck. Jinn sat in the captain's chair and Dax sat at her feet, his head resting against the side of her leg, her fingers casually tangling in his hair. The viewscreen was on. Space stretched out in front of them, silent and peaceful, their fleet drifting in a gentle arc.

He had known this moment was coming. He'd known even before they left Kepler. But he hadn't let himself believe it. 'There's always a choice,' he said, shifting his position a little so that he could look up at her.

Jinn shook her head. 'Not this time. You heard what the Shi Fai senator said. Talta left the planet undefended. Without the Virena, they've got nothing but a lot of enemies. Talta did terrible things to all the other species, not just humans, and that has made the Sittan a target.'

'I still don't see why you have to be the one to do something about it.'

She reached out and took his hand, linking her fingers with his. 'Because there is no-one else.'

'You make it sound like you think you're to blame for this.'

'Maybe I am.'

'Whatever is happening on Sittan, it's not our problem. It's not *your* problem.'

'Of course it's my problem.'

'Why?'

'Do you really need me to explain it?'

Dax could feel his temper starting to build. 'Actually, yes. We went to Kepler to put an end to the war. We've done that. Neutral space is open for business. It's over, Jinn. We're done. We don't owe anyone anything.'

'What about Ritte? Merion? The other females? What about everyone else on Sittan? Something is wrong on that planet. I can feel it.'

'The Sittan can deal with it.'

'The Sittan can't deal with it. That's the point. They've got nothing. They killed all their males. They sent their healthy females into neutral space to fight their stupid war. Everyone left on the planet is either old or a child. They relied on the Virena to protect them and it's right here with me.' She thrust up a hand and a swirling, oily cloud quickly enveloped it. 'I've got to take it back.'

Everything in him rebelled against that idea. He wanted her to stay with him, here on the *Mutant*, to freeze time and hold on to what they had. The war was over. The fighting had stopped. His dreams still took him back to the arena, but when he awoke, she let him pleasure her, and that was enough. 'No.'

'No?'

He couldn't tell her. 'The *Mutant* can't make it to Sittan,' he said, a half-truth. The ship could survive it. The problem lay with its captain.

'I don't need it. I'll go with the fleet.'

'But . . .'

'I've got to take the Virena back there, Dax. It can't stay here in neutral space. And the females know something is wrong on Sittan. They want to go home.'

'What's stopping them?'

'They won't leave their empress unguarded.'

His hand began to burn. He let go of her, holding his wrist and staring at his scorched palm in shock. What in the void was that? The dark pattern on her arm began to shift and change. It moved over her neck, curling up towards her temple. He felt as if it was taunting him. It had seen all of his most shameful moments. It knew what Talta had done to him, what she'd been able to make him do, what she'd been able to make him feel.

Did Jinn know it too? Could she become that cold, that cruel? He had told her that she wasn't like Talta. Or her mother. But with each day that passed, she gave a little more of herself to the Virena. He knew it even if Jinn did not. If she returned to Sittan, it would be only a matter of time before there was nothing of her left. He didn't think that he could bear to witness that.

With his back against the wall, Dax admitted one final, agonising truth, first to himself, and then to Jinn. 'If you go, I'm not coming with you.'

'Why not?'

'I won't go back there. The things I did on that planet, what I became . . . I won't do it. I can't.' If he went with her, and she became what he feared . . .

'It won't be the same. This time you'll know who you are. You'll be yourself. There'll be no fights in the arena.'

She was wrong. He would be little more than a slave. She might not be able to see it yet, but Dax could. 'But there will be a fight,' he pointed out. 'We already know that the Shi Fai are on that planet, and I don't think they will leave willingly.'

'It's not the same as the arena,' she persisted. 'What happened there was about power and greed. This is about right and wrong.'

'And who gets to decide what those are? Is it us? What makes us so special?'

'Is this about Talta?'

'Why would it be about Talta?'

'Because she controlled you. She won't be able to do that again. She can't make you do anything, Dax. Not any more.'

No, he thought. *But you can*. He shook his head. For the first time, he saw a flicker of uncertainty, and that gave him hope. Maybe, just maybe ... but no. 'Talta isn't the issue.'

'Then what is?'

How could he tell her, when he could barely figure it out himself? All he knew was that the thought of going back to Sittan terrified him. He couldn't do it. Not even for Jinn.

'Please,' he said. 'Don't go back there. Stay with me. Just for a few more days. Once we know what's happening on Sittan, then we'll ...'

'I have to go. I don't have a choice.'

Her skin flashed pale and familiar again, and then the Virena flashed back, and this time there seemed to be even more of it. She stood, towering over him, and he stayed where he was, prostrate at her feet. 'I'm sorry,' she said. 'But I have to do this. I thought you of all people would understand.'

Then she walked off the control deck. The doors spiralled shut behind her. Eventually, Dax moved from the floor to his seat. The lingering heat from her body surrounded him.

He could start over, he reasoned. He had his ship. Neutral space would return to normal eventually. He had Grudge, he had the boys. Maybe they could go back to the Articus and rebuild it. It wouldn't be a bad life. He had to find Eve. She'd need him, she always had. Jinn would become a precious memory that he took out and looked at in private and nothing more.

It wasn't enough and it wasn't the life that he wanted and he couldn't convince himself that it was.

He ran to the docking bay. Jinn was still there, doing something to the rear heat exchanger of a small ship.

'Jinn, wait!'

He saw the Virena swirling around her arms, the fierce blue light in her eyes. It was the first time, he realised, that he'd truly seen her for what she'd become rather than what he wanted her to be. The woman he'd met on board the A2 was gone. Forever.

He didn't move closer. He had wanted to tell her how desperately he loved her. Now he could find only the words he had already said. 'I meant it. If you go to Sittan, I'm not coming with you.'

She turned away from him. 'I know.'

'Please don't go,' he begged, hating himself for it. 'You only think something is happening on Sittan because the Virena wants you to. It wants you to go back there, and so it's giving you a reason.'

'You make it sound like it's controlling me.'

'Isn't it?'

She didn't have an answer for him.

'It will destroy you,' he told her. 'Just like it destroyed Talta. I saw what it did to her, Jinn, and it's doing the same thing to you.'

'You're wrong,' she said. He could almost hear the Virena hissing. 'You don't know anything about it.' When she looked at him, her eyes were wild. She ran up the ramp of her ship. 'You want to take it from me!'

'How can I?' he shouted back. 'I'm a man! It hates men!'

But it was too late.

She was gone.

CHAPTER

40

10th Day of the Fourth Turn

Fire City, Sittan

Heading back to Sittan had never been part of the plan, and yet here she was, and Jinn couldn't shake the feeling that it was inevitable. The last time she had left she had been running away. Her only aim had been escape. But if she had learned anything, it was that if you ran, you always left unfinished business behind, and one day it would catch up with you. She had found that out the hard way on Kepler when she'd come face to face with her mother.

She wondered if things would be different when humankind finally made it to their new home planet, and she wondered, too, if it was just another type of running away. Would they learn from the mistakes made on Earth? They would have to. There wasn't going to be a third chance. Humans were going to have to learn how to live with their new planet, not see it as something that existed simply to be used until it was used up, and then abandoned.

Sittan loomed into view. It didn't look like Earth, which was mostly white and surrounded by a dense layer of trash. It was a deep orange red, the colour of fire. Dark patches of mountain mottled the surface. There was little cloud cover. The three suns prevented it. It spoke to her of heat and fire, of something that could warm her chilled bones and bring life back to her body. She didn't need Dax when she had this.

'It's beautiful, isn't it?' Jinn said.

'Yes,' Ritte replied. She sighed. 'But being beautiful doesn't mean something isn't cruel.'

'You don't want to go back, do you?'

'No,' the Sittan female said. 'I can't say that I do.'

'Then I'm sorry to be the one making you go.' Jinn stared at that hot, red planet. She refused to think about Dax, about what he had said to her before she left, about how much she already missed him. She couldn't. If she did, she was afraid that the pain of it might tear her apart. After everything they had been through, what they had survived simply so that they could be together, she was alone.

She brought the ship down to land on a flat plane of rock at the edge of the Fire City. It was dark. The larger transporter, which contained the Sittan females, settled easily and quietly in position next to her smaller ship, guided down by a glowing stripe of Virena that Jinn willed out to light their way. The rest of her fleet was only one jump behind. They'd be here soon enough.

The females disembarked and lined up. Jinn looked them over. This, at least, was something. They were tall and strong and she wondered now how she could ever have thought them ugly. She understood the power that she had over them. She knew that they resented it.

'This is your home,' she told them. 'I'm an outsider here. I didn't come to your planet intending to take it from you, and I'm sorry that I have. But your people are in danger. Something is happening here. Whatever it is, I'm going to put a stop to it, and I'm asking you to help me. You can choose not to. You can go home, to your families, your lives. You don't have to join me.'

Ritte translated her words into Sittan, for those who were less familiar with the universal language.

None of them walked away.

So Jinn took the lead with Ritte at her side, and together, they made their way through the city. Merion and Li took up position directly behind the two of them. It was very quiet. The houses were dark, doors and windows blocked from the inside, and there was a faint smell in the air that didn't seem quite right. It was the wrong time of day for the heat to have driven everyone inside. It had to be something else.

They were almost at the palace when they caught sight of a strange group of Sittan. Li immediately moved in front of Jinn, but she waved him back. She approached the group alone. They were all males, bent and stooped with age, carrying axes and spears that seemed completely out of place in their gnarled hands.

One of them lunged at Jinn, his spear wedged under his arm and held at right angles to his body. She neatly sidestepped it and he stumbled, the tip of the spear sticking into the ground. Ritte placed a foot on it and snapped it in half.

The male looked up at her from his position with one knee in the dirt, and snarled something in Sittan.

Ritte said something back that had him paling and listing slightly to one side. He switched his attention to Jinn. One tug on what remained of the spear made it obvious that he wasn't going to be able to pull it free, so he left it where it was and scrambled back to the other males.

Another tossed down his axe and walked right up to Jinn. He dropped to his knees in front of her. Spikes rippled out over his head and neck. 'I was there,' he said. Ritte translated his words into the universal language. 'I saw her defeat Talta. The female does not lie.'

273

He held something out to Jinn. It was a long, intricate chain with a finger-sized dark ruby hanging from it.

'Take it,' Ritte told her. 'Quickly.'

Jinn did as she was told. She hung it around her neck because that seemed the most sensible place for it. Whether or not that was the right thing to do, she didn't know, but it seemed to satisfy the males.

'They come in raiding parties,' another said. 'We never know when or where they will strike, or how often.'

'Who?'

'The Shi Fai.'

Just as the Shi Fai senator at Kepler had told them. 'Any others, or is it just them?'

'A Prene ship also broke atmosphere, but it landed in the sand sea and burned up on impact.'

Jinn took a second to digest this. Just Shi Fai. But others were trying, and it wouldn't be long before they succeeded.

'Where is Talta?'

'In the palace,' he said. 'Many of the females are with her. We were refused entry.'

He didn't explain why. He didn't have to.

A horn blew somewhere off in the distance, booming out a single, terrifying note. The male immediately tensed. He turned, as if he wasn't sure whether to stay or to go.

'What is it?' Jinn asked him.

'A warning,' he said grimly. 'Their ships are approaching.' He looked up, scanning the skies, and Jinn did the same. Her human vision wouldn't have been able to see anything. Fortunately her Type One vision was a bit better.

There were what looked like huge white birds in the distance, but as they drew closer, Jinn realised that they were not birds at all, but something far more alien.

They had huge wings shimmering with scales the size of her

head. Fine strands ran along the edge of each one, almost like feathers but not quite. They had two long necks and two huge heads, their lips leathery and their open maws wide and toothless.

You didn't need teeth when you could spit fire.

'Fucking supernova,' Li said, as one of them sprayed a building a few hundred metres ahead of where they stood. The roof was scorched and crumbled away. The creature swooped up, circled, then targeted another building. The flames licked high into the sky, and then just as quickly, seemed to run out of energy and flicker out. What they left behind was a blackened, ruined mess. There would be no rebuilding here.

This was destruction, pure and simple.

'Where are their ships?'

'Up there,' Merion said, pointing to the sky. High above, Jinn could just make out the dark shapes of the Shi Fai vessels. Another dragon was coming in, and this one landed nearby, ditching a troop of Shi Fai who immediately began to scatter, rushing into the burning buildings. They didn't look like the senator she had met on Kepler. They were much larger than that, with heads elongated into blunt snouts, and six separate limbs which seemed to function as both arms and legs.

The Virena tingled in response.

'What are you waiting for?' Jinn yelled at the females, as she charged towards the nearest building. 'Go! Go!'

The females pulled free their weapons, all built from Virena, and they did as she had ordered. It was chaos. The air grew thick with smoke, and when another of the creatures rushed down, it brought with it a smell of ammonia that cut through the sulphurous backdrop of the planet. Jinn almost choked on it.

But she was not afraid of the Shi Fai, and she had done too much on this planet to be afraid of the Sittan. Instead, now, she was afraid for them. The male had told her that some of their females were in the palace with Talta, but it was quickly obvious that it wasn't all of them when a child, half-burned and screaming, ran out of one of the homes.

Jinn ran towards the creature and leapt up into the air, blades ready. Li hit it at the same time as she did. He went for one head and she went for the other. He grabbed hold of the jaws of the creature, wrapping his huge arms around them, as Jinn got a foot to its nose and scrambled along its back. The need for violence was on her now, and all she wanted to do was to bring the creature down, and she knew that Li felt the same. Her blades slashed up and then they slashed down, and the creature bled black and it fell.

It hit the ground with an almighty thump and lay there, twitching. Li jumped clear. So did Jinn. The creature tried to get up, but it couldn't, and the awkward flop of its meaty body made her feel ill. But there was no more time to think about that, because the Shi Fai were everywhere, squat, leathery little creatures.

She didn't think. She simply acted. This was her planet and her people, and they were under attack, and it was her job to defend them. So she did. It was only when the last dragon swooped away and didn't return that she realised something.

Shi Fai blood spattered her from head to foot, and she felt nothing. She stood, looking down at her arms, drenched in awareness of her body. She was sore from the effort, charged with adrenaline, but there was no pain, no sickness.

The others – Ritte, Merion, Li, the strong Sittan females and the weak Sittan males, moved to stand beside her in a group. No longer were they on opposite sides. They were allies now, of an uncomfortable and uneasy kind. But at least it proved one thing.

They could work together, if they needed to.

'Are you immune to the Shi Fai?' she asked Ritte.

The Sittan female's eyes widened in surprise. 'Yes,' she said. 'I had forgotten that humans are not.'

'Pretty sure I am,' Jinn said. 'Li?'

'Fine and dandy over here,' he said. 'Huh. All that time, avoiding them like the plague, and it turns out they're harmless.'

'I wouldn't say harmless. They've still managed to do a lot of damage here.' Jinn walked over to one of the dead Shi Fai and poked it with the toe of her boot. The creature didn't move. 'Dead,' she said. Assessment of the huge dragon, however, revealed that it was alive, although the wounds Jinn had inflicted were still bleeding.

'What do we do with it?' asked one of the females.

'Leave it,' Merion told them. He was looking the animal over, not with disgust, but with interest. He ran a clawed hand over its flank, crouched down next to one of its heads and examined one of the huge eyes. 'I have never seen anything like this,' he said quietly. 'There are stories that such creatures used to live here, but they died out ten thousand years ago. We no longer have enough food to sustain them.'

'Those are merely stories,' Ritte said.

'So are lots of things,' Merion pointed out. 'That doesn't mean they aren't true.'

'Perhaps not,' Ritte agreed. 'But the creature is the least of our concerns. They will come again. We cannot let them.'

'We won't,' Jinn told her. She left Ritte to organise the females. They would need to be divided into smaller teams and sent out to various parts of the city to get those who remained to the safety of the palace. The gates would be open to everyone who could get themselves there. Talta would just have to budge up and make room. And if she didn't, Jinn would make it for her.

'What about us?' Li asked, as Ritte and the females left. 'I'm not staying with that thing.' He pointed at the dead dragon, which Merion was still busy examining. 'It smells.'

'We're going to the palace,' Jinn said. 'It's time that I dealt with Talta.'

When they got there, they found the palace to be dark and cold and it, too, smelled.

'I don't like this,' Li said.

'I don't like it either,' Jinn told him. She sent out silent, seeking strands of the Virena, pushing them into the walls and the floor, strengthening the roof. It lit the place with a soft, shimmering glow.

One by one, females began to appear. They watched her from the shadows with glittering yellow eyes. None of them tried to approach.

Except for one.

Talta. With a crystal-studded whip in her hand. She rushed towards Jinn with the whip raised over her head and moved her hand as to swing the tip at Jinn, who knew from experience how painful it would be.

But the Virena didn't let Talta finish. It seemed to come from nowhere, flashing out in a dense cloud around the former empress. Talta screamed in rage and fought against the net of swirling black, but she had no chance against it. It pinned her in place. The only movement it allowed was the panicked rise and fall of her chest.

She spat her anger at Jinn when she approached, but there was nothing she could really do. She was completely powerless now. It was almost painful to watch.

'This will all be so much easier if you accept me,' Jinn told her.

'Never.' Clawed hands flexed against the thin strands that held them in place. 'You do not belong here, human. You are not one of us.'

'You can fight this,' Jinn said, 'but you can't change it. When I came here, the only thing I wanted from you was Dax. You could have simply given him to me.'

An inner lid flicked over Talta's eyes, turning yellow to white and then back again.

'Why didn't you?'

Talta struggled against the bonds of Virena a little more.

'Why?' Jinn asked again. 'You destroyed everything you had to keep him from me. You even gave up this.' She held up her hands, letting the Virena swirl around them.

'Because he was mine!'

'No, he wasn't.'

'He gave himself to me willingly enough,' Talta told her. 'Right here, in this very room. He pleasured me for hours. Did he tell you that?'

Jinn simply stared at her. Was it true? Had Dax done that? The Virena flashed memories at her, Talta's memories, and she saw the truth in what Talta had said. But she also saw Dax's unwillingness and his fear, and it made her sick.

'He didn't, did he?' Talta said, with a glimmer of a smile. 'Ask your precious Virena. It will show you everything.'

'It has already shown me everything,' Jinn told her. 'How you used it to cling on to power when you should have given it up years ago and let it have the new, young empress that it wanted. How you trapped it here, in this palace, when there was so much more of the universe to explore. How *bored* it was with you.'

Talta's face turned hard. 'Filthy human.'

Jinn opened her mouth to retaliate, and then she stopped. That flash of anger had gone as quickly as it had appeared. She wasn't even sure where it had come from. When she had come back to Sittan, she had known that she would have to kill Talta. It had never been said out loud, or even formed into a coherent thought, but she had known.

Now that she saw her, she knew that she wouldn't do it. Talta was pathetic and powerless. It wasn't that she thought that the Sittan female didn't deserve to die, or that she particularly deserved to live.

It was what killing her would do to Jinn.

The firepit in the centre of the room was empty. Jinn walked over to it and filled it with flame with a flick of her wrist, lighting the room. The throne sat gleaming and empty. She didn't sit in it. To do so was to claim it. She had not come here for that. So what had she come here for? If not Talta, and not the throne, then what?

'The Shi Fai are burning the villages,' she said, rubbing a thumb against her bottom lip as she stared at that empty seat.

'So kill them,' Talta hissed.

'Perhaps,' Jinn said. She could feel the Virena pressing against her mind, exploring that idea. It was not without merit. But it would not solve their problem.

Talta bared her teeth. 'What other way is there?'

'There is always a way,' Jinn said. 'All we have to do is find it. This place is for all of us, and the sooner we accept that, the better. The Shi Fai are coming here because they want something. It's not just destruction. There has to be more to it than that. You wanted the males to fight in the arena because you thought it would awaken the Mountain. We gave them to you because we wanted to be able to cross your space. It's about survival. It's always about survival. That's why we fight.'

'They needed human females to incubate their young,' Li said. 'Which means that there's something wrong with whatever did that job on their planet. Merion said there used to be creatures like that dragon they flew in on here on Sittan. Maybe they're looking for something on the planet itself. It might not have anything to do with the Sittan people.'

'I don't think I've ever heard you say that many words in one go before,' Jinn said.

'Talking is a waste of energy,' he said. 'I only do it when I have to. Most of the time I don't have to.'

Jinn turned, began to pace, her thoughts ticking over in time with each step. 'I know there are weapons in this place, Talta. Tell me where they are.'

'No! Those weapons are mine! I will not share them with you!'

'They are not for me. Make this right. Stand for your people. Defend them. Fight with me.'

'I will not!'

'Then stay here and rot,' Jinn said. She'd had enough. 'Do nothing. Let your people die.' She pulled the Virena away. Talta fell to the floor. She pushed herself up on her forearms and screamed at Jinn.

But Jinn was already leaving.

The Virena wrapped around her body as she walked, until it covered her completely, leaving only her face exposed. The weight of it disappeared. Somehow, it no longer bothered her. Perhaps because she knew now that Talta wasn't worthy of it. None of them were. She was the only one who deserved to share its power. They didn't understand it. They thought that all it cared about was violence and death, but it wanted so much more than that.

She swept through the palace, and as she did so, the Virena whispered to her the location of every single secret hiding place that had been added over the turns, and of the weapons concealed within them. Jinn opened up each and every one. 'Take what you need,' she directed the females. They ran to do her bidding. They had nothing left for Talta now.

Outside, the sky was bright, and the suns were high as Jinn walked through the empty city. This was her planet now. She would protect it. She kept walking, with only one place in mind now, and as the dark shadows began to swoop overhead, she welcomed them. She felt no fear of what lay ahead.

The arena loomed. Only then did Jinn hesitate. Only then did she stumble. For a split second, she could smell blood and sand, and she could hear death. But then it was gone, just as quickly as it had appeared. The gates opened up ahead of her, and she walked through into that place, not as a fighter, but as its ruler. She walked right out into the middle of the sand, those shadows following her, becoming lower and heavier, circling in. She breathed in the hot, dusty air, tipped her head back to let the suns warm her face. She was ready.

The first dragon swooped down. It was a huge beast, with thick, leathery skin and wings that could span a freighter. It filled the arena with darkness. Jinn sent darkness back up to meet it. She pulled that beast down and pinned it to the ground. 'Surrender,' she ordered it. The beast squealed at her, raging and spitting acid-green flame, but its wings were broken. It couldn't fly.

She dropped to her knees and pulled the Shi Fai from its back. 'Call them off,' she told it. 'End this. Now. Stop this attack, or I will end you. All of you.' The Virena urged her to do that anyway, to spill their blood and take their lives, their ships, their planet, and she was tempted. They deserved it.

The Shi Fai squealed in rage and fear, filling the air with a stink that reminded her of burning rubber. Jinn bound it in a web of Virena. Overhead, the other creatures had begun to fly higher and higher. They would soon be out of reach. The Virena flew up after them and plucked them out of the sky, jerking them back down to the ground with such force that they flew apart on impact. And then it went after the ships.

She froze it in place before it could destroy them.

The ships couldn't move. Neither did the Virena. But a single word from her and it would crush them. The sense of power was unlike anything she'd experienced before. Her modifications gave her strength, it was true.

But the Virena wanted to give her *everything*.

She sat cross-legged in front of the little creature and eyed it curiously. 'Right,' she said. 'You and I are going to have a little chat. And I seriously recommend that you listen to what I have to say.'

CHAPTER

41

11th February 2208

Park Lane Hotel, Mayfair District, London Dome, Earth

Vexler's awakening had not surprised Ferona. After all, she had directed the nurses to stop his treatment. But Bautista's reaction to it had, and she was annoyed with herself for that. She was also furious with Weston, the devious little toad. How else could Bautista have created himself a private security force of Type One agents?

But it could all be taken care of, Ferona thought, as she relaxed under the warm touch of the new beauty droid that had been delivered to her hotel room that morning. She had contemplated a return to her old apartment at the top of the Dome but decided that this option was better. Here she had an entire team of human staff at her beck and call, all of whom had been instructed not to tell anyone outside of that immediate circle where she was. And the hotel had its own oxygen generator and water recycling plant, so she could be assured of a clean and constant supply of both.

When the beauty droid finished the massage, it helped her to dress and fixed her hair and makeup. The knock on the door came at exactly at the time she had ordered it. She opened the door to find a glassy-eyed young man looking at her. 'Your car is ready,' he said.

Ferona licked the tips of her fingers and touched his cheek. 'Clean the room,' she told him. 'I want fresh flowers and a restocked Autochef when I return. Do not tell anyone that you have seen me.'

'Of course,' he said.

That would keep him going for another ten hours. She had discovered that as long as she had regular contact with the staff and re-infected them within a relatively short time period, the effects of the virus didn't wear off. It was a little irritating, Ferona had to admit that, but she did get a kick out of seeing their eyes glaze over and giving them pointless tasks to do.

Bautista had wanted to delay the competency testing for six weeks. That was completely unacceptable as far as Ferona was concerned and so she had arranged it for the following day and had the time and location sent to Bautista's office.

She was very much hoping that the president would attend.

The car journey was relatively short and very comfortable. Her driver didn't say a word. She sipped a warm Koffee from the shiny little Autochef. It had tiny almond biscuits, too, but she didn't bother with those. She had lost all interest in food. The rash on her chin had made its way to her chest. But her energy felt boundless.

The car pulled to a halt outside the hospital and Ferona climbed out, hurrying up the steps and into the building, and as she did so, she activated her wrist comm. and sent an anonymous message to various news channels.

Bautista arrived ten minutes after she did, by which time she'd already had a private conversation with the testing team. She could have left at that point. She probably should have left. But she didn't.

He was not pleased to see her. 'What are you doing here?'

'Good morning to you too, Mr President. I trust you slept well?' She smiled brightly.

His mouth turned into a tight little circle, a muscle twitching in his cheek. 'Get her out,' he said to a member of his team, who took a step towards Ferona.

But one of the testing team stepped forward. 'Mr Vexler is allowed to have a friend with him during the testing.'

'She is not his friend!'

'Mr Vexler has indicated otherwise.'

There was nothing Bautista could say to that and he was smart enough not to argue further, but Ferona could tell how furious he was and she enjoyed it very much. This was all so wonderful. She took a seat at the side of the room, smoothed out her long velvet skirt, and waited.

It didn't take long.

In less than twenty minutes, Vexler was declared competent. He wasn't. Any fool could see that. He could barely string two words together and seemed to have no idea where he was or what was going on. If Bautista hadn't had him kept in the coma, the true extent of Vexler's brain injuries would have been discovered months ago and Bautista could have had Vexler removed permanently from office and Ferona would have been powerless to stop him.

But now?

She shook the hands of the members of the testing team and thanked each one of them personally. She crouched next to Vexler and whispered in his ear, knowing Bautista could see but not hear. 'You finally did something right, you useless bastard.'

Then she faced Bautista. She made a point of pulling on her gloves rather than shaking his hand. She could have simply gone to his office and used her abilities to make him step down. But this was so much more satisfying. To see the look on his face, the rage and confusion, the fact that he didn't understand why everyone else was treating Vexler as competent when it was blatantly obvious to Bautista that he was anything but, was an utter joy.

Knowing that cameras and journalists were waiting for him outside and that he would have to tell them that Vexler had passed testing and would shortly be returning to work as president only sweetened the pot. Not even his overgrown babysitters could save him from that.

Once back in her car, she contemplated going for lunch at her favourite restaurant, but the thought of the rich food made her feel sick, so she quickly squashed that idea. Instead she activated her wrist comm. and contacted Weston. He didn't answer. That was odd. He was a difficult and unpleasant man, but she felt sure that he would have taken a call from her today of all days.

It left Ferona at something of a loose end. She intended to go to the government building, but not until later on. To appear now would be suspicious. Attending the competency testing had been too delicious an opportunity for her to miss, but she couldn't deny that it had been risky. She hadn't been able to resist seeing the look on Bautista's face when Vexler was declared competent.

She told her driver to take her to Weston's.

She passed the journey with another Koffee from the AutoChef, and the buildings passed by in a blur as she wallowed in her pleasure at the taste and the victory she had won over a man who she had hated for years.

When the car pulled to a halt outside Weston's house, she climbed out, exhaling loudly at the shock of the cold. She was half-way up the path when she noticed the door. 'What the . . . ?' She hurried towards it.

Someone had kicked it in.

Ferona risked a glance back at the street. No-one was there. She contemplated not going in, but she had to see. She couldn't seem to stop herself. She peered into the room beyond. And then she stepped over the threshold, standing just inside the doorway, and took in the sight of Weston lying dead on the floor.

The silence was incredibly loud.

She instinctively pulled the collar of her coat up over her mouth and nose.

His horrible little dog lay on the floor next to him, and the sight of it quite perked her up. She looked around the room, trying to work out what had happened. He had some horrible slime running out of his mouth, and his tongue was black. Ferona shuddered as her mind slid to a solitary thought.

Poison.

Self-administered? It wouldn't explain the door. No. Someone had been here. And that was very worrying for Ferona. There was no doubt in her mind that Bautista was behind this. But who knew what secrets Weston might have spilled under duress?

The bank of cameras at the back of the room might be able to tell her. She carefully picked her way past Weston's body over to the console that operated those cameras. How to operate them? Facial recognition technology? She looked down at the body.

No. She'd never seen Weston use it.

The console had a keypad. She tried a couple of things, neither of which worked.

She looked down at the body again, saw the dog, and narrowed her eyes. What had he called the stupid little thing? Ah, yes. She quickly typed it in. *Darling.*

A screen popped up.

It took Ferona only a few seconds to scroll back through the video feed, and what she found astonished her. A huge man, clearly Type One, and a tiny female, clearly Type Two. The man was wearing an agent's uniform and he at least made sense. The woman made no sense at all. It made even less sense when the two of them embraced. She turned on the audio, but the sound was corrupted.

'Identify the male,' Ferona told the system.

'Your voice is not recognised.'

'Oh, for fuck's sake.'

She typed it in.

On the screen, a little circle appeared around the man's face. A timer spun in the middle of it, and then his details popped up.

Adam Smithson.

His background information revealed nothing of interest. But the girlfriend certainly was. Ferona didn't know who she was, or how he'd managed to get her to the surface without being caught. It didn't really matter. A girlfriend was a weak spot. A Type Two girlfriend who would be shot on sight if anyone knew she was here was a fatal flaw.

'Well, Adam Smithson,' she said, 'I think I may have another little job for you.'

But it wasn't something that she could set up from here, however, and she had already spent far more time with Weston's corpse than she wanted to. Another journey, another Koffee, and she was outside the government building.

She walked straight in.

It was easy to find the information she needed and have a new set of orders sent to Agent Smithson and his little friend. Men like Bautista had been running the planet for far too long and they had all done a terrible job of it.

It was time to have someone in charge who could do things properly.

CHAPTER

42

13th Day of the Fourth Turn

The Palace, Fire City, Sittan

After Jinn had gone, Talta had lain on the floor of her chambers, utterly broken. Jinn had held her in place with the Virena and then had stripped it away. Talta could only imagine that this was how it felt to have a child stolen within minutes of its birth. Her exhausted body seemed to have no energy left within it, her legs too weak to support her weight. Her mind raced into agony. There was no-one to help her.

Eventually, she made it as far as the pool in the corner of her quarters. She slithered into the water, desperately wanting its soothing comfort, but she didn't find it. Without Chal Gri to maintain it the water level had dropped and what remained was thick and stinging. She had no way to change it and no energy to pull herself back out.

She rested her head on the edge of the pool and closed her eyes. She had thought, when she saw Jinn, that there was still a chance to take back what was rightfully hers, that when the Virena saw her, it would reject the human female and come back to its true empress.

But it hadn't.

Jinn had a level of control over it that Talta could only dream of. It was part of her. It had nothing left for Talta. She had clung to the throne for so long and fought off so many challengers. She had refused to let things on Sittan change but change had come anyway despite her desperate efforts to stop it. The Virena had seen to that.

It had betrayed her. She had loved it and it had not loved her back, not in the way that she wanted or deserved. She could see that now. It was a painful, shattering thing to admit, but it was surprising what you could face when you had no further to fall.

Talta dragged herself to the edge of the pool and looked out at the city. The fires had gone out, though smoke still rose in great spiralling plumes. Huge white shapes circled high in the sky. None of them had come down to the surface in almost a day. And Talta knew why.

Jinnifer Blue had stopped them

She had done what Talta could not. She had fought off the Shi Fai, and protected the planet. Talta had known that the Shi Fai were a parasitic species and that the shield was vital to keep them out. But she had allowed herself to become so drunk on power that she had stopped seeing them as a threat. When she had sent the Virena after Jinn, she had left the planet undefended, and that had been a mistake.

There was a noise in the doorway, and she turned to see a familiar female walking into the room. She pulled herself a little higher in the water, then sank even deeper when her strength abandoned her.

Ritte was dressed in strange clothing. Human clothing. Her feet were bare. There were bracelets on both wrists, the metal bright and shiny, and they jingled prettily as she moved. But time had not been kind. There were white patches on the female's face and arms.

Her back was curved, forcing her to stoop, and her eyes had the fading, sunken look of someone in their final turns.

'Why are you here?' Talta asked. 'You no longer serve me.'

'I will always serve you,' Ritte said. 'Sister.'

'What about our new empress? Don't you serve her?'

'Yes.' Ritte smiled. 'But I swore an oath to you, and I will not break it.'

'There can only be one empress.'

'You would know that better than most.'

Talta turned back to her view of the city. She did not want to look at Ritte, or the interior of the palace. It was too painful. She did not move when Ritte came to sit beside her. They looked out at the city together, the fallen empress and her guard. 'Look at it,' Talta said. 'It is ruined.'

'We can rebuild.'

'To what end? We have no males of value, and our females are so weak that they follow a human.'

There was a beat, a painful moment of silence before Ritte responded. 'If this is the end, it is only to give us a new beginning, and you would be able to see that if you were not so proud. Your vanity has served you well, Talta. But it has also blinded you. You have forgotten where your duty lies.'

Talta swung a clawed hand at her and missed.

'I always believed that the duty of the empress was to protect our planet, to do what she could to see it thrive. I believed that my duty was to help her achieve that. For a long time, I thought that meant protecting you. But I didn't understand. I was young. I didn't know that things could be different, that things should be different. My son made me see my mistake.'

'Ah, yes. The runt.'

'Merion is not weak.'

'You would not allow him to fight in the arena.'

'Death in the sand was not his destiny. It was not his purpose.'

'It is the purpose of all males.'

Ritte stretched her legs out in front of her. Her feet were bare, but she still wore her guard's anklets. 'Not any more,' she said. 'Not for a very long time. Face it, Talta. We didn't just push them into that position to feed the Mountain. We did it because we wanted to. We enjoyed our power over them.'

'And what if we had allowed them free rein? We have always produced more sons than daughters, Ritte. Unmated males are a danger to all of us. But when a male is forced to work to earn the right to a female, she becomes precious to him, and he does all that he can to protect and serve her.'

Ritte did not disagree. She did not get the chance. A huge shape was drifting down from the sky, and it caught the attention of both. 'What is that?' Talta asked.

Ritte got to her feet. 'I do not know.' She lifted a hand, shading her eyes from the sun, watching the shape as it continued on that same trajectory. 'But it is heading for the city.'

It was closer now, close enough to see that it had defined edges and a shape that Talta knew. 'It's a ship.' A Shi Fai ship. It had to be. All of a sudden, the city turned completely black, darkness spreading out from the centre so quickly that it covered everything in the blink of an eye. Talta felt a jolt as she looked at it.

She had never seen Virena do that before. It was certainly not something that she would have been able to make it do. There was a cutting feeling of jealousy, a tightening in her chest, and she gripped the edge of the balcony, claws digging into stone. It was like watching a lover choose someone else before your love for them had died.

The Virena was even more beautiful than she remembered. The shape of it, the way the smell of it cut through the air. She wanted to be near to it. She found the strength to pull herself out of the pool, somehow, and shuffled to the edge of the balcony. She did not look down but out towards the city, towards her love. She thought, for a moment, of trying to reach for it.

A heavy hand on her shoulder stopped her. 'We are going to need you, Talta, in the turns that lie ahead,' Ritte said gently. 'There is much that you know that the rest of us do not.'

'You want me to help you?'

'I want you to help all of us.'

Talta almost laughed. 'Empresses don't help. They own. They control. They rule. They *survive*.'

'But you are not an empress.'

For the first time, Talta found herself able to look at the female who had been at her side for so many turns before abandoning her. Ritte had tried to hide her changing body, had tried to stay on as a guard, but Talta had smelt it on her. She had smelt the male that Ritte had chosen and known immediately that she would kill the child. Chal Gri belonged to *her*. Ritte had no right to him.

But Ritte had left the palace. She had hidden herself deep in the city, abandoning her former life, and in the end, Talta had allowed it. She had wanted to think of herself as benevolent and generous. Perhaps the child would be female, and coming from such a strong bloodline, would make an excellent guard.

But the child had been male.

'I hate you,' Talta said. 'I have hated you for many turns.'

'Yes,' Ritte said. 'I know. But I am what you made me, Talta. As is this planet, and Jinnifer Blue. It is not our fault if you don't like it.'

With that, she turned and walked away, leaving Talta to her own thoughts.

All of them were dark and poisonous.

CHAPTER

43

15th February 2208

Acton District, London Dome, Earth

So there was a cure. It was the news Eve had been waiting for since the age of eighteen, when she'd first realised what had been done to her, and what it meant. Now there was the frustration of having to accept just how little information she had beyond that. She didn't know what this cure was, where to find it, even where to begin looking.

But there was one thing she did know.

She couldn't poison Bryant. He was completely and utterly immune to her. She kept testing this out by poking him on the back of the hand.

'Stop that,' he said.

'Just one more time, and then I will.'

He reached out, grabbed her hand and squeezed it. She could feel the warmth of his skin, the bones within, the strength in his hand. 'That's it. That's your lot. Don't touch me again.'

Eve smiled, but she kept her hands to herself after that. The skimmer nipped through the streets. It took them away from the rough area of the city, where the houses were small, the exteriors grey and the gardens non-existent, through a dead park, past an abandoned sports field, through to the centre of the city where the streets were wider, if not particularly clean, and the buildings rose tall and ornate.

Bryant switched off the autopilot and drove them the last few kilometres himself, not to the port, where they'd left their ship, but to another house.

'Where are we going?'

'None of your business.'

'Well, it is my business, given that you're taking me with you. I want to leave, Bryant. I never thought I would come back here and I don't like it.'

'You won't be here for long,' Bryant said. 'Just a few more hours, Eve, and it will be done.'

'Hmm.'

They continued down a long, wide street for another five minutes, and then Bryant took a sharp right and brought the skimmer to a standstill at the edge of the kerb. He opened the door and climbed out. 'Stay in the car,' he told her.

'Why?'

He pinched the bridge of his nose and muttered something to himself that sounded very rude. 'Just do it, will you?'

'Fine,' Eve said. 'Don't tell me. See if I care.' She pulled up her hood and busied herself chewing on her nails as he crossed the street in front of the skimmer and went up the short flight of steps to the door of a lovely, elegant house with huge windows and a green front door. A house droid greeted him.

Bryant shoved it back into the house and then was lost from view as the door closed smartly behind him. She fiddled around inside the car for a minute or so, turning the entertainment screen on and off, trying various music channels, checking the clock more times than was really necessary, trying to tell herself that she was overthinking this. There could be a million reasons why Bryant had gone in that house. Maybe his family lived there. Just because she couldn't see hers didn't mean he couldn't see his. She finally found the switch for the privacy screens and activated them. At least now no-one outside the car could see in.

Bryant still didn't reappear.

Eve started to panic. She told herself she was being ridiculous. She decided to give him another two minutes. No, another five. Then she was out of here. She scooted over to the driver's seat, but felt like that was inviting trouble and moved back again.

She had pretty much convinced herself that Bryant was not coming back and she was on her own when the driver's side door opened and he climbed in. His expression was grim. He powered up the engine and set them moving without saying a word.

Eve didn't say a word either. It wasn't until they were a good ten minutes away from that street and back into the thick of the traffic that she licked the dryness away from her lips and asked him if he was OK.

One big hand gripped the wheel of the skimmer so tightly that it started to bend. Bryant exhaled. 'I don't want to talk about it.'

'Alright.'

'I got more orders,' he said. 'About an hour ago. Another list of names and addresses.'

'But . . . '

'Weston wasn't so bad,' he said, as if he hadn't heard her. 'I could have done that one. He was a slimeball. Deserved what he got. But that guy . . . he could barely put his pants on the right way out without assistance. I don't even get why he was on the list. He was no threat to anyone.'

'Did you . . . ?'

'Yes.' A muscle ticked in his jaw. 'Anyway, I told you I didn't want to talk about it!'

'Sorry.'

'There's two more, and then that's it. We're done.'

'Do you have to do it? You can't just leave it?'

'No.'

'Why not?'

'Because whoever sent me these orders knows that you're here with me. If I don't do this, we're as good as dead. And if it's a choice between us and them, I choose us. Every time.'

He didn't bother with the autopilot this time. He ignored the speed limits, darting above the traffic, taking short cuts which took them the wrong way down one-way streets. This time they went not to a private residence, but to an office building in a part of the city that Eve had never visited before.

Whoever this was, they were important, and they worked for the government. Bryant took the skimmer down into an underground car park. Eve's sense of unease grew. Concrete walls surrounded them, caging them in, and she didn't like it one little bit. He parked the skimmer in an empty slot – there were plenty to choose from – and once again told her to wait in the car.

'Absolutely not,' she told him. She pushed open her own door and climbed out. She fastened her jacket. 'And if you so much as think about trying to make me, I'll knee you where it hurts.'

As threats went, it was pathetic. If he wanted to make her wait in the car there would be nothing she could do about it. But she stared up at him anyway, all those years of living as Type Two and having to face down pirate crews who thought they could push her around finally coming in useful.

'Fine,' he said. 'But don't blame me if something goes wrong.'

'Can I have a blaster?'

'What for?'

'In case I need to shoot someone.'

'No,' he told her.

They took a thankfully empty elevator up into the building. Eve stuck close to Bryant. He seemed to know exactly where he was going although every turn they took led them down another corridor which looked exactly the same as the one before it. Eve quickly became disorientated.

Still Bryant kept going. She almost had to run to keep up with him. Finally, he stopped outside a closed office door. He glanced back at her. 'I don't want you to come in,' he said. 'Understand? I don't want you to see this.'

Eve bit her lip and nodded. But when he opened the door, she followed him through. She didn't really understand why she did it. The impulse was just too strong to ignore. Inside the office, a tall, pale-haired man was leaning over a desk, fingers moving rapidly over a screen. He looked up when they entered, his dark eyes widening in surprise. 'Hello,' he said.

It was such a normal response, such an ordinary thing to say that Eve was quite taken aback.

'Shut up,' Bryant said. 'Put your hands where I can see them.'

The man obliged. 'Can I ask what this is about?' So far, he had only looked at Bryant, but then he looked at Eve for the briefest of moments. She saw surprise, recognition, understanding, but she didn't see anything else. There was no fear, no disgust. Just a gentle confusion.

'Never mind that,' Bryant told him. He took aim. The blaster light settled right over the man's heart. It wobbled all over the place.

It was then that Eve realised something. She understood why she'd insisted on coming with Bryant. It wasn't for her sake. It was for his. Regardless of what he might say, he did not want to do this.

She moved, slowly, carefully, not wanting to startle him, and wrapped her fingers around his forearm, then tugged. 'Don't do it,' she said softly. 'You don't have to. I know why you think you have to, but take it from me, it's not true. I spent twenty years in hiding. We can disappear. It's easy. The galaxy is big enough that no-one will ever find us if we don't want them to.'

Under her hand, his arm was like iron, the muscles were clenched so tightly. The dot wobbled even more. Eve held her breath. The man behind the desk remained thankfully silent. She sensed that if he said so much as a single word, Bryant would fire.

Slowly, painfully, Bryant lowered his arm. Eve prised the blaster out of his hand and slid it inside her jacket. The strength seemed to go out of his legs then, and he sank down into the nearest chair and put his head in his hands.

'My name is Mikhal Dubnik,' the man said. 'And yours is?'

'I'm Eve, and this is Bryant.'

'I hope you don't mind if I don't offer to shake your hand.'

'Not at all.'

'Good.' He offered her a tentative smile, then he too lowered himself slowly into his seat. 'It's not every day that someone tries to assassinate you. So, if I can be so bold, would you mind telling me who sent you here, and why?'

CHAPTER

44

1st Day of the Fifth Turn

Fire City, Sittan

The Shi Fai who had visited Sittan so far had been little more than hunting parties. What Jinn faced now was something very different, and she didn't know quite how to deal with it. She had to push aside her anger and her disgust and meet with them as equals.

It wasn't easy.

Jinn could not give in to her boiling emotions. She turned away from them, as she had done every day since she had left Dax. Perhaps all those days had been worth something after all, because she was so used to pushing aside what she felt that it came to her easily now when she needed it the most.

She climbed up onto the balustrade that edged the balcony of her chambers, feet steady on the narrow edge, and looked down at the city, her city. She did not even need to call the Virena to her now. It came easily, willingly, taking her with it when she jumped. She trusted it not to let her fall. It did not let her down. It wrapped itself around her, forming a huge cloak that billowed out behind her, letting her drift out across the streets, the broken buildings.

The Shi Fai delegation were waiting for her.

She landed several metres away from them and stood, feet firmly planted. These were different to the ones that had come here first. The ships were different. The creatures themselves were different. Larger, multi-limbed, heavy-boned and solid.

She pulled in the Virena. The Shi Fai formed a ring around her, all watching with a single eye that sat large and unblinking in the centre of each face. There was no obvious mouth, no clear way for them to communicate.

Jinn turned in a slow circle, looking all of them over.

They were all so perfectly alike that it was as if they were clones of each other, or perhaps genetically identical siblings. There was no variation between them at all. She found that undeniably creepy. She licked dry lips and felt the warm weight of the Virena in her hands. It was there, should she need it, ready to act, ready to kill.

'Welcome,' she said. 'I am glad you have come.' She didn't know if they could understand, but it seemed only right to say something. She was not Talta, and she would not rule as she had ruled. She needed this to work. It had to work.

Twenty eyes fixed on her.

The sound seemed to come from nowhere and from everywhere all at once. The Virena translated it for her in soft, easy whispers. At first, Jinn was confused, but then one of the creatures turned slightly and she saw a collection of shimmering metal scales on one side of its head. The one stood next to it had a similar device, flat everywhere apart from a solitary dark ruby embedded in the centre. A translation device, it had to be. It made sense that if humans had given such devices to the Shi Fai, the Sittan had given them something similar. It was a relief. When she had first seen them, she hadn't been sure that they would be able to communicate at all.

'Why have you invited us here?'

'I've invited you because I don't want to fight you. I will, if I have to. But I don't want to.' She held up a hand, letting the Virena swirl around her fingers. 'Do you know what this is?'

The Shi Fai visibly shrank from it. 'Yes.'

'Good,' Jinn said. That much at least meant that it wouldn't do anything stupid. 'Then tell me something. Why are you coming here?'

Its entire body flexed sinuously. 'We want what we are owed.'

'And what is that?'

'We have given the Sittan many things from our planet. Trees for oil and fruit. Dragons to spread their seed. A male called Ferriculus promised us dark rubies in return. But when we sent ships for them, they could not get to the planet.'

Because the females had discovered the Virena, and all deals were off.

'The debt is age old,' she told them. 'Let it go.'

'We will not.'

'Then I will send the Virena to Faidal and let it do what it will.'

Various smells assaulted her nostrils. A strange, burned stench. Something sickly sweet in reply. Those two mingled together, plus what she could have sworn was hot rubber. She didn't need her translation device to tell her that they didn't like it. But it didn't matter. She'd had enough of them. They looked awful, they smelled worse, and she wanted to go back to the cool shade of the palace.

'The deal is fair,' the Shi Fai senator said.

You bet it is, Jinn thought. *And it's more than you deserve, after what you did to Eve and the other Type Two women.*

She didn't wait to see the Shi Fai delegation leave. She left that to her guards, who had poured out of the palace after her and now ringed their visitors in a manner that was not aggressive, exactly, but suggested that they might not want to outstay their welcome.

But her work here was far from done. Everything that the Shi

Fai had destroyed needed to be rebuilt. The cities that Talta had left without Virena had started to crumble. And then there was Talta herself.

And the Virena.

CHAPTER

45

18th February 2208

Park Lane Hotel, Mayfair District, London Dome, Earth

Ferona had almost finished packing. She had acquired so many lovely new things over the past few days, and she couldn't bear to leave any of them behind. Everything had been perfectly folded and placed into a packing case by a droid. Four of them already waited by the door.

She had decided to go to Colony Seven. It had been a spur of the moment decision, but she was sure that it was the right one. It would be sensible for her to be elsewhere over the next few days, until the dust had settled. She would return, of course, when the time was right. Or perhaps she'd be able to move the entire government to the colony. Yes, that made sense. There would be a lot to do over the next few months, preparing for the first wave of migrants to Spes, and Colony Seven would be an excellent base from which to oversee it all.

She remembered, a long time ago, Vexler saying that statues would be erected to honour him when they reached their new planet.

Now those statues would be of Ferona. She checked her wrist unit. If Vexler wasn't dead already, he soon would be. She had an agent on the ground, primed and ready to kill. It hadn't been difficult to issue him with a new set of orders. Only three men stood between Ferona and total control, and she didn't expect any of them to be in her way for more than an hour.

Her wrist comm. buzzed. She took a second to check her appearance in her holomirror before she answered it.

'Yes?'

'Minister Blue, my name is Captain DelTonio. I work for LansCorp. We provide the security for this section of the Dome.'

'Is there a problem?'

'Well.' He paused and cleared his throat. 'I regret to inform you, Minister Blue, that Minister Bautista was found dead at his home an hour ago. It looks like one of his security droids malfunctioned. There was no sign of forced entry and the camera feed for that time is clear. We don't think anyone else was involved. It appears to have been a terrible accident.'

'An accident. I see.'

It would be inappropriate to smile. She had to keep her face straight. The agent had moved on to Bautista already? Excellent work. She blinked rapidly, as if she was trying to fight back tears. 'Thank you for informing me. Is there anything that you need me to do?'

'Not at this time.'

'Thank you.'

'Good,' he said. He paused, as if he expected her to say something else, but she didn't, so he ended the call, no doubt wondering if he had handled it correctly and if there would be any comeback if he hadn't.

Bautista was dead. Shot by one of his own droids, or at least that was how it looked. Everyone would assume that he'd killed himself after Vexler had passed competency testing. Let them think it was just a terrible tragedy. No-one would miss the incompetent twit. He'd be forgotten about within a couple of days. Everyone had far more important things to do.

There was a knock at her door. It was one of the staff, come to inform her that her transport had arrived. No shared cab for her this time. Ferona would be leaving Earth in style. Her droid busied itself moving her cases down to the street level and into the glide car. Ferona took her time putting on her coat and gloves. She took one last look around the room. It had served her well. She couldn't say that she was sorry to be leaving it behind.

A great future awaited her, one on a new planet where she already knew that she would be president. The dreams that had been squashed here on Earth would finally be fulfilled on Spes.

Her only regret was that Jinn would not be with her. Although Ferona had never been particularly maternal, and had always been more than happy to hand off childcare to nanny droids and education programmes, that didn't change the fact that Jinn was her only living relative. Jinn had Blue DNA. But it was a minor annoyance, and Ferona knew that she would soon get over it.

She followed the driver down to the street level. She'd specifically requested a human driver and crew for her ship, although she had droids as backup. She wasn't stupid.

The driver opened the door of the glide car and helped Ferona to get in. She tucked in her skirts and settled back into the seat, watching her city through the screens as it slid past.

She reached for the Autochef positioned between the seats and ordered herself a glass of pink champagne. Then she toasted her success. She had done what they had said could not be done. She had outwitted alien races that were stronger, smarter and better resourced than humankind. She had survived those who wanted to see her fall, and she had done it in style.

Soon Vexler and Dubnik would meet the same end as Bautista, and then there would be no-one to stand in her way.

She had won.

CHAPTER

46

The weather had taken a terrible turn for the worse. Snow was falling heavy and thick, the flakes big enough to fill the palm of Bryant's hand. They had no chance of getting back to the port and getting their ship out of lock up.

But Dubnik had suggested an alternative. He had a ship at a private port outside the Dome. It would be the safest way for Eve to get off planet. Why a Dome-raised politician should be so concerned about a poisonous Underworld girl Bryant had no idea, but he was willing to go along with it. All he needed was a working ship with some jump capability. He'd take care of the details later.

The three of them squashed into Bryant's hired skimmer. Dubnik didn't have a weapon. Bryant had checked. He had been somewhat surprised when the man had insisted on coming with them, but he had made a good case. Eve had to leave Earth, for her own safety as well as that of everyone here, and the best way to be sure of that was to see her onto that ship in person.

But they hadn't counted on the weather. The skimmer died when they were still a couple of kilometres from the port. 'It's not far,' Dubnik said, although he didn't sound too confident. 'We can walk from here.'

He set off, and Bryant followed him, pulling up a map on his personal comm. to make sure that they were in fact heading towards the port and not randomly wandering around in the snow. It would be easy to get lost out here. Eve kept pace with Dubnik and the two of them talked until the cold got the better of them. He asked her all sorts of questions that Bryant would never have thought to ask, and he found the answers strangely fascinating.

But eventually, she began to fall back. Bryant matched his pace to hers. The edges of her face were pale with cold, and their breath frosted in the air between them. Bryant grabbed her hand, warming it between his much hotter ones. 'It's not much further,' she told him.

'How do you know?'

She pointed to three huge black circles on the ground directly ahead of them. 'See those? They're vents for the Underworld city. The port is a kilometre beyond them. The apartment I lived in as a kid was directly underneath it. The floor used to shake every time a ship took off.'

'You won't manage another kilometre,' he told her. He looked at Dubnik. 'And neither will you.'

'We could take the skidders,' Eve said. 'There's an entrance over there.'

'Yuck.' Bryant grimaced.

'Spoken like a true Dome brat.'

He almost laughed. Perhaps he would have, if there had been more time. But Eve was already moving, heading towards one of the entrances to the underground tunnels that crisscrossed under the city, and Dubnik was following her. The wrought-iron archway was an antique, oddly well preserved as snippets of the old city sometimes were. Bryant had never been down in the tunnels below. The closest he had got had been spitting down the ventilation grates as a bored teenager hanging around with his friends. Ten points for a direct hit.

The tunnels were used by people who lived in the Underworld city as a cheap way to get around. Although droids and machines took care of most of the basic work, there were still some jobs left to humans, and some Dome dwellers who opted to have human staff.

The trains ran on magnets, drawing minimal power. They found an empty one waiting for them in the station. They climbed on board. There were no seats, because that reduced the number of bodies that could fit on board, so instead Bryant grasped a cracked strap that hung from the ceiling. It dug into his hand. Dubnik leaned back against the wall. 'I've never been on one of these before,' he admitted.

'Neither have I,' Bryant told him. 'I think we should count ourselves lucky.'

Eve selected the station at the very end of the line. The doors cranked slowly closed, the entire train seemed to sigh, and then it started to move, the three of them the only passengers. But there were still signs of life in many of the stations they passed through. Bryant couldn't understand it. 'Why are they here?' he asked, leaning closer to Eve so that she could hear him over the creaking of the carriage.

She stared up at him for a moment. 'They live here.'

'What about their families?'

'What about them?'

'Why don't they live with them?'

Eve turned to look out of the window. 'I don't know,' she said. 'Maybe their families are shit. Maybe there are already six of them living in two rooms and there isn't space for anyone else.'

All of them were silent after that. The train started to slow, grinding to a halt at the final station. The doors shuddered open and Eve was the first to get off. She stood on the platform, thankfully empty this far out, and pulled up her collar, shrinking down into it.

The wind was vicious. It scraped at Bryant's lungs and burned his exposed skin. There was no elevator here, and they were forced to climb three steep flights of stairs before emerging out into the bright light of their planet.

So white. So unbelievably, blinding bright that for a moment Bryant found himself missing the wet warmth of Faidal, something he had thought he would never do. He had never been this far outside the Dome before, never stood there and experienced the true devastation that humankind had caused. It was terrifying.

If Eve felt the same, she didn't let it show. She ploughed through the snow, dropping knee-deep into it in places, an exhausting, lung-crushing climb from the neglected station to the port, but she kept going. Thankfully it wasn't far, and the footsteps of workers had packed a pathway into the snow which was easy enough to navigate once they had found it. Ahead of him, he could see a dozen launch pads, and two remaining ships, though one of them powered up and lifted away before they could get there.

'Come on,' he said to Eve, grasping her hand and pulling her along with him. The snow gave way to the dark, smooth surface of the port and he immediately picked up speed. A team of droids was busy loading boxes onto the ship. It was not, as he had assumed, a transporter or even a long-range barge, but instead a high-end cruiser. They would be travelling in comfort. He felt a little better. But before they could reach it, a glide car pulled up alongside the ship, and a woman got out. She looked vaguely familiar.

'Ferona,' Dubnik said. His tone was grim. But he didn't lessen his pace. 'Do not get too close to her,' he told Bryant. 'Whatever you do, do not let her touch you. She has been modified with some new type of virus that lets her control your behaviour. She is very, very dangerous. Let me deal with her.'

'That's Ferona Blue?' Eve asked.

'Yes.'

'We know her daughter,' Eve told him. 'Which makes this really very weird indeed.'

'I've got a blaster,' Bryant pointed out. 'Do you want me to shoot her?'

'No,' Dubnik said. 'That's not how I do things.'

'Alright,' Bryant said, 'but if you change your mind, let me know.'

They let Dubnik take the lead after that.

Bryant took the time to study the woman. Her face was familiar. The shape of the eyes, the chin, the fall of her pale blonde hair under the deep red hat. He blinked and saw Jinn. He blinked again and saw that this was not his former partner, but someone else. She looked at them as they approached and didn't bother to hide her surprise or her irritation.

'You were supposed to kill him!'

It was directed at Bryant.

'I persuaded him not to,' Dubnik said.

'Fucking traitor!' Ferona screamed at him. She sounded like a mad woman.

'I am not the one who paid Weston to infect them with a virus so I could control other people.'

Ferona stopped dead. Her mouth fell open in shock.

'Did you really think no-one would find out?' Dubnik asked calmly. 'A strange illness started to pass around the department just before you went to Kepler. I had a couple of the junior ministers examined by a friend of mine. You're not the only one who has contacts, Ferona. Get on that ship,' he said to Eve and Bryant. 'I'll deal with this.'

'That's my ship!' Ferona screeched.

'Not any more.'

Her face twisted in rage. 'I order you to kill him!' she shouted at Bryant.

Bryant had killed angry people, and people who were high or stoned or drunk or even all three. He had killed people who deserved it, and he had probably killed some who had not. Sometimes he had even enjoyed it. He had never questioned it. It had been his job. Now he was beginning to think that maybe he should have questioned it.

'Why?' he asked Ferona instead of just getting it done.

'Why what?'

'Why do you want this man dead?'

'Excuse me?' she said sharply. 'I'm not sure exactly who you think you are but let me make it simple for you. You are an agent and you will do as I say.'

'I'm going to need a bit more than that.'

The snow had started to fall even more heavily, the sky growing dark with it. It fell in thickening heaps all around them, some of it even starting to settle on the ground as the chemical coating on the rubber struggled to melt it.

'I don't see how that is any concern of yours,' Ferona said. Her elegant mouth tightened with annoyance. She spat at him then, but missed, and it landed instead on the snow, a thin black liquid that looked nothing like saliva. Bryant felt chilled to the bone. 'All of you, treating me like I was nothing when I was the one doing all the work! No-one would be going to Spes if it wasn't for me.'

'And thousands won't,' Dubnik said. 'Thousands died in neutral space, thanks to you. And in the Underworld cities, because money that should have been spent on repairs was diverted to pay for your precious Second Species programme. What about them?'

Bryant thought of the boys. He remembered Alistair and Faidal, and the thing that had been put inside Eve. He remembered Jinn, ruining her body with dangerous prosthetics in order to escape from this woman. Had she always been mad? Dubnik had said something about a virus, and as he looked at her now, he could see how sick she was. Her eyes were wild, her hair plastered back to her head by melting snow, and she kept swinging her arms and spitting.

She started forward. And Bryant, unaware that he had even made the decision, found himself blocking her path. All he knew was that she could not be allowed to get on that ship. None of them would stand a chance with her on board. She was truly dangerous. He grabbed her, held her in place.

'Go!' Bryant shouted at Eve. 'Now!'

But Ferona was fighting against him. She was surprisingly strong, though not nearly as strong as Bryant. There was no possibility of her breaking free. Angry hands came up to pull at his ears, his hair. He got hold of her, intending to shove her as far away as he could then scramble for the ship himself, but she fought him like a wild cat.

'You, too,' he yelled at Dubnik. 'Get on that ship before you freeze to death. This place needs you.'

And then he felt the sharp, grinding pressure of her teeth sinking into the flesh of his hand, followed by a sudden bitter sting. All his thoughts began to swim. 'Get us on that ship,' she ordered him. 'Kill the others.'

Bryant shook his head. 'Go!' he yelled at Eve again, forcing himself to stay where he was and not to get on that ship and do exactly what Ferona wanted him to do.

'No!'

'Eve, I can't . . . ' The pain was growing, the urge a hot insistent fire inside him. But he could handle pain. He had lived through it before. It didn't scare him. 'I'm not a good person,' he said. 'I never have been. Just . . . go. Leave. Now. Let me be a good person just this once.'

Eve didn't move.

'Please,' Bryant said. He could feel his strength fading and knew that the pain was getting the better of him now.

Eve turned and ran up the ramp. Dubnik followed her. The ramp rolled up behind them. It was only as the drives began to rumble and the ship started to move that Bryant realised that Ferona Blue was no longer struggling, her body hanging limp and lifeless in his arms. He dropped her to the ground then sat down next to her, watching as the ship went up, up, disappearing into the white sky.

He lay back on the ground beside her, blood seeping slowly from the wound in his arm. The snow continued to fall. His arms and legs became numb. He watched the lights of the ship until they disappeared from view.

And then he closed his eyes, and let the cold take him.

CHAPTER

47

Vessel: The *Mutant*. Battleship/carrier hybrid
Location: Sector Five, Neutral Space
Cargo: N/A
Crew: 26
Droids: 7

Dax hadn't slept in days, not even snatching the odd hour that was all he had needed since he had first been modified at eighteen. Ace helped as much as he could, and the Type Two women also tried their best, but they didn't have the skills or the training. There were simply too many jobs to be done, and even one man working twenty-four hours a day was still only one man.

They had no end goal, no destination. The war was over but they couldn't go back to Earth. All they had was their ships, and now that Jinn had taken the Virena with her, most of them were fit for the scrapheap. There was no talk of heading to Spes. The ships probably wouldn't make it anyway.

When he worked, Dax didn't think of Jinn. If he slept he knew that he would. He would remember everything about her. The shape of her hands and the feel of them on his body. The scent of her skin. The sound of her voice, the way that she had laughed, the way that he had felt when he was with her. They had shared something that he had thought was unbreakable. He had been wrong.

Sittan had changed everything.

Now Jinn had gone back there.

And he had let her.

Dax swore as the laser cutter he was using slipped in his grasp, his sweating, tired hand unable to control it properly. It cut a line down the wall and into the floor, burning across his foot before switching off. He stared down at the smoking leather of his boot. They were good boots too, beautifully made, worn to just the right level of comfortable. Dax wasn't a man prone to vanity, but he liked his boots, and losing them was just a loss too far. It cut through what was left of his already thin hold on his emotions.

He was exhausted and he was lonely and he was sad and there was only so much a person could take before they hit their limit. Later, he would marvel at the madness of his ability to feel nothing over things that should have been everything and yet come apart over a pair of bloody boots. For now, there was no room for such thoughts.

He leaned against the wall, put his head in his hands, and sobbed until his entire body hurt with it. Not just for Jinn, though it was mostly for her, but for everything that had put him on this path. For the naïve eighteen-year-old that he had been and for the hardened man that he had become. For those he had hurt, and those who had hurt him in return.

He didn't know how long it lasted for. It didn't matter. At some point, exhaustion overwhelmed him and he sank to the floor and fell asleep. He awoke sometime later to find himself stiff and sore and it took him a while to unfold himself and to rub the numbness out of his legs. His mouth was dry and gritty, and his entire body felt empty.

He got carefully to his feet and made his way to the control deck, sinking down into his chair, needing its familiar comfort, but it didn't help. His problems were still there. They had simply shifted position. It didn't matter how hard he tried. He couldn't make them go away.

What to do about them was something that Dax still hadn't figured out. He was about to leave the control deck and head back to his quarters for a quick wash and something to eat when Ace came staggering through. He dropped down into what had been Eve's chair and closed his eyes, which were ringed with dark shadows. There were cuts and bruises on his hands. 'Bloody water recycler isn't working properly,' he said.

'Can you fix it?'

'I can. I just don't have the energy right now. Or the parts.'

'What do you need?'

Ace reeled off a list of various things.

'I can get you those.'

'Where?'

Dax sat up a little, turned on the near space tracker and started searching for ships. He ignored the little voice that told him that this wasn't really what he wanted to do. He was a pirate. He'd always be a pirate. That life had served him well before and there was no reason why it wouldn't do the same now. There were a few ships in the local area, several of which would meet their needs.

'We're about to cross paths with a very nice long-distance cruiser. It will have the parts we need.'

'You mean . . .'

'I certainly do.' He tracked the movements of the ship, set about programming a course for the *Mutant*. He knew how to do this. It was easy. He was good at it. 'An hour at most. Make sure you've got your tools and everything you'll need.'

'What about the people on board?'

'That's what escape pods were invented for.' There was enough traffic travelling through this sector of space that someone would pick them up. He had no concerns there.

With that hour to kill, Dax went back to his quarters and washed and changed, and if his heart lurched when his hand settled on one of Jinn's shirts, and he held it close and found that it still smelled of her, it didn't matter, because no-one was there to see it.

He strode back to the control deck to check that their target was in range. The last few minutes of manoeuvring had to be done manually. It was a relief to find that the *Mutant* was still willing and that it came to him as naturally as it always had. He watched on the screens as the jaws of the *Mutant* opened up and swallowed the cruiser, locking it safely inside the cargo bay.

And then he saw something that he did not expect.

The ramp for the cruiser lowered, and someone walked down it. She looked around, and her face split into an enormous grin. It couldn't be.

It was.

'Eve!'

Dax was off and running without a moment's hesitation. He took the quickest route he knew down to the lowest levels of the ship, and the massive rear cargo bay where the cruiser was trapped. The doors opened for him automatically and he went straight through and out into the bay. 'EVE!'

She ran at him. He didn't even have time to get out of the way. 'You're immune to me!' she shouted at him.

'What?'

'Type One! I can't hurt you if you're Type One!'

Her small body pressed up against him, the top of her head barely even reaching the middle of his chest, and she wrapped her arms around him and squeezed as tightly as she could. 'Dax,' she said, when she could finally get words out. 'Dax, I've missed you so much.'

Dax was still trying to process what she'd said.

'I've had a hell of a time of it. I've got a lot to tell you.'

'Probably not as much as I've got to tell you,' he said. 'Bryant?'

Her expression clouded, and she shook her head.

'I'm sorry.'

'It doesn't matter. Jinn?'

'Gone,' Dax said.

'Gone where?'

'To Sittan.'

'Right,' Eve said, and she tugged him away from the cargo bay and towards the elevator that would take them up to the shared areas of the ship. 'I need a decent chemicleanse and a session with your wardrober. And then you're going to tell me why you are in this sector of space, pulling pirate crap, when Jinn is on Sittan.'

CHAPTER

48

5th Day of the Fifth Turn

Fire City, Sittan

Jinn had always believed that the intergalactic senate had been set up to encourage co-operation between the species, as a way to foster peace. The things that she had seen over the past few months had corrected that misconception.

Whatever respect Jinn might have had for them was gone. But she could not escape the fact that she had been pulled down the wrong path for too long, that she had not been strong enough to resist it, to take a step back and see a different way.

And she knew why. She understood the burden she carried now, how it had changed her. More than that, she understood that the Virena was a danger to all of them. None of them were safe while it still existed. The Sittan had kept it to themselves, and as a result it had caused harm to only them, but now the rest of the galaxy knew exactly what it could do, what power it could give to those it liked.

From a safe, clean distance, it would be too easy to ignore the bloodshed and focus only on what it could give. People had fought for far less than that. And the Virena, now that it had tasted life away from Sittan, was hungry for more. It wanted to spread, to control. Already the galaxy had been seeded with thousands of dark rubies, mined from the caves below the palace and traded with the other species. They were on ships, space stations, planets. She hadn't realised that those rubies had formed from Virena, heated and pressed for millions of years. She didn't think Talta had known either. To her, they had just been a pretty thing that other species had coveted. Jinn could feel it reaching out to them even now, her skin prickling with awareness of it.

Jinn didn't try and stop it. It meant that the Virena was distracted, less interested in her, and that had given her the space she needed to accept what she had to do. It was time for her to make a choice, just as the others had made their choices.

She could, she knew, keep the Virena. That was what it wanted. She could take it off planet and to all those places that it wanted to go, let it drain them dry just as it had done this one. It was tempting. The thought of the power that she would have . . .

There would be no need for the senate. There would be no need for borders, because the Virena would allow her to control all of it. War would never happen again. Everyone would co-exist peacefully. She would make them. With Virena on every planet, they'd have no choice.

But something held her back.

There was a little part of her that the alien metal had not been able to take over, though it had tried. It was the part of her that was still human. The Virena would never stop. Nothing would ever be enough.

Jinn had only one option left to her now. She had known it for a while, perhaps even before she came to this planet, though she had been too afraid to admit it to herself.

She rose from her bed. She dipped into the cooling waters of the pool, letting her body float. She felt completely and utterly calm now that the decision had been made.

This had to be done now, before the others awoke. She couldn't let anything or anyone distract her. It was going to take all the energy she had to hide her emotions from the Virena. She could feel it, warm and heavy around her body. It wasn't restricted to just her hands any more. It swirled all round her arms, her legs, her belly, and if she hadn't been Type One, she wouldn't have been able to carry the weight of it.

She left her chambers and silently made her way down into the main hall of the palace. People from the city lay sleeping around the edge, the air filled with the sounds of their unconscious bodies.

Jinn had not been certain how she would do this, but she suddenly felt very sure that this was where she was supposed to start. The deep pool that held the heart rippled as she moved closer to it. She whispered to it softly as she dipped her hands into the thick, oily liquid, letting it come to her. She didn't want to frighten it off.

And then she left the palace, taking the Virena with her, out into the surprising chill of the early morning. A wind was blowing, kicking up sand and carrying the stench of the dead Shi Fai animal far closer than Jinn would have liked. Still, focusing on that kept her mind distracted.

It was a long way to the Mountain, and it gave her far too long to think. She didn't want to use the Virena to transport her there. She didn't dare risk it. As the path started to rise beneath her feet, Jinn could feel the muscles in her leg start to tire. She tried to increase her speed, but it was far more difficult than it should have been. She dug her heels into the dirt as she began to slide backwards.

She didn't understand why it was so hard. She was used to being alone, to doing things alone. She'd lived most of her life that way, and if there had been a brief time when she'd allowed others to carry some of the burden for her, it was over now. Dax was gone.

Alistair, Theon, both dead. She had no idea where Eve was, and even if she did, she wouldn't have brought her here.

Ritte and Li and Merion couldn't be part of this either.

Jinn stumbled to her knees, hands hitting the hard dirt, and tried to crawl, but the little stones on the path were sharp, and they cut into her skin. The pain of it shocked her a little, slight though it was, and she paused, needing a minute to catch her breath and calm down.

She bent her knee and planted her foot firmly on the ground, but she couldn't get herself upright. The weight of the Virena was suddenly too much.

She heard someone behind her, scrambling over the rock, and turned to see Li and Merion. 'What are you doing?'

'We could ask you the same thing.'

'Go back to the palace.'

Another figure slowly appeared. It was Ritte. Following her were the other Sittan, all of them, the females and the males and the children. 'No,' Jinn said. 'No! Go back to the palace! I order you to leave!'

But they kept coming anyway, until they formed a large crowd that filled the path. The younger ones scrambled up onto the rock to get a better look at her.

Jinn looked at the gathered crowd with dismay. She could feel the Virena growing hotter and hotter. Li crouched next to her. 'What's wrong?'

'Do you understand what I'm trying to do?'

'I think so,' he said.

'I can't let them stop me.'

'They won't,' Ritte said. She had moved close enough to cast a shadow over Jinn. The suns were now starting to rise, and the planet was starting to wake up.

But for Jinn, this was the end. Not the beginning. She tried to get up, but the Virena knew what she was doing now, and it had become heavier than rock. 'The weight of it . . . I can't carry it.'

'Yes, you can,' Li said. 'I'll help you.'

He held out his hand. Jinn reached out and took it. As his fingers locked with hers, she felt someone else move in alongside her.

It was Merion.

He too held out his hand, not human and familiar, but huge and six-fingered. Each of those fingers had four joints which could flex in any direction and was tipped with a lethal claw. There was a pattern carved into his palm, two interlinking circles. 'You are my empress,' he said quietly. 'It is my job to help you. I know what it is that you intend to do.'

'And you don't want to stop me?'

Spikes rippled out across his head, before sinking back into his smooth blue skin. 'It has to end,' he said. 'Look what it has made us. Look what we have become. We had everything. Now we have nothing.'

Jinn slid her hand into his. His grip was surprisingly gentle as he and Li helped her to her feet. She began to walk again, and the sound of a thousand feet crunching over gravel soon rose up around them, hemmed in by the high rock walls of the pass that would lead them to the summit. It seemed even hotter now, and sweat poured down her neck, but she kept on going.

And then they were there, at the top of the Mountain.

She felt Merion falter, and knew that she could ask no more of him. 'Go,' she said. 'I can do this.' He nodded and left her. Li remained, but only until Jinn shook off his grip.

'I want to help you,' he said.

'I know,' she told him. 'But I don't know how it's going to react, what it's going to do.'

He squeezed her hand, and then he let go and stepped back, but not too far. It was as if he wanted her to know that she wasn't alone.

Jinn walked to the very edge of the crater and looked down into the belly of the Mountain. The fall was so deep that she couldn't even see the bottom. It simply disappeared. She bit into her bottom lip and tasted blood. It was bitter. She could feel the weight of the Virena as it tried to drag her away from the edge. She would not let it. It sang at her, filling her head with sound until there was no room for anything else, and it became positively painful to hear it, but she didn't let that sway her either. It clawed at her skin, and welts began to appear, deep, stinging marks. Still she did not falter.

Sensing its fear only confirmed that this was the right thing to do. It was so desperate to cling on, even though it had taken everything from this planet, and would do the same to others, if it was given the chance.

She straightened her legs, locking her muscles, feeling all of her strength and power, and then she did what no empress before her had done. She held up her arms and called to that wonderful, greedy, murderous living metal. She called to all of it.

She pulled it from the palace and from the arena and from every single part of the city. Behind her, it formed enormous waves that crashed through the city, crushing everything in their path. She pulled it down from the sky, and from the rivers. She drained the city dry.

And she refilled the Mountain.

She poured back into it the blood of every Sittan and every human who had fallen in the arena, and she felt their souls cry out in relief. And with that, a terrible weight was suddenly lifted.

She tried to step back. She heard shouting come from somewhere behind her, thought that she heard Dax, but it couldn't be. It wasn't possible. And then a hard, heavy body collided with hers, knocking her forward. She twisted, hands reaching out to grab onto something, anything, and found herself face to face with Talta.

'I won't let you do it,' Talta screamed at her. 'I won't let you destroy it!'

Jinn caught hold of her.

The two of them fell. A wave of Virena rushed up to meet them. It wrapped itself around Talta, the darkness rising up and over her body, over her face, into a mouth wide open in a desperate roar.

But someone caught Jinn. Strong fingers closed around her wrist.

She hung there for what felt like an age, unable to see, unable to breathe, as the Virena pulled at every centimetre of her body and begged her to join it, to take her place with all the other empresses it had taken before.

But Jinn did not.

That strong hand tightened its grip, and it began to pull her forward. She swung up her other arm, and found another strong hand, and held on.

Finally, the wave was gone, and the world reappeared, and Jinn found herself looking up into a pair of familiar green eyes. 'Dax,' she said. 'You came.'

'I will always come for you,' he said. 'Never doubt that.'

He started to pull her up, the muscles in his arms bulging, but something was still pulling her. Jinn looked down to see a tangle of Virena wrapping tightly around her ankle. 'Let go,' she said.

'No.'

'You have to let go!'

'I won't. I'm not making the same mistake twice.'

But the Virena had hold of her now, and it was strong, it was so strong, and Jinn could feel her grip starting to slip. 'I will not take you with me!'

'Good,' he said, 'because I have no intention of going. Hold on to me, Jinn. Just hold on.'

But it was almost impossible. It *was* impossible. She closed her eyes. She willed the Virena away. She begged it to leave her alone.

The grip on her ankle loosened. She kicked free.

Dax pulled her up.

His arms came around her, and she threw herself against him, and just let herself breathe him in. She let herself feel his heart beat, feel his breath against her cheek, take in air and let it out. She let herself feel everything that came with knowing that it was over, that the two of them were still alive. They had made it.

His hand came up and ran over her hair. 'That's different,' he said.

'What is?'

'You'll see. Jinn, you have to know ...'

'I already do.'

She pushed up onto her tiptoes and kissed him.

CHAPTER

49

10th Day of the Fifth Turn

Fire City, Sittan

The city was a mess. The arena, the palace had both gone, brought down to nothing by Jinn. 'It was the only way,' she told Merion, as they stood together in what had been the centre of the city. Those who had been in the palace, the few remaining adults and some children, were slowly picking their way through the rubble, most still in shock.

'I know,' he said. Looking down, he shifted some orange-red dirt with his toes. 'We will rebuild.'

'It won't be easy.'

'It wasn't easy living as we did, under the control of that substance. I don't even really know what it was.'

'It was a living thing, just like you and I.'

'Nothing like you and I.'

'Perhaps not,' she decided. It felt easier to view it that way. Maybe it was even the right way to think about it. With some time, some distance, she might be able to see things the way Merion did. For now, she was filled with a strange, unexpected grief. The Virena was gone, buried deep in the core of the planet where it couldn't harm or control anyone. It had taken with it all remaining traces of her prosthetics. Her retinal implant was gone. Her blades, finally, were gone. She could still feel the slide of them, the weight, but it was a phantom, a memory. When she looked down at her hands there was nothing.

That was not to say that her body had not changed in other ways. Sittan DNA was still glued in with her own. She was still taller and stronger than a normal human woman. A dark streak ran from her right temple through the length of her hair. But Sittan was no longer her planet. She was a visitor here now, and she would not be sorry to leave.

'Will it come back?' Merion asked her.

Jinn had asked herself that question, and she thought she knew the answer. 'No,' she said. 'Not unless you start slaughtering each other again. It's buried deep in the core of the planet, cut off from everything it needs to survive. It doesn't have access to metal, or to blood. Keep it that way and you'll never see it again.'

Li walked up to them, shading his eyes with his hand. He acknowledged her with a nod, and then reached out, linking his fingers with Merion's. 'I'm not coming with you,' he said. 'I'm going to stay here. Help them rebuild.'

'Good,' she said. 'I'm glad. For both of you.'

The Shi Fai hadn't been back. But they had left something behind. Three ships, which had already split open and sent tough, woody branches snaking out over the land, basking in the heat.

The landscape of Sittan was going to change. In the distance, the Mountain stood still and silent, the Virena closed inside it, all possible exits blocked. When Jinn reached for it, she felt nothing. Not even a seed, a possibility. The life had gone from it completely. It would not come back.

She was glad to know that it had gone, but at the same time, she grieved for it. But it was a sadness that would pass. It felt natural and right. She said a silent goodbye, and then she was done. It was time to go.

Dax was waiting for her next to his ship. He had changed, as had she, and she did not know what the future held for them. For now, it was enough that he was here. That they were alive. Every breath she took felt worthy of celebration. Even the smallest things were no longer background noise to be ignored. It was all so fresh, so new.

'Are you ready?' he asked.

Jinn took one last look back at Sittan, at the planet that had been hers. It wasn't hers any more. She wasn't sorry about that. No-one should own so much, have power over so many. She closed her eyes and tipped her head back, letting the light bathe her skin. She would miss that. 'Yes,' she said. She took her first step onto the ramp that led up into the ship, then paused. 'What on Earth happened?' She jumped down from the ramp, jogged to the side of the ship, ran a hand over the scarred metal surface. It was dirty with Sittan dust, which streaked it in rust-coloured lines, but it was more than just that.

Scorch marks formed large dark splotches all over the exterior.

'I jumped,' Dax said. 'I didn't do a very good job.'

'You jumped? But it was . . . ' She counted up. 'Seven gates!'

He shrugged, didn't quite meet her gaze. 'There wasn't time to find a pilot.'

She realised then just what it had taken him to get here.

Jinn stepped back from the side of the ship and made her way slowly, carefully, back to where he stood. She didn't say anything. Instead, she walked up the ramp. The little transporter smelled exactly as she remembered, and she drank it in deep. She heard Dax follow her on board. The ramp folded up behind them, closing them in.

She blinked at the sharpness of artificial light. Even the air tasted different. Familiar it might be, but it was still going to take some getting used to. Quickly, she and Dax fell into an old routine, checking the fuel stores and the lines for the coolant system. She checked the grav generator and felt a stab of longing for the Virena. The grief at least was no longer as fierce. It hadn't gone, but it was something that she could accept.

But there could be more yet to face. 'What happened to Eve? To Bryant?'

'Eve is on the *Mutant*. I picked up her transporter in sector nine. Bryant didn't make it.'

'Is she alright?'

'She will be.'

She followed him past the small sleeping quarters. She thought he might stop her there, but he didn't, and she was both sad and grateful. She didn't know if either of them were ready for that. She didn't know yet if they would be, though as she looked at him, she felt that same pull, that same attraction. She did not know if he felt the same when he looked at her. Last time ... last time, she had been his empress, and it had been his duty to please her. Next time, if there was a next time, would be very different.

She tried to tell herself that it didn't matter, that it was enough that he was here. He was walking quickly, perhaps a little too quickly, and she almost had to run to keep up with him as he marched through to the control deck, straight to the front. He was headed for the pilot's seat, she realised, but he diverted at the last moment and dropped instead into the navigator's seat.

'Get us out of here,' he said.

Jinn took her seat. She stretched her hands out over the ports. Nothing happened. She lifted her hands up in surprise, lowered them back again, then yanked them back. She flipped them over and looked at her palms, at the controls, at Dax. 'I can't fly!'

'Of course you can.'

'No, I can't! I've got no Tellurium or Virena.'

'Here,' Dax said, and he tossed her a pair of smartware gloves. She fumbled the catch, knocking them both to the floor. She buried her hands in her face. There was a heavy lump in her throat, and she swallowed it back. She was a pilot. *A pilot.* What was she supposed to do if she couldn't fly? She pushed herself free from the seat, lowering her knees to the floor so that she could retrieve the gloves.

Dax had beaten her to it. She reached for one, and his hand closed around it right before hers did. He held out the glove and she took it, stuffing her stiff fingers into the tight fitting glove. She fastened it up.

He held out the other, and she took that too, and this time his gaze grazed her face and for a moment, she wasn't strong enough to look away quite as quickly as she knew she should. She tried to put the glove on but fumbled it again.

Strong fingers closed round her wrist, just as they had on the Mountain. But then it had been fear and desperation, and she hadn't had time to think about how the contact made her feel, how the slide of his skin against hers made her so very aware of herself.

He tugged the glove on, not easily, not smoothly, because he was not quite steady either. This time, when she pressed her hands over the ports, the gloves plugged in for her. It wasn't quite the same as it had been before, but it was good enough. She tested all drives, found them ready and willing, and then she pressed herself back into her seat as the restraints rolled around her, took a deep breath, and flew them away from Sittan.

'Exterior temp is up a little,' Dax said.

'I know.' She gritted her teeth. Smartware gloves weren't Tellurium or Virena. It was going to take some getting used to.

Patience was what mattered now. Not speed. Just ... hanging on long enough to make it through. Without her retinal implant, she couldn't leave the deck completely, couldn't immerse herself in the ship in the way that she had in the past. There was no escape from herself now.

The muscles in her legs tensed up, she was pressing her feet against the floor so hard. The lift off had been vertical, which she had thought would help to lessen the pressure on the drives, but she now saw that it wasn't working. There was only one choice. Could she do it?

'Hang on,' she said to Dax. 'This is going to get rough.'

'I thought it was already rough.'

'Well, it's going to get worse.'

She didn't give him any more warning than that. She switched off the rear drives for a second, dropping the back of the ship, and then fired up the jump thrusters. The nose went nose up, shot forward so fast that she could have sworn she was being pushed right through the seat, and broke atmosphere.

All the drives switched off.

Jinn went completely still, listening, waiting to see what damage had been done. But there were no alarms, no smell of smoke. The readings on the screen in front of her slowly went back to normal. The restraints rolled back, freeing her from the seat. The gravity generator was still working.

She slowly lowered her head to the console and let it rest there, enjoying the cool, hard press of the surface against her face. She hadn't realised how much she had missed the smell of human technology.

A hand came to rest on her shoulder. She turned her head, slowly sat up. 'Sorry,' she said.

'What for?'

'For almost breaking your ship.'

'Jinn,' he said. 'I don't give a damn about the ship. All I care about is that you are on it with me.'

She risked a glance at him then. He was watching her, his eyes heavy-lidded but just as green as she remembered. And that something in him that had always called to her called to her now. She tightened her grip on the arms of her seat to stop herself from going straight to him. There were still some things she needed answers to. Some things that she needed to say.

'You let me go.'

'I know.'

'I needed you!'

'No, you didn't,' he said. He smiled then, a tight and painful thing. 'You proved that. You did all that on your own, Jinn. You went back to that planet and you dealt with it. Me? I ran like a fucking coward.'

'You're not a coward.'

'Yes I am. And do you know what? I'm OK with that. Sometimes, you just have to accept that you aren't the strongest person in the room, that you can't do what needs to be done. And sometimes, you have to admit that the reason you can't do it is because you're afraid.'

'You were afraid of me.'

His face flushed, but he didn't turn away. 'Yes.'

'You didn't trust me?'

'I didn't know you,' he said. 'I didn't know what you were becoming. And I couldn't face going back there. I couldn't face what I had done.'

That was obvious from what he did not say, as much as what he did. She didn't press him on it. She had a few things of her own to confess. 'You were right to be afraid of me.'

Now it was his turn to look shocked. 'No, I wasn't.'

'Yes, you were. The Virena . . . I didn't see what it was doing to me. I didn't *want* to see. It made me powerful, Dax, and I *liked* it. I felt like I *deserved* it.' It was a painful, shameful thing to admit.

'But you destroyed it,' he said quietly.

'And look how much damage I let it do first.'

'It would have done that anyway. What would have happened if it had latched on to someone else, someone more like Talta? What would have happened if Talta had kept it? Don't go there,

Jinn. Don't torture yourself thinking about what might have been. There's only what is.'

'I couldn't let it carry on. It was inside me. I could see what it wanted, what it really wanted. What it would make me do if I let it. No-one should have that much power.'

His gaze met hers, and it was a moment of confirmation, of decision, and she knew that he understood. This was a man who had spent most of his life being the biggest, the strongest, the most dangerous person in the room, and who had worked every day of it to make sure that he wasn't corrupted by it.

She didn't know which one of them moved first. They met somewhere halfway, his hands closing round her waist as hers slid round his neck and they moved into each other. 'Dax,' she said, as his mouth covered hers. It had been so long. So long. Everything else that she wanted to say was forgotten. It didn't matter any more. What she needed from him now couldn't be communicated with words anyway. She wanted to know that she was still desirable to him, that they still fitted together as they always had, even though they had both been broken and put back together as something different.

He tasted of hunger and desperation and sadness. He held back, she knew he did. So she made him stop. She pulled at his jacket, stripping it away from his body, and did the same to his shirt. His skin was just as she remembered, hot under her hands, darkened by his time in the arena, the colour not yet fully softened by his time away. At the same time he was both thinner and harder, the muscle cut in with painful definition. She ran her fingers over the kill tattoos on his shoulders, forcing him to meet her gaze as she did so. She would not let him turn away from her now.

'Look at me,' she said, and as those bright green eyes fell heavily on hers, she pulled up her own shirt, tugging the fabric over her head, tossing it aside, baring herself to him. She had the same dark lines on her own shoulders. He saw them, she knew he did. But it was an acceptance, an acknowledgement, nothing more. He saw her scars just as she saw his. His throat worked as he swallowed. 'You aren't the only one,' she told him. 'You need to remember that.'

'I remember. I don't think I will ever forget.'

'Dax,' she said, suddenly aware of something that she knew now she should have always known, because she knew him. 'You are not to blame for this.'

'Aren't I?'

'I made my choices. It's my fault if they were poor.'

'You came to Sittan for me. You killed for me.'

'And I would do it again,' she told him. That much she was sure of. 'But I'm going to spend the rest of my life making sure that neither of us ever has to go through that again.'

'I'll hold you to that,' he said. He pulled her closer, buried his face in her neck. 'Do you remember the first time?' he asked her.

'I remember.'

'I was hard on you then.'

'You were hard *in* me,' she said, and felt him shake a little.

'I don't want it to be like that this time.'

'Then how do you want it to be?'

His hands were still on her, growing braver, venturing further, finding soft, sensitive flesh. She could sense his anxiousness and his fear. 'Slow,' he said. 'Gentle. I want us to be careful with each other. We never were, before. I won't let it break this time.'

She ran a hand down the side of his body, let her fingers trace a line down his belly. The muscles there shivered at her touch, but she did not go lower, not yet. She sensed that when she did, he wouldn't be able to hold himself back, and neither would she.

She pressed up against him, their bodies fitting together differently now. Better. He was still huge, still much bigger than her, still magnificent, but there was an edge to the contact now. She glanced down at him, saw the scar over his heart that had never properly healed. It was the only mark on his body. Everything else had healed as if it had never been.

She covered it with her hand. His pulse was strong. 'We will be careful,' she told him. 'But not in this.'

'Even in this,' he replied. He dug his fingers into her hair and kissed her with such restrained eagerness that she wanted to cry. But Jinn didn't want that. She didn't want him to hold back. She wouldn't let him.

She kissed him back, sliding his hands up his back. She could feel the hard press of his erection against her belly, and she rocked against him until she felt his body shudder, his breathing speed up. He needed this, she knew he did, and she also knew that he had been without for too long.

She slid one hand down his back, over hot, dampening skin. She found the waistband of his trousers, went lower, found the hard cut curve of his backside, and pulled him more tightly against her. She had been lonely for too long. She had missed him too much. 'No,' she told him. She tugged on the waistband of his trousers. 'Look at us. We will have to spend the rest of our lives being careful. We're a danger to everyone around us, and nothing will change that, because that's who we are. It's what we are. But you and I ... we don't have to do that.'

A final tug. He looked down at her, at them. A muscle tightened in his cheek. His eyes blazed green fire. He was fighting it, she could tell, but it was a battle he was going to lose. She pushed him back into his seat and he let her hold him there. The Sittan clothing she wore was basic and uncomplicated, and she didn't even bother to remove it.

She straddled him. His hands went to her thighs, then under her clothing, finding soft, sensitive flesh, the places on her body that had always been his favourites. The small of her back, the curve of her waist, the swell of her breasts.

It was easy, after that. They knew each other, and they knew this, and it was another old routine that they slid into comfortably and easily as she took him into her body, felt something inside herself adjust and ease.

He tugged at the dress, pulling it free, and tossed it aside. Jinn froze. A sense of cold began to creep in where before there had been only heat. The black marks from the Virena covered her entire body now, not just her hands and her arms, but her legs, her thighs, wrapping around her hips. The Type One modifications had made her taller, heavier, stronger. It was one thing to be aware of something, quite another to see it exposed, in the raw, to understand it.

'You are beautiful,' he said.

'Am I?'

'Like something from another world.' He squeezed her hips, setting her moving again, watching her and she knew in that moment that he had forgotten everything else. The pain was pushed back. It was just the two of them.

They tried to take their time about it, but in the end, neither of them had the patience. Pleasure came quickly and easily.

They lost themselves in it and in each other for hours. Jinn awoke to find herself curled up against him, on the floor of the control deck her head pillowed on his arm, both of them wrapped in a sheet of pure white truesilk, the kind that only a very successful pirate could afford.

'What now?' she asked him.

'I think we should go home.'

'To the *Mutant*?'

'No,' he said. 'A real home. There's a planet waiting for us, remember? One with trees and oceans, where you can walk outside and look at the sky.'

CHAPTER

50

Day 57 of the First Year

Intergalactic Senate, Kepler System, Sector Five, Neutral Space

Dax could tell that Jinn was nervous. He was nervous too. It felt strange to be here as himself. There was nowhere to hide now. Everyone here knew who they were. What they were.

'I feel stupid,' Jinn said, fiddling with the fastenings of her senatorial robe. The white fabric draped over her shoulders and hung to the floor, swirling around her legs as she moved. 'Do I have to wear it?'

'It's how they do things here.'

Her hand lingered on the fastening. 'Well, I don't like it, and I'm not going to wear it.' She unfastened it, letting it fall to the floor. Underneath she wore something much more her style, the basic uniform of every pilot.

Dax grinned as he followed her out of their pod and down the steps to the little boat that waited for them. They climbed in, closed the canopy and powered up the engine, and Jinn flew them across the water towards the central hall. They had arrived with little time to spare, partly because they hadn't rushed to get here. Since landing on Spes, they had barely had a moment to themselves. There was so much to do. The planet needed to be mapped and explored and communities set up. More and more people were arriving every day – Type Two women, Bugs, pirates. There was space for all of them.

But there were limits on what could be done, and how it could be done. Grudge had seen to that. There would be no decimation of forests, no senseless burning of everything in sight in order to power technology that they didn't really need. Solar batteries were proving sufficient to power what was necessary.

Now there was just the question of their place in the galaxy, and that was why he and Jinn were here. Dax had nominated Jinn to be their representative in the senate, and no-one had opposed it, not even Jinn herself.

So here they were, on Kepler. Jinn angled the boat into dock and Dax secured it, then helped her out. She didn't need his assistance. He just liked the way her hand fitted with his.

They walked down the wide corridor side by side. A private box had been created for them, but they didn't bother with it. Dax remained where he was, in the shadows at the end of the corridor, watching as she walked across to the central podium. He heard the whispers as the others realised that she hadn't bothered with the senatorial robes.

She planted both feet firmly inside the circle, rested her hands on the lectern, and waited for silence. They granted it to her quickly.

'My name is Jinnifer Blue,' she began. Her hands flexed. It was a tiny movement, and Dax suspected that he was the only one to notice it. 'I've come here today to represent the people of Spes.'

'We understood that Spes was for humans.'

'I am human,' Jinn said. 'Sort of. I'm a new type of human. Second Species.'

'So humans are still on Earth?'

'That's not for me to answer. I don't speak for them.'

'We are sorry to hear of the death of your mother.'

Hold it together, sweetheart. You can do this. The news of Ferona's death had hit Jinn harder than either of them had anticipated, and he knew that she still had not quite come to terms with it. It would take time and space to process a loss that had happened without the possibility of a goodbye. In death, Ferona had become a martyr. The story was that she had sacrificed herself to save Dubnik, the new President of Earth, from an assassination plot. Her story was being rewritten. She was a hero now. A few more years in the telling, and she would be practically a saint.

He and Jinn needed that version to become truth. It was what would keep them safe.

'Thank you,' Jinn said. Her voice was almost steady. Almost.

Then it was Merion's turn. He got to his feet, right on cue, his image and voice filling the hall as he spoke of the changes on Sittan. Things were still difficult, he said, but the planet was recovering, and they were finding their way forward. They were not yet ready to begin trading with their neighbours, but they soon would be. He thanked the Shi Fai senator for the deliveries of food, which were keeping the population fed.

Dubnik was next. He spoke only briefly. Dome repairs were underway, and they were about to start running the algae tanks which would purify the air and increase the oxygen supply. Things will still very difficult, but mass extinction had been delayed. There was time. He hinted at a new agreement which would, he hoped, delay it further, but didn't say what it was.

Then it was the turn of the Shi Fai.

Dax leaned forward in his seat.

This was it. This was the moment that would tell them whether or not what they had done had worked.

The little senator shuffled its way forward. A faint smell of burnt wood drifted towards them. Dax saw Jinn tense. There was one thing that she had asked the Shi Fai for, and she didn't yet know if they would be willing to hand it over.

'We would like the Sittan senator to know that we will continue to send shipments of food for as long as it is needed, as recompense for the harm we did to their planet. We would like to inform the Senator of Earth that our ships are on their way to Earth. We hope for many young. We hope that the heat generated during the fruiting process will help to raise the temperature of the Domes. We have also received a request for recompense from the Senator of Spes. We have considered this request, and we have decided to honour it.'

He stepped down from his box, walking out into the centre of the hall.

'Go on,' Dax said to Jinn. 'This is what we came for.'

She opened the little gate on the front of her box and carefully took the steps down to the main floor, then slowly made her way towards the senator. He could tell that she was trying not to rush. She met the senator in the centre. The difference in height was such that she knelt in front of it. The senator held something out to her, and Dax saw Jinn take it. A box, little bigger than her hand. The seeds for the plant that would change everything for Eve and the other Type Two females.

And so it was done.

Jinn returned to him as the rest of the senate went about the rest of their business, this dispute between the three planets of little concern now. They had their own problems to deal with, their own arguments, but Dax knew that with Jinn and Merion now part of the senate, things would be different, and that was what was needed.

They didn't wait to hear the rest of it. There would be other times for that. Instead, they took the little boat back to their pod, packed up their things, and got back on board their new transporter. It had been built from parts taken from the *Mutant*, and was big enough for long-distance travel, but small enough to only need a crew of two.

'So,' Dax said. 'That's your politician duties over, and it looks like we've got a couple of weeks before we're expected back on Spes. So what will it be? Want to map another jump? Open another space station? Save another world?'

'I've tried being a saviour. I'm not sure I liked it.'

'So what do you want to be, Jinn?'

She seemed to think about it, and then she smiled.

'I just want to be me.'

ACKNOWLEDGEMENTS

I am writing this on the 4th of April, 2020. The United Kingdom has been restricted for a little over two weeks. Schools are closed. Cinemas, restaurants and clothes shops are closed. Supermarkets have queues outside. My daughter should be preparing for her GCSEs, but her exams have all been cancelled. Her 16th birthday is rapidly approaching and I don't know what sort of celebration we'll be able to have for her. My plans were extravagant, befitting a girl born 6 weeks early and left with a lifelong disability as a result. But we're in a different world now. Everything has changed, seemingly overnight.

There will be an end to this. It won't last forever. But while it does, we're all having to figure out how to do things in a different way and how to cope with the fear that such a situation naturally creates. I have to thank my family, first and foremost, for being brilliant as always, especially as we're all stuck in the house together. I would like to thank my agent, Ella Diamond Kahn of DKW Literary, who told me that we are not working from home, we are working at home in a time of crisis, and who knows exactly what to say to fragile creative types when the world feels like it is too much for us. I would also like to thank my editor Anna Boatman for her work not just on this book, but on this trilogy, from the first phone call back in 2016 to the final edits on *Blue Planet*. It has been a privilege to work with you. I would also like to thank the rest of the team at Piatkus for the work they have done, from marketing to cover design and everything in between.

And finally, I would like to thank all those at work right now, the supermarket staff and the nurses and bin men and delivery drivers and care home workers. It has been claimed that Covid-19 sees no boundaries, that we are all affected equally, but that simply isn't true. Some are carrying more of the weight of this than others. I hope, in the future, that we'll remember that, not by self-indulgently clapping on a doorstep, but by voting for a government that believes in decent pay and conditions for all our essential workers.

Jane O'Reilly

5/10/20

MALPAS

AUTHOR LETTER

Many thanks for following the adventures of Jinn and Dax and for reading *Blue Planet*. If you've enjoyed the series, it would be wonderful if you could leave a review. It helps new readers to discover my books, and there's nothing better than sharing the book love!

If you want to find out more about me or my books, visit me at my website, www.janeoreilly.co.uk

Jane